James Daniel was born in Portsmouth, and educated at Gosport County Grammar School, Welbeck College and the Royal Military Academy Sandhurst. After a service career spanning 33 years during which he served in a variety of theatres world-wide, he left to take up employment in local government. Married for 30 years, he has one son and lives in the south-west of England.

James Daniel was born in Hertfordshire and educated at [illegible] County Grammar School, Wellington College and the Royal Military Academy Sandhurst. A [illegible] service career [illegible] 33 years during which he served in a variety of [illegible] by employment in local government [illegible] and lives in the south-west of England.

THEY TOLD ME YOU WERE DEAD

JAMES DANIEL

PAN BOOKS
LONDON, SYDNEY AND AUCKLAND

First published 1994 by Pan Books

a division of Pan Macmillan Publishers Limited
Cavaye Place London SW10 9PG
and Basingstoke

Associated companies throughout the world

ISBN 0 330 33086 1

3 5 7 9 8 6 4 2

A CIP catalogue record for this book is available from
the British Library

Typeset by CentraCet Limited, Cambridge
Printed and bound in Great Britain by BPC Paperbacks Ltd

For 'D'
who thought that I should be a writer

They told me, Heraclitus, they told me you were dead,
They brought me bitter news to hear and bitter tears to shed.

William Johnson Cory
(1823–1892)

PART ONE

CHAPTER ONE

The eyes squinting from under the helmet missed nothing. Not the group of teenagers boisterously swaggering along the wet pavements, nor the two men talking huddled in a shop doorway across the road.

The headlights of the dark-coloured Vauxhall Astra cut through the drizzle, causing the man in the helmet to withdraw momentarily into the shadow of his own doorway, closing his right eye as the lights probed in his direction. It was his master eye he closed.

His shooting eye.

The car passed, tyres swishing on the wet tarmac. The man did not move. He watched. And waited. The eyes swivelled to the right as a black taxi entered the street at the far end and drove into the glow of the red neon sign, the light diffusing into the mist and drizzle. He watched three girls get out and thought dirty thoughts as he watched. One, long-legged, in a short skirt, bent at the window to pay the fare. He liked the way the skirt rode up her thighs and clung to her hips like it was glued there. He imagined her in bikini pants without the skirt, and what he would like to do to her.

The radio clipped to his jacket whispered. The girl was forgotten. He acknowledged, calling softly to another doorway twenty yards to his left. A fist extended into the street, the thumb held vertically.

'Go.'

His voice carried no further than necessary. The man in the helmet glanced quickly to left and right before leaving his place of concealment and setting off, a shuffling, weaving run in the direction of the neon light.

The rifle, short, stubby, deadly, was carried across his body with a casualness born of long familiarity. The small group went quickly past the lights on the dark side of the road. The three girls just inside the doorway were removing their coats, looking out at them. One jeered. One spat and raised two fingers. The long-legged one with the nice tits paid them no heed at all. Music thumped out into the dark as the door opened, cut off in mid-note as it closed again behind them.

Belfast.

Now.

Jennifer McCauley was attractive, if tarty. The clothes she chose to wear were middle of the range, off the peg, and could be purchased in any of the fashion shops in Belfast's city centre. She wore her skirts short, not quite mini-length, always tight so that her panty line would show. These days she never wore a bra, leaving her breasts to roll suggestively under a silk blouse or tight sweater. The outline of her nipples and panties always got the attention she sought. Eyes focused there first before taking in the dark hair piled on her head, the intelligent grey eyes and the full-lipped mouth. Her make-up was applied just a little too heavily. To the male species, horny and hunting, the effect was devastating.

Exactly as planned.

Tonight she had gone to the club accompanied by two friends from the supermarket where she worked part-time. As always the room was noisy and full of smoke. The smell of beer was heavy in the air. Groups, all of them young, jostled at the bar or ground their bodies together on the small dance floor in the corner whenever the juke-box played.

Occasionally, when bending at the pin-ball machine, one of the men might brush against her, pushing his groin against her hip or buttocks. Mostly she took no notice, not bothering to make a comment, letting them get their cheap thrills, but if one of them came on too strongly, asking suggestively what she might be doing after, she would chop him down with cutting sarcasm.

'What're you doing later, darlin'?'

'Getting fucked. But not by you.'

They never liked having their manhood ridiculed, so would swagger back to their group and boast how they had got close enough to the girl to give her a feel of it against her arse.

Jennifer listened without concentration to the conversation of the two women at the table with her. As usual they were discussing sex in a mindless way. How well this or that boyfriend could perform. Comparing notes.

Her grey eyes swept the room, apparently casually but missing nothing. It was the group over by the fruit-machine that had caught and held her attention. Three men, older than most of the club members, were sitting hunched over their glasses of stout, talking, their heads close together. There was something sinister in the way they held themselves. She wasn't sure why she had singled them out. Just that they were different. Two of the group sat facing her but the third had his back to her and she couldn't see his face.

'I'm going to play the machine,' Jennifer told her friends. 'Here's a fifty. Be a darlin' and put a record on the juke-box. Anything will do, but not too noisy.'

She stood and squeezed past her friend, smoothing the green, soft leather skirt against her thighs before walking long-leggedly towards the table where the men sat. One of them noticed her and nudged his companion, leaning close to make a lewd remark. A dirty laugh followed. The third man didn't bother to turn.

The fruit-machine was beside their table, and as she approached she noticed that the one who had not turned round had no drink in front of him. Nor was he smoking. She tried hard to hear what was said, but with her arrival they had lowered their voices. She waited for the record to play, knowing that as the music crashed into the room they would be forced to raise their voices to combat the noise.

'. . . Hammer between eight and nine. They'll know then for sure.'

'. . . what about the . . . I'll need at least . . .' It was the one whose face she had been unable to see. He was leaning forward, checking points off with his fingers. Jennifer watched him out of the corner of her eye while still playing the machine, pushing money in with studied concentration. She noticed that the little finger on his left hand stuck out awkwardly. It didn't bend when he made a fist.

'. . . it'll be at one fifty . . . easy for . . . After . . .'

Jennifer strained, trying to make sense of the broken dialogue, hearing only the occasional phrase. She won two pounds then waited helplessly for the machine to cough the coins noisily into the tray, the clatter drowning their voices.

'. . . white Escort outside . . .' The crowd was now applauding the dancers at the end of the number. The three men returned to their muted discussion and she was unable to hear any more. At last the two facing her got up and left. There were no handshakes, no backward glances as they weaved their way through the crowd and slipped unobtrusively through the door. The last of them lingered, but she knew from his movements, the way he shifted in his seat, that he intended to stay no longer than was necessary. Perhaps he didn't wish to be seen leaving with the others. She wondered if it was important.

The machine paid out another win, spewing out coins

so that they rattled into the tray once more. Jennifer, apparently gleeful, threw out her hands, letting the coins she already held spill into his lap.

'Oh, my word. I'm sorry,' she gasped. 'You'd better be handing me my money back. Unless you want me rummaging down there for it.' She let her eyes drop to his lap, the innuendo left hanging as she appraised him coolly from under long lashes. He had to scramble around looking for the coins, finally needing to stand up to let the last of them fall to the floor.

She was struck by the greenness of the eyes that stared levelly at her, firstly at her breasts, then rising slowly to her face. She would later recall that she remembered no expression in them. Two bright green marbles set back in the sockets under dark brows.

No humour. No sparkle.

No life.

He returned her money with his right hand, rough from manual labour, and she cupped both hands to take it, gazing at him indolently through the haze in the room.

'Could I get you a drink?' The voice, like the eyes, was without expression, thick with the harsh, flat sounds of the Falls Road.

'Bacardi. With tonic. And a twist of lime.'

The long drink would keep him there. Unless he walked out on her.

'This is Belfast. Not bloody Kingston Jamaica.'

Educated, she thought. Not your average thick Paddy, who didn't know Kingston from the railway station.

Jennifer sat in one of the chairs recently vacated by his earlier companions. It was still warm. She watched him push his way through the crowd to the bar. The table was bare. Just wet circles where the glasses of stout had stood. She saw the green eyes bore into the barman who was about to serve another party that had been standing there longer. His order was taken.

With authority, she noted. Used to getting what he wanted, when he wanted.

The drinks were paid for with a five-pound note. He waved away the proffered change.

Not short of a bob or two either.

He returned to the table with her drink and a glass of mineral water for himself.

'Not drinking? A proper drink, I mean?' she asked. He hooked out the chair opposite her and sat in it.

'Early start. I need a clear head tomorrow. Can't afford to be bleary-eyed, not with what I have to be doing.' He looked over his shoulder and glanced casually around the room before returning his gaze to her. His eyes once more dropped to her breasts as if he liked what he saw. Something at last registered in the green marbles, a brief spark flaring, then extinguished.

Lust.

'Jennifer McCauley.' She offered her hand. 'Most people use Jenny. Especially close friends.' She flirted deliberately and obviously.

'I'd better be calling you Jenny, then.' Her hand was taken and again she felt the roughness of him.

'And what should I be calling you?'

'Patrick. Never Pat. Patrick.'

No surname.

They talked and he bought her another drink. She thought she might be appearing a little tipsy to him. He waited for a slow number to come on the juke-box before asking her to dance.

'I came with a couple of girlfriends. They'll be mad if I desert them,' she replied, although she knew she would dance with him.

She stood, this time leaving the short leather skirt hitched up on her thighs. The marbles took in her legs. She came out from behind the table and walked in front of him to the dance floor in the corner, letting him get a good look at her backside where the panty line was indenting into the soft leather. They pushed through the swaying dancers, most of whom were fondling and kissing open-mouthed. They reached the back of the floor.

She was a good dancer, moulding into him as they walked in small circles on the creaking floor, she compensating for his lack of rhythm. She could feel the hardness of him against her thigh and when their hands dropped to waist height, she let the back of her hand slide along the length of it until, at its end, she ran her thumb in light circles. His response was to put his hand under her skirt on the soft part of her thigh above her stockings. She murmured approval as his fingers pushed her panties to one side, then stroked her with a tenderness she found surprising.

'You'd better be getting me out of here before we're swimming in come.' His voice was ragged, choked.

Jennifer led him off the floor, telling him to wait while she got her coat.

She was gone five minutes. He did not see her use the telephone, punching the buttons quickly, talking into the mouthpiece in a low voice. When he came up behind her she was telling the taxi where to pick them up.

Her flat was small but neat with an adjoining bathroom and kitchenette.

'Not bad.' He was looking around appreciatively. The double bed seemed to hold his attention.

She had been working on him in the back of the taxi and now she could see the outline of his penis as it pressed against his jeans, angling down his thigh, a spreading damp at its end. She pushed her skirt and panties down together, standing high-heeled in front of him, legs encased in shiny stockings, spread provocatively. He moved towards her, standing close, letting her fingers work his belt buckle open. The jeans dropped stiffly to his ankles, and free from its confines at last, his penis slammed upward as he ground it against her belly. His hands clamped around her buttocks and he dipped his knees, eager to be inside her.

'Patience, Patrick. We need to be safe.'

She moved away from him and bent to the bedside table searching for a contraceptive. She didn't hear him come up behind her, just felt the heat of it as he rammed into her.

'No!'

Her hand reached quickly behind her, a manicured thumbnail digging painfully into the base of his erection. She wound her fingers into his pubic hair and jerked hard. He yelped, pulling out of her as she turned to face him, anger flaring in her eyes, her body tense, rigid.

'No johnny, no fuckee.' She was adamant.

He shrugged then tore the foil packet open and peeled it over himself. She lay back on the bed and let him do it to her then, making whimpering noises into his shoulder, telling him he was the best, the biggest dick she'd ever had in her. At his climax he raised himself up on his hands, impaling her, growling deep in his throat then shaking uncontrollably as he came.

'John-ny-get-your-gun,' he muttered, then collapsed on to her, breathing hard, his hair moist against her breast. She had moaned and cried out with him, knowing he would think he had given it to her. Now she lay spread-eagled under him, stroking his back with long fingernails, whispering things she knew he wanted to hear, knowing that he felt good, masculine, that he'd satisfied her and made her come with him. Had he bothered to feel her breasts he might have wondered why the nipples were soft and unresponsive, not hard and erect.

Even Jennifer McCauley could not fake that.

Now she lay on her back and waited for him to start talking. She knew he would. They always did. She listened to everything he had to say. Later he came out of her, saying that this wouldn't be doing and that he ought to be sleeping in his own bed, that he couldn't afford to make a mistake today.

'Would you call me a taxi?' he asked her.

'This is a working-girl's flat in Belfast, not a posh room in the Europa Hotel,' she quipped.

'Then I'd best be on my way. An hour to walk if I can't find a cab at two in the morning, leaving only three hours in my pit to sleep you off.'

He went to the toilet before he left and she heard the heavy splashing from where she lay. It was still flushing noisily as he left. At no time had he tried to kiss her.

Jennifer lay unmoving after he had gone, listening to the small noises of the flat. She got up at last, put on a robe, then opened the drawer of the second bedside table. She pulled out a telephone. Sitting cross-legged on the bed, she dialled a number. It was answered on the first ring. She could picture the tape running.

'Yes.'

A man's voice.

'This is Rapier. There's something on. Starting today at 0600 or thereabouts and completed by nine. A three-man team possibly. One of them is called Patrick—'

'Surname?' the voice interrupted.

'No, I couldn't get it.' She paused. 'He has an injury to his left hand. Told me he did it on a building site back in 'seventy-six. The little finger sticks out straight. He can't bend it.' She gave a complete description.

'Address?'

'Don't know. I arranged a tail before we left the club, to pick him up from my place.'

'Any more?'

'I heard a word. Can't be sure but it sounded like hammer.'

'Hammer.' The voice spelled it out.

'Yes. And there's a car. A white Escort.'

You're sure they're Provees?'

'Bet on it. I was close enough to smell the bastard.'

'Thank you, Rapier.' There was a pause. 'I'll pass this on. Do you wish to allocate a codename?'

Cucumber entered her mind. Instead she said: 'Yes. Marbles.'

'Marbles is confirmed.'

The line went dead.

She remade her bed then, throwing the soiled sheets and pillow-cases into a wicker basket in the bathroom. She looked at herself in the mirror, hating the reflection, the expression that stared defiantly back at her. She looked down at herself, seeing where he had put himself into her. She vomited into the sink, retching noisily. For half an hour she washed herself, scrubbing hard, finally using a vaginal douche. Still she could feel where he'd been, the greasy sensation of the condom as it had been pumped in and out of her. She fell on the bed. Burying her head in the clean pillows she sobbed raggedly. She begged her father to forgive her.

Inspector John McCauley had been blown to pieces by an IRA car bomb in the driveway of their house. It was the only time he hadn't checked under it. She had watched in fascinated horror from the bus-stop further down the road as she had waited for the bus to take her to school, the searing white heat of the explosion, the ear-shattering impact as pieces of metal were slammed into the air only to clang and patter back to earth. Then, the awful stillness.

One of his fingers had landed at her feet.

Now, she was WPC Jennifer McCauley, Royal Ulster Constabulary, two years an undercover operator.

Her codename was Rapier.

*

Outside in the cold of the November early morning, Patrick Donnelly turned up the collar of his denim jacket, looked hopefully around for a taxi before trudging off in the direction of West Belfast.

He didn't see the figure in the donkey jacket step out of a darkened doorway across the street and follow at a tactful distance.

There was much on Donnelly's mind.

CHAPTER TWO

Patrick Donnelly felt the cold eating into his bones, forcing him to hurry along, cutting in and out of dark alleys to avoid being picked up by an Army patrol. He knew which routes to follow, but with no desire to walk the whole way home in the crippling cold, he headed for the bright lights where he might be lucky and get a cab. At the junction, he hesitated, glancing over his shoulder.

The man in the dark donkey jacket, trained in the art of covert pursuit, was already in a doorway as Donnelly's head began to turn. Not that Patrick Donnelly was expecting to be followed. His mind anyway was filled with thoughts of Jennifer McCauley, of how she had looked standing in front of him wearing nothing but a thin silk blouse and a pair of stockings held up by a frilly white suspender belt, framing her pussy like it was a fine old masterpiece. Couldn't tell if she'd been wet for him, though. The condom had spoiled that. Grinning, he scratched the sore part at the base of his dick where her fingernails had dug into him.

Bitch.

Dismissing the thoughts of her, he let his mind drift back over the years that had brought him here. He saw segments of his life through a diaphanous curtain, catching glimpses here and there of his childhood as he had grown up in the harshness of Belfast in the fifties and sixties, the times before the Brits had arrived to trample all over them. His mother, a thin wisp of a woman, had told him of the earlier bad times, when it was almost a sin to be Catholic, when all the proper work went to the Protestants.

She had told him after his father had died how she'd almost killed herself giving birth to him, Patrick, in a damp house in a narrow street when his old man had been out pissing it up with the labourers he worked with. If it hadn't been for the neighbours hearing her screaming bloody murder, she would have died there on the bedroom floor amongst the bits of gravel and hardened cement that had fallen from her husband's work boots.

He also learned why he was an only child. She had secretly gone on the Pill. She had told nobody of her dreadful arcanum, afraid of being excommunicated. Not that she ever went to church. His father, she told him, could never understand why she was never with child again. It wasn't through lack of trying on his part. Every night he would stagger home, full of stout, and lurch up the narrow stairs to where she would be lying huddled under a thin blanket, with him, baby Patrick, asleep in the next room.

She would see him sway into the room, heavy and ponderous, reeking of booze, collapsing on the foot of the bed as he sat to remove the working boots. He had once been a powerful and muscular man but the constant drinking had turned his belly to flab. In an uneven contest between working at the site and drinking at the club, the drink had won. Now, she recalled bitterly, he was soft all over. Except for his dick. One thing your father never suffered from was brewer's droop, she had said.

And so she would suffer the humiliation and pain of having the whale-like figure humped over her trying to make another child. He was slow to come and she reckoned it had to be the booze. Sometimes he would fall asleep in the middle of it, and she would wait for the pain to ease as his penis softened and slipped out of her. Then she would struggle out from under him, leaving him snoring and snuffling into the pillows while she went down to the freezing kitchen to make herself a cup of tea, having first looked in on Patrick. Most nights he would come though and in the morning remember. But he could never work out why she was never pregnant again. She had told him that there was no lead in his pencil. It had been worth the swipe across her face, to say that.

Donnelly had now reached the bright lights of the centre, but still saw no sign of a taxi. He cursed himself for following his dick earlier, like a bloody compass, to Jennifer McCauley's flat. He blew into his cupped hands, trying to restore some feeling as he peered hopefully to left and right. Nothing but privately owned cars. He considered trying to flag one down, but thought better of it. There was no way anybody would stop here, at this time of night.

He had struggled at school, not because he was unintelligent, but because the facilities were never sufficient to induce good teaching. The school building was in a poor state of repair; books were in short supply and those that were available were covered with brown paper to prolong their lives. Everything was decrepit, or dilapidated. Everyone left as soon as they could.

Patrick Donnelly had learned about one thing at school: sex. Not through sex education, for this was unheard of in those days, but from what he later termed practical application. He learnt to masturbate by the time he was eight.

He had gone into the outside toilets at break-time, where it stank of stale piss, and had walked in on a group of the older boys, in their early teens. He had seen their hands flashing back and forth on the hairy stumps and wondered what they were doing.

'Wanking, Patrick,' is what they had told him. It was the first time he had ever seen a hard-on. He tried it, on himself when he got home. He was amazed at the change to his dick. He liked the sensation. He loved the way it made him feel. He was hooked. He did it whenever he could after that, sometimes several times a day. He didn't go blind. Nor did he grow hair in the palm of his hand. Only at the base of his prick and around his balls. He supposed that the hair had grown there instead of in the palm of his hand. He'd never heard the word puberty.

He was thirteen years old.

The real thing came to him when he least expected it. He couldn't even remember what class it was. But the urge to do it had come over him. He was sitting at the back of the room on a stool behind the long bench that served as a desk. A boy he knew vaguely, perhaps younger, was sat beside him. Donnelly had worried a hole in his trouser pocket and was working on himself, paying no heed to the teacher at all. It was near the end of the class and she was giving out work for the next day. Patrick concentrated on what he was doing, trying to imagine what a cunt looked like. He heard the boy next to him ask him what he was about.

'Having a wank.'

'Shall I do it for you, Patrick?'

He let the boy put his hand in his pocket, felt the fingers close round his shaft and start the gentle rubbing.

'You've a whopper, Patrick. And hair.' It was awkward the way they were fooling around, kids playing with each other. Patrick saw the mistress gather up her books and dismiss the class. He undid his fly under the bench so that the boy could do a proper job on him. He felt himself beginning to come.

'Donnelly!' The voice slapped him back to reality. 'Just what are you two doing? It's disgusting.'

Shit.

The mistress had been watching them through the glass window in the door at the back of the class. Now she had come into the room, and seen the boy's hand playing with him.

'You.' She spoke to the other boy. 'Go to the staff room and wait for me there.' He scampered out, his face flushed with fear and embarrassment.

'As for you, Donnelly, turn round.' He tried to get his dick put away before he pivoted on the stool but there was too much of it. The bloody thing sprang out again as he swivelled to face her. He saw her look down at him, saw her lick her lips making them wet.

Donnelly noted the indecision, suddenly apprehensive. She had been holding her lesson notes in against her shoulder with one hand, the other was clenched tight at her side. There was a long pause. Patrick saw her decision. She took a pace forward and placed her notes on to the bench, leaning over him to do so. He smelt her perfume. She stepped back.

Donnelly saw a look in her eyes he didn't understand, knew only that he was going to see cunt for the first time. He knew. Instinct. He sat quite still, doing nothing, waiting for her, leaving the initiative with the woman. She dragged up her skirt so that it was hitched up around her waist and Patrick Donnelly saw the tufts of dark hair curling out from the panties, before she hooked her fingers into them and pushed them down. He smelt her again, different this time. She stepped forward, leaving the panties in a pretty little pile on the classroom floor.

Even in her high-heeled shoes she had to stand on tiptoe to get him into her. Donnelly came the instant he felt the warmth of her envelop him, unable to control the violent shaking of his body. But she hadn't done with him yet. Oh no. She had come this far and was not going to stop until she had her satisfaction. She began to bounce him and young Donnelly let the initial discomfort pass, watching the muscles in her thighs contract and expand, as she rode up and down on him. He listened to the noises they were making, the sucking mingled in with the hoarseness of her breathing. He didn't know what to do with his hands. She showed him, taking them and placing them on her buttocks so he could feel the smoothness and where he was in her.

Quicker now. His back was hurting pressed against the bench. She was smothering him, her breasts in his face so that he could feel the softness of them through the lambswool sweater. She was noisier too, animal sounds he'd never heard before. The sensation building in him overcame his fear. She had risen right up on the tips of her toes so that only the head was held in her. The ecstasy was delirious. She held herself like that, teasing, until at last she slammed down on to him. He felt her come. He marvelled at it. Feeling the wondrous sensation as she worked unconsciously on him, softly, caressingly, tightly, loosely. He had also climaxed for a second time. Maybe it was the third. He had learned about sex in those short minutes which felt like for ever. He knew now what the others only imagined.

He was still hard when she came off him. Like getting off a bike, he thought. She didn't look at him again, just gathered up her notes and hurried out looking at the floor. She had left her knickers behind. Young Patrick Donnelly bent forward and scooped them up. He screwed them up into a ball and put them in his pocket. The incident in the classroom changed his life. From that day he lived for one thing only. Sex. It ruled his every action. He lived and breathed for nothing else.

Until they taught him to kill.
After that the two were synonymous.

The taxi's horn caught him unawares. It had come up behind him, cruising slowly as it sought out a late fare. Patrick slid gratefully into the rear seat feeling the warmth envelope him. He gave the address of the car-hire firm where he worked and lived, then sat back, watching idly out of the side window as the cab sped through the deserted streets.

The man in the dark donkey jacket cursed, then looked about him for a telephone.

Inside the taxi, the seats were stained and it smelt of the dampness of Belfast and stale cigarette smoke. Donnelly leaned back and let his mind wander, not following any particular pattern, just letting it meander from one train of thought to the next. He made no attempt to come to terms with himself, nor to justify his actions. What he did, had to be done. It was the only way to get the Brits out. They understood no other language. He tried to remember how long he had been involved but his mind could not cope with the problem. He knew the Brits had been there twenty years. Twenty years too many.

In the early days their presence had not bothered him. He had work at the site and he kept out of trouble. He, like most of the Catholic population of Northern Ireland, recognized that they, as the minority, got the short straw. The jobs, the perks, the housing, went to the Protestants. Everyone knew that. He had seen the discontent growing, festering in those early years, the riots, the bloody B Specials savagely putting them down, the RUC trampling all over them as they protested the only way they knew how. On the streets. With bricks and bottles, and finally petrol and nail bombs.

Donnelly had kept out of it. He saw no need to man the barricades. But Derry and Belfast became battlegrounds. The rioters were getting the better of the Establishment. The RUC and the B Specials were knackered, unable to maintain the relentless pressure night after night. And so, on that fateful day in August 1969, the decision was taken that was to alter the course of the historv of the Province for ever. The British Army was called in. At first they had been welcomed by the Catholic population, who gave these fresh-faced lads in their steel-tipped ammunition boots, with white banners and shiny bugles, cups of tea on the streets. All very civilized. It couldn't and didn't last. The Army was seen to be on the side of the Establishment. The Protestants. The killing started, slowly at first, some of them, some of us.

Donnelly, in the back of the warm taxi, remembered.

Still he had remained aloof. At that time he saw no reason to man the barricades. But Molly couldn't keep away. She had to get involved. Her barricade was the biggest. It had withstood the onslaught night after night, and the defenders would jeer derisively as yet another attack was beaten off. One night, the Establishment had decided that it had to go. The symbol of defiance had lasted too long. A combined Army and RUC effort was launched against it. Donnelly shuddered as he remembered.

He had been walking home. He had had to pass behind the barricade to reach his road. He had been able to see the figures of the soldiers silhouetted against the flickering light of smouldering petrol bombs, huddled in behind the protection of their armoured 'pigs'. He had seen Molly rallying her defenders, magnificent in her dirty jeans and anorak, her hair flying in the wind. He hadn't been close enough to tell but he knew that the wildness would be in her eyes. Like it was when they did it, grinding together on the couch in her mother's front room.

Three years his senior, she had taught Patrick Donnelly how to make a girl go wild. He had been a good learner and she gave him all the practice he needed. The teacher, reflected Donnelly, in the back of the classroom, was just the tip of the most exciting iceberg.

Donnelly was in love.

The charge, when it had come, was ferocious. There was no possibility of them holding out. They broke and ran as the rubber bullets rained about them, hitting the running defenders in the back and shoulders as they had fled. Molly, his Molly, had lingered on to toss one last defiant petrol bomb. Donnelly had watched her as she tried to light the damp match, scraping it down the sloping piece of paving-stone put there for that purpose. The charging soldiers were closer, he could see long riot sticks, others with rifles staying with the vehicles. He had screamed at her to get out, to leave the bloody thing and run with the rest. Christ, they were close. Donnelly saw the burly sergeant ahead of the others, his boots thudding through the rubble and mess of the riot.

He saw the match flare, a pinprick of light blossoming as the fuse of the petrol bomb caught. Triumphant, Molly had scrambled up the barricade, the flaming bottle in her hand. Her arm had been drawn back, ready to hurl it at the oncoming line.

The rubber bullet hit her full in the face, flicking her head backwards. Donnelly had heard the thud of it. The petrol bomb fell at her feet, breaking on a sharp edge of the barricade. It ignited with a dull whoosh, enveloping the girl instantly. Her screams, as the nylon anorak she wore had melted and burned on her flesh, were horrifying. Donnelly had seen her hair go as the soldier reached her, ripping off his combat jacket and covering her in an attempt to smother the flames. But the nylon burned into her like phosphorus. Her screams of pain and terror continued long after the flames had been put out.

They hadn't let Donnelly near her. They'd formed a cordon which he couldn't penetrate, a circle of grim young soldiers, facing out, their rifles and riot sticks held across their bodies. The ambulance had eventually come and taken her away. A soldier had given her a shot of morphine, and Donnelly had felt the first beginnings of hate when he heard one of them say not to waste it on the Catholic bitch. It was her fucking petrol bomb. Let the cow fry.

Molly had died in the ambulance. His Molly who had taught him how to love.

The next day he had joined the Provisional IRA. He was seventeen years old.

Donnelly felt the taxi slow for a corner and realized that he was almost home. His mouth was dry with the bitterness of memories and he swallowed saliva to ease the discomfort. The IRA Command had not made use of him in the early years, despite his protestations. He wanted to be at them. Give us a bloody Armalite and I'll show you what I can do. But Command had plans for Patrick Donnelly. He was made to sweat it out, hearing of the gallant deeds of the other brigade members, feeling inadequate in not being able to contribute. One day in August they had sent for him.

'You're to go to the mainland, Patrick. There's a place for you to stay in Kilburn, and a labourer's job to keep you in money. When you're eighteen, you're to join the British Army. They'll teach you to kill.'

He had done it. He loathed every living minute of it, the drill, the bullying, the piss poor food, the barracks in which he was imprisoned. He hated Command for making him join the people he most wanted to kill. He did the bare minimum required to keep him out of the guardroom. The instructors thought of him as a thick mick, hardly worth their attention.

All except the weapon training instructors.

They didn't much care for Donnelly's attitude either, but at least in weapon training he had paid rapt attention. He had kept the pamphlets in his barrack room and would study them at night when the others were out on the piss in some downtown German *Gaststätte*. He knew them by heart, and could strip and assemble all the company weapons blindfolded. He was the best shot in the platoon, especially with the automatic weapons. Command was getting its money's worth out of the young Patrick Donnelly.

The weekly letter from his mother had arrived and Donnelly almost didn't bother to read it. Her handwriting was thin and characterless, as if someone had dipped a spider in ink, then allowed it to walk across the paper. The letter had been filled with the normal depressing Belfast news and her complaints of him not sending her enough money. Right at the end, where he had almost missed it, was a small insert. A man had come round to the house and given her a telephone number for Patrick to call. He was to do it as soon as he got the letter.

He had squeezed himself into the *Deutschebundespost* call-box and fed his money into the machine, before dialling the number he had been given. It was picked up almost before it had rung.

'Yes?'

'I was told to ring this number.'

No names were given.

'You're to buy yourself out of the Army and come on home. There's work to be done.'

At last.

He was going to get into it. And now he was ready.

When he got back, he was allocated the M60 machine-gun which had been stolen in America. On each mission it was brought to the place of the killing, assembled for him, then dismantled and taken away when it was done. All he ever did was to fire it, kill with it. It was the only weapon he ever used.

It was his.

CHAPTER THREE

Johnathan Norris watched the shaving foam form a symmetrical pattern in the palm of his left hand. He transferred it to the stubble on his face, not knowing as he picked up his razor that this was to be the last time he would see his reflection in the mirror of this room. The diagonal crack across the glass gave his face, handsome in an untidy sort of way, a lopsided and out-of-proportion appearance.

He finished shaving and dressed quickly. The camouflage suit was still damp from yesterday's patrolling and he felt uncomfortable in the confines of the jacket. Sore patches had appeared at the top of his thighs where the constant chafing had inflamed the skin. Somehow he had been unaware of it. Too busy zigzagging along the pavements of West Belfast trying to present a hard target to any Provo who might have him in his sights.

He laced up the combat boots and glanced around the small box of a room that had been his home for the last three and a half months. There was just sufficient space for the camp-bed in the corner and a low square table against one wall cluttered with his belongings. A metal wardrobe, the door secured by a heavy brass padlock, stood across one corner. A stainless-steel wash-basin with the cracked mirror above it completed his rude quarters.

Any remaining space was jammed full of his gear. A camouflage-pattern rucksack stood at the foot of the camp-bed, open, with a heavy military pullover spilling untidily from the innards. A flack jacket, sweat-stained and greasy, was hung across the back of the chair. Not the most luxurious of places, he thought. But then he had only another two weeks to spend here. What the hell.

He bent down to his sleeping-bag and straightened out the mess. It smelt of body odour and gun oil. He pulled the zip fully open to allow the air to circulate. At the same time he hefted the rifle into his hands from where it had lain like a lover beside him in the sleeping bag. It was still warm from the heat of his body. He picked up a loaded magazine from under his pillow, checked the alignment of ammunition and let it drop into his thigh pocket. With a last quick look around the room, he left by the narrow door, the gun crossed over his arm gamekeeper fashion.

He was never without the rifle. He even slept with it. The men found this trait amusing, but he didn't feel remotely self-conscious. He accepted the banter, remembering an old Western he had watched as a boy with his father. In it, two over-the-hill gunfighters, one of whom was bringing the other to face justice, the other with his hands tied as a result, had been caught in the open in a hail of fire from a rival group hidden in a barn. The two had dismounted from their horses and run for cover in a ditch, only to find that the bad guys were out of range of their hand-guns.

'Where's the rifle?' asked the one who was tied.

'Still with the horses.'

'In the old days you *never* would have left the rifle,' replied the other disgustedly.

Norris thought it had been Randolph Scott and Joel McRea yet he couldn't be sure. But he took the rifle everywhere. No way would he ever be caught without it.

The door creaked shut behind him as he stepped out

into the cold November morning. It was drizzling and his jacket was soaked by the time he had crossed the square. The dreary building which housed the dining room was hidden by a high corrugated-iron fence and wire netting, which served as protection against the home-made mortars which were becoming ever more sophisticated and accurate. They'd not been attacked here, but he had once seen the devastation in a similar base, where a bomb had landed without warning amongst the occupants.

The dining room was overpoweringly warm and he let the heat wash over him. There was one occupant, already seated at the table, wolfing down his breakfast. He was the last of the RUC patrol to eat, the remainder having skipped breakfast in favour of sleep, albeit in a damp sleeping-bag on an uncomfortable camp-bed. The constable had removed his flak jacket and sweater and looked up only briefly in acknowledgement as Norris entered, before continuing with his meal. He ate ravenously and noisily, as if it were his last breakfast. Who knows, thought Norris, maybe it was.

Through the hatch, he could see the duty cook moving soundlessly amongst the pots and pans in the warm, friendly atmosphere of his kitchen. Whenever a patrol came in, there was chow. No complaints with that.

The cook looked out of the hatch and grinned.

'Usual, Mr Norris, sir?'

'Got it in one, Peterson,' he replied. 'Have you heard from your wife yet? I know you've been worried.'

'Got a letter yesterday. Great. It's another boy. Seven and a half pounds. We're over the moon. One breakfast special coming up.' It was no more special than for anyone else, but the banter passed between them daily. It helped break the monotony of the cook's day, thought Norris. Sweating amongst his steaming pans, waiting for the combined patrols to come in was a dull job, one that he himself wouldn't care for.

Norris pulled off the camouflaged scarf he wore and wiped the moisture from the rifle before placing it carefully next to his chair. It lay within easy reach. He collected his meal from the hatch and sat down to eat, wondering what the day might bring.

Two more weeks. A lifetime.

He dallied over his coffee, steaming hot in the mug, letting his mind wander aimlessly through the kaleidoscope of memories that cascaded through his brain. He loved the Army as he loved life, as his father before him had loved it. Strangely, he was second generation serving in the same theatre as his father had done twenty years before. In the bad old days, the old man had joked.

He had inherited his father's technical bent and was gifted with a high level of raw intelligence. His decision to join an infantry regiment had been consciously taken, and, although his mother had wanted him to, he had not followed his father into a technical corps. Nevertheless he had opted for a graduate entry commission after the successful completion of a science degree at Bristol University.

'More coffee, Mr Norris, sir?' Peterson's head was poked through the hatchway. He had noticed the empty pot on the hotplate in the corner and replaced it with a fresh brew.

'Thank you. Yes. I'll help myself.'

Johnathan got up and refilled his mug before letting his body drop into a battered armchair, the mug perched on the arm. He could reach out and touch the rifle with the tip of his toe.

He closed his eyes and breathed deeply.

After a year out in America, getting ready for the Regular Commissions Board – where he would be either accepted or not into Sandhurst – was a rush. His mother fussed about him while his father sifted through the paperwork and travel documents to make sure all was in place. Then, on a sunny Monday morning, he boarded a train to Westbury in Wiltshire, seeing others bent on the same career course as himself, some apparently calm and relaxed, others pinched and nervous.

The next three days were to sort them out. At the end of it, his brain hurt.

It had begun easily enough with written intelligence tests and he was not overly concerned. The interviews had been probing, though, with questions, apparently innocent, loaded with innuendo. He noticed the notes written in red ball-point pen when, in his own mind, he had answered badly.

'Be *yourself*, Johnathan. Anything else and they'll find you out.'

He had remembered his father's advice.

The buff envelope arrived two days later. He had been accepted into Sandhurst as a graduate entry.

His stint at the Academy flew by and he was commissioned almost before he had time to take stock. At his graduation ceremony his mother had cried, dabbing her eyes with a useless little handkerchief which did nothing to stop her mascara from running. His father had hugged him and for the first time in his life Johnathan had felt a touch of embarrassment.

He had made it.

To Belfast on a wet November morning.

He came out of his reverie, finished the cold coffee and looked at his watch. Time for a letter to be written before he reported for duty in the operations room.

'Thank you, Peterson.' He picked up the rifle. The cook's head, pink from the heat of the kitchen, was thrust through the small hatch. The white hat had been knocked out of true and Peterson looked comical, unable to get his hands through the hatch to straighten it.

'In for lunch, Mr Norris? Stew and dumplings. Only instant potato powder though. No resupply till tomorrow.' Peterson looked anxious.

'Should be in by thirteen hundred if there's nothing unusual. Keep me a meal warm in case I'm late. And thanks.' Johnathan was already heading for the door, standing aside as two RUC constables hurried in out of the rain.

He heard the telephone ringing as he crossed the square. The door of the operations room was flung open. A shirt-sleeved figure stood framed against the light.

'Mr Norris, sir. Telephone. Battalion. Sounds urgent.' The door swung shut as he ran towards it. The duty corporal handed him the telephone. The room was cramped and smelt of the stale cigarette smoke that hung in the still air at ceiling height, almost obliterating the upper half of the large-scale street map on the wall.

'Johnathan?' He recognized the voice of the second-in-command. 'There's a bomb. A big one. Between two and three hundred pounds. Home-made explosive. Location, junction of Cregah Road and Hamel Drive. Got that?' Norris scanned the map. The corporal found it first and stabbed a finger.

'Got it. Cheeky, that close to Castlereagh.'

'Felix has been scrambled and is on his way. But he wants another brick in support. You're flavour of the month. How long before you can be moving?' Felix was the nickname given to the Explosive Ordnance Disposal officer.

The corporal was already on the second telephone alerting the duty section.

'Ten minutes. What's the plan. Will Felix zap it?'

'Can't. It's right outside a residential home. No time to

evacuate so he'll have to defuse it. We got the call from the RUC, who received the info from the *Belfast Telegraph*. Anonymous caller.'

'I'm on my way.' He could hear the vehicles revving up outside. He moved quickly but without apparent haste across the square and into his room where he put on the flak jacket and his helmet. He checked his equipment and switched on the radio clipped to his pocket. Outside, he snapped the magazine on to his rifle and contrary to all regulations cocked it so that the live round was fed into the breech. He thumbed on the safety catch.

The two vehicles were drawn up in line just inside the high gate, bursts of purple-blue smoke belching from the exhausts as the drivers revved the engines in an attempt to warm them. There were four soldiers in each. Norris waited for the sentry in the tower to give them the all clear before ordering the gates to be opened. They swung inward as the ground sentry pulled them on unoiled hinges. Norris climbed into the first vehicle.

'Go,' he ordered, and the two vehicles roared out into the open, past the concrete chicane and quickly down the road in a cloud of spray.

Behind them the gates clanged shut.

They drove fast through the wet streets, almost empty at this early hour. A section of the large-scale map had been cut and pasted to the butt of Norris's rifle then covered with acetate to keep it readable. He used this to guide the small convoy towards its destination.

Everyone looked everywhere.

Another routine patrol.

Just another day.

The reluctance to transfer intelligence between the security forces of the world is unquestionably the weakest link in the fight against terrorism. Intelligence and its sources are jealously guarded and the lack of success in the apprehension and conviction of terrorists is, more often than not, due to the reluctance to pass on intelligence tips from one service to another. Most branches of the security forces like to gain the credit for arrests and subsequent convictions rather than giving the chance to their opposite numbers. This practice is less evident in Northern Ireland, where it has long been recognized that to contain and eventually defeat terrorism a joint police and army effort is necessary.

Thus it was that a transcript of Rapier's report was sent from RUC headquarters at Knock to Headquarters Northern Ireland in Lisburn. The package was taken to the barracks by an RUC courier vehicle and handed in at Receipt and Despatch.

It was 5.17 a.m.

The document was registered, and because it was marked as priority it was hand-carried to the Intelligence section and given to the duty warrant officer, who duly signed the transfer slip and tossed the envelope into the in-tray on the desk, while he completed the Intelligence log for the previous evening. Half an hour had passed before he took the envelope and carefully slit it open, removing the single sheet of paper. The warrant officer noted the secret classification and that it was graded Class One which meant the source was undercover and could not be further identified. He lit a cigarette, the twelfth of the night, and squinting through the smoke, began to read.

Whistling silently through his teeth he swivelled his chair to face the mainframe computer terminal and began to tap the keys, accessing the on-line data. As the screen scrolled out the information he sought, each menu was intently studied, more keys tapped, more information called up, each piece cross-referenced and checked.

Nothing of note under Patrick.

The warrant officer was a diligent man. He persisted. An hour passed.

Without a name or address he had little to go on. He drew a blank when he keyed in the general description. He stretched, yawned, his shoulders aching, his eyes watering from the smoke that curled up from the cigarette in his mouth and incessant staring at the screen. He tried another tack, initiating a stepped scan search.

'Come on, old girl.' He was drumming his fingers on the table. He looked down at them, paused, and remembering something in the report about fingers, began searching in the free text section of the menu. The screen filled. The cursor blinked.

He called up INJURIES, scanning the screen. He keyed in HAND and watched the prompt. He entered LEFT. The screen filled, unfolding the data.

He keyed in F – I – N.

Nothing.

He tried again with FINGER. There it was:

FINGER: FOURTH: LEFT HAND

The ash fell from the cigarette and dropped into his lap. He called up the reference, feeling elated, fearful. He read from the screen:

REFERENCE: FILE: T/NI 457–3/76: ARCHIVES

There was nothing in the archives of the computer. He realized the date was 1976. He rechecked the times given in Rapier's report. It stared out at him. Between 0600 and 0900 hours.

His watch said 7.26 a.m.

He picked up the telephone and dialled quickly. It rang. No answer.

'Shit.' He was running out of the office, along the corridor and down the steps to the basement. The duty

NCO was walking towards him with a mug of tea, whistling, unconcerned.

'Why the hell aren't you manning your phone? Get in here. Find me a three-series file. Nineteen seventy-six, number 457. And move.'

In his hurry, the NCO slopped tea on his desk making the ink run on the ENQUIRIES sign. He moved along the racks of dusty files counting out the years, seeing the impatience in the warrant officer's eyes.

'. . .'seventy-nine, 'seventy-eight, 'seventy-seven . . . Here, 'seventy-six.' He began to thumb through the boxes of files. '. . . 450, 455 . . . 6 . . . 457. This the one?'

The Intelligence officer took it, flicked open the faded cover. Clipped inside was a single piece of paper with neatly typed notes and two photographs. He began to read.

INTRODUCTION

1. The enclosed photograph and negative were received from the RUC at 1430 hours on 4 May 1976. The RUC had 'obtained' them from a freelance photographer named Joseph Bannerton who works for several provincial newspapers in Norther Ireland. Whilst he was 'handing over' the photograph to the two RUC constables, they were able to 'persuade' him to tell how he had come to take them. [The main photograph has since been published in all the mainland nationals.]
2. He was apparently reluctant to divulge his source but eventually admitted that he had been contacted by a low-level IRA member who had told him that if he wanted to obtain a scoop photograph he was to go to Crossmaglen at 1400 hours the following day. On his arrival at the appointed RV he was guided to a side-street and told he could photograph whatever he chose.

3. The photograph of the M60 machine-gun and its operator is the only one of real interest. From his position behind the gun, it is apparent that the firer has received professional training. He is lying in a classic position and he is holding the weapon correctly, the butt close into the cheek and right forefinger on the trigger.
4. The enlargement of the section of the photograph showing the hands reveals two points of interest.
   a. The first pad of the index finger of the right hand is resting on the trigger, confirming he has received formal instruction. (An untrained operator would use the finger at the second joint.)
   b. The little finger of the left hand stands up vertically and is not curled round the butt as with the rest of the hand. If, indeed, the firer has undergone training, and he was holding the weapon correctly (which in all other respects he is), all the fingers of the left hand would be gripping the butt.
5. It is also evident that the firer is used to wearing a beret. It is clear from the photograph that it has been pulled correctly down over the right ear and does not stick out 'cow-pat' fashion as is so often seen when berets are worn by the various paramilitary groups operating in the Province.

ASSESSMENT

6. The firer of this weapon could be professionally trained and will be competent in the use of the M60 machine-gun. He may even be ex-British or Irish Army. From the way he is holding the gun there is an indication that he either has a personal idiosyncrasy or, more likely, the little finger of the left hand is injured and the firer is unable to bend it.

The report was signed by a Major T. P. Johnstone, Intelligence Corps, and dated 5 May 1976.

It was the twelve-by-nine-inch glossy black and white photographs that held the Intelligence officer's attention. They showed the figure of a man wearing a balaclava mask and black beret lying behind an M60 machine-gun. A section of the photograph had been enlarged to show the hands. Where the left hand held the butt close to his cheek, the little finger stood up vertically.

The warrant officer knew Major Johnstone, was aware of his painstaking care when examining intelligence. He pictured him poring over the photographs with a high-powered magnifying lens, sucking air over his teeth as he tried to identify the make of jeans from the patch on the rear pocket, the brand of boots the firer wore. There would have been a slow, satisfied smile when he noticed the fingers.

He heard the big clock out in the quadrangle strike the quarter hour.

It was 7.45 a.m.

He started running again.

The corporal took a sip of his tea and wiped his desk where it had spilled. He started to whistle again, still unconcerned.

The two Land-Rovers turned into the top end of Stirling Gardens, pausing briefly to let the traffic scurry by, propelling its occupants to their places of work. The rain was heavier and the windscreen-wipers slapped back and forth clearing the rain from the scratched windscreens. To Johnathan Norris everything looked peaceful, ordinary. Rain slanting down on a Belfast street, spattering on to the wet tarmac, forcing the few pedestrians into the middle of the pavement to avoid the rainwater gushing from broken gutters. The people he saw looked pinched and resigned. Robberies, killings, bombs. Norris saw it in the hunched figures, a dull acceptance somehow. Some time, this would end and they could go back to living normal lives.

Norris saw the police road-block two hundred yards from him, the red and white tape stretched across the road to prevent further access. Two RUC constables stood beside their Land-Rover with its engine running, and he could see the irregular coughing of the exhaust fumes as the engine laboured.

His two vehicles drove along the length of Stirling Gardens. The furniture lorry and the dirty van parked in front of it, in a side-street to their right, were noted but not registered in minds busy with the problem ahead.

What held his attention was the vehicle slewed across the junction of Hamel Drive and Cregah Road, two hundred yards further on, opposite a white-painted mock-Tudor building which he recognized as the Residential Home. There was no one to be seen and he knew it was the vehicle housing the bomb.

He ordered his driver to stop just short of the road-block and heard the thump of rubber-soled boots on the wet road as his brick dismounted and moved quickly away from the vehicles and into the shelter of doors and alleyways.

Satisfied that the men were in cover, as best they could find it, Norris walked forward to the RUC checkpoint along the road. When he asked them where Felix and his team were, one of the constables pointed to an alley in the direction of the suspect van. Norris moved there quickly in a shuffling, zigzagging run, bobbing his head forward as he moved. His rifle was held to his shoulder, pointed down across his body at a forty-five-degree angle. He turned thankfully into the alley, feeling less exposed than he had on the wide expanse of Hamel Drive.

Felix was in deep discussion with an RUC sergeant and

Norris waited until they stopped talking before he introduced himself.

'Charlie Barnes,' said the Bomb Disposal Officer. 'Where are your chaps?' Norris told him, quickly without preamble.

'OK. We're not sure about this one. The RUC found it at about 0600. One of their constables has been up to it and peeked inside. It's a beer keg, so if it's live we're looking at between two and three hundred pounds of home-made explosive. The reporting constable couldn't see any command wires, but I'm not happy. This could be a "come on", which is why I asked for another brick – yours. I'd like you to do a sweep,' he stabbed a finger on the map, 'from Thiepval Avenue, that's where the RUC road-block is, and along Hamel Drive, where the suspect vehicle is located, out as far as and then beyond the RUC road-blocks. My chaps will provide close protection here. Anything out of the ordinary, *anything*, let me know. Flick your set on to my channel if you need to report.'

Norris listened without taking notes, nodding to show he'd understood.

'Where do you want *me*?' he asked.

'Close by,' said Felix. 'I may want to hold somebody's hand.'

Patrick Donnelly sat with his back to the sides of the van with his knees drawn up to his chest. Now that the time for action was approaching he was calmer, more relaxed. He yawned more from nervous tension than tiredness, although he had to admit that he could have used another couple of hours in his bed. He let his mind remember Jennifer McCauley. Now that was what he called a fuck and a half. He recalled how she had moved beneath him, panting and moaning as she had come, her stockinged legs drawn up under his armpits so that he could feel the nylon rubbing against his neck. That had been a really neat trick. There was something odd about her, though. He couldn't put his finger on it exactly, but she had seemed, at times, a bit too refined.

'Brits.' The voice was pitched low, full of disdain and disgust. The other occupant of the van was sitting in the driver's seat and had seen the two Land-Rovers speed past the entrance to the road in which they were now parked. Donnelly didn't bother to look. Time for them later.

'Keep a sharp eye out for the signal,' Donnelly said, 'it won't be long coming. Better get the engine started.' He listened as the starter whirred. The engine coughed and finally caught. The driver watched the man in the black work jacket standing in a doorway across the road from their vehicle. The engine laboured under the effect of too rich a mixture, letting the acrid fumes seep into the rear of the vehicle where Donnelly now sat.

'Shut the bloody choke off before you gas me,' he snapped. 'How the fuck am I supposed to see?' The pitch of the engine evened up then, but the driver had to work the accelerator to prevent it from stalling. Donnelly looked once more at the gun. It was laid out on the floor of the van on an old stained mattress, its bipod supported by sandbags. To him it was the most beautiful thing he had ever seen. It possessed him like an evil being and he was a slave to it, and its ability to spew death. The ammunition glinted in the dull light inside the van, each bullet destined to send its message of destruction at his bidding. He felt the stirrings of sexual arousal as he stared at the M60. It was allocated to him. No one else was allowed to touch it except when carrying their section of it to him. He let his hand caress the oiled metal, raising his fingers to his nose so that he could breathe in the smell. His penis had erected.

'That's it. The signal.' The driver had seen the man across the street light a cigarette then drop it to the ground and immediately step on it. The van moved slowly forward and turned into Stirling Gardens. Behind them they heard the high-sided furniture van cough into life and knew that it would be pulling forward to the position that they had just vacated. Patrick Donnelly stretched out behind the gun, adjusting his body position to absorb the recoil when the weapon leapt into life in his hands. He lay relaxed in his place and waited.

The driver dismounted and closed the door without slamming it, then moved to the rear with the canvas screen and a blue traffic-diversion sign. He placed them around a manhole and then returned to the front of the van and climbed into the driver's seat. The man opposite crossed the road and joined the other two. Once aboard, he climbed into the rear through the space where the passenger seat had been removed, and knelt by the rear doors to report the actions of the group of soldiers at the far end of Hamel Drive.

'I see him.' The observer sounded excited. 'He's on his way to the suspect now. He won't be in there five minutes before he realizes it's a fake. You'll get just the one chance. Are you ready, Patrick?'

Patrick Donnelly lay on his stiffened penis and nodded.

He was more than ready.

Johnathan moved to the corner of the alley and looked to his left. He could see the whole length of Hamel Drive as far as the junction with Stirling Avenue where the morning traffic was already building up. To his right, eighty yards away, was the suspect vehicle, angled across the junction with Cregah Road, doors closed, rain pattering on to the roof. He talked into his radio, short sentences, listening for the acknowledgements. He gave the command and saw his soldiers appear from their places of concealment and begin the shuffling run, occasionally lifting the short stubby rifles to their shoulders and sweeping the buildings with them.

He turned back to the Felix team. Already the remote-control device, like an ungainly toy tank, was whirring along the road in the direction of the van, guided by a corporal with a control box in his hands. A good operator could do just about anything with this contraption. It was a life-saver. The Army called it Wheelbarrow.

Johnathan watched fascinated, at the same time admiring the skill being demonstrated as the machine was guided around the van, its TV camera relaying pictures through the cables spewing from its rear. The watchers peered intently at the monitor in their vehicle.

'What do you reckon, boss?' It was the corporal talking to Felix.

'Looks clean. Bring Wheelbarrow round this side and take the door off.'

'I enjoy this bit,' Norris heard the corporal say. 'I hope he's got his insurance in order. At least third party fire and theft.'

'Get on with it.' There was no rancour in the reply and Norris could feel the comradeship between the two. He thought that they had probably been through this routine a hundred times before.

Wheelbarrow was positioned alongside the vehicle and, using the TV camera, the corporal aimed the on-board shotgun at the door handle.

'Right, I'm ready.' Charlie Barnes spoke briefly to the RUC sergeant, who in turn talked into his radio, checking with his road-blocks. Norris did the same, warning his brick.

'Zap it.'

The sharp crack of the gun reverberated in the narrowness of the street as the heavy shot slammed into the door. More work on the controls and the door was pulled open by a remote arm. A switch was pressed and the inside of the van was flooded with light as the spotlights came on. The three of them scanned the screen, eyes screwed in concentration.

'There it is.'

Norris too saw the beer keg lashed to the side of the van, ugly, sinister.

'We won't get our little friend in there,' muttered Charlie Barnes, 'too much shit around it. Besides, it's too high. Tucked back at that angle we can't get a clear shot at it. Did you see how they've welded steel bars across the back door to deny us access?' He paused. 'I'll have to go in.'

Johnathan saw the look that passed between them.

'Body armour, boss?' An unnecessary question, but the corporal asked it anyway. He began to dress his EOD Officer, pulling the heavy suit over his chest and shoulders. The armour protected the whole of the front upper torso and Norris heard the quip as it was fed between the officer's leg and the straps tied at the back.

'Got to protect the wedding tackle,' said the corporal. 'That's one bit we have to look after.'

Norris saw that, despite the banter, the laughter had gone from their eyes. It was replaced by apprehension. And something else. Trust.

'Helmet, boss.' Not a question this time, more like an order. 'I know that it hurts like hell, but wear it.'

'You're a worrier, Taff.' But he pulled the helmet on, wincing as the foam pinched his ears against the arms of his spectacles. They both knew that once inside the confines of the van, the glasses would mist up and he wouldn't be able to see through the visor of his helmet.

Charlie Barnes's mouth had dried up. It always did when he was this close to a job. His training helped, kept him clear-headed, but it never really made up for the fear that crawled around his guts like a dose of salmonella. He was afraid. Shit scared. It made no difference that this was his twenty-third bomb, that he had done it all before and that by now it was all routine. Something about this one felt unusual, he wasn't sure why. But sure as hell it was different.

Each awkward step took him closer to the van. It looked ordinary, as if it had been abandoned by joy-riders who had stolen it and run it out of petrol. But he was nevertheless unhappy. It wasn't right. It didn't smell right.

He stopped ten yards short, wishing he had a cigarette. He smoked too much, and knew it. He thought of the notices from the Surgeon General, warning him that smoking was hazardous to his health. So was dismantling bombs.

The van.

It was as he had first seen it. He realized that he was now very close to it. He crouched, the movement made awkward by the heavy body armour he wore. He thought briefly that this, perhaps, was how the Ninja Turtles felt just before they went into action. Inwardly, he chuckled at his own childish thoughts. But, for a fraction of time, it had kept his mind off the thought of entering the van.

The van with the bomb in it.

Christ, he hated it. Every time he was called out, he hated it.

In the beginning he had been able to control the fear, when he had felt the first stirrings of doubt, and the uncertainty in what he was doing, that his training might somehow let him down. He remembered the time when it had gone wrong. God, he had been so lucky. He had missed the simplest anti-handling device, and had got away with it. A fluke. The bombers had screwed up and got it wrong, and Charlie Barnes had survived, when he ought to have been splattered all over the walls of the warehouse.

Charlie Barnes tried not to notice the sweat trickling down behind his right ear.

He looked once more at the van, squinting through the rain-covered visor, seeing the huge drops splashing off the roof. He wondered again why on earth he had ever become an EOD officer. For the second time in as many minutes, he wished he could light a cigarette.

He came back to reality. Young Norris and his boys were in position and sweeping the area. And Taff was on the monitor. It was OK. Just another suspect bomb. He'd done it before. Twenty-two times in fact. He approached the van, feeling the evil coming from it. He walked round it twice, looking at it from every possible angle, checking for command wires, anything that might give him a clue about the means of detonation. He glanced over his shoulder and was reassured to see his group of vehicles, their image made hazy by the rain, grouped in the distance, their silhouettes bristling with antennas.

He took a deep breath. The door had been wrenched open by the remote-control device and he was able to see the mess of the interior of the van, the plethora of implements and equipment scattered haphazardly, put there to keep his concentration from the bomb. He saw it at once, and was careful to keep his body out of the line of the camera recording his every move.

Don't lose me, Taff.

Slowly, he reached up and took hold of the sides of the door. He placed a booted foot on to the floor of the van, then shut his mind to the uncertainty. He pulled himself into the dark interior, hearing nothing except the roaring in his ears and the rain splashing on to the roof in an uneven staccato that filled his head with the sound.

He looked at the bomb. The beer keg. He squatted uncomfortably down on his haunches and studied what was in front of him. His spectacles began to mist. He couldn't see. He altered the angle of his vision, seeking a gap in the murky Perspex of his helmet that would give him a clear view, tilting his head to see under the line of the condensation. It worked for a while, until condensation won the uneven contest and spread over the whole of his visor. With a sigh he reached up to the helmet and slowly pulled it over his head.

He placed it carefully on the floor of the van within easy reach. He sighed deeply, massaging the sore patches behind his ears where the helmet had rubbed. He tried to avoid licking the cold sore that had formed on his top lip. Instead, he ran his hand across his mouth, ending the movement by scratching the side of his face absently.

He was calm now and he could see what he was doing. The fear was gone. This was routine. He reached for his bag. Even in the noise of the rain he heard the sound of the zip as he tugged it open.

Right.

Let's be having you.

CHAPTER FOUR

The Chief of Staff at Army headquarters in Belfast was a man of habit. Each morning he would walk his big Labrador around the perimeter of the barracks, calling in to the operations room for an update on the previous evening's occurrences before strolling over to the officers' mess for a leisurely breakfast. He liked to mull over the problems at the big polished table in the dining room, only half-listening to the muted conversation around him. It always struck him as odd that nobody talked at breakfast in a mess, but he had learned to live with the tradition. He was unique in not taking a newspaper to the table, preferring instead to let his mind grapple with the oncoming problems of the day.

The operations room was quiet save for an occasional telephone ringing. For once the radio was silent. He picked up the log and scanned it briefly. Nothing of importance or untoward. He looked at the duty watchkeeper, who was busily writing on a message pad.

'All quiet, Peter?' he asked.

'Yes, Brigadier. The usual minor incidents and reports of gunshots. Patrols are out following up but it's unlikely they'll find anything. There's been an RUC report of a suspect vehicle and Felix is dealing with it now.'

'Right, I'll be off to the mess then. I'll be in at my usual time.' The Chief of Staff turned to leave, but paused as the Intelligence Warrant Officer came quickly into the room, panting and agitated.

The Brigadier felt a surge of anticipation. He listened.

'We got an RUC report in at just after five this morning. It's a Class One grading so it's from one of their undercover operatives. I'm not sure what it all means yet, but I've been doing some cross-referencing on the mainframe and I'm not sure I like what I've found.' He took a deep breath. 'The report indicates an upcoming Provo action, thought to be planned between 0600 and 0900 hours today, any time now, that is. All we have to go on is that it could be a three-man team, that one of them is called Patrick and that he has an injury to the little finger of his left hand.'

'Not much. Any more?'

'Yes. Going through the archives I found this.' He placed the glossy photographs carefully on the table. The Brigadier studied them, not seeing the significance at first.

'Look at the enlargement. Of the hands. The little finger.'

'I'll be damned.' The Chief of Staff went over to the map

and stared at it. 'What was the word that was intercepted by their people?'

'Hammer. But they weren't sure.' The Intelligence Officer was still wheezing from his dash up from the basement.

'Peter,' the Chief of Staff turned his attention back to the duty watchkeeper, 'remind me again what we have deployed.'

The watchkeeper came over to the map, the lights glinting from his spectacles. He pointed out the incidents which were recorded there with symbols stuck on the Perspex covering the map. He was succinct, accurate, wasting no time.

'And the suspect vehicle? Where is it?'

The watchkeeper showed him.

'There. The junction of Hamel Drive and Cregah Road.'

The watchkeeper was an observant man. He saw the alarm jump in the Brigadier's eyes.

'Hammer? Hammer?' The Chief of Staff was deep in thought. 'Oh my God. It's Hamel Drive. That's what was heard.'

He hurried to the map and bent to it, looking at the position of the suspect vehicle, its relation to the length of Hamel Drive, the traffic system that would keep the road clear from the top end. The scale of the map showed it to be at least three hundred yards.

'They're after Felix. The bastards are after Felix.' He'd seen it all at once. 'Get him out of there. Tell him to abort. But get him out. Now.'

The watchkeeper picked up a telephone, the direct line to Brigade, and started talking rapidly into the mouthpiece.

Johnathan watched as Charlie Barnes walked the eighty yards to the suspect vehicle, where he skirted carefully around it. He did this twice before gingerly, awkwardly climbing into it. He held the bag of equipment in his hand like a GP going off on his rounds. They watched him disappear.

'What happens now?' Norris had a fair idea but wanted to hear from the quiet corporal who wouldn't take his eyes off the monitor screen.

'He'll be shitting bricks. Bloody great breeze-blocks. He'll be using all his bits of kit, following the drill. It ought to get easier the more you do it, but it doesn't. Every bastard's different, HME, Semtex, tilt switches and God knows how many other types of anti-handling devices.' The corporal stopped talking, concentrating on the flickering screen. He went on. 'That's why he follows a procedure. Trouble is he can't see once his specs mist up. He'll have the helmet off as soon as he's out of sight. He's good though, this one.'

The corporal's eyes never left the screen.

Charlie Barnes's face appeared from the van. His thumb was stuck up in the air.

'A hoax. I'm going to hook it, though, just to be sure.'

He was without his helmet.

'OK.'

Norris saw relief flood the corporal's eyes. He knew what the term hooking meant. That Charlie Barnes would select a hook from the assortment he carried and attach it to the device, then paying out the nylon line he would make his way slowly back to the safety of the alley before yanking the bomb over.

'If it has got a booby on it, there'll be a fucking great bang,' said the corporal, 'and they won't be needing a window cleaner round here for a long time. But if he says it's a hoax then you can bet your life on it. You would though, wouldn't you?' The corporal was grinning now. It was all over, bar the shouting.

The radio in the vehicle came alive.

'. . . This is Zero. Fetch Felix. Over.' There was urgency in the voice, controlled, but Johnathan recognized it.

'Zero. Felix indisposed. Over,' the corporal spoke briefly into the mike, looking at the monitor.

Another voice came on the air. There was no mistaking the authority in it.

'This is Zero. Fetch Felix. Fetch Felix. Over.'

The NCO thought for a moment.

'Zero, Roger, wait out.' He released the pressel switch. 'Boss. You're wanted. On the radio. Sounds like top brass.' He was yelling down the street. Norris could see the annoyance in the corporal's eyes. Nobody ever asked for Felix in the middle of a job. Not unless it was vital.

'Right. I'm just about through here. Hold on a tick.' Charlie Barnes was backing out of the truck, paying out the nylon cord as he came, pausing only to unhitch the snags. There was no noise. Just the sound of the rain splashing out of the gutters.

It was quiet inside the dirty van with the clean rear windows. One of the three-man team sat in the driver's seat, a second knelt at the rear door with his face pressed against the window, while the third, Donnelly, lay behind the gun. He was breathing shallowly, evenly, eager now that the time was near.

Donnelly saw the van window mist up as the man positioned there spoke, his face close to the glass. Suddenly the watcher winced and ducked his head below the window. Donnelly chuckled, knowing that outside one of the patrolling soldiers had suddenly, without apparent reason, snapped his rifle up into his shoulder and aimed it at the van. He knew too that if nothing had been registered the weapon would sweep away seeking another unseen target.

'Patrol coming.' The voice of the watcher sounded nervous.

'How far?' Donnelly was not overly concerned.

'About two hundred yards, maybe more. Other side of the street from us. Four men.'

'Forget them.' Donnelly was dismissive. 'Concentrate on the target. He's the one Command wants. He's the one we've come for. Stop pissing yourself and get a grip.'

The man behind the gun saw the watcher's gaze return once more to the window, saw him stiffen and heard the words he had been anticipating.

'OK. He's getting out of the truck. He's working his way back to the alley.'

The watcher took hold of the two wires which, when pulled, would raise a small panel set into the rear door of the van. Once in the upper position, the gunner would have a clear field of fire down the length of Hamel Drive.

The observer was breathing more heavily now, anticipating what was to come. He gripped the wires tightly in his fists, ready to jerk the door upward. Donnelly moved his position slightly on the mattress, raising his pelvis to take some of the tension out of his straining penis, now so hard it was hurting him. He fought to regulate his breathing, knowing that this was essential if he was to control the weapon which he fondled and caressed so lovingly. At last he was at peace, ready.

Watch and shoot.

How many times had he heard that command as he lay on the range firing points so many years ago, waiting for the plywood targets, the picture of a running man pasted on to them, to pop up out of the redoubts three hundred yards away? The sergeant's voice echoed in his ears.

'Now!'

The sliding door slammed quickly upwards on greased pulleys. Donnelly immediately identified the target. A man in a heavy suit of body armour backing slowly towards him, paying out some sort of line. The range, exactly as had been paced out. He looked through the aperture sight with both eyes open, seeing the figure moving towards him in sharp focus.

The excitement boiled in him. He had to shake his head, blink, to bring the figure back into focus. The sensuous feeling in his loins became unbearable, and his body throbbed in anticipation. Gently, lovingly, he squeezed the trigger with the pad of the first joint of his index finger. His eyes were an intense green, unblinking as he poured his concentration into the kill. The gun, his gun, shuddered deliciously as it erupted in his hands. A five-round group of bullets crackled, hissed on their way.

'John-ny-get-your-gun.'

He counted them out to the staccato rhythm, feeling the shudder of the gun in his shoulder, smelling briefly the acrid smell of burning cordite as the rear of the van filled with the stench of it. He heard the empty cases rattle on to the floor of the van.

Three hundred yards away, at the top end of Hamel Drive, Charlie Barnes pitched forward into the wet puddles.

Patrick Donnelly felt the excruciating pleasure of his climax as the semen seeped out of him, clinging to his belly in a warm damp pool.

Corporal Geordie Shaw acknowledged Lieutenant Norris's orders and stepped out of the doorway in which he had taken cover. He signalled for his half section to follow. He spoke into his radio then directed the three soldiers behind him with signals from his hand. Satisfied that they were in position, he led the way down Hamel Drive in the direction of the main junction about two hundred yards in front of him.

Everything seemed normal. The road ahead was clear, free of moving traffic, the way he preferred it when on a job like this one. Not so much to keep track of. The only vehicle in sight was a van parked at the side of the road where some council workmen had erected a screen and a diversion sign to direct any oncoming traffic wide of where it stood. He raised his rifle quickly to his shoulder and sighted on the rear windows before sweeping the barrel away toward some windows high in the building to his left. The rain pattered on to his already soaked helmet.

He signalled for his half section to halt and take cover as best they could. He glanced over his shoulder at the suspect vehicle. He couldn't see Norris, probably still concealed in the alley, but beyond the gap he saw Felix alight from the suspect vehicle and work his way slowly backwards in his direction, paying out the nylon cord as he went.

The burst from an automatic weapon took him by surprise. Without pausing for thought he dashed forward a few yards and hurled himself into the cover of a vacant doorway, wondering where the hell the fire was coming from.

A bullet makes a distinctive noise as it passes close by, a nasty, zipping, buzzing noise which runs instantaneously into a savage crack. This is followed by a thump from the weapon that fired it. Soldiers recognize it instantly. They move fast then, shit scared, instinctively searching for cover.

Johnathan Norris knew it was a five-round burst from a machine-gun. It passed the alley where he was crouching, watching the action a short distance from him. Worse, much worse than the hissing crack of the passing bullets, was the sickening, unmistakable sound of three of them hitting their target.

Thwack-thwack-thwack.

All running into one. Norris watched in horror as

Charlie Barnes, whom he'd only just met, pitched forward as if he had been jerked by an unseen force yanking on the cord he held. He saw clearly the neat holes appear in the unprotected back of the body armour as the copper-jacketed bullets tore through the neoprene and entered the chest through the lower back, chewing through the vital organs before flattening on the body armour, designed to protect its wearer from the front.

Charlie twisted as he fell. A bullet had entered the back of his skull and exited through the cheek under his left eye. He was dead before his body tumbled to the wet pavement. Most of his face was missing. He lay there, his right hand twitching.

Johnathan Norris started running in a low, fast zigzag. Charlie Barnes was lying face down about forty yards in front of him and slightly to his right. He wasn't sure why he had started this mad dash, only that Felix was down and needed help. Johnathan's boots pounded on the wet cobbles as the gap between the two narrowed. His mind was crystal clear. He knew exactly what he had to do.

Donnelly, satisfied, was about to give instructions to move when he saw the second figure break cover and begin running in a low weaving pattern towards the body crumpled in the road, a Guy Fawkes discarded by bored kids. He realized that he was being given the opportunity to get two for the price of one. The voice of the weapon training instructor echoed in the dim recess of his mind, haunting, mocking, the words thick with the Glaswegian accent.

If he's running in a low zigzag pattern, you may have to squeeze off a longer burst. Not by much. Two more rounds, making seven all together. That will see him away with the fairies.

Patrick Donnelly broke his own golden rule.

He fired a second, slightly longer burst.

It was to have fatal consequences.

'John-ny-get-your-gun-a-gain.'

He counted them away, thrilling as he saw the running figure stumble, pirouette like a ballet dancer, then pitch headlong into the road, close to the body of the first victim. The rifle he had been carrying spun out of his hands and fell clattering into the road. It was done. Time to be away. He shouted for the driver to get them out of there, in time to see the big, high-sided furniture van rumble into the crossroad blocking vision in both directions down the length of Hamel Drive and Stirling Gardens.

Exactly on cue.

Geordie Shaw crouched in the shelter of a doorway still hearing the reverberation of the burst of fire as it crashed and echoed in the narrow confines of the street. He was breathing heavily from the effort of the short dash for cover, yet his instinct told him to search the buildings around him looking for the tell-tale signature of the smoke that would show him the direction of the fire. Suddenly, without warning, another burst, this one fractionally longer. The sound was evil in its intensity, frightening in its power, hurting the eardrums as it clattered past. His eyes scanned the street, windows, doorways, rooftops, chimneys, vehicles.

The van.

The council van a hundred yards in front of him, parked on the opposite side of the road behind the diversion sign. It had to be. Corporal Shaw brought his rifle up into the aim, seeing the rear windows clearly through the optical sight. He hesitated. If he was wrong and the fire was coming from elsewhere, he'd be right in the shit for blowing away some innocent Paddies. He could almost see the headlines.

He thought of the little yellow card in his pocket which told him if and when he could shoot.

He made up his mind.

He snapped the rifle into his shoulder, saw the back of the van magnified through the 4 × optical sight. He breathed out, held it, then pressed the trigger.

Once.

Twice.

From the corner of his eye he saw the big high-sided furniture van pull out from a side-street to his left. It drove ponderously across the junction, completely obscuring his target. By the time it had cleared the junction, the dirty van had gone.

From over his shoulder he heard the bomb NCO yelling into his radio. Felix was down. So was callsign two two alfa. Looking, he saw two bodies lying in the road, close enough to touch.

'Oh, shit.'

He yelled at his half section to cover him, had time to register their frightened, alarmed faces peering at him, before he was running flat out in the direction of the bomb disposal team.

Christ.

They'd got his Lieutenant.

He was running. The ground underfoot was softer now and he could no longer hear the sound of his pounding feet. He had watched the greasy ball bobble back through the opposing scrum, like a prehistoric monster laying an egg through the mass of scrabbling legs. He saw too the white-shirted scrum-half scoop up the ball and spin a long pass out to the opposing outside half. He was already sprinting towards the line of players coming fast towards him, angling across the pitch. With the score at eighteen to fifteen and only a minute left to play, the game was in the bag.

But now the opposition had taken one against the head and were running it from their own twenty-two.

Johnathan saw the pass was fumbled, not taken cleanly, giving him the yard he needed. The roaring was loud in his ears as the opposing spectators saw a chance. It died as they realized that the flank forward with the straw-coloured hair was going to intercept their man. The big centre took the pass neatly and came fast and hard down the field.

Already the stand-off was looping outside the ball carrier, creating the overlap that would leave their winger free. Johnathan knew he had to make the tackle and smother the ball all at once, preventing the pass at any cost, holding on to him until his own forwards got round to ruck the ball back. The big centre with the tree-trunk legs would side-step off his left foot. He hadn't come off his right the whole match. He timed his lunge perfectly, hands high to pin the centre's arms to his sides.

His legs seemed to have gone. He was losing his momentum. Somehow he'd come off worst. Must be a real hard case. He nose-dived to the ground.

Christ, I hurt.

He couldn't move his legs.

Come on, ref, can't you see there's a player down?

He was bleeding into the puddle in which he lay. There was a chunk of his shoulder like a bloody lamb chop lying there in front of him. A rough game this one. He lay there on the wet cobbles, unable to smell the grass.

He couldn't hear the radio properly. Some silly sod was shouting something about Felix being down and sunray two two alfa. Who the fuck are they? Rain falling on to his face and the cold spreading up from his legs.

Some back-row forward he'd been, bouncing off the opposition and getting dumped in the mud. He supposed that the centre had come off the right foot after all. No reason to take a bite out of his shoulder though. Again the roaring in his ears. Maybe they'd scored. They were carrying him off the field towards the dressing room. He knew that he wouldn't be at the after-match party that night.

Damn. Been looking forward . . .

Donnelly watched as the high-sided pantechnicon drove forward across the junction, ready to cover their escape. Their own vehicle was accelerating away from their killing position and Donnelly was flung about the interior as it lurched along Stirling Avenue. He gripped the sides of the van as both he and his observer knelt looking out of the window, seeing the gap across Hamel Drive narrow as the furniture van moved into their vision, cutting out the scenes of death which they had just created. The gap was almost closed. Donnelly was flung to the floor of the van as the driver wrenched the steering-wheel hard to his left. The observer was still clinging precariously, his face close against the glass.

'The Brit. He's got his gun up!'

'Forget the bastard. He'll never fire.'

But the soldier did fire.

Twice.

Donnelly and the driver both heard the bullet slam into the metal of the van door. They heard, too, a noise that sounded like a piece of timber slapped against a side of beef hanging in a cold store, flat side on. The observer at the back of the van coughed as the 5.56 mm bullet, twisted beyond all recognition by its passage through the door, tore through his lungs and exited through his back leaving a gaping messy hole. The bullet was deflected slightly upwards into the ceiling of the van where it once more changed direction, ricocheting downwards, out through the windscreen to the left of the driver. He felt the wind of its passing, heard the angry buzz as it sped by, close to his ear. Blood and pieces of flesh were splattered on to the glass obscuring the driver's vision.

'Patrick. What the fuck's goin' on? What's happened?' The driver dared not look round, afraid of what he might see.

Donnelly was lying on his back where he had been thrown by the violent swerving of the van. He had seen the bullet explode through the back of the man who had been looking out of the window, and who had been pitched backwards on to him. For a dreadful moment, before Donnelly could throw him off, his face was forced into the wound as the man lay helplessly twitching on top of him. He felt the mess of it warm and wet on his skin, then he was able to force the weight of him away.

'He's been shot. They fuckin' shot him. He's a goner for sure,' Donnelly was screaming, yelling, his voice echoing in the confines of the van. It was the first time he had seen death close up. He hated it.

'What do we do?' The driver was in a blind panic, the van swaying over the road.

'Stick to the plan. Turn left. Here, you stupid bastard!' The driver had almost missed the escape road, a narrow turn to their left. The van careered round the corner, almost on two wheels. The wounded man rolled back on to Donnelly.

'For Christ's sake! Slow down. You'll draw attention to us.' Donnelly was becoming more rational, his instinct for survival. He heard the sucking noises coming from the wounded man. The van turned left again at the next junction. They were now travelling parallel to Stirling Gardens, in the opposite direction to their line of escape. A short distance along this road was a set of double doors leading into a corrugated-iron garage, a repair shop with a faded sign above. A man who had been waiting for their arrival opened the doors wide as the van drove in. He closed up quickly and quietly.

Donnelly and his team were less than a hundred yards from where the killing had taken place. They were as safe as if they had been a hundred miles. The sounds of sirens were loud in the next street.

The driver stalled the engine as they turned in off the road. His head fell forward on to the steering-wheel. He beat it with clenched fists.

'Jesus,' he said. 'One bloody burst you were supposed to fire. One. One. And you, you stupid arsehole, had to be bloody clever and fire two. Donnelly's Golden Rule you told us. Now we've a wounded man on our hands. Command will have your balls for this. A good man down because Patrick fucking Donnelly couldn't keep his trigger finger from twitching like it's in a whore's cunt!' He had turned round in the driver's seat, facing Donnelly, trembling with fear, delayed reaction, apprehension. Donnelly saw the spittle showering out over the yellow teeth as he spoke. He hit him very hard with his gloved fist just under the right eye, a short punch that hurt his knuckles. He saw the dark bruise appear instantly, high on the cheekbone.

'Shut your face, y'hear? Just shut your fucking face. Get the gun team in here and get my gun safe away. I'll see to him on the floor.' The driver looked sullen, malevolent, but he jumped from the van and called over the group that would spirit the gun away, broken down into its component parts. It would not be assembled again until the next killing.

One section was already being concealed in the false bottom of a pram, the crying baby lain gently over it on her covers, before the mother walked out of the building, going about her normal business. Doing a bit of shopping for her man. The rest would go by equally ingenious methods. Donnelly paid them no heed. The less he knew about the location of the gun, the happier he felt.

He wouldn't touch it or any part of it, until he had to fire it again.

The retching cough brought his attention back to the casualty. Donnelly opened the back doors and looked in on the mess, screwing up his face at the sight of him. The man was dying. Each time he sucked air into his lungs, Donnelly could hear the faint whistling through the hole. The eyes were pure agony. Donnelly lifted one shoulder and looked at the carnage of his back. Dead. But when? The driver had come up behind him and was looking over his shoulder. Donnelly could hear the heavy breathing. He didn't turn to face him. He picked up the vehicle jack.

'The gun's away . . . what the hell?' The driver had seen the jack and the murder in the bright green eyes as Donnelly turned to face him.

'Go home. Go home to your woman. You've finished here.' He saw realization in the other's eyes.

'You can't. You bastard, Donnelly. He's still living, breathing. You can't do it.' He was wiping his nose with the back of his hand, almost crying. He pointed a shaking, accusing finger. Donnelly saw the shiny mark, like a snail had crossed it.

'He'll be dead anyway. You want him talking to the RUC, the Brits? They'll recognize him from the mugshots. I'm not taking that chance. If you've not the stomach for it, bugger off. Now!' Donnelly looked at the other in disgust, then turned his back on him. The wounded man looked up pitifully, a spark of hope in his eyes as he recognized Donnelly. He held out a hand as if he wanted to be pulled into a sitting position. He coughed more blood on to his chest, pink, frothy, like milkshake. Donnelly smiled at him, saw that he was reassured.

Then he hit him with the jack. He hit him in the face and about the head. The jack rose and fell in a steady rhythm. It became slippery in Donnelly's gloved fingers. Blood spattered on to the sides and ceiling of the van. Donnelly stopped hitting only when the head had been smashed into a flat mess of pink and grey, with broken teeth amongst it. The torso was headless. Just pulp where it had been.

The driver was puking in the corner of the workshop, his body heaving as he spewed the dark stout over the paved floor. Donnelly walked over to him and yanked him to his feet. He wiped his gloves on the other's lapels.

'His blood is on you now.' Donnelly was cold, menacing, frightening the man he held so disdainfully. 'Now get the fuck out of my face. You're off my team.' Donnelly spun him away.

A new group had come to dispose of the van. It would be driven away to waste ground, doused in petrol and torched.

One of the newcomers looked into the van.

'Jesus,' was all he said.

Donnelly left via a door at the rear of the building. He crossed a small yard and entered an alley through a broken wooden gate, barely hanging on its hinges. He could see the stolen white Ford Escort. It was parked a short distance away with its engine running. Exactly where he was told it would be. This vehicle too would be gutted once it had done its work. No detail had been overlooked.

Donnelly was unworried about Command's reaction to his killing of the observer. The observer was expendable, but *he* was indispensable. It had been recognized long ago that for him to remain effective, he would need complete freedom of movement. For this reason, Donnelly had to stay clean. No record. Not entered on to any police or Army computer. Nobody to finger him. Patrick Donnelly was a valuable commodity. Command was going to make damn sure he was well looked after.

But Patrick Donnelly was not clean.

Not quite.

CHAPTER FIVE

The Royal Victoria Hospital, Belfast, has the best gunshot-wound surgeons in the world. They get more practice than most. A team worked on Johnathan for three hours, with surgeons probing, débriding, packing. They had done the best that they could under the circumstances, but the senior surgeon knew, deep down inside, that it was almost impossible to recover from the terrible damage inflicted by three 7.62 mm bullets. He had made a study of bullets and their characteristics. It was his business to know.

Each weighed 9.65 grammes. At three hundred yards it would, if fired by a US M14 rifle, be travelling at a velocity of 642 metres per second, creating 1,988 joules of energy. He supposed that there wasn't a great deal of difference if it was fired from the M14 or the M60. It wouldn't matter too much. Especially if you were on the receiving end. He was no scientist, but wondered what could be done with that amount of energy, converted to electricity. Boil a kettle, maybe.

He thought that the hideous shoulder wound would eventually recover, but the smashed spine, where a bullet had entered under the protecting flak jacket, would ensure that he never walked again. But it was the one that had entered the back of the neck and which had been deflected upwards by the rim of the helmet that had done the real damage. If the boy were to survive, it would be as a vegetable.

After surgery, Johnathan was wheeled to the Intensive Care Unit, accompanied by the anaesthetist and one of the theatre team. Together they checked that the patient was correctly positioned and that ventilation via an endotracheal tube connected to the OHMEDA CPU1 ventilator was functioning properly. Blood was fed intravenously into the cephalic vein of the right wrist together with Hartmans solution into the dorsal vein in Johnathan's foot. His blood pressure was monitored continuously through a CVP line inserted into the vena cava ensuring that this pressure was kept low to minimize intracranial pressure and bleeding.

There were other monitors. After the surgeon had gone, the young nurse was left to keep a careful watch on the wounded man. She checked continuously, the pulse oximeter, temperature probe, and the electrocardiograph with its three probes connected to the young officer's chest. The pips were irregular, hesitant, one minute beating strongly, the next faltering as Johnathan fought his silent battle to stay alive. She felt a deep sadness at the cruel taking of life, the maiming and crippling of healthy young people as the troubles continued. She saw no sense to it, no rational reason. She was sickened by what she had been forced to witness.

She looked up alarmed as the ECG stopped momentarily, only to start again with its irregular, hesitant pattern.

He was a fighter. Death would not take him easily.

He was warm at last. Except for his toes. It was quiet. It was dark. He swam in a sea of blackness, screaming silently in his fear of not being able to see the sun. He spoke, but was unheeded. He shouted, feeling the panic.

'Where's my rifle?'

Nobody answered him.

He wept silently in the dark, suddenly feeling the cold.

The nurse was alarmed. The pips from the ECG had converted to a continuous tone, the loudness filling the room. She placed her fingers, butterfly light, on the wrist to confirm that there was no longer a pulse. She felt nothing. She looked at the head swathed in bandages, at the drain to remove surplus blood and serous fluids.

There was no life, no feeling in her probing fingers.

The monitor piped into the room.

She reached over to press the alarm that would summon the ward sister.

In the overly warm dining room at Johnathan's base, Private Freddie Peterson, Army Catering Corps, duty cook, collected the plate of stew and dumplings and potato made from powder, about which he had been so anxious. It had been on the hot plate for young Mr Norris, who was late for lunch. Now he scraped it into the waste-bin. He threw the plate in after it, the knife and then the fork.

'Fucking bastards.'

He was crying.

She scanned the newspaper, reading the report of the killing of the two British officers. She felt the sadness. Everyday someone would be feeling sad in the Province, regardless of occupation, religion or political upbringing. This was Northern Ireland. The sickness was never-ending, endemic and incurable. Jennifer thought the leaders sometimes didn't want it to end. With the violence in progress, they had certain status. They spoke and were heeded. Without the violence, they were nobodies. Just little men who could shout their mouths off until they were blue in the face and nobody would give a shit. The violence was their life blood. They thrived on it.

After the murders she had submitted a full report of her encounter with Patrick Donnelly, although she had been reluctant to discuss how she had learned so much about a man who was, until that evening, a stranger.

'Mind your own bloody business,' she had yelled down the phone at her unknown controller when he'd pressed for details. She didn't know it but her controller had been a close friend of her father. He was sympathetic. He understood Jennifer McCauley's desire to see justice done. That didn't prevent him being persistent. He had worn her down until she had told him.

'When he climaxes. He says "Johnny-get-your-gun." He says it in short sharp bursts, but all strung into one.' She had been defiant. Her control had understood.

'Thank you, Rapier,' was all he had said. He thought of Inspector John McCauley. He sympathized.

The idiosyncrasy was passed to Army Headquarters in Lisburn.

The Intelligence Officer who had spent so long on his computer recorded the information. He looked into the far distance, whistling through his teeth.

'I wonder,' he muttered.

He picked up the telephone and dialled the mainland.

In the Ministry of Defence, Main Building, a telephone rang. A man in his shirt-sleeves lifted the receiver to his ear.

He listened.

'I'll do what I can. It's a bit thin, but we'll do our best. It may take a while. I'll send the information by classified signal. That way we won't be talking on an open line. If you get any more, let me know soonest. Good hunting.'

The shirt-sleeved man replaced the telephone in its cradle slowly. He made some notes on a pad, then started dialling numbers.

The hunt for Patrick Donnelly had begun.

*

She had learned years before that her body could get her anything she wanted. Her figure had developed when she was still young, and at school she was conscious of the effect she had on boys, especially those in the senior classes. She found their attentions flattering and it was not long before Jennifer McCauley was experimenting with sex. She had had a terrible crush on one particular older boy, and had let him know how she felt. He had led her into a secret spot in the midst of the rhododendron bushes behind the sports pavilion and spread out his blazer for her to lie on.

It was her first time, and although he had not let on, it was for him too. He had knelt in front of her and taken it out, so that it was sticking up in the air at an angle. It had excited her. He came towards her on his knees and she had pulled her knickers across to expose herself to him. But as soon as he had touched her down there with it, he had started shaking, and stopped poking it into her. She had been holding her breath in anticipation, and was frustrated and disappointed when he stopped for no apparent reason.

The second occasion was several months later, when she had gone with one of the prefects into the scout hut at the far end of the school grounds. He was much more experienced. He had done it before. He carried a condom in his wallet, and she had seen the mark where it was pressed into the leather. It was the first time she had seen one, and she wanted to giggle when she saw it stretched over him with the teat full of air, like a little balloon. He wasn't as big as the first boy. She had not been sure if that made a difference. He had pulled her knickers off and they had caught on her sensible school shoes, an insignificant thing that made her want to giggle again. But he got it into her and it hadn't hurt. She had supposed that it was due to the lubricant on the johnny.

It had been good, when he started to do it. Jennifer McCauley had liked it. She liked it a lot. Funny things were starting to happen inside her. Nice tingling things that were getting more intense. Then he stopped. Just like the other berk. He left her so that she felt empty, pulling it out of her without saying a word.

She had looked up at him as he stood. The condom looked ridiculous now, but she hadn't felt like giggling then. He had tried to pull it off while he was still hard and it wouldn't come. It was stuck fast, and she had watched as he tucked it away, still with it on. She had had a vision of it falling off, when he had shrunk back to normal, and slipping down his trouser leg and landing on his shoe. *That* had made her giggle. Not knowing the reason for her amusement, he had stomped off, pissed off that she had not been impressed by his performance.

Then came London. Wonderful, beautiful London. Her father had been seconded to the Metropolitan Police, to the Anti-Terrorist Squad, for a six-week period during a marvellous summer when it had been warm without the oppressiveness that usually oiled the city each time the sun came out. For Jennifer McCauley, it was her first time out of the Province and she had felt a sense of relief as she had walked freely in and out of the magnificent shops, without a soldier or armed policeman in sight. She could have been on another planet. Her father, whom she loved, was enjoying the attachment. She had never seen him so happy and relaxed. He seemed younger, and was once more lively. Laughing and contented as she remembered him as a child.

Jennifer was seventeen and in her last term at school. It was the summer holiday, and she was in London, and happier than she could ever remember.

Then her stepmother spoilt it all.

She began an affair with their host, Inspector Brian Chesterton. Her father never guessed what was happening. Yet to Jennifer it was obvious, even at her age. She noticed the closeness, the touching of fingers at the dinner table, the looks full of eagerness that crossed the room when her father wasn't looking, how Chesterton would follow her stepmother out when she made an excuse to leave the room, to come back minutes later, her eyes alight with some bright shared secret, her face flushed. Chesterton would follow, walking awkwardly, his hands in his pockets, a smug but sheepish look on his face. He was damned good-looking though, this Inspector from the Anti-Terrorist Squad. Smooth and urbane. Not in the least avuncular.

She was not going to see her father hurt, no matter what. She thought she hated her stepmother, more so after she had, through a crack in the kitchen door, watched him with his hand up her stepmother's skirt. She had never seen an expression like it on anyone's face. Eyes closed, mouth open. Ecstatic. Jennifer heard the words spoken quite clearly.

'Do it. Fuck me.'

Jennifer was shocked. She ran, face burning, her heart lurching in her chest. Couldn't her father see this happening? He was supposed to be a detective. Jennifer had no proof. But she knew they were doing it. Fucking. It was in the dreamy expression on her stepmother's face, in the eagerness with which she looked up when she heard a car in the driveway, in the music she listened to on the hi-fi. Mrs Inspector didn't know what was going on either. She was too busy keeping her nice detached house clean so that she could impress her visitors from across the Irish Sea.

The affair continued after their return to Belfast. Once, by chance, Jennifer heard her stepmother on the telephone to him, listening from her bedroom as the other sat at the foot of the stairs, the handset close to her lips, saying dirty things about how she would make him come, telling him about the feeling she had down there that wouldn't go away, and that she would die if he didn't do it to her soon. Chesterton was due to come out to the Province for his six-week attachment to the RUC. Jennifer was dreading it. She could see her father's life ruined unless she did something. She got her chance the third day he was there.

Her parents for once had gone out shopping together, leaving the Inspector in the house. It was after he had come back from a game of squash and had gone upstairs for a shower. There might not be another chance. It was now or never. And for Jennifer, the time was right. She crept up the stairs and into her room, where she took off her school clothes quickly, discarding them in the corner. Hunting through her drawers, she pulled out the frilly underwear she had bought without her stepmother's knowledge, put it on and stepped into white high-heeled shoes. She looked at the effect in the mirror, thought briefly, then took it all off again. Instead she put on a silk dressing-gown embroidered on the back with a Chinese dragon, tying the belt loosely around her waist.

She adjusted the angle of the mirror so that as he passed her door on the way to his room, he would see her reflection as he walked by. He would see her breasts and the dark hair below the swell of her belly where she had left the robe open. If that didn't get the Inspector into her room, nothing would. She buffed her fingernails and waited. She heard the shower stop running and the bathroom door open, then his footfall on the step as he mounted the landing, the floorboards creaking at that spot a yard from her room. He was in the doorway looking. He stopped whistling and hesitated, looking back the way he had come. The house was very quiet.

She looked up knowing she would see him watching her in the mirror. She gave a small gasp, as if surprised, pulling the top of the robe across her body with the fingers of one hand, a maiden protecting her modesty. She didn't pull the robe far enough to hide the hair though. She was very careful about that. He had wrapped a towel around his waist and she could see the droplets of water on his shoulders, the dark hair on his belly wet from the shower. She saw the bulge appear in the towel.

Got you.

He came into the room, the posters of pop stars and Winnie the Pooh on the walls. He closed the door quietly behind him.

She turned to face him, holding the robe closed across her body, conscious that it was still open at her waist. She watched his eyes flick down, and tried not to look down at him. Her heart beat rapidly, her breathing quickening in anticipation of what might happen next, frightened that she had already overstepped the mark. Not knowing how to get out of it. Then she remembered why she was doing this, and steadied her resolve.

He was very close to her now, and she felt him lean forward, seeing the uncertainty in his eyes, realizing that for him this must have been new ground. She felt herself flush as his hand rested gently on the softness of her breast, his fingers lightly tracing small circles on the nipple. She saw the look on his face as he felt it harden under his fingers. He pushed her robe to one side, then bent his head to take the tip of her breast in his mouth, gently running his teeth over the swollen nipple. Jennifer held her breath, letting him do as he wanted. He sucked the other, gently, till it was hard like the first, then ran his hand down over the swell of her belly and across the soft hair. His fingers explored her gently.

She was dizzy, afraid yet excited by what was happening. It was a feeling she hadn't experienced before, and she was uncertain. Perhaps she had done enough already. But she was aroused and, without meaning to, was responding. The gown had slipped from her shoulders, she didn't know if it had been by his hand or hers. Almost in a dream, she put her fingers to the towel at his waist and gently tugged it away, knowing he would remember afterwards.

His hands were gently holding her shoulders as he kissed her face and mouth. She felt him push her away from him on to the soft duvet with pictures of Rupert Bear on it. She let herself fall backwards then turned her head to one side as she felt him part her thighs and run his hand along the softness.

She wasn't supposed to be enjoying this. But oh she was. She was helpless, had allowed it to go too far, but didn't care. Don't stop, Mr Inspector. This is bloody wonderful. She felt him lift her legs over his shoulders, first one then the other. He kissed her on the inside of her thighs, softly, then where she was open. She gasped aloud. Nothing had ever been like this. She let him do it, rolling her head from side to side into the feathers of the duvet, sucking her thumb and biting her fingers. He took his time and she knew that he was aware of the effect he was having on her.

He lowered her legs, stood between them as she looked up at him. His eyes were half-closed, bright and intense as he looked down at her. She knew now that it was going to happen. He spoke, his voice calm, a little detached, yet earnest, eager.

'You know what we're doing? Say you know what we're doing and that you want to.'

'Do it. Fuck me.' She remembered her stepmother's words, saw the puzzlement in his eyes.

They did it.

Together.

She had known nothing like it. So good. The lovely slow motion of his movement. She looked up at him, seeing the closed eyes, the head bowing then lifting. Moving against him she felt the beginnings of her climax, and tried to concentrate on what she had to do. His movements were quicker, more urgent and she wondered if he was feeling as she was. He was grunting, gasping as he worked his body. Heaven. Oh, don't stop.

She remembered in time.

'No!'

He hadn't heard.

'No!'

Now he looked puzzled. The motion slowed, imperceptibly. But he was still moving in her.

'No!' Louder, insistent.

Now he realized. He jerked out of her and she felt the warm fluid splash on to her belly. He was breathing heavily, his chest heaving, his expression pained. His arms were supporting his weight on the bed and he was half-kneeling between her legs, still immense, hard and not fully satisfied. She saw anger where seconds before there had been only lust.

'What the . . .?'

She had to speak. The room moved. She had to tell him, so that he would know. She gathered her resolve, still feeling the warmth where he had been inside her. Another few seconds and she knew that she would have been unable to have said the word that made it rape. She shoved him hard in the centre of his chest.

'Did you enjoy me, Mr Inspector, clever one from the Metropolitan Police?' She shoved again. 'That is the last time you do it in this house. I'll not let you hurt my father by carrying on with my stepmother the way you have been. Your mess is all over me, and on my bed. You raped me.'

He was scrambling off her.

'I said no, which made what you were doing to me rape.' She saw the fear, panic in his eyes and felt the triumph. She had done it.

'Get out of our house.' He was on his feet, looking as if he couldn't wait to get away. 'Go back to London and leave us alone. If you don't, I'll tell what you did to me. I don't care about my stepmother, but I won't see my father hurt. If you ever try and contact her again, I'll tell on you. You'll go to prison. You'll be finished.' She saw him shrink, his hard arrogance gone.

She cried then for what she had done for her father. She was sobbing as Chesterton walked quickly from her room, picking up the towel to cover himself. She was still crying when she heard the taxi arrive in the driveway. She stared through her tears as she watched from behind the curtains as he left the house. He didn't look back.

Her parents found his letter when they arrived home from the shops. Her father read it quickly and Jennifer heard him tell her stepmother that Brian Chesterton had been reçalled to London to help in a major case that had just broken.

She saw the anguish in the woman's eyes but felt no sympathy. Just hate. Yvonne McCauley moped around the house for days, wondering why the Inspector never telephoned her or even wrote.

Her father was killed by the car bomb a week later. Her stupid bitch of a stepmother had told him about the affair at breakfast. The blinding row had made him late for work.

So late he didn't have time to check under the car.

The one and only time.

Jennifer forgave neither herself nor the stepmother she had learned to hate.

Instead, she had waited until she was old enough, then joined the Royal Ulster Constabulary.

She became Rapier.

PART TWO

CHAPTER SIX

King Khaled International Airport on the outskirts of Riyadh in Saudi Arabia is the unfriendliest airport in the world. It is a place of engineering genius, built from the finest stone and marble, with fountains and ornamental trees, set into alcoves, standing proudly astride the concourses. Whispering escalators transport arrivals to baggage-collection areas, where passengers stand in confused groups, wondering what lies in store for them. It is deadly quiet. There is neither laughter nor careless banter, no relatives to greet the newcomers with embraces or kisses. Here, in the strictest of Islamic countries, such behaviour is both offensive and obscene. To show such affection can lead to stern admonition, or even gaol.

There are no carefree holiday-makers meeting in happy laughing groups, for nobody, apart from children of expatriate workers visiting for the school holidays, ever travels to Saudi Arabia, unless it is to make money.

Richard Norris stood in line, waiting to clear immigration and customs. He refused to allow the apprehension he felt show in his features. His grey-blue eyes looked around the arrivals lounge, noting the other passengers, many of whom were less comfortable, more confused than he, perhaps worried about their visa or other documentation. He pushed the fingers of his left hand through his hair, an attempt to keep it off his forehead, only to feel it fall back untidily almost immediately. Realizing that he had done little to improve his appearance, he shrugged, then shuffled forward, pushing his flight bag with his foot, reminding himself again that he wore his hair a little too long for a business executive, even if he did own the company.

The tiredness at the corners of his mouth did not hide the strength or aggressiveness of his character. It was a mouth that could smile easily or set in a determined line if the odds were against him. Those who paused to look at him sensed immediately that he was a man who would not suffer fools and would prove a hard adversary if riled. And yet there was humour in the features, haphazardly arranged, as if put there as an afterthought.

He glanced at his watch and wondered what his family would be doing. Felicity was probably at another of her meetings and Johnathan no doubt would be manning the operations room radio, unless he had been sent out on patrol. Richard was not overly worried about his son. He knew, he told himself, how to look after himself. Although he would never admit it to Felicity, he occasionally felt apprehensive, as any father might over the safety of his only son.

He let his mind dwell on his reasons for being in Saudi Arabia. His British Embassy briefing, like that of his sponsors, had been clear enough, perhaps overly cautious. They had done little to dispel the disquiet, the gloom he now felt. He shuffled forward, moving slowly with the remainder of his fellow passengers, stooping to pick up his case, watching as the immigration official scrutinized every passport handed to him. Norris thought that he probably couldn't even read the English, realizing that to an Arab, one European face looks very much like another. This, and the officialdom found worldwide, was probably the cause of the delay.

At last he was through immigration, standing patiently to repeat the process at customs. He knew what to expect here, but was still surprised when an advertisement for Scotch whisky in a passenger's newspaper was unceremoniously torn out and discarded in a waste-bin under the counter. An advertisement featuring women's tights torn from a glossy magazine followed, except that it didn't accompany the first into the waste-bin.

Outside, the night was pleasantly warm, although he noticed that the British Army major who had come to meet him was dressed in a khaki pullover in addition to his lightweight uniform. The man was tanned, fit, lean like a runner.

The two men shook hands.

'Tony Meredith,' said the Major, 'sorry about the delay in immigration and customs. It's always the same though, so don't think you were being singled out.'

Norris laughed, following him to the underground car park. He stowed his bag in the back of a Japanese 4-w/d, and climbed in.

'Nice,' remarked Norris.

'Perks of the job. Courtesy of the Saudis. Don't worry. It doesn't cost the British taxpayer a bean.' They sat in silence, Richard gripped by the beauty of the desert as they drove through the sunset along a modern highway in the direction of downtown Riyadh. The new university building stood grandly, reflecting the red glow of the dying sun. Such splendid architecture seemed at odds with the sight of Arab families sitting on rugs beside their cars in the desert at the edge of the road, watching portable TV sets.

His hotel was comfortable enough, clean and modern, and after arranging a time for collection the following day, Norris said good-night. He unpacked, lay on the bed and began to read the prepared briefing which he was to present the next day. He read for an hour, considered ringing room service to order a nightcap, then, remembering he was in Saudi Arabia, decided against it. Stuff the fruit juice. He would have killed for a gin and tonic. He thought of phoning home to tell Felicity where he was staying, but realizing the time difference, decided to leave it until the morning.

It wouldn't matter.

'Gentlemen, that concludes my presentation. Are there any questions on the capabilities of Seeker?' Richard gazed at his audience, his mouth dry from the sales pitch he had delivered to the mixed group of Saudi and British officers. It had gone well, and Richard was pleased and encouraged to see the Saudi officers talking amongst themselves, occasionally looking to their interpreters to clear up a point. They looked impressed. Mentally he braced himself as the senior Saudi officer began to question him, mostly on back-up and after sales. He was ready, answering smoothly without hesitation, noting the bobbing heads, the quiet asides muttered behind hands. There followed the inevitable queries. Discounts, contractor's percentage charges. Richard had noticed his sponsor shaking his head almost imperceptibly. He took his cue.

'With Your Excellency's permission, I would prefer to leave your query until after today's field trials. I would like you to see a complete demonstration of Seeker before discussing the points you have raised.'

'Of course.' The Saudi stood, turned to look at the group behind. He spoke rapidly in Arabic, then in English. 'Are there any further questions for Mr Norris? No? In that case I will thank him on behalf of us all for the most excellent presentation.' He looked at a fat gold watch, too large on the thin wrist. 'We are scheduled to meet at the Jebel Al Shifa at lunchtime when we will see the equipment working.' His English was perfect.

After they had gone, Richard packed up his presentation and joined the group which had remained behind, re-emphasizing various aspects when asked. He felt light-headed with relief, knowing that once they had seen the kit in action, any lingering doubts would be dispelled. Seeker was the best piece of equipment he had designed and built since forming his company. It was going to launch him in an aggressive, competitive market. More importantly, it would give Johnathan, should he want it, a decent inheritance. Something to get his teeth into when he, Richard, retired, and his son had decided to leave the Army.

He arranged with Tony Meredith for his equipment to be stowed into the rear of a Land-Rover, the 110 LWB model. Satisfied it was stored securely enough for the cross-desert journey, he climbed into the front. He remembered then that he still hadn't called Felicity to tell her where he was staying.

'Get one of the clerks in the office to do it for you,' said Meredith. 'We need to be on our way or we'll be late for your demo.' Richard ran quickly back into the building and located the clerk's office. He handed over one of his business cards and asked if his hotel address could be telephoned or sent by fax.

He rejoined Tony Meredith, scrambling into the front passenger seat beside him. They drove through busy Riyadh streets, Richard alarmed at the traffic chaos at the Petromin flyover. Relieved, they drove on to a wide freeway heading west towards Kashm Al Am.

'Take your life in your hands every time you try that,' said Meredith, grinning at Richard, squirming in his seat. 'Safer than it looks though.'

Once out of the city, Richard was able to concentrate on the demonstration he was due to give to the Saudi and British officers somewhere out in the desert. He was confident that at the end he would have convinced his potential customers of the advantages of his design parameters, ease of operation and maintenance. He let his mind dwell on the procedures.

He knew them backwards.

*

They left the main freeway, climbing a steep escarpment, with tall red and white communication towers, neat white buildings nestling under them, set back off the road and protected by wire-mesh fencing. Soon these were left behind and the tarmac road petered out, gradually becoming a rough track. Finally, they were in open desert.

'How will you find the place?' Richard was curious, remembering his own days in the desert with sun compass and sextant, all those years ago.

'We use this navigation aid, a Loran, same as you get on a sail-boat.' Meredith pointed to a square box, a mini computer, fitted between the two seats. 'I've already plotted and entered our start and destination. The kit does the rest. Gives me course and bearing. I use the vehicle compass to keep me going in roughly the right direction.' He pointed to the dash. 'There's always a track running on the bearing you want. I just follow the track. Every now and then the navigator tells me if I'm off line. I make the corrections, look for another track going our way and follow it. Easy. I used to think it was a black art, but I'm sold on it now. The Saudis have never yet worked out how we find our way about in the desert. White man's magic!' He chuckled, his tanned face looking younger, more at ease. 'It will even give off an audible alarm when we arrive, so even I can't get lost.'

An hour later the 4-w/d ground up a steep bank in low ratio, on to a plateau high in the desert. To Richard it felt pleasantly warm, but he saw Meredith shiver in the light breeze. Their group was located about two hundred yards away standing in a small knot, the red-and-white-checked *ghuttrahs* fluttering in the wind. The senior Saudi officer was talking agitatedly into a mobile telephone. He looked up as the Land-Rover stopped, its engine switched off, the hot metal plinking in the silence.

The officer with the telephone stepped forward, desert boots scuffing through the dust, small explosions as each foot was placed on the ground. He looked anxious in his attempt not to look grave. Richard was suddenly apprehensive, alarmed, but could not explain why. He could hear the engine ticking as he watched the officer approach him through the heat haze rising from it. The group was no longer talking.

A black bird, wide-winged – he had no idea what kind – hovered on a thermal in the white-blue of the sky.

'Mr Norris.' There was no expression in the dark eyes. 'I have been talking to my headquarters. They have received a message from the British Embassy in Riyadh. They in turn have been talking to your Foreign Office.'

Relief.

It was something to do with his export licence. Or his visa.

Wasn't it?

'You are to contact this number immediately.'

Alarm lurched queasily in his throat.

The Saudi officer held out a piece of paper, torn from a notebook.

'I understand it is most urgent.' The Saudi broke off, avoiding looking at him. Richard felt the tightness in his chest. He looked at the single piece of paper held between brown fingers, the wind picking, tearing at it. Slowly he took it. He read the figures printed there in an unfamiliar hand.

Arabic.

He looked at Tony Meredith, controlling his emotions. He handed him the note, watching as the Saudi walked back to the group. He listened as the numbers were read to him, slowly, one at a time, as Meredith struggled to translate.

After the first four he knew.

His telephone number.

The big old farmhouse not far from Cheltenham.

*

It was lunchtime on a beautiful autumn day and Felicity Norris felt serene and happy with her life. The coffee morning held at the hall to raise funds for another of the charities was over and now she drove the small Peugeot towards the converted farmhouse at the far end of the village which had been their home since Richard had left the Army. Her blue eyes reflected her contentment and a smile of sheer pleasure played round her mouth, making her look younger, vibrant and full of life. It had been wonderful news to learn that Johnathan was to be home for Christmas after all and that his tour in Belfast was not to be extended as they had all feared. The regiment was coming home.

Felicity lived for two things: her son, and the beautiful old farmhouse. Oh, she loved Richard too, but it was her son, Johnathan, she idolized. She frowned as she thought of him in Northern Ireland, patrolling the streets, spending long hours in the operations room. Little wonder he looked so pale, washed-out whenever a tour was completed. Never mind, perhaps when Richard returned from this latest sales drive in the Middle East they could take a holiday together. Somewhere warm. They could, if Richard pulled off this contract. That ought to put some colour back into Johnathan's cheeks.

She drove carefully through the village. The white-painted walls shone cleanly in the late autumn sunshine and she realized that she felt as happy as she had ever been. The weather forecast had threatened rain sweeping in off the Irish Sea, but as yet there was no hint of it, except for a few darker clouds behind the square tower of the church.

She parked in front of the double garage. Out of the sunshine it was chilly in the courtyard. Felicity shivered then turned up the collar of her blue mid-length coat, glad of the thick tights she had worn. The wind tugged at the blonde curls circling a pretty face, still young looking. She hummed quietly. Life, she thought, is good. It felt wonderful just being alive.

She was in the big kitchen drinking her third cup of coffee when the doorbell rang. Puzzled, she glanced at the small gold watch, thinking the caller must be from the committee she had left half an hour earlier. She walked along the wide passage, reminding herself again that the big old clock had to be repaired the next time she went into Cheltenham. She was still humming as she approached the door. Twisting the catch she drew the heavy oak in towards her, unconcerned.

The tune and the smile died together on her lips as she saw the short figure in Army service dress uniform standing in the porch.

It was in his eyes.

The sadness, the awful dread of having to tell her, half-concealed in his embarrassment. He shuffled awkwardly on shoes that were too shiny, twisting brown leather gloves in his fingers. The whole face spoke of bad news, and she knew, without him saying a word, why he was there, standing so uncomfortably in the doorway. A terrible feeling struck her and she felt fear wrench at her stomach. The officer opened his mouth, about to speak.

'No! Please. Don't say anything.' Her voice was too high-pitched, quivering. 'Just don't say a word. If you say anything, anything at all, I won't believe you. It can't be true. He's due home in two weeks. Nothing's happened to Johnathan. So,' she felt calm again, 'if you'll be on your way . . .'

'Mrs Norris . . .' the officer spoke at last, his voice gruff, gentle.

Felicity Norris broke then. She shouted at him. There had been nothing on the news. They had received a letter from their son just two days ago. Nothing had happened. Anyway, he had come to the wrong place.

Despite the briefings he had received on how to deal

with bereaved parents, the Casualty Reporting Officer was unprepared for the effect his standing there had had upon her. She was weeping, trembling, beating small fists on his chest, hurting herself on the shiny buttons of his uniform. She collapsed, slowly sinking to her knees, her head bowed, her grief utter.

'Perhaps if Mr Norris . . .' He didn't finish.

'He's away, out of the country. Middle East. Saudi Arabia. He's not telephoned yet. I don't even know his hotel.'

The officer pulled her gently to her feet, and with an arm to support her, guided her back into the big, low-ceilinged sitting room. He went to the telephone on the small oak table near the cushioned window-seat and dialled quickly. His headquarters would know what to do.

The telephone was replaced with a soft click. Felicity continued to cry, rocking back and forth on the couch. She was vaguely aware of the Casualty Reporting Officer thumbing the pages of her private telephone book which he had found on a ledge under the table. Finding a number, she saw him dial, the telephone held up under his chin. He asked for the parish vicar.

Outside, it was beginning to rain, big heavy drops that splashed into the gravel of the driveway. A cold wind started to blow, moaning round the corners of the buildings, across the chimney pots. For Felicity Norris, her beautiful day had died like a discarded match in a puddle. Life, as she had known it since the birth of her son, ended as the heavens cried their tears in sympathy.

Johnathan was buried on a cheerless grey day at the end of November. It was two weeks after Remembrance Sunday, when those that had fallen previously had been remembered. The sky behind the granite tower of the village church was an angry yellow, consuming the stone, cold, cheerless and mournful. Most of the village was there to witness the burial and sat quiet and sombre in the bare wooden pews. A bearer party of Johnathan's brother officers stood in a nervous knot at the small lych-gate at the entrance to the cemetery, awaiting the arrival of the big black car which would bear the body of their comrade.

It crunched to a stop on the gravel driveway.

Felicity sat with Richard and watched as the coffin, draped with the Union Jack, was carried into the church.

Johnathan's dress cap, sword and medal looked lonely in their isolation. Felicity was outwardly calm, in control, dressed in a simple dark-grey coat and matching hat with a wide brim, the veil hiding the empty eyes. She had spent long hours on her make-up, reapplying it each time she was not satisfied. Anything to keep her mind off what was to come. Now it was perfect. And yet there were no tears. The heavy sedative she had been prescribed was effective enough to prevent her registering the words spoken at her son's coffin. She remained calm, benign even, hearing neither the whispered prayers nor the mournful notes of the organ.

The polished wooden coffin was borne out of the church, the bearer party expressionless, staring straight ahead. The hole was neatly dug, the wet brown earth hidden under clean green Astra Turf in an attempt to disguise its purpose. A hole in the ground into which they would shortly lower her son. A grave. It was next to the village memorial stone and in passing, Felicity saw Richard bend and pick up one of the poppy wreaths. As the bearer party stood each side of the hole, the coffin suspended on strong nylon straps, he stepped forward and placed the wreath of poppies on it. She could see the muscles working in his jaw as he stepped back beside her.

The volley of rifle fire crashed out, reverberating around the cemetery, frightening the rooks in the bare oaks beyond the tower, making them rise raucously into the air.

She was vaguely aware of the bugler blowing breathily into his horn, warming it, so that when he played, the notes would come clean and pure.

Felicity did not hear the prayers the vicar spoke as the box bearing her son was lowered into the ground. She heard instead those melancholy words as the wreath of poppies disappeared.

They shall grow not old,

Why, dear God?

as we that are left grow old:

Why my son, whom I loved and cherished?

Age shall not weary them,
nor the years condemn.

He was my life.

At the going down of the sun and in the morning

He was so young, so full of life. He was coming home for the birth of Your Son. Why then have you taken mine?

We will remember them.

The commanding officer of the regiment joined her when it was done, telling her that Johnathan had been a fine young officer whom everyone had liked and respected. He would be missed. At the gate, the vicar offered her his deepest sympathy, the words sounding empty and hollow to her, despite the genuine warmth with which they had been uttered. She listened, hearing, it seemed, for the first time. A brief spark of life came into her eyes. She met the vicar's look of practised sincerity.

'There is no God,' she said clearly. 'If there were, Johnathan wouldn't be lying in that hole in the ground.' The vicar recoiled, shocked.

At the entrance to the cemetery, a television reporter, microphone in hand, stepped forward, approaching them as they were leaving. Felicity's sole thought was to be away from this place. But the reporter was persistent – on the way back to the studio she had been diverted by her station to capture the funeral on film for the lunchtime news. The pictures were to be transmitted live.

The young female reporter pushed into the knot of mourners and thrust out her microphone.

'Mrs Norris, would you tell our viewers of your feelings towards those that perpetrated this crime. Can you find forgiveness for them?'

The microphone was held out expectantly, the reporter conscious that these pictures would impact on millions of lunchtime viewers. Felicity paused, ignoring the gentle pull on her arm from Richard. She lifted her head to look directly into the camera, then slowly raised her veil. Her vacant blue eyes gazed out of a multitude of television sets all over the country. What she said was completely out of character, spoken slowly, every syllable enunciated. None of the crew gave a thought to stopping the transmission.

'I hope somebody cuts the pig-shits up with a machine-gun. Just as they did to my son.'

She would never know the effect those words were to have on the people who watched, nor on Richard who stood trembling at her side.

At the farmhouse, the conversation was muted, stilted, polite. The mourners recognized the sorrow that the two parents were suffering, but knew that the time for words of comfort had passed. Those who stood in awkward groups, quietly sipping drinks, were conscious that they would soon be able to leave, get back to their normal lives, knowing that for Richard and Felicity Norris life would not return to normal. Not ever. They had lost their son, taken from them when life was just beginning.

Felicity went upstairs to lie down, telling Richard that she felt drowsy, that she needed to rest. He followed her as she left the room, making her apologies, saying that Richard would see to everything. Richard watched her heading for the stairs, her body exuding despair, worried that she might have had too much to drink.

He felt empty, lost, with no real idea of how he was going to face life without his son. They had been close, could talk easily together, without the barriers that often appeared between father and son. He tried not to think of the good times, sitting at a table in the sun at a pub on the banks of the Thames outside Reading, planning the next skiing holiday when others' thoughts were on summer breaks on the Costa del Sol.

People were beginning to leave. It was dusk and would soon be dark. Richard saw them out, then stood on the step as the last of the cars crunched past on the gravel driveway. He was glad they were gone. He suspected that they, too, were relieved at leaving. He looked at his watch and saw that Felicity had been gone for several hours. He would leave her a little longer, then awaken her with some tea. They could cry together then in the privacy of their own bedroom. No need to put on a brave face any more.

He poured another whisky and stood in front of the big fireplace where the logs crackled and spat. He felt cold, despite the heat coming from behind him, warming his legs.

The anger started to build in him.

Then came the hatred.

Belfast.

He saw it all before him. Christ, it had been going on for ever. He had been there. Twenty years before. He could remember as if it were yesterday. The hatred and the bitterness, the endless, mindless violence. And they'd got Johnathan. They had left him without a son. They had left him without life. He finished his drink, pouring another immediately.

Richard stood his glass on the mantelpiece, not caring about the stain it might leave on the polished wood, and went to the telephone. He dialled, listening impatiently to the empty ringing, replacing the receiver when he heard the Ansaphone, concerned, even in his grief, that he had been unable to contact Felicity's brother, the only family she had left. But Alex Howard was like that. He worked for himself as a financial adviser, answered to nobody and was probably abroad again researching one of his overseas accounts.

Richard would not have met Felicity if Alex had not invited him down for a weekend after one of their climbing trips in north Wales. How to tell his best friend what had happened? He thought of leaving a message on the Ansaphone, but decided against it. Better to meet, tell him face to face.

The carriage clock on the mantel chimed, reminding him he ought to look in on Felicity. She'd like some tea, he knew, and went into the kitchen and filled the kettle, switched it on and waited impatiently for it to boil. The kitchen, normally so cosy at this time of the day, seemed sterile to him now; the copper pots and weave baskets hanging from the oak beams, the tasteful bunches of dried flowers, skilfully arranged, appeared artificial and out of place.

Richard saw only a wet street, the rain rebounding from the surface, a body crumpled in a wet combat uniform, not moving. Why? Why did it have to be you? All we had. Now just each other.

Johnathan.

*

It was dark in their bedroom. In the dimness he could just make out Felicity on the bed, curled up facing away from him. He put the tray on the table just inside the door and turned on the light. There was no movement from the bed. Normally she would have woken up as soon as he switched on the light. The bottles, five or six of them, were scattered on the carpet near her outstretched fingers, a whisky bottle standing out amongst those that had held the pills.

Oh God, no.

He took a quick step to her, frantically, roughly pulling her over on to her back, lifting her wrist, searching for a pulse. Nothing. Am I feeling in the right place? Where's the pulse? Nothing, cold flesh, but nothing. He snatched the telephone from her bedside table, an old-fashioned heavy instrument which she had wanted, which he had bought for her at a car-boot sale. He'd had to rebuild it in his workshop before it would work properly. Now he wished it had buttons he could press, not this dial that wouldn't accommodate his fingers. It distorted his voice and the operator had to ask him twice which service he wanted. He knew his shouting was not helping.

The ambulance took twenty minutes. Slapping her wrist, shaking her, had done nothing in the end. He sat with her on the bed, her head in his lap, stroking her hair, resting her carefully back on the pillows when he went to answer the doorbell. They were quick. They were efficient. They wanted the empty bottles. In the ambulance, he held her hand as the medic worked on her.

He didn't find the note until he came back.

By then he had lost his son and his wife.

It had been a combination they had said, the whisky complementing the effect of the pills. The doctor had looked at him sadly as he had told him, knowing that it was her lack of will, her not wanting to live that had really taken her. He suspected Richard knew.

Richard Norris went outside to the log pile, lit by the security lamp that came on as he passed. The axe, embedded in the stump, came free as he yanked at it. The handle felt smooth, strong in his hands, the edge, keen, glinting in the light. He raised it above his head, then roaring with all the force of his lungs, swung the axe-head downwards, splitting the seasoned log with such force that the wood spun off into the night. He worked for an hour, unaware of the blistered, bleeding hands, before sinking to his knees over the pile of freshly cut wood, holding the handle of the axe close to his face.

His body shook as he wept.

There, in the garden, under the hard stars of the cold November night, he made a vow.

Wherever you are, I will find you, seek you out and send you to your maker.

Whoever he may be.

CHAPTER SEVEN

Alexander Howard, Alex to those who knew him well, was a contented man. He pushed his chair away from the desk, unbooting the computer as he did so, taking off his frameless spectacles, rubbing his eyes with his thumbs. His small office, part of the flat he owned in a beautiful converted Georgian house, was neat and organized. As he glanced around him, he felt justifiably proud of the business he had formed. It had taken him longer than expected to build his client base, but now he was well established, able to live comfortably. Self-employment suited him, and once he had left the Army, he had decided he would never work for anyone other than himself.

He was a big man, proud of his physical appearance. Long hours in his work-out room ensured he was in good condition. Middle-age had treated him kindly, and women found his outdoor ruggedness attractive, wanting to harness his independence. The grey eyes and whimsical mouth suggested he might be good in bed, and those who made it there would confirm it.

Alex had never married and had been in love only once. She was American, beautiful, and had been working in Pan Am's London office when he had met her while on a duty trip during his days in the Army. Their affair had been wild and wonderful, but she refused to leave America and he would never move there. Parting had been a wrench, and for years he had felt lost and alone without her. More than once he had considered abandoning his career and joining her.

Somehow, he never did.

The telephone ringing startled him. Glancing at his Rolex, he reached over and lifted the receiver, wondering who it might be this late. It was probably not a client, but he said nevertheless, 'AH Financial Services.'

'Alex? It's Richard.' Alex recognized the voice of his brother-in-law. His best friend. 'I'm here, in Reading. I need to talk. Can we meet?'

'Richard! Great to hear from you. You sound a bit rough. Been pissing it up again?' The banter was light-hearted, instantly regretted when he heard Richard speak again.

'Alex. They got Johnathan.'

'What?'

'The Provos. Last week. I tried, couldn't get hold of you for the funeral. You being his uncle . . .'

'Richard, dear God, I . . .'

'But that's not all. Christ, Alex. Felicity, she was never strong. You know better than anyone. She loved our boy so much. She's gone too. She took an overdose, the evening of the funeral.' His voice was ragged, choked, words tripping over. 'I tried to call you, Alex, all last week. But you must have been away on one of your trips. No contact number. I couldn't leave a message. It didn't seem, well, right. You getting home to hear of it like that.'

Alex felt the dull hard shock.

Felicity and Johnathan? Dead? Both of them? His brain tried to register, to cope, refusing to believe, accept what he had heard.

'Richard, wait,' he strove for calmness, 'we can't talk on the phone. Can you come to the flat?'

'Yes, of course. I've hired a car.'

'Then come at once.'

Alex replaced the receiver, realizing he was trembling. He gripped the arms of his chair, pushed himself up and strode around the room, big steps taking him nowhere. His legs felt weak. Half-stumbling, groping for the chair behind him, he sat once more at his desk. A fly tiptoed across the computer screen, paused and rubbed its front legs together. He watched without seeing.

Felicity dead?

They'd been closer than most brothers and sisters. United somehow after their parents' divorce. Their mother, a volatile woman, had entered a no custody plea and Felicity and Alex had spent their childhood farmed out with whichever family their father could persuade to take them. Each found in the other the only permanence in a bewildering inconstancy of aunts and uncles and cousins.

'Are you there?' Felicity would call out in the night across one of their many shared bedrooms.

'Yes,' he would say, 'I'm here.'

Where had he been when she'd really needed him?

And Johnathan.

Wait. Wait. He didn't believe all this.

Had he spoken aloud? Alex bowed his head on to his hands. Great displays of emotion were not his style, but as the horror of it welled up, washing over him like a tidal wave, he fought to hold back the tears. He hadn't cried for years.

Now, he almost did.

Alex was shocked at the sight of his friend. He had lost weight and there was a gauntness he had never seen before, even on their long alpine climbing expeditions when they had spent nights freezing in snow caves, or bivouacked on rocky ledges high on a mountain face. There had always been humour, even then. Now, he looked ragged, haunted, his eyes bloodshot, yellow mucus in the corners. He hadn't shaved, the stubble grey-flecked on his chin. His clothes, normally immaculate, were crumpled, stained, and the tie, pulled half-open, showed his Adam's apple.

He wanted to hug him. Instead he squeezed his shoulder, leading him into the flat, up the wide stairs to the comfortable lounge.

'Alex. God . . . Oh, Alex,' Richard wandered aimlessly, agitated. 'What the hell am I going to do now? I still don't believe this has happened. I keep thinking I'll wake up, see the sun through a gap in the curtains, feel her beside me. Get up, go to work, find her cooking dinner when I get home, seeing her sipping sherry in her delicate way, telling me it was only her second. As if it mattered . . .'

Alex listened to him rambling, not making sense.

'And you, Alex? Christ, I'm so wrapped up in my own sorrow, I've not even asked how you feel. I know you were close. She talked about you a lot. And Johnathan

. . .' Richard turned away, but could not hide the shaking of his shoulders.

Alex went to the sideboard and poured whisky.

'Richard, come on. Sit down.'

He sat his friend in a big old armchair and put the crystal glass, half full of whisky, into his hands, wrapping his fingers round it to make it secure. He waited, uncertain.

The whisky was gone. One second it had been there, the next, swallowed down in a gulp. A thin trickle had run down Richard's chin and dropped unheeded on to the lapel of the untidy suit.

He said nothing, controlling his own sorrow, waiting for Richard to talk. It tumbled out, words slurred, half-formed.

'He was on protection duty, guarding the back of a bomb disposal officer. They think it was set up so that they could take Felix out. They shot the officer to bits as he was backing out of a suspect vehicle and Johnathan – ' His voice cracked, tears squeezed from eyes closed in anguish. 'The stupid, brave . . . oh Christ, Alex. He ran to help him, not knowing he was already dead. He was chopped down. They carved my boy up with a fucking M60. I got a phone call from one of his corporals. Johnathan just stopped running and went down. Said he saw the van where the fire came from and that he'd got a couple of shots off. Then a lorry crossed in front. Alex, they hit him three times, three fucking times.'

Richard was weeping openly now, unable to control his grief. He looked up wildly.

'Corporal Shaw wanted me to know. Said he'd get his balls chewed off if it were ever discovered he'd spilt the beans. He thought it wasn't proper, that a father should have the right to know how brave his son had been. So he told me. For the love of God. Johnathan was twenty-three.'

Alex got up and refilled his friend's glass, letting the whisky do its work. He didn't try to speak, to offer words of comfort until this had been said. When he spoke, Richard's voice was harsh, expressionless.

'There's no end to it. Over there,' he said. 'Two officers killed in a day and it isn't even front-page news.' He gulped the Scotch. 'If a reporter hadn't been diverted on her way back from another take, it wouldn't have been on television.' His voice had thickened, cynical, his words clipped. 'No interest. Too much else going on in the world for them to find the time to report the death of a young subaltern on a Belfast street. More interest in the value of the pound against the Deutschmark, the state of the economy.'

The whisky was sipped now, not gulped.

'Then we get one of them, legitimately, and the bastards are yelling "shoot to kill" from the rooftops. Yet they blow up a busload of ours and nobody except the parents gives a shit. Some minister gets on the box, with his fat jowls shaking, pronounces some crap about the Government's resolute determination in the fight against terrorism. It's shit. It makes me puke. Let the SAS loose and take them out. Give them an alphabetical list of all the ones we've got fingered so that they know their turn is next.' Alex noticed the wildness in the eyes, almost madness. 'The law is useless. It's time we, the good guys, recognized that this is war, that we should fight dirty.'

Alex kept silent, letting the man opposite calm his breathing, waiting as he drained his tumbler. He made to stand, to fetch the decanter, but Richard shook his head, placing his hand on top of his glass. His voice was calmer when he spoke next, almost in control.

'What saddens me is that the IRA is the only terrorist organization funded and supported by a democracy. Oh yes. I know Gaddafi has been providing arms and Semtex, but it's America, good old Uncle Sam, who gives them cash.' He looked at Alex, wondering if he understood. 'Misguided Irish Americans who don't even know that

Northern Ireland is a part of the United Kingdom, that a referendum was held to give them the choice of remaining. They still think it's the emerald isle, that we're an army of occupation. They gather in their Boston and New York bars and hand over their hard-earned dollars thinking it's going to a good cause. Don't they know it goes through Noraid, ending up in the Provos' coffers, then is used to buy their hardware? I mean . . .'

Alex let his friend talk, relieved he seemed more controlled and rational. Richard got up, walked to the window where he stood, legs spread, looking out over the town, fiddling with the change in his pockets. He was quiet.

He turned and looked squarely at Alex then went back to the chair.

'I'm going to take him out. The one who killed Johnathan. He's going the same way, with a stolen American M60. What's more, the bastard is going to know what's coming to him. And I'm going to cut off their money supply. I don't care how long it takes or how much it costs, I'm going to do it.' The voice was calm, detached, convinced. 'I need your help, Alex. I can't do it alone.'

Alex studied his friend. He tried to absorb everything, to arrange his thoughts, wanting revenge as much as Richard. Yet instinct told him this was wrong. Unconsciously he recoiled at Richard's suggestion. The police, the law. That was the way to get back at them. He was still mourning, hurting, unable to register, to see where this was leading.

'Richard, I don't know. It's been a shock, learning of Felicity's death. I need time. Maybe we should sleep on it, give it more thought.' His voice faltered when he saw the impassioned, haunted stare. He hurried on, 'I'm shattered. I can hardly believe it, even now. I hate them just as much as you for what they've done, but I'm not sure that what you're suggesting is right.'

Alex stood in front of the chair and looked down at

Richard. He was sympathetic, consoling, despite his own sorrow, this utter wretchedness. Richard dipped his head, staring into his glass, swirling the whisky in the bottom, then raising it to his mouth and draining it. He spoke without looking up.

'I've ideas, Alex, churning about in my head, maggots in a bowl, all squirming in different directions, then coming together. There are people I know, people who owe me, can provide information. And you, you've got contacts, from the regiment and in the States.' Richard was undeterred. 'I've a basic plan, one I've been mulling over ever since the funeral, when I found Felicity upstairs with the bottles scattered on the floor.' He paused, got hold of himself. 'I remembered something she'd said outside the church, to a television reporter.' His expression had turned hard, cruel, his lips pressed against his teeth, a sudden ripple in his jaw muscles.

'I'm doing this for Felicity. God, Alex, I wasn't even there when she was told. Away on a trip when she needed me most, to comfort her, give her the strength she lacked. She loved Johnathan, perhaps too much. He was all she lived for.' He looked embarrassed. 'More than me. She loved him more than she did me, Alex.'

'Look, Richard.' Alex rolled big shoulders. 'I understand, I know what you're going through. But it's too soon to talk of revenge, of personal vendettas, rushing headlong into something so . . .' Alex spread his hands, searching for the right words. 'So utterly wrong.' He made fists, punching air. 'We'd be sinking to their level. The security forces, the police. They'll get him, eventually—'

'And then what?' Richard interrupted, shouting. 'What'll they do? Put the bastard in prison for a few years, release him later on a technicality, the forensic evidence disproved because some smart-arse scientist devises a way of showing he'd been shovelling shit instead of firing a weapon, or was somewhere else at the time? A prick of a lawyer, standing in court, claiming that the police didn't conduct their interview properly, that his precious client had been denied three square meals a day and had been coerced into giving a confession? Fuck it, Alex. Leave it out.' He was panting, red-faced, his features tugged out of shape, untidily ugly.

There was a tense, awkward silence, neither wanting to break it. At last, Alex spoke.

'Sleep on it, Richard. In the morning—' He didn't finish.

'Alex,' Richard said through clenched teeth, 'I'm going to get him. Through shit and molasses if I have to.' He looked levelly at his friend. 'We've been through a lot, you and I. There was a time once, when . . .' He got up from the chair and crossed to Alex, leaning on the mantelshelf. 'Can I count on you, mate?' He gripped Alex's arm, hurting, the bloodshot eyes imploring.

The low growl of the distant traffic threading through the city steets filtered into the room, barely heard, yet loud in the silence. It was the only sound. Alex made up his mind.

'All right,' he said.

There was no need to say more. The two men looked at each other, feeling a bond, strong, forging them. Something had come alive in Richard's eyes. It would come to Alex later, as he lay in bed trying to sleep, to forget his own plan.

It was murder.

That's what he'd seen.

Sleep would not come.

Alex got out of bed, put on a robe and went down the three short steps to the kitchen. He made tea, strong, black, splashing whisky into it, then sat in his big armchair, the mug on the rosewood table beside him. His thoughts cascaded, following no particular pattern, each superseding the next as they jumbled aimlessly. He tried not to think about his sister, of what had happened to her because of Johnathan's death.

He was alone now.

Yawning, he stood, stretched, then walked over to the wide window with its view of the twinkling lights of Reading, sharp in the night's pre-dawn cold. He remembered Richard's final comment before going to bed.

'Alex,' he had said, 'we've been trained to put a battalion on to its objective, co-ordinating the fire power of an all-arms battle group. I'm damned sure we can take out one poxy Provo between us.'

Alex nodded, turned from the window and went back to his room.

Norris was right, had been all along.

This time, he was soon asleep.

Richard stayed a week, seldom going out, wandering morosely around the flat when he wasn't at the table hunched over a block of A4 paper, his forehead in his hands. Sometimes he would stare absently at the wall, then concentrating, scribble notes, or sketch a diagram with bold strokes of his pencil.

Alex abandoned his clients.

He, too, buried himself, consumed, working mostly from his armchair, a reporter's notebook on his knee, a road map beside the whisky glass on the adjoining table. He grappled with the problem, his head resting on the back of the chair. Sometimes he would pause, sip Scotch from the tumbler, write notes on the pad, frequently referring to the map, nodding when satisfied. He had compiled a list of names and places. Taking his address book, he matched them with telephone numbers. Finished, he lay down the pad. Later he would burn the pages, then flush them down the toilet.

He glanced at Richard, seeing him absorbed. He got up.

'It can be done,' said Alex. 'We can do it.'

He walked over to the table, and looked over Richard's shoulder, trying to decipher the arcane scribbling, the jumbled notes and diagrams. Richard leaned back, threw the pencil on to the table. He twisted to look at Alex, huge behind him.

'We'll need money. A lot of it.'

'Plus a car, a fast one.'

'And a gun.' Alex paused. 'We'll need a gun.'

The course was set.

There was no going back.

Norris looked better as time passed. The two worked independently, coming together at the end of the day, comparing notes, each eager to see what progress had been made by the other. Alex had watched as the hatred had smouldered, much like his own, listening as Richard repeated again and again what he was going to do.

Richard was at the breakfast bar, watching Alex cook.

'I meant what I said, Alex, the night I arrived. I'm going to find the one who murdered Johnathan and take him the same way.' He hesitated. 'And I mean the same way. Exactly. I'm going to America to steal one of their M6os and bring it back, just as they did. Then, I'll set him up and blow his balls off. And he's going to know what's coming, and why. And I'm going to watch it, as he would have done from the back of that van when he murdered Johnathan.' There was a cruelness in his features which Alex, in all the years he had known him, had never seen. He was alarmed, a little afraid of the intensity, the commitment.

'Is that necessary? Going all the way to America?' Alex asked, concentrating on the eggs in the beater. 'Can't we buy one somewhere, black market or whatever?'

'Yes, we probably could, but I've no idea how, have you?'

Alex shook his head.

'It's important to me, doing it like this. I won't be satisfied else. My way is the just way. I'll know then my justice has been done.'

They were eating now, and Richard spoke through a mouthful of scrambled eggs and toast, the words muffled.

'Alex.' He looked across at him, suddenly contrite. Uncharacteristically, he hesitated. 'This isn't your fight. I realize now that I've been selfish, coming here like the ghost of Jacob Marley, forcing my way into your life. If you've had second thoughts, I'll understand. In the beginning I had a feeling you weren't too taken with this hair-brained scheme. If you want out, just say the word and I'll piss off.'

'I told you, I'm with you. All the way.' Alex wanted him to be sure, convinced of his own commitment. 'She was my sister. I have no family now. *They* did it to her, Richard, indirectly maybe, but they're as guilty as if they'd poisoned her. And Johnathan, well, you know how much I loved the kid. Fuck it. We're in this together.' He picked at the food on his plate, pushing it round with a fork, his appetite gone. 'My business won't miss me, so don't worry.'

Richard ate in silence, finished and set the knife and fork down carefully.

'The plan. It's all but complete. I've a few more calls to make, some people to meet, then we're ready. I'm happy enough with what I need to do, how about you?'

Alex went through it again, occasionally poking the breakfast bar with his finger for emphasis.

Norris listened, and though he'd heard this before, couldn't keep the anxiety from his voice as he said: 'Alex, that's risky. You'll be exposed. You can be fingered. Are you sure we need the gun?'

'Richard, you are one of the most technically gifted men I've ever met. Your electronic wizardry, designing this gear your company makes, amazes me. I couldn't do it. But you've no idea how to steal a car. And nor have I.' He got up, poured coffee for them both. 'This way we spread our dirty deeds around all over the place, do a bit here, a bit there, keep old John Law guessing, tying their computers up. Yes, we need a gun.'

Richard recognized the finality, but was still worried about the dangers. But he had to admit Alex was right. He could design and build anything electronic, but hadn't the faintest idea how to steal a car.

'Agreed?' Alex was talking again. 'I have a plan to cover my tracks. I called someone, made the arrangements. What we do now is tidy up the loose ends, map out a timetable, from now until the Provo is frying his arse in hell, wishing he'd gone to confession more often.' He got up and went to his desk in the other room, returning to hand Richard a sheaf of papers.

Alex watched him read through the notes, offering a pencil if a hand was held out for one, or when he needed to make notes, or query a particular section. Finally, Richard looked up.

'Looks good. Can you count on this . . .' He looked down at the notes again, reminding himself '. . . this fellow Willis?'

'Absolutely. And you with Nobby Clarke?'

Richard looked into the distance, for the moment elsewhere, perhaps remembering.

'My life on it. No question. I know he's still with the same firm. I checked. Can I use the phone?' Alex passed him the cordless telephone, watching him key in directory enquiries.

He heard him ask for an Ambleside number.

*

It was finished.

They had shaken hands.

Norris had gone, leaving him alone with his thoughts. He still wondered, despite Richard's confidence, how they would identify, then find, the Provo. He could be anyone, anywhere. If the security forces, the RUC, couldn't nail him, what chance had they? Alex had been less certain than Richard, despite the other's confidence. Someone owes me, Richard had said. A man in the right place who will give me a steer. It may take a bit of luck, he had said, but I'll find him. I know, I feel it . . .

Alex went to his bedroom and hunted through a drawer in the bottom of his dresser. Finding the cardboard box, he carried it over to the big double bed where he picked through its contents. The military identity card, with the photograph of himself when he was younger, slimmer, with fewer creases around the eyes, shone in the light. He recalled the night he had lost the bloody thing after a mess party, how he had reported it and stood before the brigadier to be disciplined. He hadn't been marched in like a squaddie, but it had been just as embarrassing.

'A prevalent offence.' The brigadier had been stern. 'Alex, for God's sake, I'm supposed to put you up before the GOC. How do I explain that one of my commanding officers has lost his ID card?' Alex had said nothing. He had known the rules.

'I'm not going to fine you, Alexander.' The brigadier had been formal. 'Not officially. But you can bloody well donate two weeks' salary to your unit funds. Get the damned thing certified destroyed and fix yourself a replacement. And, Alex, for heaven's sake tie the bloody thing round your neck with a chain. You're as bad as one of your recruits.'

As a result of the brigadier's decision, the ID card was

never officially lost. Nothing was entered on to Alex's military documents. He'd followed the procedure to get himself a new one.

A week after his new card arrived he had found the other in the lining of his mess kit jacket. It had slipped through a tear in the silk and was tucked into the material, missed by his probing fingers. He had never surrendered it, just tossed it into a drawer and forgotten about it.

Until now, when he wanted it.

The other document he found was a neatly folded NATO travel order, needed when he had been posted to the States for an individual exchange programme. His American hosts called this an Index P. It was out of date, but that didn't bother him.

At the walk-in wardrobe he pushed the plastic suit-bags along the rails until he found the one he wanted; the strong smell of mothballs as he pulled open the zip. He took out the service dress uniform and shook it.

Memories stirred. Faintly he heard again the sounds of the band, the crash of rifles as the regiment presented arms. For a moment, the unmistakable whiff of cordite filled his nostrils as weapons popped at the distant range.

The uniform was tight, not because he had put on weight, but because the daily work-outs in his small gym had made him more muscular. The jacket was tight across his shoulders and the buttons pulled. He considered having it tailored, but decided it was too risky, another unnecessary connection. There was time before he needed it, while Richard was putting his bits of kit together.

Maybe he would lose a few pounds.

Richard drove slowly on the motorway in the direction of Cheltenham, unworried by the fog descending as he had crossed on to the M5. He was in no hurry, following traffic in front, tail-lights flaring angrily, forced to stop and start every few miles. For once drivers were heeding police warnings, careful for a change. He found his exit and followed the minor roads into the village.

The farmhouse was in darkness, foreboding, even when the security lamp diffused light into the courtyard. He dreaded entering the house but knew he had to. It was cold in the porch, not much better in the hallway. He stood, listening to the emptiness. Even the big clock in the hall was silent. Pain, sharp in his chest, remembering Felicity was to have had it repaired before . . .

Closing his mind, he went to the utility room where he turned on the heating, hearing the reassuring plop of the boiler kicking in, the constant roar as it struggled to warm the big old house. He thought about eating, dismissing the idea when he realized that apart from food in the deep freeze there was nothing. He looked at the whisky bottle, a third full on the dresser, discounting that idea too. That was behind him now. Only the future lay ahead.

He shivered, then glancing at his watch, switched on the television for the evening news. The last item, almost an afterthought, concerned a shooting in Belfast. This time, the victim had been an RUC constable, leaving a wife and four children. From deep within him a hatred seeped up into his throat. He could taste it, feel it as the sensation spread through his body.

He switched the TV off in disgust, then left the house, crossing the courtyard to his workshop. He went directly to the drawing-board by the window, sat on a high chair, thought briefly, then started to design the first piece of equipment he would need for his revenge. He worked for a little over two hours, and content with his work, pushed back his chair. Studying the circuit diagram once more, he traced a pattern with the point of a pair of dividers.

A picture formed, at first hazy, then suddenly in sharp focus. A faceless Provo jerking, falling as the heavy-calibre bullets punched into him. For an instant there was a face. Then it was gone.

Richard closed his workshop and went back to the house. He couldn't face the bed they had shared, cuddled in on cold nights, lain apart in after some quarrel, made love in. Instead he went to the airing cupboard and took fresh linen to the spare room.

Alex let the plan gel.

There was much to do, contacts to make, lists to be compiled, committed to memory, then burned and flushed away. He spent more time on the telephone talking with directory enquiries, using a call-box rather than his own phone, always careful. He packed a small overnight case, collected the aired uniform in its plastic bag, the dress cap, Sam Browne belt and shoes, placing them ready. From his dressing room he selected various items from his amateur dramatics kit, choosing each with care. These were packed in a separate case where he could get at them easily.

Alex allowed himself few leisure activities, preferring instead to spend time in his gym. He did, however, enjoy the sessions with the amateur dramatics society, where his ability to mimic accents of famous personalities was always in demand. If the role required an unusual accent, the part always went to Alex.

Taking his private telephone book, he flicked through the pages. Finding the number he wanted, he stabbed the 0101 code, whistling silently as he waited for the Seattle number to be answered. It rang four times before it was picked up, the handset thumping against something solid, probably a bedside table, as the man, waking from a deep sleep, scrambled in the dark to find it.

'This is Jamieson.' The voice was heavy, stifling a yawn.

'Jim? Alex Howard.' He grinned. 'The Brit. Sorry to wake you. Are you sensible enough to talk?'

A short pause.

'Jesus, Alex! What the hell's with you guys? Shit, it's as dark as your ass over here. What's up? You need something, else you wouldn't be calling at this hour.'

Alex grinned again, picturing the American lying next to his partner. He was sorry to be calling so late, but time was critical.

'Jim. You're right. I need something. And fast.'

He told him.

Jimmy Jamieson whistled, but wasted no time with questions.

'It'll cost. Almost as much as the real thing. Where do you want it sent?'

Alex gave an address, waiting while it was written down.

'OK, Alex. I don't know what you're up to, but take care. You hear?'

'Don't worry. And, Jim. There's more. I'm coming over to the States in a few weeks, maybe sooner. I'll have a friend. There's something we need to talk about, but not on the phone.'

'Right, Alex. Look forward to seeing you again, have a few beers and talk about old times. You need a bed?'

'Maybe. I'll let you know nearer the time. Bye now.'

He hung up.

It took a week for the parcel to arrive. Alex used the time refining, fine-tuning the plan, and keeping tabs on Norris's progress. He spent long periods in the gym, different exercises that would keep him supple, agile, fast on his feet.

The contents of the package were better than even he could have hoped for.

He called Richard to confirm their rendezvous. Then gathered what he would need. With a final look around, he closed and locked his flat. His clients would have to make do with his answering machine.

He took the bus into Reading.

From the bank he collected five hundred pounds in French francs.

In the post office he had four passport photographs taken.

At Thomas Cook he booked a two-week skiing holiday in Val Thorens, France. The snow was already good. He was given a discount because he had booked early.

Like Richard, Alex knew that the riskiest part of the plan was in stealing the gun. Alex knew about insurance. He sold it to clients all the time.

The gun was their insurance.

It took a little time for his eyes to adjust to the dim interior of the crowded, smoky pub. He did not immediately find the person he was looking for, until he saw a beer glass raised and waved at him by someone over in the corner. Alex pushed his way through the crowd, excusing himself to an attractive girl forced against him in the crush. She smiled up into his eyes, not trying to move away. Alex recognized her perfume. Coco. He smiled, slid past her, putting a hand on her shoulder.

At the table he shook hands with the man who rose to greet him, thinking that if it were not for the other's moustache he could have been looking in a mirror. The two men were strikingly similar.

'Chris. It's good to see you again. How are things with you?'

'Can't grumble,' said ex-sergeant Chris Willis. 'You're looking as fit as ever.'

They ordered pints, Willis emptying his glass in one

long pull. The two made small-talk, mostly about the good times in the regiment. Sometimes about the bad.

Alex had always liked Willis, remembering his own laughter when the sergeants had put on a sketch at their Christmas ball, where Willis had impersonated Alex, commanding officer at that time. It had been professional and tasteful, and although they had worried about Colonel Howard's reaction, in the end it had been a huge success. The Regimental Sergeant Major had watched with relief as Alex had stood and applauded with the rest.

Alex got down to business.

'We spoke about this briefly on the phone, Chris. Are you still game?'

'No problem,' Willis grinned. 'I'm not due to start my job until January, and this will be a great chance to kill a few weeks. Sod all happening at the moment.'

Willis was a BASI ski-instructor and had got a job in one of the fashionable French resorts for the coming season. But, in common with others like him, Willis was having trouble with the French Ski Instructors Union who resented the intrusion of the British instructors on their patch, jealous because the English-speaking skiers sometimes preferred to be taught by a British instructor, without having to struggle with the language.

Alex sipped his beer, letting his eyes drift round the room, the cheerful, flushed faces, the conversation far too loud, the suden bursts of raucous laughter. He saw the girl who wore Coco staring. He locked eyes, felt the chemistry, before returning his attention to the man opposite. Alex reached into his inside pocket and pulled out a thick envelope.

'It's all there. Money, photographs, Greencard, and passport, just in case. The car is in the garage under the flat. I've included a street map of Reading so you should have no trouble finding it. All my stuff is loaded, bulky kit on the roof-rack, but take your own as well. Just make sure that mine is used. And one other thing,' Alex grinned, 'don't bend the car too badly. Leave your notes in the glove compartment when you bring the car back. But leave it outside. Don't put it away in the garage.' The grey eyes twinkled briefly. 'I wish I were joining you.'

Willis flicked through the envelope, asked a few more questions. They agreed an emergency contact procedure.

'OK, Colonel. I don't know what you're up to, and I don't care. You did a lot for me when I left, and without your help I'd still be unemployed. I owe you this one.'

'Chris, you owe me nothing. Just make sure. It's important. Anything else? Right, I'm off then. Good luck and,' his eyes twinkled again, 'have fun.'

'And you. Careful on your way out. The looker in the sheepskin has been eyeballing you all night. As if you hadn't noticed.'

'Now, would I miss something like that?' They laughed, shook hands as Alex made to leave. A thought came to him.

'Chris, you'll have to shave off the tache. I know you think it's macho, but I'm sure as hell not growing one.'

'You'd look better with one than I would without,' protested Willis.

'So how come the girl in the sheepskin is fluttering those baby-blues at me, instead of you?' The two chuckled. 'And, by the way, if you want to impress, she's wearing Coco by Chanel. That's her perfume, not her underwear. I haven't had a chance to check that out. Keep in touch, Chris.'

He punched him gently on the shoulder.

Alex strode out of the room. Chris Willis looked at the girl in the sheepskin, shrugged when he saw she was looking at Alex as he slipped out of the door.

He fingered his moustache and wondered.

CHAPTER EIGHT

Richard yawned in the confined heat of his rented car, watching the motorway signs warning him of his approaching exit. He left the M6, turned on to the A590 driving west, remembering the directions Nobby Clarke had given him. On the Broughton-in-Furness road he spotted the Torver junction. He turned, taking the narrow road skirting Coniston Water. It was cold, sharp, with brilliant sunshine.

He felt better than he had for days, and now that the plan was going, more relaxed, able to come to terms with his sorrow. Alex, a tremendous source of strength, despite his personal grief, had listened quietly as he had poured out his hate, not interrupting until it was out of him. He had worried at the start that Alex might not be as committed as he, but as the days had passed and the plan had developed, he'd been reassured.

Alex, solid, dependable.

He had reached a junction, and glancing to his right, found the inn. He turned the car into the car park and switched off the engine. He got out and stretched, listening to the silence that surrounded him. He was hungry for the first time in many days, but did not consider trying to get a meal at the inn. The fewer people who saw him here, the better. Safer for Nobby, too.

Opening the boot, he heaved out a rucksack and a pair of walking boots, which he put on while seated on the rear bumper. He closed and locked the boot before unfolding an Ordnance Survey map, spreading it on the warm bonnet. Satisfied, he refolded the map showing the section he would need. Crossing the road, he set off in the direction of Coniston, the inn on his right.

He walked briskly and after a few hundred yards turned left up a track past a granite farmhouse. It was early and he had the track to himself, able to concentrate on gaining height quickly. Despite his circumstances he felt the stirrings of long-forgotten enjoyment, boots crunching on the stones of the track. The beginnings of a light sweat glistened on his forehead.

From the bottom of a slate gully, he saw a man sitting on a boulder a couple of hundred feet above him. Even at that distance, after so many years, he recognized the big, strong-framed figure. Nobby Clarke sat easily on his rocky seat, tossing pebbles into a puddle formed from the earlier rain. He got up as Richard approached, the sun over his left shoulder throwing his shadow into the heather, long-dead and brown. There was a big rucksack at his feet which Richard knew contained his mountain rescue gear, needed when called out. The two men shook hands. Richard felt the strength in the big, hard hand, comforted by the genuine warmth in the grip.

'Long time no see, Nobby. Donkey's years. If we hadn't kept each other on our Christmas card list, I might have lost contact with you yonks ago.'

'Never, Mr Norris.' He insisted on this formality, despite protestations from Richard. But with Nobby Clarke, old habits were ingrained for ever. 'The missus, Millie, said I was to pass on her regards to Mrs Norris . . .' Instinct silenced him.

'Let's walk. I'll tell you everything as we go. You'll know then why I've asked you to meet me like this at the arse end of nowhere, alone.' The two men turned up the hill and headed in the direction of the Old Man of Coniston. Richard told this big friendly man how the Provos had killed his son with an M60 machine-gun. He wasted few words. It came easier the second time of telling.

Nobby Clarke let his former officer speak, release the pent-up hatred. He knew not to ask questions. He listened, quiet, sucking on an empty pipe as they strolled leisurely up the track. He could understand what Norris had been through and tried to imagine how he, Nobby Clarke, would have felt. He thought of his own son, working as a climbing instructor in an Outward Bound school in north Wales. Nobby had no idea how he and Millie would cope without him.

They were approaching a fork, and Nobby asked if Norris would prefer to go via Brown Pike and Dow Crag or the direct route from Goat's Water, saying it as much to get Norris out of the black mood into which he had descended, as to seek an opinion. Richard snapped out of it and agreed the Crag. Accordingly, they took the left fork and continued over steeper ground, crossing a beck by a pretty stone bridge. They walked in silence, Nobby waiting for Norris to tell him why he was there, Richard lingering until the time was right.

They were climbing along a steep ridge, a sheer drop to their right. Richard remembered when he had been good on rock, picking his way with feline precision, the rope heavy on his waistline, the karabiners, pitons jingling from his belt.

That had been before the Kaiser-Gebirge.

He was sweating, as he did when he remembered.

He was unfamiliar with this part of the Lakes and asked Nobby to tell him about the place.

'We had to come out on a rescue, last year. A party had got into trouble in that gully.' He pointed with the stem of his pipe. They sat on an outcrop at the top of Dow Crag and let the sun warm them, Richard listening, picturing the desperate struggle, the rescue team labouring to carry the injured men off the mountain.

'Funny,' Nobby looked pensive. 'It reminded me of that time in Aden. Only difference being we was going downhill, colder than a witch's tit.'

Richard also remembered. All those years ago. But it

was Nobby Clarke who recalled the experience more vividly. Had it not been for the man beside him, he wouldn't have been here, sitting on this track. Nobby let his mind drift, remembering the tension, the fear on that dreadful night.

Shit, he thought. If it hadn't been for the young Lieutenant. The radio operator in the Land-Rover had told him what had happened in the command tent as he and the rest of them had raced up the jebel, trying to get to the top before the dawn. They were all in a panic down in the wadi, losing faith in Norris and his team. But Nobby Clarke had known that they would make it, that Norris would get them out of the shit. He was that sort of man. Once he had set his mind to something, he saw it through. Mind you, thought Nobby, it had been touch and go . . .

Brigadier Leslie Fairthorne pushed back the sleeve of his combat jacket with a gloved finger. He peered at the dial of his luminous watch. For half an hour he had resisted, knowing that his staff officers were watching him, gauging his reaction, caught up in the tension inside the command tent attached to the back of the Land-Rover.

Two minutes.

He glanced at the Signals officer, stood with his back to the tailboard, head thrown back, staring up at the tent roof where the red lamp swung jerkily in the cold pre-dawn desert wind. Eerie shadows danced erratically across the faces of the operations staff, accentuating the fatigue lines etched into the corners of their mouths.

'I hope to God your chaps have made it,' the Brigadier said. 'We've been after this bastard for years. Shame if we lost him now.'

He smiled, an alternative to grinding his teeth, making his jaw muscles stand out. It wouldn't do for him to show any apprehension.

Or fear.

'They'll be there. And on time,' said the Signals commander. He looked away, then up at the light, jerking as the tent-frame moved, the wind flapping the stiffened canvas.

One minute.

The sweep hand on the operations clock pecked towards the vertical. The Brigadier took a deep breath, swallowing to relieve the tightness in his throat.

'Right. Break radio silence,' he ordered calmly. 'Let's catch a rat.' Everyone listened to the operator transmit the code word. A staff officer passed Fairthorne the radio handset. He was aware of the clammy feel of sweat on it. Despite the chill of the air, he could smell the perished rubber on the mike as he raised it to his mouth.

'Hello, all stations, this is Sunray. Rat trap. I say again, Rat trap, over.' Through the faint buzz in the earphones he listened, waiting for his units to repeat the code word, acknowledging they were ready.

'One, Rat trap, over.'

'Two, Rat trap, over.'

The earphones buzzed into emptiness.

Silence.

Only the tent creaking in a sudden squall.

Where the hell was callsign three? The Brigadier looked once more at the Signals commander, who held his gaze levelly.

'One and two, Roger, wait, out to you. Hello, three, nothing heard, I say again, Rat trap. Rat trap. Over.'

Nothing.

The Signals Major punched a gloved fist into his palm, wondering, willing an answer. The Brigadier felt a twinge of regret, his mind racing. He bent over the map, weighing, assessing, balancing, finally deciding. Recrimination would come later.

Damn.

A perfect plan, about to become a military cock-up. Callsign three, the cut-off unit, the anvil on which he would smash the Red Wolves as they were forced out of the rat-holes by the other two units.

Had they reached their blocking positions? If only he could *talk* to them. Abort or go in?

Slowly he raised the microphone to his mouth.

Nobody in the command tent looked at him.

They had been moving since darkness fell, a single file of men hunched under heavy loads. Across the desert and through the foothills they had initially made good time, despite the improvised litters loaded with equipment which four of the party carried. Now the angle of the track had steepened and the ground underfoot became rougher, sharp rocks protruding to catch the unwary boot. Any discomfort was suffered in silence. They were too well trained, had campaigned too long to allow pain to convert to a gasp or a curse. Besides, there was too much at stake. They were painfully aware that success depended on them. With this ever present, they laboured upward towards the ever lightening sky.

Corporal Nobby Clarke was the biggest in the party, as was the load he carried. On his back, two radio batteries lashed to a stripped-down rucksack frame. The webb belt held two ammunition pouches. A rifle, slung casually, lay across the front of his body, the weight borne by the sling and one of the pouches. He held the pistol grip lightly, finger along the trigger guard, thumb on the safety catch. Despite his size and the heavy load, he was light on his feet, at home in the hostile environment of rock and scree.

Occasionally he caught a glimpse of the figure five paces inb front, young Lieutenant Richard Norris. Clarke had been duty operator when Norris had discussed the plan in the command tent, putting his argument forcefully and convincingly. Finally, they'd accepted the risk, told Norris to get on with it, train up a team and put the plan into operation. Who would have thought of manhandling two radios, normally fitted into a vehicle, to the top of a three thousand foot jebel to provide a rebroadcast?

Two radios, each weighing around three hundred pounds, to be lugged up a mountain and connected together by cable to provide an automatic relay to units out of range from Base. Whose idea? Mr Norris. Nobby grinned into the darkness.

Ever alert, he was instantly aware of the Lieutenant's movements and signals. One moment he was moving, a shadowy silent figure in front, the next he had stopped, frozen into immobility. Clarke's heart leapt as he saw the signal. Norris's arm was out from the shoulder, forearm at right angles, first and second fingers raised.

Two enemy spotted.

Shit.

Clarke relayed the signal to the men following. Without looking, he knew they would be melting into the cover of the rocks at the side of the track, easing their weapons from aching shoulders ready for action. He waited, wondering how Norris would react. From further up the hill he could now hear the sound of soft voices in conversation.

Arabic.

Norris had heard them as soon as the stone was dislodged. He squinted into the darkness, trying to make out the direction. Suddenly a match scraped on rock and he saw the brief flare before the light died in cupped hands. Then the dull red tip of a cigarette passed across a sharp gap before it glowed brightly as someone dragged deeply, coughing as the pungent smoke was drawn into his lungs.

A pause, before the cigarette was passed back. At least two, then. Maybe more.

They were sitting in a scoop about thirty yards away, oblivious of the party's approach. Probably a forward observation post with orders to report any movement in the wadi below. Norris slipped the rucksack from his shoulders, lowering it carefully to the track. Realizing he was holding his breath, he forced himself to breathe slowly, silently, through parted lips. Sweat prickled his shoulders, ran down his spine. He couldn't see Clarke further down the track but knew he would have copied his actions, that he would be watching him intently. He signalled with his right arm, jabbed his thumb up and brought his open hand down in a swift chopping motion.

Go right. Up. Kill. Silently.

Norris moved quietly off the track to the right.

There was silence below as Clarke moved his big frame in pursuit of Norris's figure, a ghostly flicker a few yards above him, rolling on the balls of his feet as his desert boots stepped softly on the rock. Their progress was painfully slow, noiseless as they inched closer. Foot forward, lowered on to the outside of the sole, test for loose stones, rolled flat. Pause, listen. Repeat the process.

With ten yards to go they eased down on to their bellies. Progress even slower now. Weight on to the elbows, tips of the toes, raise the body, rock forward, lowering the torso, toes pointed rearwards, the tops of their desert boots flat on the ground. Fingers gently searched for loose stones, pebbles, debris. Anything found was carefully placed to one side. Elbows then moved forward a few inches, toes were drawn forward at right angles to the leg. Slowly the body weight was raised, transferred to elbows and toes, then slowly rocked forward, lowered. It was agonizingly slow.

The loud trumpeting of a fart surprised them. Clarke was balanced delicately when he became acutely aware that someone was crapping a few yards in front of them. The perpetrator grunted, hawked a blob of phlegm on to the rock in front of him. A slow sigh of satisfaction.

Norris crouched, hesitated. The bayonet, if withdrawn from its scabbard, would be heard. Instead he took a jagged rock in his hands. Raising it slowly above his head he focused on the figure squatting in front of him, *thawb* hitched around his waist, sandalled feet straddled. The Arab reached out his left hand towards the plastic bottle of water at his side, intent on cleaning himself. As his fingertips touched the bottle, the rock in Norris's hand sliced down on to the skull protected only by the casually wound checked *ghuttrah*.

The head disintegrated, a rotten melon. Norris felt no resistance to the downward thrust of his arms, all his strength behind the blow. The Arab sighed, collapsed on to his own faeces. Then silence, until the plastic water-bottle, its delicate equilibrium upset by the outstretched fingers, began to rock. Gravity did the rest.

The bottle tipped forward. Water gurgled from the neck, trickling down the slope. Niagara Falls.

'Khaled . . .'

The question, pitched low, carried down the hill. Norris, Clarke, heard it clearly. Norris, already on his feet, had the advantage. Glancing over their shoulders the sentries were beginning to scramble to their feet, although the softly spoken question had been mild curiosity rather than any sense of alarm. Norris leapt forward, pushing off the balls of his feet, the bayonet held forward, belly high.

He gave no thought to the support he knew would be coming from Clarke a few paces behind him. Arm stiff, he angled the blade upwards, hurling himself at the Arab on his left, off balance, weight on his right hand as he pushed himself up from his cross-legged position.

The bayonet pierced the sternum just
pectoral muscle. Propelled by Norris's m
blade cut through sinew, tissue, bone. E
touched, Norris felt the gush of fetid breath on his che
Time stopped. Norris waited for him to die. His charge forced the Arab back, slamming him into the hard gravel of the scoop. Norris went with him, landing hard, full weight on the bayonet, twisting the handle with both hands. Warm blood, mucous, spat into his face, clinging to the stubble before dripping into the open mouth below him.

He rolled from the body, crouched, looking right, left.

Where the fuck was Nobby?

Clarke had seen the Lieutenant's mad charge, drawn himself into a crouch ready to follow. He pushed off with his right foot, twisting sideways, unaware that the lace of his desert boot had snagged on a projection of rock. Thrown off balance, he fell flat on his face, the rough gravel ripping the skin from his chin, bringing tears, winding him.

Instinct.

He rolled, knew he was too late.

The second Arab, initially confused, recovered. Without looking at the other fight, he leaped up the hill, pausing to draw a sword from its scabbard. The blade hissed as it came free.

The Arab was above him now, sword held in both hands, eager anticipation in the dark eyes. Slowly the Arab raised the sword.

Nobby Clarke stared at death.

He did not hear the Arab die, just saw it. The heavy blade of the sword stopped in its upward path, held at shoulder height. The blade trembled, gently, then

-ently. It clattered on to the rock between his out-
etched legs.

What the . . .?

A bayonet protruded from the Arab's right eye, blood spurting from the socket on to the cheek. He had neither seen nor heard Norris appear, materializing, ghostly in the darkness. Norris was breathing heavily. A foot on the dead man's shoulders, the bayonet yanked free, a hard tug.

The Lieutenant looked at his watch.

'We're late. To hell with being quiet. Let's move.'

Nothing about keeping the Arab off him. Just get on with the job. A hard bastard, this Norris. Nobby shrugged. Fear would come later.

The two ran back to the rest of the group waiting anxiously under cover at the side of the track. They felt the urgency, reshouldering their loads then lumbering up the mountain, stumbling as they ran.

Two hundred feet below the summit, Norris jabbed a finger, showing where he wanted the radio set, a flat piece of ground just off the track. Some stopped, unburdened their loads and began to assemble the radio. Despite the urgency, there was no panic. Everyone knew what to do. Nobby Clarke, impressed with the efficiency, remembered Norris's bloody relentless rehearsals, even making them do it blindfolded.

'Check the frequency.'

The Lieutenant's voice was sharp, driving them. He led the remainder upwards. Behind, Nobby watched the signaller spinning the controls, needles swinging across dials, stabilizing as the frequency locked. Norris, grunting, uncoiled field cable from a small drum as he lurched up the hill, the others, their loads heavier, staggering after him. The men carrying the litter were gasping, one crying, dragged by the stronger, faster men in front. Clarke, drenched in sweat, forced himself on, fatigue beginning to win the battle of wills.

Christ, it was almost light.

The code word, breaking radio silence, burst from the set down the hill. Fingers scrabbled, cables connected, the antenna up, earthed. Cursing, sockets refusing to mate with cable ends, a frenzy to get it done.

Rat trap.

Callsign one acknowledged.

Then callsign two.

A pause.

If the commander felt tension, it wasn't apparent in his voice. He repeated the code word to callsign three.

Norris had finished, squeezing the second of the field cables into the J-box. The radios were linked, a rebroadcast. They could do no more.

The squelch-lights glimmered, startled red eyes.

Fairthorne's voice again, tense now.

'One and two, Roger, wait, out to you. Hello, three, I say again Rat trap. Rat trap, over.'

The relays in the set chattered momentarily, loud in the silence. The red lights flickered, held steady. Nobby Clarke stared at the radio, willing.

Silence, interminable.

The command tent, stifling, moved in the wind. The Brigadier paused, mike to his mouth. He made his decision. His index finger began to depress the pressel switch. Suddenly, from the earphones, crystal clear in the stuffiness of the tent:

'Three Rat trap, over.'

Euphoria.

'All stations Rat trap now. Out.'

The first of the 105-mm shells whispered across the sky.

*

From the summit of the jebel, the men watched the battle unfold in the valley below, artillery shells exploding where, minutes before, men had been sleeping peacefully. Rocks, sand spewed into the air. Feeling remote, they saw the dun-coloured figures advancing through the smoke, the deeper crump of the close-support mortars mixed with the sharper crack of small-arms fire. The forward troops were in amongst them, individual fire-fights breaking out, small personal battles, soldiers killing to stay alive. It was one-sided, soon over. Surprise had been complete.

Nobby Clarke looked at his Lieutenant squatting, an Apache, trying to clean the mess from his face. He remembered the Arab, the sword, and shivered in the heat of the new sun climbing into a cloudless blue sky. The best part of the day. Unless fighting hand to hand in an unnamed battle somewhere in the Radfan. He took the towelling scarf from around his neck, damp with his sweat, offering it to Norris. The Lieutenant looked up.

'Thank you.'

The sounds of the battle in the valley were fading. Nobby could see soldiers moving amongst the positions below, winkling out the few remaining fighters. It was quieter now.

'It's finished,' he heard Norris say. 'Tell control we'll wait up here until they've done. Then we'll come down off the mountain. And.' He paused. 'All of you. Well done.'

The carnage in the valley was over.

'You look miles away, Nobby.' Richard Norris brought him out of his reverie.

'Remembering Aden, the Radfan. That time when you took us up the bloody jebel with the rebro. When the Arab was going to slit me from brain to bollocks until you stuck him from behind. Shit that was close. Flat on my back, nowt between me and that oversize carving knife but fresh air. Scared shitless. I never did thank you properly. Words just didn't seem right at the time.' The big man was gruff.

'Nobby Clarke. In all the years we spent together, that was the only time I had to sort you out. Normally you were the one who kept me out of the shit. Don't talk about it again, you hear?'

Clarke took the pipe out of his mouth and knocked it on the palm of his hand. It was empty anyway. He had never smoked, but he found sucking on the stem relaxing, especially in the hills.

'You said you wanted to ask a favour.'

Norris had known that the subject would be raised, sooner or later, and was surprised Nobby had waited so long. He looked at Nobby squarely, holding his gaze before his spoke.

'At Johnathan's funeral, Felicity said something. It went out live on television. You couldn't have seen it or you would have known.' He saw Nobby shake his head. 'I made her a promise after she . . .' He struggled, remembering the bottles haunting his waking hours, denying him sleep. 'She couldn't face life without the boy. So I promised her I'd get the bastard who murdered Johnathan. I've got a partner, no need for you to know who, and we have a plan. We need money, a hell of a lot of it.'

He saw realization in Nobby Clarke's eyes, hating himself for asking, knowing that he must. He knew, now that Aden had come up, that it would seem as if he were asking for the return of a favour, calling in his marker. Committed, he pressed on.

'You still work for that security firm, Securitall.'

Nobby's head jerked up. Richard hurried on. 'We're going to heist one of their vans. I need your help, Nobby. You won't be involved in any way, apart from what I'm about to ask you. It won't be anywhere near here, so there's no way it can be traced back to you. Nobody has seen us together. You'll be in the clear.'

He waited, the sun on his shoulders, the breeze suddenly cooler.

'You'll do it anyway, with or without my help.' It was a statement. Nobby Clarke looked into the distance, at the sun reflecting from Goat's Water below them.

For the first time Richard felt doubt, wondering if he had asked too much, had overstepped the delicate line bonding them. But Nobby had been right. He and Alex would do it anyway. The silence stretched. Neither spoke. The man in the mountain rescue team who owed his life to Richard Norris battled with his conscience. At last, he spoke, slowly, evenly.

'What you're asking me, Mr Norris, goes against my principles. I do have principles, y' know. If you don't have principles you don't have no honesty. Without honesty a man's not worth a spit. I try to be honest.' The pipe tapped against his palm as Nobby, never one for speeches, searched for the right words. 'But because it's you, who's lost a son and wife, and because I know's you have the highest principles, I'll do what you want. But if anyone gets hurt . . .' He left it unsaid.

'No one will get hurt. You have my word.'

'Tell me what you need to know.' Nobby Clarke was committed. Staring across the Fells, he listened as Norris told him, not asking questions until he was finished. Occasionally he grunted, looking quizzically at the other man.

At last he said: 'We've a good record, not easy to rob. There's a system called "Lock Slam". If a van gets attacked, the inside man hits a button on the dash. The safes in the van lock electronically, can't be opened until a technician resets them. An alarm is automatically transmitted to our base.' Nobby nodded, seeing the gleam of satisfaction in Norris's expression. 'The crooks know this, that as soon as they appear with their cannons, we're going to shut them out. Bastards can dance around outside the van threatening what they like, but there's no way the safe can be opened. That's why they leave us alone.' Nobby sounded proud.

'You said that the button is up on the dash. Can you see from outside the van if Lock Slam is being switched in?'

'Ay,' Nobby Clarke answered immediately. 'A big red button, on top of the dash, left of the steering-wheel. If you know where to look, you'll see it easy enough. The alarm being transmitted can be intercepted, if you've a radio tuned to that frequency.'

'How does the driver talk to the despatcher outside?'

The wind tugged at Nobby's hair, blowing the dark curls into his eyes. He flicked them away with the stem of his pipe.

'Radio. In the helmet. Voice-activated switch. Despatcher tells the driver what to send out. The bags are serial numbered. Coins, they're in bags with a number starting with a two. Used notes, which is what you want, are in the four series, so you won't want to be pissing about taking any others.'

'The radios,' asked Norris, 'what frequencies are we talking about?'

'They're standard countrywide, so low powered that two vehicles can't interfere. You being a technical whiz-kid will understand that. Maximum range, less than a couple of hundred yards. The sets work on 476.80 MHz.'

'Do you know all the schedules, nationwide?'

'Ay. If you tell me where and when I can work it out. It may take a bit of time, though. They're always being changed. The most I can give you is a week. Long enough?'

Norris nodded. 'I'll call you as soon as we decide where to pull this off.' Norris looked satisfied, relieved.

'Anything else?'

Richard thought for a few moments.

'Nobby,' he said, 'when it's all over and I've blown the

bastard away, this is how I plan to finish it.' He told him then. All of it.

When he had finished, Nobby Clarke studied him.

'You're a bloody bandit, Mister Norris. Born 'undred years too late. If anyone can pull it off, the way you tell it, you can. I feel happier now.' He looked up at the sky. It was colder now, and the two men felt the need to get moving.

They descended from Dow Crag to the col at Goat's Water, then began the gentle stroll to the summit of the Old Man of Coniston. They were a little below the cairn that marks the summit when they heard the voices of other climbers drift towards them.

'You'd best go back the way you came.' Clarke didn't want to be seen in Richard's company. 'The weather is set fine so you'll not get lost.'

The two men shook hands. Norris watched Nobby walk up the hill. He called up, saw him look back over his shoulder.

'Thanks. I'm glad I kept the Arab off your arse. You've been a real friend. Felicity and Johnathan – they won't forget.'

He waved briefly, turned and strode down the hill.

CHAPTER NINE

Catterick. North Yorkshire.

Parents entering the barracks were smartly dressed, eagerly anticipating the Pass Off parade. Today, the culmination of ten weeks' training under instructors who had controlled the lives of their young offspring since their joining the Army. And the difference. Gone the pimply undisciplined youth who had left home in Leeds. Now there was a broader, leaner, bright young man, laughter, comradeship in his eyes. They had gone through the basic training together. A proud day.

The corporal guard commander leaned out of the guard-room window, watching parents streaming into the barracks. He noted how the sentry on the gate did his best to account for them all, knowing it was almost impossible to ensure that everyone had a pass.

A good day for the parade, cold, clear blue skies with just a touch of a breeze to keep the lads on their toes. He was sad to be missing it. But then, someone had to be guard commander, keep the place secure. He left the window and returned to the guard report he had to finish before lunch. In triplicate. Bloody bumf.

He parked the car, a place reserved for parade visitors. He had no car pass. A risk, but necessary. If all went well he would not be there long. He picked up the briefcase from the passenger seat, got out of the car and locked it.

He looked smart in uniform, the shoes, Sam Browne polished to a lustre, not overly done. He was conscious of its tightness as he crossed the road, striding towards the unit guard room. He no longer resembled the officer who had driven into barracks. The sentry who had so closely scrutinized his ID card a few minutes ago, had he looked, would not have recognized the dark-haired, brown-eyed, moustached officer now walking across the road less than thirty paces from him.

Alexander Howard was indeed a changed man.

It had been a worrying moment at the gate. The sentry, thankfully young, probably had not yet finished his training. Nevertheless, he had given both the ID card and Alex a close look, matching the colour of hair and eyes against those shown on the card. Fair, grey. The sentry was to remember the details later.

It had taken Alex less than a minute to duck below the

dash, insert the brown contact lenses, stick the false sideburns and moustache on to his face, and fit the hairpiece.

The briefcase was not heavy, but what it contained was frightening, an American imitation hand-gun, perfectly moulded from lightweight plastic, indistinguishable from a real weapon, even down to the plastic hollow-point bullets, clearly visible in the chamber. To anyone not knowing, it was real, a 357 Colt Python, nickel-plated, eight-inch barrel. The gun had arrived courtesy of Jimmy Jamieson, American citizen, currently residing in Seattle, WA. Alex climbed the steps to the guard-room window. Seeing nobody there, he took a deep breath before tapping on the glass to attract the attention of the corporal writing at the table.

The Corporal heard the tap on the guard-room window, immediately alert. There was an officer outside, knocking with the knuckle of his index finger. He stood up, walked to the window, and noting the single pip and crown of a lieutenant-colonel's insignia on the shoulders, snapped up a smart salute.

'Sir?' The Corporal was defensive. He'd not seen the officer before but recognized his seniority. Perhaps a fussy parent wanting to know if he was in the right place, or where his seat was on the parade ground. He noted the tightness of the uniform, faintly smelt mothballs, saw the briefcase in the officer's hand.

'Corporal.' The voice was Scottish, broad. 'I'm due to meet the Adjutant here at ten thirty. Has he not arrived yet?'

'Sorry, sir.' The Corporal was apologetic. 'We weren't briefed on your arrival. If you'd like to come in out of the cold, I'll give him a bell. Won't take a minute.'

The Corporal looked across at the gate sentry, who

would have checked the ID. He indicated the telephone, greasy from countless dirty hands, mostly calling the cookhouse to ask when the next meal was coming.

'Thank you.' The Colonel walked round to the main door, entering the guard-room behind the Corporal, who had picked up the telephone. His finger was in the dial.

A voice, harsh, uncompromising.

'The phone. Put it down. Stand away from it. Out of the light of the window.' The Corporal, duty NCO of the day, heard a double click, a noise he'd heard before in the cinema, on television and during weapon training. The sound, a gun being cocked.

In the distance the band began to play as the parade marched on. Soldiers of the Queen. Parents, beginning to applaud. He looked into cold brown eyes. He saw the barrel of a 357 Colt Python held steady in a massive hand, not in a two-handed grip like they did on television, but one-handed, like a duellist.

Maybe it was some kind of security exercise. He was isolated until the roving picket came in. He tried to think when they were due back, but his brain would not function. He watched the officer walk over to the telephone, lift the receiver, dial one digit, then leave the instrument on the desk. Cut off. Where the fuck was the roving picket? The officer was looking around the guard-room, seeing the posters on the wall warning of car bombs, terrorist attacks, notice-boards listing prisoners held in the cells, the duty roster. A big sign gave the state of alert.

Bikini black.

'The keys. To the armoury. Get them.'

'You'll not get away with this.'

'That's my problem. The keys? Do this right and nobody gets hurt. Try and be a hero, you'll regret it. You may even be dead.' The eyes said no bullshit.

The Corporal got the keys.

'Right. Take me through to the armoury. Now.' The

Corporal looked at the Python. It followed his every move, aimed at a spot somewhere above his nose where the close-set eyebrows met. He could see the hollow points in the chamber. There was no shake in the hand that held it. No shake at all.

'This way.' He went through a connecting door leading to the armoury, seeing the Colonel close behind, but not close enough for him to make a grab for the gun. A pro. The armoury, dimly lit, reeked of gun oil. The weapons were neatly chained in racks, gaps showing where rifles had been taken out for the parade. The officer didn't even look at them.

'Show me the privately owned weapons.'

The Corporal hesitated, saw the arm that held the Python straighten a fraction.

'There. In the steel locker. The keys are in the key press.'

'Get them.'

He did as he was told, removing the Chubb key from its hook behind the glass.

'Open it.'

His hands shook, but eventually the door opened.

'Stand back. Over there in the light, where I can see you.' The officer looked into the steel cupboard, scanning the World War II Luger, the P38, the Belgian 9 mm. His eyes settled on a walnut gun case with a brass name plate. He picked it out, flipped open the lid. The Corporal saw the look in the officer's eyes, certain he had made his choice.

Alex snapped the gun case closed, dropping it into the briefcase. He motioned with the Python for the Corporal to lead the way back into the guard-room, allowing him to relock the doors as he went. There were two young soldiers carrying pick helves looking surprised as the two came from the direction of the armoury.

'Sir!'

They had seen the officer and sprang to attention. They waited, rigid. The Corporal swore.

'He's a fake, a phoney. He's just stolen a weapon from the armoury. And you two berks are at attention like he was bloody royalty. Get a grip!'

'Nicely put, Corporal.' Alex tried hard not to smile. Nothing had changed. 'If you've finished your bollocking, get the keys to the cells.'

'They're open.' Sullenly. 'The keys are left in the locks.' The Corporal, surly, angry at being taken in, was dreading explaining to the Military Police when the shit hit the fan. Most of it was going to spatter down on him.

Alex told the Corporal to lead, following at a distance as the three trooped off to the cells.

'It seems as though you three are your only inmates,' he said. 'You won't be there long enough to starve. You know when your next roving picket is due in. If you holler loud enough, they'll come and let you out. They'll have to search around for the keys though, or get the duplicates from the Adjutant. I need a start on you so I won't be leaving these where they can be found easily.'

As he swung the heavy door shut, he saw a resentful Corporal glaring balefully at him and two frightened recruit soldiers more concerned that they would probably miss tea.

Alex heard the band in the distance playing the 'British Grenadiers'. The Advance in Review Order. The parade was drawing to a close. It was time to leave. He crossed the road without looking at the sentry, and walked back to the car. Inside he quickly removed his disguise. He drove slowly to the gate, returning the sentry's salute. On the main road, he turned, accelerating in the direction of Richmond. He relaxed. Now to meet Richard for the next phase.

Gateshead.

And all going well.

Davey Rogers was fifteen years old going nowhere.

The estate where he lived on the outskirts of Gateshead was a hell-hole. The fittest, the cunning, survived. To survive required credibility. Contribution ensured acceptance. Davey Roger's contribution was his ability to steal cars, and to drive them at reckless, breakneck speed. He had never been caught by the police in their white patrol cars with the red stripe, 'jam butties' to Davey and his gang. But the police drove with skill and care, concerned the car they were chasing might crash, killing innocent bystanders. Young Davey Rogers didn't give a shit. Somebody's insurance would pay.

The lad was well dressed, surprisingly because neither of his parents had work. The Berghaus ski jacket, expensive roll-neck sweater, designer jeans and Reebok trainers he wore were spoils from ram-raiding. It was the easiest, quickest and safest way of stealing yet devised. The requirement was easily met. Two vehicles, one to smash through the plate-glass window of the store, the second to carry off the loot. A slick team of ram-raiders could clear a store in less than a minute, goods selected earlier during a casual visit. It was easy pickings, over and done before the pigs had even got off their arses.

Tonight, another raid. He had already stolen the getaway car, a white Ford Cosworth, from the posh estate across town. Another of the gang had stolen a Range Rover. Neither theft had been difficult, both completed in under ten seconds.

Easy, if you knew how.

*

Young Davey Rogers was in his element, unable to contain his excitement. It was dark. No lights showed from the indoor shopping mall across the road from the Range Rover, parked with its engine running evenly. The Cosworth was stopped close behind, the teenager behind the wheel, tense, nervous. There were few people about, but the boy in the Range Rover bided his time, waiting until the last of the pedestrians had turned the corner out of sight.

Satisfied, he slammed the vehicle into gear. Tyres spinning, burning rubber, he drove fast towards the big glass doors a hundred yards away. The Cosworth, close behind, almost touching. The doors were ripped from their hinges, glass shattering into a million tiny pieces as the heavy Rover burst through. The boy driving gripped the wheel, laughing deliriously, rocking violently in his seat.

The shop to be looted was at the end of the lower concourse. With considerable skill, the boy swung the vehicle into a handbrake turn, bringing it with its rear facing the shop window. The Cosworth stopped twenty yards short, the driver blipping the accelerator, spewing fumes into the concourse.

The Range Rover, front completely damaged, reversed towards the window, which was protected only by a lightweight steel mesh. It was no match for the heavy vehicle which smashed into the shop. The back doors were flung open. Four youths tumbled out, immediately collecting television sets, video recorders and other expensive electrical appliances selected earlier. Its work complete, the Rover was driven quickly forward leaving the way clear for the Cosworth, which now came to take its place, its boot lid already raised to carry off the spoils.

Davey Rogers was satisfied.

He ignored the alarm ringing ineffectually. He leaned across the passenger seat, watching the progress of the rest of his gang. He could see one of them carrying the first of the television sets towards the Cosworth. Another few seconds and they would be loaded, away, abandoning the Range Rover.

A good haul.

Nothing to it.

The Filth didn't even know they were on the job. Even if they came now, he could outrun them in the Cosworth with its beautiful motor and four-wheel-drive better than anything they had. Fucking jam butties. Useless sods. They didn't have the balls for a high-speed car chase. Davey Rogers was derisive.

'Hold it right there!'

The voice was loud, metallic, artificial. Davey Rogers, car thief, ram-raider, spun in his seat. Twenty paces in front, a figure in a black one-piece overall and balaclava helmet, wearing a gas mask. But it was the gun he was holding that really got Rogers' attention. Even from there, it looked like the Channel Tunnel. The man in the overalls was holding it in a two-handed grip, not crouched down like Crockett and Tubbs, but with his arms out straight, the right foot drawn back.

From the corner of his eye Rogers saw a similar figure coming at the run from his left. He also had a big gun in his hand, silver, not black like the one he was looking at.

'All of you. Stand still and don't even think about moving.'

Davey Rogers felt real fear for the first time in his dishonest young life. But he was cunning. His cunning had kept him a survivor. He balanced his options. If he made a run for it, the gang members still in the shop would be a diversion, covering him. He gave them no other thought. Tough. He was in the driving seat, they were in the open, exposed. *Their* problem. Anyway, he reasoned, these guys weren't about to shoot. Not for stealing a few TV sets.

He had the briefest moment of doubt, then shrugged it off. He slipped the big Rover into gear, holding it on the clutch.

He waited. It had gone very quiet.

He'll never shoot.

Will he?

Davey let out the clutch, drove his foot hard on the accelerator, spinning wheels on the smooth marble, the smell seeping into the cab. The vehicle leapt forward directly at the man in the black suit, holding a gun that looked as big as the Channel Tunnel.

Davey Rogers screamed in exhilaration.

Alex and Richard had spent two nights in the shopping mall. They had reconnoitred the area carefully during the day, spending the evenings staking out from two ends, hiding in the toilets until the last of the shoppers had gone. They had no idea where or when the raiders would strike, but knew that two or even three times a week was not unusual. They had been lucky.

Alex had been closest when they heard the splintering of the main door, the screech of tyres, the roaring of the engines as the raiders had sped past in low gear. It was luck that Alex had stationed himself, hidden in a clump of ornamental shrubs, as the two vehicles had torn by with neither driver looking to left or right.

Alex had heard the screech of tyres as the Rover had spun on a handbrake turn, able to identify his target as the vehicle smashed its way through the shop front, leaving shattered glass and twisted metal from the protective screen all over the floor.

Speaking quickly into the short-range radio, he told Richard where to come, then broke into a run, pulling out the big Smith and Wesson. He could see the group of teenagers leaping from the back of the Rover, saw it pull forward to let the Cosworth in close, the driver, his arm across the passenger seat, looking over his shoulder.

The driver of the Cosworth got out, leaving the door open as he dashed round to open the boot, ready for the first of the loot. Richard, dressed like him, in a black one-piece overall and military respirator, came sprinting from his right.

The Cosworth.

That will do nicely.

Alex shouted, 'Hold it right there! All of you. Stand still and don't even think about moving!' His voice, distorted by the tiny amplifier Richard had fitted into the breather in the respirator, sounded frightening. They froze. Richard had the Python up, a professional, aggressive stance, looking the part. The yobs were convinced. Alex stared at the boy in the Rover. He heard the engine revs gradually increase, saw the gear lever pushed forward into first. The little shit. He's going to try it.

Alex thumbed back the hammer, adopting the Weaver Stance, pushing his right arm out stiff, pulling back with his left, holding the beautifully moulded grips with both hands. The right foot was drawn back. He saw the indecision on the acned face, before it blurred as he focused both eyes on the foresight.

For Alex Howard and young Davey Rogers, the world stopped.

It started again in a roar of the engine, the squealing of the tyres. The vehicle leapt forward. Alex felt the big gun jump as he squeezed off a bullet, pulling the barrel off aim as he did so. A neat hole appeared in the windscreen right of the driver. The banshee yelling was cut off by the bang of the gun. The Rover stalled. The boy fell from the driver's seat, landing in a mess on the floor, the designer jeans stained darkly at the crotch. Suddenly, a rat, running low to the ground, arms flailing in his haste to be gone.

There was a crash, one of the gang dropping a television set. The raider, open-mouthed, looked at Alex.

'Don't shoot, mister!'

Then he was gone, the rest following. Nobody looked back. Richard, already in the Cosworth, manoeuvred to get a straight run at the door.

'Alex! Come on! For God's sake. The police will be here in a minute.'

But Alex was standing in front of the Rover, aligning the bullet holes in the windscreen and rear window.

'The bullet. I have to find it.' He ran forward, leapt on to the bonnet of the Rover, kicking out the windshield, all of it. He jumped down, dashed to the rear of the vehicle, smashing the back window with the gun butt. At the marble wall, he searched at the point where he had lined up the bullet-holes, found the indentation, the impact of the soft lead bullet.

The hee-haw, hee-haw of a police siren in the distance, getting closer.

Alex looked vertically below the point where the bullet had struck. Shrubbery in big terracotta pots. Shit, where was the thing?

'Alex!'

He was down on his hands and knees, scrambling in amongst the dirt and dead leaves. The rubber gloves found something hard. A pebble. Damn. There it was. Like a ten-pence piece, flat and spent. He picked it out, scuffing over the leaves, then rubbed the mark on the wall with a gloved finger. No time for more.

As soon as he dropped into the passenger seat, Richard accelerated, taking the car up to sixty in the short distance to the doors. He braked hard, then, thinking only of escape, tore out into the road, ignoring the blaring horns as he cut through the traffic.

He drove fast for a while, then slowed, turning at an

intersection, following the circuit to a multi-storey car park opposite the shopping mall they had just left. Richard took the new number plates, changing them quickly while Alex kept watch. The two walked away. Tomorrow, or the day after, they would collect it and drive it respectably down the motorway.

South, to Willingford, Devon.

CHAPTER TEN

The man paused outside the gunshop. He wore a light-coloured trenchcoat, a caricature of a private detective. The plastic carrier bag in his hand looked garish, out of place. He glanced casually about before pushing open the door and entering the dim interior.

It was an untidy place lacking order, except in the layout of the weapons cased at the far end of the shop. Here, at least, some care had gone into the presentation and Alex was able to see that the weapons were secure behind strong steel bars and armoured glass. He noticed a number of rifles, two revolvers and assorted spares lying beside a big automatic.

His entrance had been recorded, relayed via a security camera mounted above the door to a room at the back of the shop from where a figure now emerged. He was a swarthy character, with thinning, greasy black hair plastered across his skull. The eyes in the dark face were hooded, indifferent, though a spark of recognition flared briefly once he had identified the caller. He was dressed in a dirty roll-neck sweater, an open cardigan with imitation leather buttons. A piece of cotton dangled where the middle one had once been. The dark trousers were stained with oil. The owner of the gunshop shuffled forwards on sandalled feet. The expression when he looked at Alex was resentful and malicious, the eyes smouldering, greedy in anticipation.

'You're late.' He was looking at an old clock on the wall. 'You should have been here an hour ago.' He walked to the door, sandals scuffing on the tired carpet. He reversed the sign, the closed side facing the street. Alex said nothing. The man was loathsome, as he had remembered him when he had been unit armourer.

'Where do you do the work?' was all he said.

'You mentioned a price. Show me.' The gunsmith looked cunning, his greed measurable, the anticipation apparent on the wet lips. Alex reached into a pocket and took out an envelope which he tossed disdainfully on to the counter. He controlled his feelings.

'Five thousand, as agreed.'

He knew that the money would be counted. He curbed his impatience as delicate brown fingers picked through the notes, lips moving soundlessly as each was registered. Satisfied, the gunsmith slipped the envelope into his hip pocket. He looked up.

'Where is it?'

Alex held up the plastic carrier bag.

'Come into the workshop.' The grubby figure led him through a dirty curtain, along a narrow passage where wallpaper was peeling, exposing the damp plaster. Alex, dubious, followed. At the end of the passageway he entered a workshop. The contrast between this and the front was marked. The dimness was replaced, bright lights accentuating a clean efficiency. Tools neatly held in racks on the wall. A partially assembled rifle on the larger of the two work-benches.

At the second bench, the gunsmith switched on a powerful light. As he pulled on a pair of thin rubber surgical gloves, Alex had a mental image of a surgeon about to perform an illegal abortion. A gloved hand was held out.

Alex passed the bag, watching as the walnut gun case slipped out. Four small screw holes showed where the owner's brass plate had been. The gunsmith said nothing. Instead he lifted the lid and whistled, sucking air through yellow teeth.

'Nice.' Reverent. 'Smith and Wesson model 586. Six-inch barrel.' He flicked open the chamber, spun it with the palm of his hand, and confirming it was unloaded, snapped it back into place. He dry-fired the weapon six times, rapidly, then snicked the hammer back with his thumb. Alex noticed the transformation in the man. Suddenly, he was absorbed, hefting the blued revolver in the palm of his hand. As he lifted the gun to his nose, Alex saw the nostrils flare open revealing dark tufts of hair as the gunsmith sniffed.

'Parker Hale 303 gun oil,' he pronounced, 'no trouble matching that. Pachmeyer combat grips. Pattridge foresight. Feels like he's fitted competition Woolfe springs. I'll know for sure when I get the grips off.' He looked down into the box and whistled again before carefully picking out one of the objects from the recessed green baize.

'Safariland speedloaders. Shouldn't be left with the shells in, though. It strains the springs.' He looked at Alex accusingly before emptying the cartridges out on to the bench. One was selected delicately, then examined under a powerful magnifying glass held close to his eye. 'Winchester brass, Federal primers. The bullet looks like . . .' He jiggled it in his hand '. . . a 158-grain semi-wadcutter.' The gunsmith had already noted the single empty cartridge case with the black powder stains on it.

'Has this killed anyone?' The question was too casual. 'If it has, the price is double.'

'None of your damned business.' Alex hated being there. 'Just reload the empty then scrub the gun. I want it like it's never been used.'

'I can do it all. The reload is easy. But I won't be able to identify his powder. I'm a gunsmith, not a bloody chemist. Any powder with it?'

Alex thought hard, remembering the collection of containers in the metal locker where the gun had been.

'Maybe. Name some.'

'Vitarhouri N310?'

'No.'

'Bullseye?'

'No.'

'Hodgdon?'

'Yes.' Alex concentrated hard. 'Yes, that's it. I'm sure.'

'In a black plastic bottle?' Alex nodded. 'Then it's Hodgdon HP 38.' The gunsmith went to a cupboard and held up a bottle for him to see.

'Yes.'

'Then let's get on with it.'

'Talk me through it,' said Alex. The man looked at him and shrugged.

'You're paying.'

'I'm paying,' confirmed Alex.

Despite his dislike of the man he recognized an expert when he saw one. He was fascinated to see the long effeminate fingers at work on the ammunition, his dark skin showing through the thin rubber of the gloves. He watched as a bullet and cartridge case was inserted into a hollow-headed plastic tool shaped like a hammer. The gunsmith noted the interest.

'A kinetic bullet puller,' he said curtly. 'I have to take one apart to find out his load before I can match your empty. Once it's clamped, I give it a sharp tap, so.' The bullet spat out of the brass case, and was put carefully to one side while the powder was painstakingly transferred to a scale and weighed. Alex could read the printing on the instrument. RCBS 505.

'Three point six grains.' A satisfied nod. 'A grain, what one grain of corn used to weigh. In the early days, this was all a bit hit and miss.' It was an aside, the man showing off. 'I could have guessed the load. But you said you wanted it exact.'

'Precisely.'

The empty cartridge case was then placed in a single-stage rock chucker, as Alex watched the gunsmith take a set of tungsten dies, using the first to resize and decap the cartridge. The open end of the brass case was then flared with an expander die, before a new primer was fitted. The fingers in the rubber gloves were quick, nimble. The case was adjusted in a roll crimp die.

'Now. Once I've weighed out the powder, I transfer it through the funnel into the empty case. Then,' Alex watched, 'I insert a new bullet, made to match the original. I'll use eighty per cent wheelweight lead, the balance Lino type.'

'No, use this.' Alex tossed the flattened bullet on to the bench. It was the one he had fired at Gateshead. The gunsmith picked it up and jiggled it in his hand. He looked quizzically at Alex.

'It won't be exact. Bits will have been lost when it impacted. I'll still have to add some lead but only a tad. You really do want this thing exact.' The work went on as the lead was melted and moulded. Alex could see there was an element of trial and error as the new bullet was fitted using seating punches and a vernier to measure the exact depth. The man working assured him that it was more precise than it looked.

He had not noticed the time pass. He had been absorbed, watching as adjustments were made an eighth of a turn at a time, until, with a last critical look at the vernier, the gunsmith straightened up.

'What was the stuff you put on the bullet?'

'Lube sizer. Your shooter uses Black Widow. I've matched it. All I have to do now is to resize to 357, and I'm done.' Finally, he held the new bullet up, squinting at it into the light, examining it minutely with the big magnifying glass. He nodded, satisfied. 'I'll wipe off the powder stains, then clean the gun. It's done.'

'The bullet. The new one. It's shiny.'

'It hasn't had time to oxidize. I can make it look old. Don't panic.'

The gunsmith put his handiwork back into the speed-loader before reluctantly replacing them both with the cleaned gun, back into the case. Still wearing the gloves, he transferred the box to the carrier bag. He handed it to Alex.

'And the other item? The specialist piece of equipment I asked for?' Alex watched as the gunsmith crossed the room to a cupboard under the work-bench. He bent, then pulled out a cylindrical tube about eighteen inches long and four inches in diameter. He handed it to Alex.

'Will it work?'

The gunsmith looked pained.

'I didn't have a model to try it out on. I got the data from the technical manuals. It fits over the flash hider. Pull it as far back as it will go, then tighten the grub screws. It won't interfere with the foresight, which on your weapon is offset to the left.' The gunsmith demonstrated with a jerking, twisting movement, then showed Alex where the grub screws were located. 'I wouldn't recommend trying to use it at ranges in excess of two hundred yards.'

'Ammunition?'

The gunsmith looked unhappy.

'That could be a problem.' He looked cunning, greedy.

'I can only buy and sell ammunition against a valid firearms certificate. The regulations are tight now. Since Hungerford.' Alex remembered the incident, someone running amok with an AK47 assault rifle. 'And 7.62 NATO isn't easy to come by.' The gunsmith went to a drawer. Pulling it towards him, he took out a bullet.

'This is what you're after.' He had a school professor's expression. Alex knew he was in for a history lesson.

'As a bullet, it's crap. Developed by the Americans from the 30 odd 6 when there was a requirement for a short round. The 7.62 mm was really a compromise, neither one thing or the other. It lacks real hitting power, yet is too powerful for an assault rifle. The Americans adopted it anyway, and the rest of NATO had to follow suit. Then, of course, they developed the 5.56 mm and everyone had to change again, despite the fact that the British had developed a better bullet – the 280 – years before, in the fifties.'

The gunsmith looked disgusted. He scratched his fingers across his scalp, examining the flaked skin, dandruff under his fingernails. Alex wrinkled his nose in disgust. Probably he'll pick his nose in a minute. The armourer was talking again.

'The non-military equivalent is the 308 Winchester. They come in a variety of loads. If you can get some 308s you won't go far wrong. You'd get some easy if you knew a man in the States. You can buy it over the counter there.' He tossed the bullet back in the drawer and slammed it shut, its contents jumping around inside.

'I'll see what I can do about the ammo.' The greedy look. 'But it'll cost you.'

Alex smouldered, then played his trump.

'I've kept a record of the serial numbers of the notes I gave you.' Alex saw the hatred. 'Insurance. In case you fail to keep your end of the bargain.'

He walked out of the workshop without looking back. Behind him, the gunsmith said some uncomplimentary things about his former commanding officer. But he was more than a little curious about the 357 magnum hand-gun and the flattened bullet.

It puzzled him even more that he had been asked to design a silencer for an American M60 machine-gun.

Finally, he shrugged, looked at his watch and decided not to reopen. Instead he went into the small living room behind the workshop. He poured himself a stiff shot of neat vodka, plonked himself down into his favourite armchair and, for the second time that day, took the banknotes from the dog-eared envelope and began counting them.

CHAPTER ELEVEN

The young gate sentry and the Corporal of the guard were grilled extensively by the Special Investigation Branch of the Royal Military Police. The sentry had racked his brains, trying to remember if he had admitted a dark-haired, brown-eyed officer wearing horn-rimmed glasses into the barracks on the morning of 6 December. A lieutenant-colonel, Scottish, he was reminded. Try as he might, he could recall only one. Fair-haired, grey eyes, matching the ID card.

Oh, yes.

His military number began 47. His blood group was A Negative. He had remembered that because it was unusual.

The sentry was dismissed.

'Anything unusual about the officer?'

The RMP sergeant was interviewing the Corporal. It was the third time he had been asked the question.

'I told you, his uniform was a bit tight, like he'd grown out of it. Smelt of mothballs. But he was a real officer, not someone dressed up.'

'What makes you think that?'

The Corporal, scornful, didn't answer. If the bloody RMP couldn't tell a proper officer when they saw one, well, it was a different time of day.

'We don't understand why he should steal a gun, when he already had one.' The SIB man was persistent.

Bloody obvious, thought the Corporal. Either he wanted a second gun, or the one he was threatening me with was a fake. He was fucked if he was going to find out which. Not when he had been looking down the barrel of the bloody thing.

The RMP came to the same conclusion.

Eventually.

As a result, the police made enquiries with every supplier of replica weapons in the UK. None had provided a Colt Python 357 recently, but their records were available for checking. In conjunction with the North Yorks Police, the RMP concentrated their enquiries, looking for an officer whose uniform no longer fitted, who might have retired. His military number began 47. His blood group was A Negative. His regiment was known. It was the thinnest of evidence.

Central Records came up with seventeen names.

One was Lieutenant Colonel A. T. Howard.

Alex returned the rental car to Newbury and took the train to Reading. From the station he caught a bus to the shops, where he bought some groceries. He walked home, the collar of his coat turned up, hiding his face. He didn't see anybody watching the flat. His car was parked in the reserved space opposite his door. He grimaced, seeing the ugly scar on the nearside front wing, showing where it had collided with a stone or plaster wall. He collected the sheets of paper from the glove compartment and put them into his pocket, before going into his flat.

There was a letter lying on the hall carpet. It was postmarked Birmingham.

Alex went to the window, carefully drawing back the curtains. The road was empty, except for his car, the skis on the roof-rack.

He read the notes he had collected, then the Birmingham letter written in an unfamiliar, girlish hand. He grinned, then whistled.

'You bastard,' he muttered.

An hour later the doorbell rang. Alex went to the window and looked out. A man wearing an unbelted raincoat was walking slowly round his car. He couldn't see anyone in the doorway, although he knew there were two. They always hunted in pairs. The bell rang again, then the antique brass knocker thumped on the heavy wood. The second man appeared, craning his neck to look up at the window. Alex stepped back, watching the two men walk away.

In step.

They would be back.

In his dressing room he sifted through his stage make-up, then started working on his face. It didn't take long.

The bell rang as he waited in the kitchen. It was early evening, nearly dark. Alex took a deep breath, went downstairs pausing at the front door as he gathered his thoughts.

He pulled the door open.

Detective Sergeant Clive Manley stood in the porch, hands behind his back, bouncing on the balls of his feet. He was a patient man, as yet unconcerned that he had been unable to contact the owner of the flat. This was his third visit, and judging by the car outside, it looked as if, at long last, Mr Howard was at home.

He studied the well-built, middle-aged man who stood looking at him with a gentle, inquisitive expression. The policeman noticed the tanned face, slightly less so about the eyes, the broad shoulders and muscular figure. He recognized an athlete.

'Mr Howard? Mr Alexander Howard? Detective Sergeant Manley, Berkshire Constabulary.' He produced his warrant card from the pocket of his mac. 'I wonder if my colleague and I could ask you a few questions? May we come in?'

Satisfied with their credentials, Alex led upstairs to the comfortable lounge.

'We're making some enquiries, sir, in connection with a recent crime. Perhaps you can help?' He was polite, looking tired, slightly bored.

'Sure. I'll do my best. Am I allowed to know what this is all about?'

'That's no concern at the moment, sir. I wonder if you would be so kind as to account for your movements on the morning of December the sixth, from ten o'clock?'

Alex paused briefly, looking at the date on his Rolex.

'I was skiing. In Val Thorens, France.'

'And where were you staying, sir?'

'At the Hotel Val T. I'm sure they will verify that.'

'And who might "they" be, sir?'

'Monsieur Charles Dubois, owner, proprietor, barman and bouncer.' Alex grinned.

'And how did we pay our bill, sir? Credit card? Cheque?' The detective looked uninterested, as if his mind were elsewhere.

'I paid my bar bill by Eurocheque. Incidental expenses

with cash. I paid in advance for the holiday at the travel agent, Thomas Cook, here, in Reading.'

'You've ferry tickets, of course? We assumed you'd gone by car.' He looked smug. 'The ski-rack on the roof.'

'I've got them somewhere,' said Alex. He crossed to his desk and rummaged through some papers. 'Yes, here they are.'

He handed the ferry tickets to the Detective Sergeant, who passed them to his companion without looking at them.

'The other document, sir? You dropped something, on the floor.'

The detective had noticed the ski-lift pass, dated, Alex's photograph fixed under the clear plastic.

Alex bent, picked it up and handed it to him.

'Ski pass,' he said. The detective studied it, then handed it back.

'It seems there was an accident, with the car, sir. Care to tell us about it?'

'Bloody silly of me. I stopped for lunch on the way down in a little village.' Alex paused, thinking, trying to remember. 'Pouilly-sur-Loire. A little place, Le Bistro des Chats. I clipped my nearside wing while reversing. Damaged the old boy's wall a bit, but he wouldn't accept payment. I bought him a cognac and he told me to forget it as the place was falling down anyway.'

'I see, sir. And when you were skiing at Val . . .?'

'Thorens. Val Thorens,' Alex reminded him.

'Can you recall anyone who might corroborate your story?'

'Look, what the hell is this?' Alex was indignant. 'I've told you where I was. You've seen my tickets, papers. What more do you want?'

'I'm sorry, sir.' The anger had been noted. 'But we have to be sure.' He waited, seeing Alex's look of embarrassment.

'There was a girl, no, a woman. I met her on my last night. We had a few drinks and laughs together. We ah . . . we spent the night together in her room. We got on rather well, you see.'

The policeman took note of the discomfort.

'She wanted to keep in contact, for me to write. I haven't yet. I had a letter from her, though. There, on the table.'

'And what would her address be, sir?'

'Look for yourself.'

He went to the cabinet to pour himself a drink, while the junior detective wrote in a notebook. There was a photograph in the envelope, showing a man in a Head ski-suit with his arm round a youngish, attractive woman. It was blurred, out of focus, but clear enough to see who it was. The junior passed it to the Detective Sergeant.

'Is this you, with the lady, sir?' Alex nodded. The policeman snapped his notebook closed.

'That's all for now, sir. I'm sorry to have taken up so much of your time. If we need to contact you again, you'll be at this address?'

'I may be going abroad, after Christmas. I'm not sure yet.'

'Thank you, sir. We'll see ourselves out.' He paused by the door. 'A nice tan, sir. From the skiing? The area round your eyes, it's not caught the sun.'

'From wearing ski goggles. I doubt if the tan will last long, not in this weather.' The policeman nodded, understanding.

They left.

Alex watched from behind the curtain. At his car, the junior detective bent to the damaged wing and scraped a sample of the dust into a plastic envelope.

Neither looked back.

*

Later, Alex picked up his telephone and dialled a number from memory.

'Chris Willis,' said a voice.

'Hello, Chris. It's Alex. Thanks for getting noticed. I hope you enjoyed the skiing. And the rest.'

'Better, even, than the skiing. I hope I didn't go too far?' Willis was chuckling.

'No, but you'd best call her and tell her you've been moved overseas. Did you get the job in France?'

'I'm still working on it.' There was a pause. 'Don't worry yourself. It was one of those holiday romances. I don't think she'll be turning up on your doorstep. I'll phone her anyway.'

'The Eurocheque.' Alex needed to be sure.

'As I said in my notes. I played the dumb Brit abroad and got them to fill it out for me. Told them I never could fathom the damned things. He hardly glanced at your cheque card, just comparing the signatures, making sure it was valid. Otherwise I used cash, like you said. And, by the way,' Willis sounded mischievous, 'there's no change. And I don't think I'll regrow the tache.'

'I didn't expect any. Thanks again. I suppose I'll be hearing from my insurance company about the prang?'

Willis was still chuckling when Alex hung up.

The gendarme stood in the snow watching the laughing, brightly dressed skiers clump past in their heavy boots, towards the ski lift behind the hotel. It was cold after the warmth of the bar, and the gendarme pulled his cloak tight about him. The brandy glowed pleasantly. On recollection, he reckoned that the journey up from Albertville had been worth the trouble. The traffic in Moutiers had been bad, as usual, but Monsieur Charles Henri Dubois from the hotel had made his investigation as pleasant as possible.

Dubois had recognized the photograph of the Englishman, received by fax from Interpol at the request of the chief inspector from the North Yorkshire Police.

Not a particularly good photograph, it seemed to have been copied from some sort of identity card. It was him, though. No mistaking the handsome Britisher. He was older than in the photograph, but it was definitely him. Dubois would swear to it. So would the waitress, still besotted. Dubois had the Eurocheque he'd signed to pay his bill, intending to bank it the following day.

The gendarme trudged off through the snow, climbed into the Citroën chewing a peppermint to kill the smell of the brandy on his breath. He drove down the mountain, through Les Menuires towards the N91 and his station in Albertville. There, he would send his report to New Scotland Yard confirming that a Monsieur Alexander Howard had been in Val Thorens over the period of their enquiries.

The major drove home from the gun club, irritated at coming second in the annual pistol competition. He had borrowed a fellow shooter's hand-gun. Some bastard had stolen his from the unit armoury. Typical. Not permitted to keep his Smith and Wesson at home for lack of security, he had obeyed Standing Orders and kept it with other privately owned weapons, locked in the armoury.

He had stuck to the rules and what happened? In broad daylight, somebody had just walked into the armoury and lifted it. His gun. The one he would have used to win the competition. Angry, he slammed the car door shut and went inside.

It was nearly Christmas.

Glad tidings were far from his thoughts.

The major could think of nothing, other than losing the

trophy, the trophy he won every year. Full of self-pity, the injustice, he forgot to lock his car.

He did not look outside again. Had he done so, he might have seen someone stealthily approach his vehicle and carefully try the doors. Finding one open, the figure slipped something inside under the seat where it would slide into view as soon as the vehicle braked.

It was a walnut gun case with a brass name plate screwed on to the lid. In it, a Smith and Wesson model 586 with a six-inch barrel and Pachmeyer combat grips. Recessed into the green baize were two Safariland speed-loaders, each charged with six 158-grain semi-wadcutters.

It was the gun that would have won the trophy.

Close examination later would show it had not been fired.

Detective Sergeant Manley called his opposite number in North Yorkshire. Holding the receiver against his ear he stared dejectedly at the pile of files on his desk which seemed to grow taller by the hour. He had enough work, without being diverted to make enquiries about the theft of a gun from a military armoury in Catterick.

'Oh, hello. Manley, Berkshire. Let me talk to the case officer on 561 please. Yes. I'll hold.' He tried to open one of the files and hold the telephone against his ear at the same time but failed. 'Hello? Yes. The man Howard you asked us to check on? He can account for his movements on December the sixth. Yes. He was skiing in France. Interpol confirm he was there for two weeks, from December the second. Positive ID from two people at the hotel. Also a girl he met there. She corroborates it. We also had French forensics check the dust from his car where he had allegedly hit a wall during his journey. It checks. Anything else?' Manley looked irritated as the pile of files slipped off the desk and slapped on to the floor.

'What? The gun's been returned to the owner?' He whistled. 'Not been used?' Bending, he tried to gather the files. 'Well, I'm damned. Seems we've taken a lot of trouble over nothing. Never mind, North Yorks will be picking up the tab. Any time. Bye now.'

He hung up.

Alexander Howard was deleted from the list of suspects.

CHAPTER TWELVE

The headquarters of the Devon and Cornwall Police is located at Middlemoor on the outskirts of Exeter.

The driver of the blue Datsun examined the building carefully as he drove round the big traffic island. He had left the motorway a few minutes earlier, and seeing the car park of a nearby public house, pulled in and switched off his motor.

He could have been anyone, breaking his journey to check his bearings, studying a road atlas open on his lap. A casual observer would not have noticed the flesh-coloured earpiece. Had they done so, they might have suspected the traveller was slightly deaf. Occasionally, he cocked his head, listening to the radio fitted under the dash.

It was a frequency scanner.

A vigilant observer would have noted that each time a police vehicle or motor cycle turned into the headquarters using the police radio, the man in the car wrote on a pad concealed in the road atlas.

The listener sat at his post for an hour, sometimes appearing to fall asleep. But he missed nothing. After a while he closed the atlas and placed it carefully on the passenger seat. The notebook was studied thoughtfully, then concealed in a pocket, much of its contents committed to memory.

Satisfied, the man drove off, rejoining the M5 motorway a few minutes later. In the notebook, he had recorded the frequencies used by Police Control and the retransmission frequencies of their repeater station. Also noted, the call-signs of every police vehicle and motor cycle entering the grounds. A tape-recorder had been silently running throughout his vigil.

Richard Norris had got what he had come for.

He hoped Alex had been as successful.

They drove round the circuit of the small market town again, just to be sure.

It was a quiet, largely dull place, the raw December weather doing nothing to improve it. Some effort had been made to enliven the town, but, already, early frosts had attacked the plants, killing most. People scurrying along the windy pavements took little notice of the bright fairy lights strung across the main street, put there in a vain attempt to elicit some Christmas cheer. Most were intent on finishing their shopping and returning home, before it got any colder.

Not a day to be out and about.

Alex drove the Cosworth easily, carefully, enjoying the feel of the powerful car, comfortable in its warmth. The lock-up garage, rented the previous week, was tucked away in a small courtyard set back from the one-way traffic circuit. Alex stopped the car in front of the up-and-over door, which Richard unlocked with the agency key. The door, probably not oiled in years, squeaked loudly as he lifted it. A small 250cc motor cycle stood leaning against one wall, leaving just sufficient space for the car.

Richard Norris was smartly dressed in a dark suit. The chill biting into him, he put on a Crombie overcoat, before opening the boot and taking out a metal case, larger than might be expected of a middle-aged executive. He pulled on a pair of dark sheepskin gloves, shivered briefly, watching Alex pull the motor cycle out of the garage.

Unlike Richard, Alex wore dirty jeans, a checked woollen shirt, a puffy, grease-stained anorak and heavy boots. He pulled on a crash helmet, raising the visor to look at Richard. The two men nodded briefly. Richard turned, left the courtyard, lifting his collar as he walked away. The motor cycle started behind him, but he didn't turn to see it ridden smoothly out into the road.

Richard Norris walked swiftly against the flow of the traffic until he reached the high street. He paused opposite the tall grey building across the road, waiting for a gap in the traffic as it sped round the one-way circuit from his left. He could see the bank a hundred yards away. His glance was casual as if, like the others waiting to cross the road, he was merely ensuring that it was safe to do so. Finally, apparently changing his mind, he stepped back on to the pavement, walking in the direction of the bank but on the opposite side of the road.

He waited at a pedestrian crossing, thirty yards further on, where he studied his watch as he listened to the pips. Finally he crossed, reversing his direction, passing the bank on this side of the road. Norris looked in casually.

When he reached the main door of the town hall, opposite his original crossing place, he strode confidently past the reception room on his left. He turned right, up a wide staircase, making no sound on the thick pile carpet. At the top, on a landing, he paused, checking his watch, as if making sure he wasn't late for an appointment. He studied the plan of the building fixed to the wall, although he knew exactly where he was. From outside the council chamber he could hear muted voices behind the thick oak doors.

There was a small door to his right, recessed into the

wall, unnoticed if its whereabouts were not known. From a previous visit, he knew a flight of narrow wooden stairs led from behind the door into a disused public gallery.

Certain he was alone, he stepped quickly to the door. He climbed three short steps and, holding the narrow metal railing for support, yanked the door towards him. He went through, pulling the door quietly closed behind him. He waited, listening.

Nothing.

On the balls of his feet he took the stairs two at a time to the gallery above. The place was dirty, smelly, littered with broken furniture and pieces of discarded carpet. Mouse droppings were everywhere, and the air was thick, stuffy, unpleasant to breathe.

Norris found the iron spiral staircase to his left. Going directly to it, he squeezed between the wooden pews which had once served as a spectator's auditorium in the days when people took an interest in what their elected members were doing. Now, it was deserted, unwanted, unused. A screen partitioned the auditorium from the main chamber below. The voices he had heard were louder. Clearer, now. From the sound of the legal language floating upward, he supposed that the court was in session.

At the top of the spiral stairs he found himself in a smaller, darker room. A ladder led higher still, up to the town-hall clock. But Norris was high enough.

Immediately to his right, a small door, held in position by four sliding bolts, led out on to the roof. He snapped back the bolts, pulled the door inwards, placing it carefully against the wall. The wind, colder now, whistled through the narrow gap. Norris stepped out on to a narrow lead-covered ledge behind a low wall. He came out bent double, not standing until concealed by a granite rampart. Above him the wind tugged at the halyard lines, slapping them noisily against the flagpole.

He placed the case at his feet, flicked open the catches and raised the lid. The sheepskin gloves were removed to reveal the rubber surgical gloves beneath. He pulled out an extending antenna, then a pair of small binoculars from a foam recess in the lid. Next, he took a headset fitted with a boom mike. With the earphones on, Norris flicked a switch, nodding as the power light glowed dully from the case. He checked the dials, LED indicators and, from habit, blew briefly into the mike, nodding again when he heard the reassuring side-tone. It was short and sharp and he did not repeat it.

He was ready.

It was bitterly cold on the roof. Even sheltered by the rampart, he could feel the wind cutting through his coat, making him shiver, whipping his hair across his forehead. The cold crept up through the soles of his shoes. Although determined to see this through, he hoped he wouldn't have too long to wait. He glanced once more at his watch. If Nobby Clarke's information was correct, he would soon be in action. The slap of the halyard on the flagpole was the only sound. Below, the noise of the traffic was muted, remote.

The security van appeared from the far end of the high street. It stopped at the pedestrian crossing, waiting for the light to change. Norris focused the field-glasses on the cab, studying the two occupants inside. They looked unconcerned, a little bored.

Another collection and delivery day.

Just like yesterday.

The heavy square van stopped outside the bank, its nearside wheels on the pavement. Beyond, Norris saw a motor cyclist pull into the kerb and stop between two cars parked illegally on double yellow lines. He recognized Alex's bulky figure. Through the glasses he could clearly see the gold letters painted boldly on the maroon van.

Securitall.

His heart beat faster as one of the guards jumped on to the pavement, then closed the door behind him carefully. The guard walked into the bank. In under two minutes he returned, accompanied by a bank employee who spoke briefly, before hurrying into the warmth of the building. He opened one door, securing it with a heavy brass hook.

The motor cyclist kick-started his machine, looking casually over his shoulder. When the lights on the crossing changed to red, he rode slowly towards the maroon security van.

Shivering, Jim Dalby stood in the lee of his vehicle ready to unload the money for transfer into the bank. This close to Christmas, there was more than usual. He would be relieved when it was finished. A retired police sergeant, he had been working with Securitall for seven years, knowing the routine so well he could do it in his sleep. He was a conscientious man who reckoned he earned his pay. It wasn't much but, with his police pension to supplement it, he and his family lived comfortably.

Ever conscious of the threat of armed robbery, he lived in constant fear of being confronted by it. Desperate, hard-eyed men, their faces hidden by stocking-masks, sawn-off shotguns grasped in their hands. During his police service he had seen the damage this weapon could inflict at close range, when a hostage-taker had turned one on himself. Take the bloody money is what Jim Dalby would say. No bloody heroics from him. He shivered again at the memory. Noting the signal from inside the bank, he switched on the radio inside his helmet, speaking quietly to his driver still seated in the cab.

'OK, Harry, we're ready out here.'

'Right. Two coming. Serial numbers 2781 and 2782.'

Dalby recognized the code numbers. Coins. Heavy. The door at the side of the van slid upwards, closing immediately he had taken the bags. He walked across the pavement into the bank where he hefted them on to a low trolley. Returning to the van, he stood with his back to it, looking left and right, anxious at this vulnerable moment. A motor cyclist passed the van, but Dalby took no notice. Nor did he hear the dull, metallic thud, drowned by the snarl of the rider blipping the throttle open and speeding away. He waited for the next consignment.

'Mr Security man.'

The voice was loud in his earphones.

Dalby could hear the caller breathing. Slow, deliberate.

'Yes, you. Beside the van outside the bank. Raise your arm to show you can hear me. We don't want you missing anything.' The voice was harsh, menacing, authoritative yet refined. Dalby was frightened, puzzled. Someone was talking on his radio, had broken through on his frequency. But who? His eyes scanned the street to the left and right. Nothing.

Shoppers hurrying by, unaware.

'The two of you. You in the cab as well. I can see you both clearly, even the warts on your chin.' The voice paused.

'There's a bomb. Two sticks of gelignite attached to the back door of your van. It's on a timer. You do anything, anything at all that I don't like, and you go up. So high they'll be picking your balls out of the fairy lights. I don't give a shit about anyone, pedestrians, women, kids. Do just as I say and nobody gets hurt. Both of you, nod to show you understand.'

Dalby did so, his driver the same. Then he spoke into his mike.

'Hey, listen, whoever—'

He was cut off, frightened by the savagery in the voice.

'No. You listen. Now. I know about "Lock Slam". Try to use it, the van goes up. Use your alarm, or try to radio your base, and I'll know. Then bang. You're scrap metal and offal. You outside. Go round to the back of the van, take a look and tell your friend inside what you see. Then wait there. Go. Now.'

Why today?

Seven years without a sniff of a robbery. Now this. He walked around to the rear of the van and saw the bomb. Fear spread from his bowels. The device was attached to the rear door by a heavy magnet. Two greasy sticks of gelignite, looking unstable, were attached to a sophisticated timer, the coloured wires bright against the dark paint of the van.

The timer was running.

Dalby watched the red digital numbers flashing from the panel on the front, showing the minutes, seconds and one-hundredths of a second. It was set to detonate in four minutes and thirty-seven – no six, five seconds. The hundreds spun round too quickly.

'Right. You see it?'

'I see it,' said Dalby. Then, to his number two in the vehicle. 'Harry, he's right. There's a bomb with a timer. There's about four minutes left on the clock. Don't do anything unless he says.' Dalby looked at people streaming by, hurrying in the cold, unconcerned with his plight. Or his fear.

The voice came again, cruel, relentless.

'Watch the clock. See what I can do. I can stop it. Like this . . .'

The figures on the square face read 3:58:17.

'Or I can rewind it like so . . .'

The figures spun, finishing on 6:00:00.

'If I really feel like being a shit, I can bring it forward. Watch.'

The figures whirled, settling on 2:37:06 where they stabilized for a hundredth of a second, before restarting. Dalby's heart leapt.

'OK. OK. I get the message. Shut the bloody thing off. We'll do as you say. Anything. Anything at all.'

'Good. You learn fast. The next two bags out. Used notes. I'll know from the bag serial numbers if you try to pull a fast one. Make sure the numbers are in the four series. Hold them up so that I can see them. Rotate them so I get a good look at the numbers.'

'Right, I hear you.' Dalby was puzzled by a cracking noise in his earphones. His ex-policeman's mind working.

'Look to your left. You see the motor cycle with the panniers. In front of the pedestrian crossing. When the lights turn red, he'll ride up to your van, on the offside. He'll be close, but riding slowly. Drop the bags in the panniers. Got that?'

'Yes.'

'When the bike's gone, he'll check the bags and call me on another set. If they're OK, I stop the clock. If you've tried to pull a fast one I'll know. Then woomph. Kiss your arse goodbye. Have another look at the clock, then come back to your station.'

Jim Dalby did as he was told, thinking he'd rather be facing the sawn-off shotguns. From the clock, the red digital figures glowered angrily.

Two minutes, forty-seven seconds, and running.

He went back to his position at the side of the van ready to collect the bags before the motor cycle arrived. Looking to his left he saw it, in front of the crossing, pulled into the side of the road where it wouldn't interfere with the traffic.

The lights were green, remaining so for what seemed an eternity. Terrified, the clock running, he pleaded silently for them to change. At last, a pedestrian, an elderly woman, wisps of grey hair blowing about her face from beneath her blue fake-fur beret, hesitated at the crossing, pondering. She seemed frightened of the busy traffic. She raised a hand, thin, frail and big-knuckled. It hesitated by the button then dropped to her side. She turned away, continuing along her own side of the busy street.

Dalby had been counting the seconds under his breath, thinking of nothing except the clock.

Somebody press the button.

A child, a boy, ran to the light, standing on tiptoe. He pressed. Twenty seconds passed before the security guard heard the pips, the lights changing to amber and finally red. Relief. He saw the bike pull into the road, the rider glancing over his shoulder. It came slowly towards him.

'Harry. The bags. Quick!'

The side door shot up and Dalby ripped out the bags, holding them aloft and spinning them, letting the voice see. The bike was alongside, its exhaust popping. Dalby walked round the van, not daring to look at the clock. Pray God it had been stopped. Time must be nearly up. He couldn't make out the face under the visor, the chin-guard. There might have been a beard but Dalby wasn't sure.

He stuffed the bags into the panniers and the bike accelerated away, the red light at the crossing giving it a clear run. Dalby noted the registration, knowing it would be false. Finally, he looked down at the clock. He swallowed hard.

It was stopped on 00:02:03.

He waited, sweating in the cold.

Two minutes passed.

'OK. The money's good. I want five minutes. Try anything before them and I'll incinerate you and half the town.'

The airwaves went dead.

Dalby gave him the five minutes, eyes staring at the clock. He heard a soft click. Terrified, he waited.

The figures on the clock read 00:00:00.

It clicked again, softly. Dalby thought about making a

run for it, or wrenching the wires off. His legs refused to move. He sucked in his breath, squeezing his eyes shut. He looked once more as the mechanism clicked quietly again. The red letters glared at him.

MERRY XMAS.

From the device came a tinny voice singing 'Jingle Bells'.

Weak with relief, Jim Dalby sat down heavily on the kerb. He started to laugh.

'Well, I'm buggered,' he said.

From the town-hall roof, Richard Norris had seen it all, the fear and apprehension on the faces of the two security guards, hurrying to do what he told them. He had not enjoyed it. But it had been necessary. They had done exactly as he had instructed. Especially after he had used the remote-control device to operate the timer attached to the back of their truck. As he had worked the controls, he had watched his own clock, knowing whatever showed there was duplicated on the other timer.

Later, when the police examined the device, they would discover the gelignite was two pieces of a broom handle wrapped in greaseproof paper.

Repacking the case, he collapsed the telescopic antenna. He looked around carefully. The security van was still parked outside the bank, the guard looking at his watch. Norris squeezed inside the clock tower, closed and rebolted the small door, and stood listening. Only the sound of the halyard slapping the flagpole, muted now, and the wind whistling through the cracks in the door. He went back down the spiral staircase and across the auditorium.

The narrow stairs, silent during his ascent, creaked loudly now. At the bottom, he paused, ear to the door, listening. Alarm jangled in his brain as he heard voices, not six feet from where he stood. A group of people talking, their voices mingling with the clink of crockery and the tinkle of spoons in saucers. He looked at his watch. The Cosworth would be on its way. Norris had to move now, or he would miss the rendezvous.

He was trapped.

There was no way of knowing how long the group of coffee-drinkers would remain on the landing beyond the narrow door. He tried to work out where the car would be. From their rehearsal last week, he knew it took two and a half minutes for the motor cycle to get back to the garage. It would take Alex another five minutes to replace the number plates. Then he had to change his clothes, set up the equipment in the boot of the car, reverse out, then close and lock the garage. After that, it was only a matter of joining the traffic and driving round the circuit, past the bank and the security van to a point fifty yards beyond the town hall. Norris reckoned that would take another three or four minutes, depending on the lights at the crossing.

He had less than two minutes.

At the door, he listened, holding his breath. There seemed to be fewer people now. They were drifting back into the chamber. Then, quiet except for the sound of crockery being collected, the sound gradually fading. Norris opened the door a crack. A woman in a black dress and white apron was carrying a tray loaded with crockery across the landing. She went into a room to his right. He heard her talking to someone, another helper perhaps.

He tugged the door open, glanced quickly in both directions, then ran across the deserted landing. He went down the stairs, two at a time, out into the street.

The Cosworth whispered past.

CHAPTER THIRTEEN

Police Constable Trevor Wilkinson was peeved.

He was sitting astride his white BMW police motor cycle in a lay-by at the side of a wide, three-lane link road, his arms folded across his chest, not only to keep warm, but to disguise the fluorescent lettering identifying him. In spring or summer, he enjoyed operating the speed trap, checking vehicle speeds, pursuing offenders, then issuing them a ticket or warning. Which one, depended on his mood.

There was a calibrated stop-watch clipped to the right handlebar under the Perspex windshield. The procedure was simple. On spotting a vehicle which he thought might be speeding, he would lean forward and start the watch, trying to synchronize with his quarry as it passed a brightly coloured cone three-quarters of a mile away.

There was a similar marker opposite, and as the vehicle passed this, he would stop the watch. Any time under forty-five seconds meant that the sixty-mile-an-hour speed limit had been exceeded. He was sometimes a bit out with the stop and start procedure, and because of the thick gauntlets he wore, operating the watch was perhaps not as precise as it should be. He had never been challenged, though.

Today, he was in a foul mood. He had been called in at short notice when a colleague had telephoned in sick at the last minute. So now, instead of out shopping with the wife, he was freezing his bollocks off in a lay-by, with a north-easterly blowing in off Exmoor, slicing through his protective clothing as if it wasn't there. He didn't mind missing the shopping, boring at best. He would rather have been downing a few pints with his mates in the Police Club.

There wasn't much traffic. Anyone with any sense would be at home with their feet up in front of the fire watching the box. Grey-black clouds tumbled southwards across the orange sky. His breath condensed in the sharp cold and he had to keep removing the scarf from around his face to prevent his visor misting.

Suddenly, a red hatchback, coming fast down the hill towards the first cone. He unfolded his arms, placing his finger on the button of the stop-watch, clicking it smartly down as the car flashed by the first marker. Wilkinson watched the hand jump round the face of the watch. He stopped it as the hatchback broke a line between him and the second cone. The driver looked to his right and saw the policeman. Wilkinson knew he would be cursing. The brake lights flared briefly as the car slowed, the driver trying to make amends.

'Too late, pal,' muttered Wilkinson.

He had glanced at the watch. The hatchback had taken 37.6 seconds to cover the measured distance. The table of figures Sellotaped to the petrol tank of the BMW gave an instant conversion of time to speed.

He would enjoy confronting the young driver, telling him importantly that he had been timed at 37.6 seconds over three-quarters of a mile, meaning he had been travelling at an average speed of 71.8 miles per hour. Wilkinson liked to stress the decimal point, hoping he had impressed, showing off his ability at maths. Without the crib sheet, though, he was unable to do the sums. But they weren't to know that. Nobody had ever challenged him. They couldn't do the sums either.

He pushed the self-starter, feeling the bike throb into life. Rolling it forward off the kick stand, he set off, following the hatchback, now driven legally. As he approached the roundabout at the end of the link road, he accelerated to keep in contact, realizing that the driver had now seen him in his rear-view mirror. The hatchback drove directly across the roundabout, taking the twelve-o'clock exit, on to the dual carriageway, heading east.

It accelerated to seventy, but traffic from his right forced Wilkinson to stop. There were three vehicles. The first was a white Ford Cosworth. The driver looked casually at him as it passed, but Wilkinson didn't look at the car or its occupants. He was only concerned with the red hatchback disappearing into the distance.

A bit of excitement after all.

Alex saw the police motor cycle approach the roundabout from his left. It slowed to allow him and two more cars to turn on to the dual carriageway. He drove steadily, accelerating to the speed limit, but careful to stay within the law. His heart was beating more quickly than usual but his breathing was steady. The police bike entered the main carriageway moving rapidly into the outside lane.

'Where the hell did he come from?' Alex kept his voice calm. 'Were we spotted, back there, in the town?'

'God knows. My fault, being late.'

'Couldn't be helped. He's coming. Fast. I think we're going to need your kit. Let's hope it works.'

Richard Norris worked quickly, adjusting the modified radio fitted under the dash, flashing lights reflecting from his face as he made minor corrections, fine-tuning, as Alex concentrated on the rider behind. They listened, trying to identify each caller using the police radio net. Richard studied his notebook, flicked switches, then looked at Alex. There had been no reference to their vehicle, and he hoped there would be no need to use the equipment he had fitted in the car, for just this purpose. Better safe than sorry, though.

'How's he doing?' Norris tried to keep his voice calm, neutral. His mind was busy, going back over the events in the town, wondering. Maybe they'd been spotted after all, a result of the Cosworth having to make a second pass.

Alex kept looking in the rear-view mirror, watching the bike. Suddenly the blue light came on, flashing ominously, the distance between them closing as the motor cycle picked up speed. Alex knew what to do. Slamming the gear lever forward, he jammed his foot down on the accelerator. The Cosworth transformed. The tachometer swept up into the red, engine howling. Their heads jerked back as the turbo kicked in.

'We're losing him.' Alex flicked his eyes to the mirror. 'Oh, shit. Here he comes again.'

The BMW was gaining on them.

They listened to him calling his control.

Wilkinson had slowed at the roundabout to let priority traffic from his right on to the two-lane highway. The red hatchback was almost a mile ahead by the time he was able to cross the roundabout and give chase. There were three cars between him and his quarry, and to prevent them from pulling out into the fast lane, holding him up, he flicked on his blue light.

Suddenly, for no apparent reason, the white Cosworth in front tore away from him. The big bike surged forward as he twisted the throttle back, the front wheel almost rearing off the ground. Wilkinson was not stupid. He knew there had to be a reason for the Cosworth to pull away from him as soon as he'd used his light. With luck, he could be in for a good collar.

The freezing wind knifed through him as the needle of his speedometer swept round to the ton. But he couldn't close the gap between them which stayed stubbornly constant. If anything, it was widening. He flashed past the red hatchback, briefly seeing the driver glance at him, relieved he was no longer being chased. Wilkinson knew he could not catch the Cosworth. His petrol tank was less than a quarter full. He was supposed to be manning a speed trap, not involved in a sustained, high-speed chase.

He tried to think, ignoring the numbing, buffeting wind.

The best he could do would be to radio base where a car would be despatched to intercept the Cosworth five miles further on, where the road joined the motorway. He flicked the send switch on his handlebar.

'Alfa one two three this is Mike Zulu one.' He was shouting over the roar of the wind. 'I am in pursuit of a white Ford Cosworth heading east on . . .' He sent his location and the vehicle registration number. He waited for an acknowledgement, irritated when, instead, he heard control talking to another vehicle. He tried again, with the same result.

What the hell was the matter with them? Here he was, a chance of an arrest, and the silly buggers wouldn't acknowledge. Too busy gassing to each other like old women at the WI. He tried again, yelling into the mike, the noise filling his helmet, then ripped away on the wind.

At last, control.

Calm, remote, unimpressed by his excitement. But at least they were answering.

He grinned as he prepared to carry out the instructions he had been given.

We'll have you, mate.

The Cosworth flew along the dual carriageway as each of them busied themselves with their individual jobs. Alex concentrated on driving, while Richard fiddled with the electronics. Timing was vital. There could be no error. He waited tensely for the policeman to use his radio. Almost at once, Richard recognized the Mike Zulu identifier. He flicked a series of switches, smiling tightly as he transmitted the police broadcasts recorded earlier at Middlemoor.

'That'll confuse the poor sod,' he said, satisfied. 'It's up to you now, Alex. This has to be good. I hope you're in good voice. This has to work, or we'll be intercepted as soon as we hit the motorway.'

He passed over the mike.

Alex continued to drive, one-handed, looking frequently in the rear-view mirror, then back at the road.

'Here goes,' he muttered. Coughing gently to clear his throat, he spoke calmly into the mike.

'Mike Zulu one, Mike Zulu one. Your transmission is acknowledged. Delta twenty-one and four are diverted. Disengage and return to your station. Confirm. Over.' The imitation was perfect. The police rider, wind howling in his ears, was completely taken in. Alex saw the motor cycle slow, falling further and further behind, the rider acknowledging the call.

Richard was impressed. He had heard his friend mimicking famous voices at mess parties and admired his talent. This was the first time he had seen him perform in earnest though. Alex had spent only a few minutes listening to the voice of the controller on the tape, and yet he had copied it exactly.

'He's off.' Alex grinned, relieved.

'I bet their controller is a bit confused,' Richard had relaxed, 'wondering why the hell he could hear his own voice repeating something he said yesterday.' He punched Alex on the arm. 'There's an exit coming up. We'd better cut across country for a bit, then rejoin the motorway further up.'

'You're the boss.' Alex changed down through the gears, leaving the dual carriageway at the next exit. He drove fast but skilfully through narrow Devon lanes, taking care through the villages, not wanting to draw attention to themselves. Half an hour later, they rejoined the motorway continuing their journey at a normal pace.

The communications officer at police headquarters pushed back his chair from the console and stood, stretching as he got up. He yawned, turned away and walked over to the coffee machine in the corner. Another hour and his shift would be finished. He poured coffee into a stained mug and raised it to his lips, blowing across the steaming liquid to cool it. He cursed silently, scalding his lips, careful not to allow the WPC to hear.

He was about to talk to her when something odd happened. He could have sworn he could hear Mike Jones on the radio. Bloody funny. Jones wasn't due to take over until he himself went off shift. He looked at his watch again, frowning. Was Jones out in one of the patrol cars? Can't be. He's using our callsign, the one allocated to this console.

'Bloody odd,' he said, 'I could have sworn that was Mike Jones talking. What the fuck's going on?' He had forgotten the WPC. She didn't even blush.

'Odder still,' said a voice behind him. 'That's me talking from my patrol car. So how come I'm standing here listening to myself?'

'I don't get it.' The communications officer was about to step forward to investigate when the airwaves came alive with frantic calls. Every car in the division seemed to be talking at once.

'What the fuck is going on?' he said again. Leaving the coffee to get cold on a table, he slid into his chair, picking up the mike, eyes scanning the despatch board.

A security van had been robbed in Willingford. That was what all the excitement was about. No wonder the circuits were jammed, messages passed with such urgency. He started talking, trying to sort the confusion on the net, gradually restoring order as reports of the robbery started coming in.

Mike Jones was still on the air, confusing everyone, preventing units talking to one another.

Bloody strange . . .

It came to him. They were being jammed.

Some bastard was jamming them.

It was quiet in the country lane.

No birds sang. It was too cold. The passenger of the sporty car climbed out into the muddy entrance to the gate, keeping watch along the lane as the driver snapped off the front and rear number plates from the original plates underneath. The false plates, wrapped in a piece of sacking, were stowed in the boot.

The car drove off.

The same car left the motorway, re-entering from the opposite direction. At the next service area, it was driven to a car wash, given the full treatment, leaving it shiny, clean, the wheels and chassis scrubbed. It looked almost new, left in a free parking space. The two occupants climbed stiffly out, transferred the contents of the boot to two other vehicles, then walked casually over to the restaurant.

They stayed fifteen minutes, leaving independently.

One carried a larger than normal briefcase, the other a black, Gold Pfile overnight bag. In all other respects, they looked like any other travellers.

In the car park, the man with the briefcase got into a blue Datsun and drove north-west. Five minutes later, the other followed in a green Volkswagen.

Neither looked at the shiny white Cosworth.

*

A wintry sun splashed into the narrow street, bringing a fraudulent promise of spring. Filtering through the wide windows of the showroom, it reflected weakly off an assortment of cars lined in two rows close to the walls. It was cold in the office, an area partitioned at one end. A man sat blowing on his hands, warming them while he waited for the radiators to heat the room. It was sparsely furnished, unimpressive, with a wide, light-coloured wooden desk, badly scarred, covered in ball-point scribbling. A chair, its padded seat deeply indented, stood behind it. Hanging tiredly from the walls were various schedules, charts, and a large, out-of-date, much-fingered Pirelli calender. Dowdy, dismal, the limp, insipid pot-plants did little to enliven it.

Looking without interest along the narrow street, he saw a few pedestrians drawing their coats tight as they hurried along, heads bowed as the wind plucked at them. Each ignored their surroundings, derelict houses to the right side of the road, neater houses on the left, one for sale opposite the junction at the far end.

There was a sudden tenseness in him as a car turned into the street and drove slowly towards the showroom, the sun briefly reflected from the windscreen when it passed a narrow alley.

The car drew up outside. The man at the desk made to rise as it stopped, resting his hands on the desk in a half-hearted attempt at standing. The driver hesitated, glanced about him before getting out, then entered the showroom and walked quickly between the lines of cars into the office. He stood, hands thrust deep into the pockets of his anorak. He stared. Neither spoke. A set of ignition keys was tossed, followed by a thin wad of used banknotes, plunking on to the table, the sound of their landing contrasting with the musical jingle of the keys.

The visitor nodded, turned and strolled casually from

the office, out of the showroom, leaving the red Vauxhall Cavalier parked outside. He walked quickly away.

The money, uncounted, was tossed into a drawer. The man stood, picked up the ignition keys and went outside. Once in the car, he drove round the back and parked next to a Honda Prelude. Leaning over to the glove compartment, he flipped it open, removing the small piece of paper from the document holder, folded neatly in half. He slipped it delicately into the top pocket of his shabby suit.

Back in the office, he spread the paper on the desk, smoothing it with the fingers of his left hand. His little finger stuck up stiffly. Absently, he rubbed it on his trouser leg, enjoying the warmth the friction created. He stared, startling green eyes, unblinkingly, reading the boldly written print.

From the drawer, he took a cigarette lighter and burned the paper in a heavy ashtray, the flame hesitating, not catching fully until he coaxed it, poking with a pencil. Crushing the ashes, he stirred them into a pulp, mixed with the cold tea dregs from a chipped mug. He took the mess to a dirty toilet at the rear of the office, pulled the chain, holding the ashtray in the bowl, until everything was flushed away. He watched the few pieces of ash left floating then settling in the bowl. He pulled the chain again.

He would remember the details.

Soon, it would be time.

CHAPTER FOURTEEN

The civil servant looked prosperous, comfortable, pleased with life. He was sitting at a table in a small Italian restaurant on Buckingham Palace Road, not far from the Rubens Hotel. He had enjoyed a splendid lunch, and was now warming a large brandy, swirling it in the goblet he held gently in the palm of his hand, waiting for the man opposite to get to the point of their meeting.

Fairthorne hadn't seen Richard Norris since leaving the forces, but remembered him from Aden. Fairthorne had been commanding his Brigade, and had been awarded the CBE after a successful action against the Red Wolves in the Radfan. The whole operation had hinged round Norris and his signallers.

A bloody close-run thing.

He remembered authorizing the plan.

If they hadn't got there with the radios there was no way of knowing what might have happened. Fairthorne would have lost his job. Sacked. No doubt about that. Early retirement and a piss poor pension to live on. Nobody would have employed him with such a record of failure. As it stood, he was very highly placed in the Civil Service, looking forward to a further pension at the end of a second successful career. He was due to retire shortly. This time for good.

He was employed in the Northern Ireland Office.

Ungrudgingly, he knew he owed a great deal to the man opposite, who looked as if he hadn't slept decently for weeks.

He listened to what Richard Norris had to say, the cigar smoke eddying gently on the air between them. Almost as though not listening, he half-turned away, his fingers playing with the corner of the table napkin. In fact, he missed nothing.

'The list you want is not a problem.' The white damask slid through first and second fingers. 'I confess I find this a most unusual request, but why you need it is no concern of mine, unless my giving it to you threatens the security of the nation.'

He drew reflectively on the cigar, blowing gently on the tip as he exhaled. A fragment of tobacco leaf had stuck to his bottom lip, which he picked off delicately with a fingernail.

'The name you are asking for. A different matter. One outside my sphere of operations, not covered by my directorate. I'll have to obtain this information from another department. That is if, and it is a very big if, the information is available.' Rubbing his thumb and forefinger together, he dropped the piece of tobacco leaf into the ashtray.

'I have, as yet, seen no memorandum. Nothing has been minuted. That doesn't mean there's been no progress in finding him.' He was beginning to sound pompous. He balanced the cigar carefully in the ashtray while he dabbed at his mouth with the napkin. He dropped it on the table and without looking up, asked Richard directly, 'Why do you want to know? What's so important about this man in particular?'

'He murdered my son.'

Fairthorne cursed himself for his crass forgetfulness. Of course. Norris. Johnathan Norris. He hadn't made the connection, hadn't seen the significance.

'My dear chap, I'm so sorry. I didn't connect. Unforgivable of me.'

Contritely, Fairthorne picked up the cigar, staring at it. He thought he knew now why Norris wanted to identify this particular Provisional. He let his mind drift, remembering Aden, Norris's expression when they'd come down off the jebel, the debrief, when he'd told of the fight with the enemy patrol.

Just to get a bloody radio on top of a hill.

He owed him.

'Look,' he said. 'There's a chance I might get to hear, if I ask around. Military Intelligence, RUC reports. They pass across my desk occasionally. If I get anything, and I repeat, it's a bloody big if, how do you want it passed on?'

Richard gave him a contact number.

'It will be a single telephone call. Unattributable. This conversation did not take place. You do of course appreciate my position.' Fairthorne was short, not wasting words. 'The leak must not be traced to my department. I will deal with it personally. No one must know of this.' He stabbed the cigar into the tray, twisting to extinguish it, preparing to leave. 'That was a splendid lunch, for which I thank you. The 'eighty-one Barolo was exceptional. Anything else?'

Richard thanked him.

Fairthorne got up from the table and walked to the coat stand. He wrapped a regimental silk scarf across his shoulders, covering his throat, then shrugged into the British Warm held for him by a waiter. As he passed the table, he nodded briefly, then walked out into the traffic.

Relieved, Richard watched him go.

The list he had asked for arrived at the post office box sooner than he expected. A computer spreadsheet longer than Richard had thought possible. He studied it, suddenly dispirited, feeling inadequate. He read the neat, dot-matrix print, representing twenty years of sorrow. Page after page into a thick sheaf.

There was no name.

Not yet. But he could wait.

*

Despite the cold outside, the man working so late wore no jacket. Progress had been slow. Central Records had made no breakthrough in its search. He studied the few clues he possessed, listing them on a clean sheet of A4 paper.

First name Patrick. Never Pat.

Home. West Belfast. Somewhere.

Little finger of left hand injured.

Green eyes. No expression in them.

Johnny-get-your-gun.

Not much to go on. Sod all, in fact.

As the man in the shirt-sleeves was putting on his jacket ready to leave, his superior, a colonel from the top floor, poked his head into the office to say goodnight.

'If there's nothing on, I'll be off. Anything I should lose any sleep over?'

He surveyed the untidy room, sniffing disapprovingly, glad his own office was up on the top floor.

'No, Colonel. I'm about to leave too. I've been late every night this week. Jean is getting a bit pissed off with me.'

'What's been keeping you?' The Colonel was sympathetic. The work wasn't always fun.

'We're after a Provo. The Int boys think he may have served in the Army at some time, British or Irish. Thin evidence really. An old photo, taken in 'seventy-six, shows he can put a beret on without making it look like a plate of cow shit.' He grinned. 'There may be something in it.'

The Colonel was looking at the paper on the desk.

'What's this?'

'Johnny-get-your-gun?'

'Yes.' The Colonel looked thoughtful.

'It's something he says.' The other grinned. 'Er . . . when he . . . you know, when he comes. And don't ask me how the RUC found that out!'

'You sure about this, Brian?'

'That's what I'm told. Bloody odd, but still . . .'

'You've no name?'

'Patrick, Colonel. Apparently he doesn't like Pat.'

The Colonel looked thoughtful.

'Well, I'm damned.'

'Something, Colonel?'

'Perhaps. I wonder. We once had a weapon training instructor who used that phrase. It was his favourite training aid.' The Colonel folded his arms, sitting awkwardly across the corner of the desk. He held up his hands, as if firing a machine-gun. 'It's a way of helping a machine-gunner count the number of rounds in a burst. Broken into syllables, John-ny-get-your-gun equates to five rounds.' He got up from the desk, pulled out a handkerchief and noisily blew his nose.

'It's out of date now. It stopped the firer letting go too long a burst, causing the barrel to overheat. We had a weapon training instructor in the battalion when I was a platoon commander. Always hammering it into us. A Jock. From Glasgow. Let me think . . .'

The Colonel walked to the window and looked out on to Horse Guards. Without turning he said, 'McKinnon. Sergeant Doddy McKinnon.'

'You think there could be a connection? Do we know where he is now?'

'God knows. Doddy liked it on the pop. But bloody ace with the machine-gun. I don't know of anyone else who might use that expression.' The Colonel was getting ready to leave. 'He'll be pissing it up somewhere. If he's still alive.'

'Well, I'll be . . . It's a long shot, but anything is worth a try.'

The jacket was off again, flung untidily over the back of a chair. He seemed comfortable without it, sitting once more behind his desk, reaching for the telephone. He dialled a number in Military Intelligence.

*

The South Glasgow Working Men's Club was full with men drinking, some on their way home, others with no home to go to. The air was hot and smoky, and it was difficult to see across the bar, or talk above the noise. One occupant of the club was obviously uncomfortable, his dress different from the others. Urgent business was his only reason for being there.

He was from Military Intelligence.

Allowing his eyes to get used to the dim light, he walked to the bar, squeezing through the group of drinkers who watched a darts match at the far wall. But it was information he had come for, not drink. He leaned close to the barman in a filthy, greasy apron, shouting above the din. The barman cocked his head, cupping a hand to his ear, but still had to ask the stranger to repeat his question. Finally, wiping a beer glass with a wet tea-towel, he jerked his chin in the direction of a booth in the corner.

The barman watched him cross the room.

Police.

He knew. What had old Doddy been up to this time?

The man approached the booth, looking at the unhappy-looking sot clasping a pint beer glass in one hand and a whisky glass in the other. Both were empty. The man spoke briefly, went to the bar, returning with a tumbler half-full of whisky. He let the man pull at the glass, feeling the distaste as it was held out for another. It was refilled.

The man spoke again, this time urgently.

'Mr McKinnon? Doddy McKinnon?'

The old boy nodded, squinting through the booze. The drink seemed to have steadied him, brought him to life. He held the glass out again.

'Later, Doddy. Let's talk.'

The man leaned across the table, avoiding the wet circles from the glasses.

'How long have you been out, Doddy?'

'Prison, or the fucking Army?' McKinnon stared at the glass, then over the man's shoulder at the bar. He held the glass up, waving it unsteadily, looking into it again, then raising it to his mouth and licking round the rim.

'Army, Doddy.'

'Who the fuck wants to know?'

'Me, Doddy. I want to know.'

'Get me a dram. Helps the memory.'

He drank it down in one gulp. His eyes seemed in focus now.

''Eighty. Court martial. Drunk as Orderly Sergeant.'

The man nodded. He had known.

'We're looking for someone, Doddy. An Irishman. We think he came out in 'seventy or 'seventy-one.'

'Why ask me?'

'We thought you might know him.'

'North or South?'

'Does it matter?'

McKinnon shrugged.

'Does he have a name? This Irishman?'

'Try Patrick. May be handy with a machine-gun.'

There was a faraway look in the old boy's eyes, remembering, seeing the ranges at Sennelager, the sand, the pine trees, targets popping up in the distance. The yammer of the gun.

'Doddy?'

'I'm thinking. Patrick, you say. Anything else?'

'Johnny get your gun?'

'Donnelly,' said McKinnon, without hesitation. 'Patrick Donnelly.' He stared down at the table. 'Eyes like frozen green piss-balls. He used to say it out loud when he was behind the gun. Thick mick probably couldn't count to five otherwise.' He hesitated, looking at the glass. 'Bought himself out in 'seventy-one. Fucker owed me a fiver. Said he'd pay it back on pay-day. Bastard never did. I remember him.' Doddy McKinnon held out the glass. 'He was the best, Donnelly was. If only he could count . . . Bloody fiver. Not a sniff of it.'

The smartly dressed visitor reached into his jacket and pulled out his wallet. He took out a new five-pound note.

'Have one on me, Doddy,' he said. 'You've earned it.'

With that, he got to his feet and left, looking straight ahead. Doddy McKinnon watched him go, then looked at the note in his hand, before folding it neatly down the middle.

'Johnny get your gun,' he said.

Chuckling drunkenly, he got up and weaved to the bar, holding up the note.

Christmas came and went.

For Richard, it was lonely and depressing. It should have been a happy break with them all together. Felicity excited, making plans, lists, arranging parties, meals and days to go shopping. Johnathan, perhaps looking tired, but relieved to be away from it. Until the next time.

But there was not to be a next time.

In early January, seven weeks after Johnathan's death, the telephone in the old farmhouse rang. Richard Norris listened to the cultured voice of the ex-brigadier, now employed in the Northern Ireland Office.

'The name you wanted. Donnelly. Patrick Donnelly.' A description followed.

'You're sure?'

Fairthorne didn't answer straight away. Richard heard his hesitation.

'It's the best I can do. There was a good lead, followed up by those who know their business. Everything fits. Too much for it to be a coincidence. Although it's not cast-iron, if it were me, I'd bet on it.'

'Your life?'

Richard wanted to be sure.

'If it's a certain, how come he's running free? Not in "stir" where he belongs?'

'There's something you should know.' Fairthorne took a deep breath. 'He's squeaky clean. Spotless. There's nothing on him, not even a motoring offence. We've nothing, us, the RUC, anyone for that matter. But they'll be watching him, you can count on that. As soon as he does something wrong, anything at all, they'll lift him, bring him in for questioning.'

Richard understood.

He had paid particular attention when he heard about the injury to the left hand.

He didn't write the name down. It was seared into his brain and he would take it to hell if he had to.

Patrick Donnelly.

The little finger of the left hand. Indentification would be easy, irrefutable.

He'd collected dole.

There was an address.

Belfast.

He was going back.

PART THREE

CHAPTER FIFTEEN

The bar was noisy, full of smoke.

A guitarist, seated in the corner, dragged his pick across the strings, the chord reverberating around the room. Voices were lowered. It was quiet, the crowd waiting until he broke into another rousing rebel song, the notes nasal and flat. An old squeeze-box joined him, a thin, wailing sound. Tears were shed as the drink took its toll. Voices sang, supporting the boys fighting against the British in Ireland, as their own forefathers had before, at Bunker Hill, and at Yorktown, where it had ended. When the British, defeated, had surrendered and finally left.

Glorious days.

A young man in a green jacket, a pretty young girl with him, passed a box around the bar. Dollar bills were stuffed in, until it was thick with the money. The letters painted on the side of the box had been crudely done with an aerosol spray. The message was simple, easy to read:

BUCKS FUCKS BRITS

There was no shortage, everyone was generous. As the stout and the Bushmills flowed, tired, faded eyes cried their tears. Arms were hugged around shoulders as bodies swayed to the lament. Yet none there had ever heard of the Falls Road, Divis Street, the Creggan Estate or the Bogside. The boys were fighting for their freedom, the Old Country, that green land, which long ago, before their parents had grown up in the excesses of the United States, had been home. Nothing else mattered.

Later, there was to be a speaker, a fighter on the run. The Brits had applied for his extradition. He was going to tell them what it was really like, where the dollars were going, and how they could, if they really put their minds to it, screw up the army of occupation once and for all.

The young man and woman weaved amongst the drinkers collecting the money. They didn't stop until the box was packed tight with crumpled notes and could hold no more.

In the parking lot, the cash was transferred into a canvas flight bag and zipped up. The girl tossed the empty box into a trash can as the car drove off, the young man with his arm around the pretty girl's shoulder.

Boston, Massachusetts.

New York, January, freezing.

Driving into the city from John F. Kennedy Airport, the view from the cab was cheerless and depressing. Powdery snow drifted from a dark sky, a harbinger of worse weather to come. But, for the man in the cab, this journey into the city was necessary, only because it was an indirect route to his real destination, Boston. He would stay here for the shortest time possible before continuing.

Alex was relieved at getting into America so easily. There had been an awkward moment, waiting to clear Immigration, when the official had scrutinized the NATO travel order and his bogus identity card. Alex had been prepared to brazen it out.

'You here on temporary duty, Colonel Howard?' The question was casual.

'Yes. TDY.'

'Where will you be for the duration of your stay?'

'Fort Carson, Colorado. A few days sightseeing first.' He had decided to stick with somewhere he knew. The official looked at the documents again, letting his eyes flick once more to Alex's face.

'You have orders cut?'

Alex, expecting the question, answered confidently, 'Not until I get to Seventh Division. I was told that any orders cut in the UK were invalid without the sponsor unit authentication stamp.' The official seemed satisfied. He folded the document and handed it back.

Have a nice day.

So far, so good.

After he had seen the ease with which the date stamp on the NATO order had been altered, he had been worried it might not stand up to close scrutiny. The English forger had earned his fee. Alex moped round the city, killing time, thinking of what lay ahead.

After two days he was fed up with New York, the claustrophobia, buildings pressing in on him. He caught an internal flight to Boston, checked in to the Intercontinental Hotel, and waited for Richard Norris to make contact. Richard had already arrived perfectly legally, a business trip on behalf of his company.

Richard had been busy. Already he had found and had been watching the tall imposing structure in downtown Boston where Noraid was located. The place reflected corporate success. Security was tight, the best that money could buy.

Entry through the front door was impossible unless the caller was recognized by the guards. Even then, the correct code had to be entered into the electronic switch and an individual entry card swiped through the lock. Everybody entering the building was registered from information stored on the magnetic strip.

Once inside, the security guard checked credentials before issuing a further magnetic key to gain access to individual offices. This second card was given only on the receipt of a signature.

'Tight as a drum,' commented Alex after surveying the building over a period of days. 'Can you crack it? The electrics, I mean?'

'Not without a card. Even then we'd never get by the guards. See how they check in everyone. And I mean *everyone*? Even the regulars.'

'Then we'll need to find another way, bypass their security system somehow.' Alex, deep in thought, scratched his head behind his ear, wondering how they would get into the offices.

They rented an office in a block on the same side of the street, separated by an alley perhaps twelve feet wide. From behind drawn blinds they carefully inspected the building across the alley without being seen. Richard soon identified the accounts office, one housing the big computer terminals, the steel safe with the time lock. This was their target.

They just had to find a way in.

And out.

'I've been up on the roof. We can get in that way.'

Alex had just entered the rented office, where Richard was staring across the alley, examining the building through powerful field-glasses. Rubbing his eyes, he turned tiredly to look at Alex brushing dust marks from his coat-sleeves and trousers. The desk, littered with plastic coffee-cups and fast-food packages, showed how long they had been there.

Richard stared. Briefly, Alex thought he saw a spark of alarm in his eyes, a movement of his jaw muscles, something Norris could never control when angry.

Or afraid.

'We can get across from the roof. There's a metal pipe about eight inches in diameter, leading from our building over to Noraid. It's about thirty feet lower than our roof, but, once we are down on it, we can just walk over. It's a bit trickier to get to the actual office we want.' Alex paused, pointing with a hot dog he had started to eat. He looked at it with an expression of mild disgust, then tossed it half-eaten into the litter on the desk.

'We'll need to traverse round the building on that ledge, the one leading towards the accounts office. The trouble is,' he frowned, 'we'd be blocked by that wide sill sticking out above their window. We know the window's opened early in the evening.' He leaned forward, his face close to the glass. 'It's probably hotter than hell in there. I'll bet you a tenner he can't regulate the heating, and leaves the window open for about ten minutes to let real air in before he starts work.'

Alex looked at Richard. He was scratching the side of his face, sipping coffee. Not enthusiastic.

'We'll need ropes, snap-links, climbing harnesses, God knows what else. I'm not sure—'

'It's the only way,' Alex interrupted. 'We've been climbing stuff like this since we were sprogs. It's a doddle compared to Cenotaph Corner. The tricky bit is the timing. We need to be there when the window is open, otherwise there's no way in. We'd be dangling there tapping, asking to be let in out of the cold.' Alex laughed, excited, like a schoolkid off to the seaside. He had already made up his mind. 'Tomorrow we'll buy the kit, not locally. We watch two more nights, and go in Friday.'

Richard had turned his back. He was staring out of the window with a faraway look in his eyes. Something else was there.

Doubt.

He shrugged.

'OK,' he muttered. 'Friday.'

*

Henry Mikovitch stepped smartly along the sidewalk towards his office block. The collar of the expensive camel coat was turned up to keep out the penetrating cold. It was almost 9 p.m. when he slid his entry card through the magnetic lock to let himself into the Metropol Building. He keyed in his personal code without looking at the buttons, listening instead to the tones as they piped out. It was warm inside, too warm, as usual. At the security-guard's desk, he held out his hologrammed ID.

'Evening, Mr Mikovitch. Looks cold out. How long do you expect to stay? I'm askin' cos we got a new guy on tonight when I'm done. I need to let him know who's still in before I leave. He'll also be up to see you in the office so's he can recognize you in the future. I'll let him find his own way up to the tenth, if that's OK with you.'

'I should be through by eleven or eleven thirty. You know how busy we get Fridays.'

''K, Mr Mikovitch. I'll make sure he knows. You're the only one in tonight. Mr Donnovan and his secretary left about thirty minutes ago. She sure is a nice piece of ass that secretary. I wonder where *they* were off to?'

'George, you got a dirty mind.' The accountant laughed. He let his own mind go into fast forward. He knew where *he* was going to be after he was through here tonight. With his latest hooker. Now she *really* was a nice piece of ass. He had already decided what he was going to do with it, once they were alone in her apartment, the apartment *he* paid for. He walked to the elevator and hit the button for the tenth floor, thinking about the girl all the way up.

He opened the office door using another magnetic card and two keys. As usual it was stifling; the heating, controlled by a central thermostat and set too high, had been on all day. He switched on the light at his desk, placing his attaché case carefully on the leather surface.

At the computer, he daintily tapped at a bank of

switches, waiting as the screen flickered into life. Fitted to the south wall was a large walk-in safe, which Mikovitch opened, spinning the combination, waiting for the magnetic relays to operate, then turning the big handles. He heaved the heavy steel door open and looked in, satisfying himself that the money was still there, used notes neatly bundled and stacked on the shelves. His nose wrinkled at the whiff of stale air filtering into the room.

Later, when he had finished work and relocked the combination, the safe could not be opened until the timing mechanism was activated the next morning.

At the window, he stood looking at the lights of Boston sparkling in the sharp cold, before pressing the electrical switch to open it. Icy air came in on the breeze. In ten minutes the office would be much more comfortable. When it was, he would close and lock the window.

Henry Mikovitch was a magician with figures. In his thirty years as an accountant he had processed billions of dollars, shifting them through a complicated system of accounts, escaping the attention of the Inland Revenue Service and the FBI. He adjusted the accounts constantly, ensuring always that they were where they were most needed. Currently, he was working for Noraid, an organization providing American money to the Cause in Ireland. Although he had no proof, he suspected that the money was used to buy weapons and explosives. He didn't really care.

From his desk, he worked at the computer, moving money, adjusting figures, checking profit margins, calculating, balancing. Occasionally he wrote notes in a small leather-covered notebook with a small, solid-gold pen. Large amounts had been collected from donations that week. Mikovitch shifted the cash into shadowy companies and corporate groups, until, eventually, it was deposited into numbered accounts, controlled by the Provisional IRA.

Small amounts, multiplied many times, were diverted into accounts controlled by Henry S. Mikovitch. How else could he afford the most expensive hookers in town?

He worked busily, unaware of the time. After a while, he stretched, yawned and scratched his genitals. He pictured what was in store, later.

There was a loud thump as something heavy landed on the floor behind him. Swivelling in his chair, he gasped aloud at what he saw.

Impossible.

It was dark, bitterly cold in the easterly wind.

Two men crouched under the low parapet, blowing on their fingers to warm them, thankful for the thermal underwear under the black one-piece suits. Richard shivered. It wasn't just the cold. He tried to keep his mind clear, ready for the action ahead, running through the plan in his mind.

Nothing to it.

Once they were in.

He saw Alex look at his watch again, envying his calm. The coil of 9-mm climbing rope spread about their feet, ready when needed. For the tenth time he checked the climbing belt around his waist, his movements jerky, his fingers clumsy. Like Alex, he had rubbed the soles of the black trainers on the rough surface of the roof to give more friction, a better grip.

It was so long since he'd been on rock. He tried not to think about the last time, to shut it from his mind. He had started remembering with Nobby Clarke astride Dow Crag. How long ago? It seemed a lifetime.

Alex picked up the coil of rope and tested the anchor point. He looked over the edge, at the alley fifteen floors below, the street, traffic hurrying, toys in a child's playroom, muted, distant, remote.

'All clear,' said Alex. 'Ready?'

He didn't wait for an answer, instead tossing the coil of rope over the edge, down into the night, hissing through the air. Too short to reach the ground, it hung, swinging in the breeze, level with the pipe which Richard could just see in the darkness. Alex, already up on the parapet, ignored the exposure, clipping the rope into the aluminium *descendeur* attached to his climbing belt with a karabiner. He was leaning back at an angle, ready to start the short abseil down to the pipe.

Richard felt the fear then. The fear long hidden, which until now had been private. He thought he might be sick. Alex was looking at him, his left thumb in the air. OK? But it wasn't. Not for Richard Norris standing terrified behind a parapet on the roof of an imposing building in downtown Boston, USA.

He spoke, his voice wretched. 'Alex. I can't. I can't do it!'

Alex was looking at him, puzzled, still poised, balanced on the edge of the roof, leaning, ready to go. He waited for what seemed an eternity, then pulled hard on his left hand to bring himself back into balance, to step down on to the roof.

'Richard? You OK? Christ, you look dreadful. Here.' He pulled the flask from his pocket, unscrewing the cap with numbed fingers. Richard gulped the malt whisky, would have finished it had Alex not taken it from him.

The two men sat in the cold, Richard with his knees drawn up to his chin, hugging them in an attempt to stop his body shaking. Alex waited. Was this where it ended, then? Richard spoke through clenched teeth, forcing the words through bloodless lips, ground out, unable to hide the pent-up fear.

'The Kaiser-Gebirge. It's because of the Kaiser-Gebirge.'

The new man was settling in.

George, the old guard, had shown him the ropes, familiarizing him with the procedures. No one else in tonight, George had told him, only Mr Mikovitch, up on the tenth, working as usual. No one understood why the man worked so late every night, instead of being home with his family. But then they weren't to know about the call-girl, the expensive apartment.

The guard settled himself comfortably behind the bank of TV monitors, glancing at them occasionally to make sure there were no intruders in the building. There was one other TV, unauthorized, showing the NFL preview. The Washington Redskins were playing the Miami Dolphins. The new man was an avid supporter of the Redskins. He spent more time looking at the game than the monitors.

He would watch a little longer, then go up to the tenth and introduce himself to Mr Mikovitch. He didn't want to make any mistakes, not on his first night. The job was important, meant a lot to him.

Alex studied his friend closely, seeing the fear without understanding. They had climbed together for years, since they had been subalterns. Alex knew Richard was a natural, gifted climber, able to pick his way up the hardest rock faces, despite the frightening exposure. As a pair, they had excelled: a pitch requiring strength was always led by Alex; where finesse and delicate balance were needed, Richard would lead. The two complemented each other. Alex envied Richard's finesse. Yet he knew Richard sometimes wished he had Alex's power when hauling himself over the overhangs.

The story unfolded, slowly, haltingly at first, then in a rush, as if Richard was eager to purge himself of some sin. Alex listened in silence. He, too, remembered the day.

Austria. The Kaiser-Gebirge. The *Wilden Kaiser*.

A climb started too late in the day. The day they were caught in the dark.

Richard was talking, his face screwed up, squinting as if in pain.

'When you fell and were dangling on the rope under the overhang, I really thought we'd had it. You felt like a ton weight. The rope had practically taken the skin off my hands. I didn't think I could hold you. God knows how, I tied you off, safe on my piton so's you couldn't fall any further. You didn't answer when I yelled down the face. Well, you wouldn't. You were out.' He paused, shivering again.

'I climbed down, no fucking rope, black as your arse, to a ledge opposite where you were dangling. You were a bloody mess, literally. You had a great hole in your head.'

He sniffed in the cold wind.

'I undid my waist-line and tied a snap-link to it to make a weight that would wrap itself around your rope when I. . . I used it like a bolas. It worked. I hauled you on to my ledge. No first-aid kit. You know what mad bastards we were. Off on a major climb without so much as a fucking Elastoplast between us. Not like today when these tigers have got enough gear hanging off them to do El Capitan twice over.'

Alex took out the hip flask, passing it. Richard sipped. He had never spoken before of this desperate fight for life. Typically modest, he'd merely said he had been a bit pushed getting Alex down off the face. The words, slower now as he went on.

'I used a snotty handkerchief to plug the hole in your head and wondered what the hell to do. I sat for an hour with you bleeding into my lap. I knew if we stayed there we were fucked. If you didn't bleed to death, we'd freeze. I made up my mind.' His eyes had a tormented, faraway look. He went on. 'I rigged up a pulley system using pitons and karibiners, and lowered you down, a bit at a time until I'd got you to a ledge. I climbed down to tie you off so you couldn't fall. Then I had to climb back to get the rope.' He held out a hand for the flask, wanting its comfort.

'Sometimes I was able to lower you on a double rope, that wasn't so bad because I could recover it by yanking it through the runner. You slipped Christ knows how many times. My hands.' He held them up, staring at them, seeing in his mind the deep burn marks, feeling the nylon rope slicing through the flesh. 'I couldn't hold you. You were moaning a lot. That was the only thing telling me you hadn't kicked the bucket and gone off to join those others in the happy climbing school in the sky.'

'Richard, I never knew . . . How come you've never told me?'

'It didn't seem important. You know me, Alex.' He shrugged, uncomfortable. And Alex learned how his life had been saved by this unpretentious man beside him. Their present mission was forgotten for the moment.

'We were doing OK. It was taking for ever, but we were coming down. Bit by bit, chipping away.' He paused, sipped at the flask, then shivered. 'Then I fell. The rock. It was rotten as hell on that part of the face. One second I was there on the mountain, the next I was gone. The hold, I saw the fucking thing break away in my hand, like it was in slow motion. I just fell out backwards into the darkness, still with the piece of rock in my hand.'

He let his head fall on his forearms, his knees drawn

up. The flask slipped unnoticed from his fingers. Alex recovered it, replacing the cap without screwing it up.

'But somebody up there,' Richard gestured with his chin towards the stars, speckled, puncturing the blackness of the sky, 'must have liked me. I fetched up jammed in a gulley between two dirty great boulders. Nothing beyond them except space. That's when I lost it. My nerve went. The rest of it is a dream. How the hell I ever got back up to you I'll never know. I was crying like a fucking schoolkid, shit scared that the mountain was going to fall apart around my ears.' He paused, perhaps wanting another drink.

'When we finally got over the *Bergschrund*, sitting in the snow, a chamois cantered past. We must have disturbed its kip. I prayed then. I actually prayed, said thank you, I suppose. You were starting to come to, mumbling all sorts of crazy shit.'

Alex looked at Richard.

Suddenly it all made sense.

'You know the rest, Alex. I piggybacked you down. Just kept walking till we got to the car. I bundled you in and drove to Ellmau – it was only a village then, not the fancy ski resort it is now. I've never been on a rock face since. Just being up here on the roof . . .' Richard looked miserable. Alex put out his hand to his shoulder.

'Shit, Richard, I didn't know. You should have told me.' He slapped his hand to his head. 'You saved my fucking life.'

'Maybe. But I can't go through with this now. I thought I could, but now that we're here . . .'

Alex got up and looked down at Richard, then at his watch.

He made up his mind.

'I'll go alone.'

Richard looked up, alarm flaring.

'You can't work the system. You may be able to piss

around with your own personal computer, but you need me once you get into that office.' He was looking up, his eyes full of anguish.

'Then tell me how to crash their program.'

He listened as Richard told him.

On the parapet, Alex grinned, trying to reassure. He stuck his thumb into the air, then walked over the edge of the roof, down into the darkness, feeding the rope through his hands as he went.

Richard watched.

He had been talking too long. He knew the chance of Alex getting to the window before it was closed was almost impossible. He hated himself for his weakness. He sat, wretched, hugging his knees.

He had blown it.

CHAPTER SIXTEEN

The new man reluctantly tore his eyes away from the game, the Redskins needing a yard for a first down. He wished he didn't have to work and could stay and watch it finish. But this was his first night. Not a time to be caught out. Get some time in first, like old George.

Resignedly he strapped the belt and holster around his waist, hooking the leather thong over the hammer of his gun to prevent it falling out. He unpeeled a stick of gum and fed it into his mouth, chewing noisily as he adjusted the belt and holster, making it comfortable on his waist. Turning his back on the TV monitors, he walked towards the elevator.

He pressed the button for the tenth, tugged at the short jacket of his new uniform, sucking in his belly. The peaked cap, set at a jaunty angle, accentuated his dark, handsome features. He looked good. Felt good. At the tenth floor, he stepped out, turning left in the direction of the lighted office at the end of the corridor. Through the half-glass door, he could see a grey-haired man, wearing thick horn-rimmed glasses, working at a computer on a big leather-topped desk.

The window behind was open.

Richard Norris was petrified.

Alex had gone.

He stood looking into the distance, the lights of the city blurring as the wind blew into his eyes. Could Alex get to the window in time? The telling had delayed him. Restlessly he walked back and forth, hating himself. Closing his eyes brought a vision of a teenage boy flying down a ski-slope, laughing, the smiling face, teeth white in a tanned face as his son beckoned him to tackle the steep mogul field below. Remembering, now, the breathless exhilaration.

'Come on, Dad.'

Johnathan.

The roof was empty. He was alone with his fear, confused, stumbling to the space where Alex had stood before stepping off into the darkness. A deep breath, the cold air hurting his lungs, dizziness filling his head, he moved towards the wall, a sleepwalker, unaware of what he was doing, for the moment reliving the nightmare.

The Kaiser-Gebirge.

Alex, he needs you.

Clumsy, uncoordinated, he climbed on to the parapet, his hands, body, shaking as he tried to feed the rope through the *descendeur*. He stopped, tried to concentrate. At last, done.

He waited, summoning his courage, terrified.

Make the move.

He stood still, fighting the spasms, forcing himself to step off the parapet and abseil down the wall as Alex had done – how long ago? He shouted silently, forcing blood into his head, willing his reluctant body to execute that one, simple move.

Come on, man. Kids abseil, for fun, at adventure parks. He gripped the rope. Too tight. A beginner. It wouldn't feed through his fingers.

Donnelly.

Johnathan.

He stepped off the parapet, tense, awkward, the rope not running. Relax, Norris, you silly sod. How many times had he done this? Easy does it. Better. Moving now.

The pipe. Don't look. Where is it?

He felt his feet touch. Delicately he tested its strength, gradually lowering himself on to it. Frightened, face pressed into the cold stone, he gathered himself, his breathing, short, sharp gasps.

OK, so far.

Now the difficult part. A delicate manoeuvre requiring total concentration. Reluctantly, he unclipped the karabiner at his waist, then slowly, carefully, turned to face the opposite wall. The rucksack forced his body away from the rough stone. His breathing, too fast, shallow, not letting enough air into his lungs. He tried to relax, to stop the trembling in his knees. He forced himself to breathe more slowly.

The gap was ten feet.

Four steps.

Only four.

Nothing to it. In the old days.

Arms extended like a tightrope walker, he set his feet at an angle on the pipe. Breath held, finely balanced, he waited until the moment was exactly right. The wind blew spitefully across his face. His eyes watered. He blinked, shook his head, clearing them. He sucked in air, took one tentative step, paused, controlling his fear, gathering himself for the move that would take him over the gap.

Tense, waiting.

A cat yowled from the alley below as it fought with another. The crash of a garbage can shattered his concentration. He wavered, teetering on the narrow pipe, then fell back against the wall, squeezing his eyes closed, desperately shaking his head. Below, two cats fought a noisy battle over disputed territory. They fell silent at last. He shook himself. Concentrate. He took a short pace, paused, then:

One two three four.

He was over.

Sweet relief.

The ledge on which he now stood was narrow as a boot. He pressed his face into the cold stonework, shuffling to his right, arms stretched out, fingers walking across the rough surface. Looking down from the corner of his eye, he could see the light shining from the accountant's office, cutting a rectangular pattern into the night. He inched his way towards it, moving first one foot, then drawing the other into it. The weight of the rucksack dragged him into the gap. He stopped, dragging his centre of gravity back inside his heels. Despite the bitter cold, he was sweating, his breathing still quick, irregular.

Although he was now above the window he could no longer see it, hidden under the projecting ledge. He had reached the ornate piece of stonework, seen through the field-glasses earlier, but too far away to identify. Now he saw it was a lion's head, about the size of a soccer ball.

Alex had fixed the rope to it.

He breathed deeply, drawing cold air into his lungs. Sweat trickled down his forehead, into his eyes. The street, silent below him, except for the sound of a distant horn occasionally floating up to him. He shut his mind to the height, the narrowness of the ledge, the numbing cold.

Testing the lion's head for stability, he clipped into the rope and carefully, slowly, abseiled on to the ledge.

He lay on the narrow platform and looked over the edge, forcing himself to relax. The window was ten feet below. It was open. The warm smell of centrally heated air drifted up to him.

Alex had made it.

Richard stood up, heart thumping. He paid out the rope behind him, estimating the amount he would need. Lining up, he took a last gulp of freezing air.

Donnelly.

Johnathan.

Sweet Jesus.

He jumped backwards off the ledge.

The new man hesitated, fist raised, ready to tap politely on the office door before going in and introducing himself to Mr Mikovitch. He cleared his throat, hoping he didn't sound nervous, tugging the jacket down for the second time, wanting to look his best, create a good impression on his first night.

At that exact moment, Alex swung into the room.

'What the . . .?'

Standing at the half-glass door, the guard saw a figure wearing a black one-piece suit and ski mask come flying in through the open window, then disappear temporarily behind the big wooden desk. Mikovitch spun in his chair, gasped, then lurched sideways, grabbing at the drawer. The intruder, fast on his feet, dived, beating him to it, slamming his knee against the drawer, trapping the hand. Mikovitch yelled. The new man wrenched open the door, trying to unthong his gun and draw it, all at the same time.

He ran into the room.

*

Alex swung smoothly into the office, relief flooding through him. He had arrived in time, the window was still open. He saw at once the comical, pathetic look on the face of the man who had been working at his desk, spinning in the office chair to face him.

The accountant made a grab for the drawer. There would be a gun. Alex leaped, slamming his knee against the desk, jamming the hand. He held on, gripping him hard by his bony wrist, ignoring the gasp of pain. The man glared balefully but made no further attempt to get the gun. Alex shoved him back into his chair, preventing him getting up. He walked round the desk, his back to the door.

Leaning over the leather top, he pulled the drawer open. The snub-nosed .38 Bodyguard Airweight gleamed dully amongst some papers. It looked dusty, unused. He reached for it. As his fingers touched the butt a voice behind him yelled: 'Freeze! Touch the gun, you're one dead sonofabitch. Mr Mikovitch, you OK?'

Mikovitch, spread in the chair, rubbed his wrist, looking up in surprised relief as the security guard came into the room, gun drawn, held, crouched in a two-handed grip.

'Yeah, sure I'm OK.' He sighed. 'I guess you're the new man? George told me you were on. Good job you came when you did. No knowing what this bastard would have tried.' The accountant was recovering some of his composure.

The guard covered Alex with a big nickel-plated automatic. It looked as if he knew how to use it.

'Asshole. Over here.' Gesturing with the gun, making it clear he wanted him the other side of the desk, an obstacle between them. Alex, hands still at his sides, skirted the desk and stood facing the window.

Handcuffs.

Alex despaired, watching as the guard pulled a pair from a holder on his broad leather belt, then walked purposefully round the desk, holding the gun in one hand and jiggling the handcuffs in the other. He chewed gum noisily, his mouth open.

'Turn round. Kiss the desk, mister.'

Alex did as he was told. He didn't speak. Light, on the balls of his feet, he waited for a chance. Any chance. Once he was cuffed he was done for. He tried not to think of the consequences.

The guard took Alex's wrist and pulled it up hard behind his back, trying to force an arm lock, ready for the first of the handcuffs. Alex countered, bunching his muscles, forcing his arm downwards, levering it against his elbow. The guard, surprised, grunted, suddenly realizing that this was real, not a practice at the training school.

Alex felt the gun barrel jabbed hard in his ear, hurting him. He stopped struggling, letting his hands drop to waist height, behind his back. He felt the cuff go on to his right wrist, wrenched against his skin, painfully tight.

Finished.

Now what?

Richard felt the briefest sensation of falling free through the air before the friction of the rope drew him up sharp. His momentum swung him through the open window into the room. His shoulder slammed into the left-hand side of the wall, spinning him off line. The blow was hard, all his body weight behind it. Momentarily, his left arm was numb, useless.

He landed with a thump on the thick pile of the carpet, then pitched forward until the rope brought him up sharp. He unclipped, rolled to his feet, all in one movement.

Alex was in the shit.

A security guard had an arm lock on him and a big shiny automatic pressed against his left ear. Richard knew he had to get a hand on the gun. He leaped forward, reaching desperately.

Alex felt the guard slam into him, forcing him down on to the desk. He couldn't move, unable to work out what had happened. Suddenly the guard's breath was forced out of his lungs. A wad of gum spat on to the desk. Alex twisted his face sideways, trying to see what was going on, unable to understand why he could not throw off the man's weight, nor why he had not fired and splashed his brains on to the desk.

At last he could see. The big automatic in the guard's hand had been forced on to the desk. Another hand, bleeding profusely, was wrapped round the gun. The hammer, on its way to strike the firing pin, had pierced the flesh between finger and thumb.

That was why Alex hadn't been killed. As the hammer snapped rhythmically on to the mangled hand, small droplets of blood spurted on to the desk, spoiling the inlaid leather. If this continued, the hammer would eventually chew through the damaged skin, discharging the first cartridge in the chamber.

He made a superhuman effort, putting all his strength into his legs in one mighty heave. As he rose, Alex saw the accountant, crouching terrified in the corner, no longer the man he had been when Alex was about to be handcuffed.

Alex jabbed with his elbow, hard, into the guard's belly, hearing him gasp. He felt him drop to his knees, winded, for the moment out of action. The gun was on the carpet. Alex bent quickly, picking it up, the firing pin and part of the grip sticky with pink flesh. Behind the guard, a hand in his mouth in an attempt to stem the bleeding, was a masked figure in a black one-piece.

There was no need for him to say anything.

'Glad you could make it.'

The voice was Michael Douglas.

Richard didn't answer, shaking his hand to alleviate the pain. Alex hauled the guard to his feet and led him over to the massive walk-in safe.

'What time is this set to open in the morning?'

The accountant looked at him malevolently.

'Nine o'clock.'

Alex shoved the guard in. He staggered against the shelves. The money, wads of used banknotes, was stacked in neat bundles above the plastic flight bags on the floor.

'Fill the bags.'

The guard hesitated, looking at the accountant for a lead. Seeing only fear, he shrugged and began stuffing money into the bags. He filled two before the money had disappeared.

'Toss them out.'

They landed near his feet. Alex went to the safe. He swung the door on the guard, leaving the heavy door closed, but without spinning the combination to lock it.

Henry Mikovitch was not happy.

He was afraid, with no idea what the two men wanted, only that he was there alone with them, shit scared. Especially the big guy. Real mean eyes through the ski mask. Goddamn, he just came in the window, an angel of death, out of the night, black, evil, like a vampire bat. How the hell did they get in here? They were paying good bucks for security, and two guys just fly in out of the night, like they got goddamn wings.

Mikovitch cowered in the corner. The bigger of the two, the one he feared the most, heaved him to his feet, dragging him, struggling feebly, to his chair. He crumpled into it. He felt the strength in the man's hands as his arms were lifted, placed on the sides of the chair, then tied tightly with lengths of thin nylon cord taken from the rucksack the second man had been carrying.

'Fatso,' said the big one, his voice familiar, 'we need to—'

'The name is Henry. Henry Mikovitch.' He tried to show some authority, but knew he had failed. The big one with the mean-looking eyes seemed not to have heard.

He went on: 'Henry, we need to access your computer. And do it fast. How about your telling us the access code?'

Michael Douglas?

Sure sounds like him.

But he was a dead man if he gave them the code. They could spread all sorts of shit around if he gave it them.

'Piss off.' He was just as afraid of his masters.

'Have it your way, Henry.'

Mikovitch tasted real fear then. It was the quiet way it was said, with finality. There was no mercy or compassion in the voice. He felt sweat break out on his forehead, running into his eyes. He blinked, shook his head trying to clear it from his eyebrows. His hands left wet patches on the leather arms of the chair.

The big bastard switched off the table-lamp. Slowly, with a gloved hand, he unscrewed the bulb, placing it carefully on the desk. He jerked something with his foot. Mikovitch looked from one to the other, his head twisting from left to right trying to keep sight of them. The one he was more afraid of came round from behind, standing huge in front of him.

'Henry, clichés aside, this is going to hurt you a lot more than it does me.' There might have been a sadistic grin under the mask. Mikovitch couldn't tell. 'You want to reconsider the access code? And your PIN while you're at it. Then you can tell us the emergency procedures, used when you want to move money in a hurry. Like when the Feds are after sequestering your funds. An organization as shady as this one has got to have one.'

The accountant felt the bile come up into his throat, burning, making him cough.

'Fuck you.'

He wished he'd never said that. The instant it came out, he knew he shouldn't have said it. The big guy stepped forward, putting his gloved hand on to the zipper of his fly. He jerked, ripping it open.

Hell, what is this?

Mikovitch soon found out. The thin brass of the lamp was used to expose his penis. It hung over the lamp like he'd picked up a rattler out in the Arizona desert. The big guy jiggled with the lamp until the head of his penis was in the bulb-holder. Mikovitch looked down at himself. Like a fucking plum in a brass eggcup, was all he could think of. His body shook, trying to jerk himself out of the lamp, but the big bastard just jiggled him back in. Wait. This ain't where my dick is supposed to be. In her mouth, that's where it was goin' to be, not in the end of a goddamned table-lamp.

'Henry. The procedure.'

Mikovitch could not speak, his fear total. He shook his head.

Click click.

The lamp was switched on and off, with hardly a pause. Mikovitch went rigid in the chair, the veins in his neck purple as they stood out in the loose flesh, his teeth bared, eyes screwed tight shut.

He screamed.

'The number.'

'No.' A wretched sob.

Click, pause, click.

The scream was terrifying.

'Henry . . .'

'OK, OK. Do me a favour. No more. Please. The access code is PIRA-USA. My PIN is 02-17-40.' It had spilled from him, the words jumbled in his eagerness.

'The PIN looks like a birthday.'

'Mine.' Mikovitch looked wretched.

'OK, you're doing good. Now the crash procedure.'

Mikovitch hesitated, saw the lamp move imperceptibly, threatening.

'There's a sleeper, a sub-manager in the bank, Boston First City. He handles all our financial business. Normally, to move funds me and the president have to give the authorization.'

'Can you do it alone?' The hesitation was fractional. Mikovitch looked at the lamp, feeling naked, his penis hanging limply.

'Yes. In an emergency.'

'I'd call this an emergency, Henry . . .'

'Man, I'm dead if I tell you.'

'At least your dick won't be fried to a cinder.'

'We got numbered accounts in Grand Cayman, Switzerland, Liechtenstein and Jersey. Tax havens. The accounts are run by local firms who have their own lawyers. All legit. They get their instructions from Boston First City, who tell them where to transfer the funds. It's all done by inter-bank Swift, Express or sometimes Fundsflow procedures. It varies.'

'Go on.'

Mikovitch gulped. His mouth was dry. He needed a drink. His soul for a bourbon over ice. The table-lamp kept twirling, the flex twisting, untwisting.

'The front companies don't know who the principals are. They never visit the countries concerned and they ain't permitted to correspond directly with the account holders. Security. There's a lot of money involved.'

'How much?'

Mikovitch shrugged.

'Millions. Not all in one account. Spread around for security reasons, like I said.'

'What happens when you want to dump the money fast?'

Henry Mikovitch had said enough to sign his own death warrant. He wasn't thinking about the table-lamp any more.

'There's a code word. Only three people know it, me, the president, the sleeper. He gets a fax, signed by either or both of us, and he dumps the money. There's no questions from him. He does as he's told on pain of death and he does it pronto, before the Feds or the IRS can move in.'

'Then what?'

'Four things.' He tried not look at the lamp. 'He splits the funds and express transfers it to the four overseas accounts. He closes the account here, obliterating all records. Then he either uses E-mail or sends a fax to the front companies instructing them to transfer all funds to a nominated destination account. They then close the numbered accounts and destroy all records. They ignore all enquiries, instructions and correspondence, from whatever source, concerning these accounts.'

'You're doin' great, Henry. And how do you protect your sleeper?' The big guy was leaning across the desk, holding the lamp so Mikovitch could see it.

'He fucks off, leaves the bank employ. He's got a hide-out and a special fund set up for him for just such an emergency. I don't know where it is – Canada, somewhere, leastways that's where the account is. He vanishes for three months, until the heat dies down. The sleeper is the only guy who knows the identity of the front companies and the numbered accounts.'

'So what's in the computer?'

Mikovitch shrugged.

'It's just a record of where everything is at. We got several accounts at Boston First City Bank, brought together if we need to crash the funds in a hurry.'

'Write me a fax, Henry.' The big one stood menacingly above him as he untied him. The accountant made to reach for his drawer, showing his hands, palms upwards when he saw the automatic come up.

'I need a pad. And a pencil.'

'Slow and easy, Henry.'

They weren't taking any chances.

Mikovitch took the pad and wrote quickly, a neat accountant's hand. He printed in bold capitals:

ALCATRAZ

He signed it.

'Can he – the sleeper – do the job any time?'

'Sure. Anytime. He's got fax, E-mail at home.'

The big guy walked out of earshot, talking with his partner. He came back.

'Send it.'

'I'm done for. You know that?'

'Send it. Use this bank. There's the account number.'

Mikovitch looked down at the pad, at the name of an English bank in the Channel Islands. He let his head fall forward on to the desk, muttering quietly into his forearms. He looked up, pleading.

'Send it.'

He fed the paper into the fax machine on his desk, reluctantly pressing the auto-dial. They heard it ringing on their speaker, then the tone of the answering fax. Henry Mikovitch watched in horror as the single sheet of paper slipped down into the machine. The pips confirming receipt were a death knell.

But they hadn't finished.

Mikovitch saw the second man, the smaller of the two, at the computer entering his access code and PIN. The screen came alive, information displayed as the keys were tapped. Whistling, fingers flying over the keys, he read, keeping notes in a small black book. The green light reflecting from the screen gave him a ghostly, sinister appearance.

His eyes, unblinking, never left the screen. He worked for perhaps an hour before he got up and beckoned over the other. He whispered to the bigger man, who looked mockingly at him.

'Naughty accountant. Ripping the company off. Taking a little but often. Creaming away some funds for when that rainy day comes along? I wouldn't be in your shoes when this gets out. You better get the next plane outta here to somewhere remote, Henry.'

He had finished.

Mikovitch had a pretty shrewd idea what had been done. They had probably transferred money from the investment accounts. The computers would have acted on instructions, once the correct access code had been keyed in. And it was Mikovitch's own PIN. Traceable to him. Now the bastard would probably feed in a download virus. Anyway, Henry Mikovitch was dead.

'OK, pal. You get to go into the safe with the security guard. It's big and airy in there so you won't run out of air.' He was led towards the big safe; the oak panelling, heavy leather furniture, the tasteful prints of Renoir's *Two Sisters* and Monet's *The Seine at Argenteuil*, unnoticed.

The drinks cabinet with the bourbon, tantalizing.

'You can't get out of the building. It's electronically sealed. They'll get you, in the morning.'

'Our problem, Henry. You let us worry about that.'

'Listen. I have to know. If I hadn't given you the codes. What would you have done to me?'

'Henry.' He *did* sound like Michael Douglas. 'In that case I would have had to plug the lamp back into the supply. All you got, pal, was a big shock of imagination.'

'You fuckin' sonofabitch.'

Henry Mikovitch would have sworn the big bastard was grinning under the ski mask.

The two men looked round the office. They had cleaned up the desk. Everything looked normal. The safe was locked and would remain so until the next morning. It was time to go.

'Can you make the abseil?' Alex was still amazed Richard had got into the office.

'Yes. I'm fine now. Once I'd crossed the alley, it was as if I'd never been off a rock face. I still don't understand it. I thought of Donnelly. And Johnathan. The fear just went. Anyway. Enough said. Let's get the hell out of here.'

They used the single rope to rappel out of the window. It took no time at all as they abseiled down in heart-stopping bounds, until they were in the safety of the alley.

The rucksack was heavy with the money.

At nine o'clock the next morning the two men in the stuffy confines of the walk-in safe heard the loud click of the timer mechanism and watched thankfully as the door swung open. The new security guard walked out quickly, collecting the big automatic from the desk and sliding it into its holster.

Mikovitch went straight to the computer, waiting nervously for it to come alive.

'Mr Mikovitch, I gotta go. Get down to the front desk. There's going to be hell to pay for this. I'll need a statement from you when I file my report.'

The accountant was hardly listening. He stared at the screen, tapping keys. He felt sick.

'OK. You did all right. Pity there was two of them. You go on now. I got things I need to do here.'

He was appalled. The Mikovitch accounts had been left intact, there for anybody with half a brain to see. He looked at his watch realizing he could do little to unscramble the crash procedure. The damage had been done while Uncle Sam slept.

If he really moved his ass, he could get a cab to the airport and catch the next London flight, and then on to . . .? He had no idea. Get out and survive, that was all that mattered.

The office was freezing now. Before leaving, Henry Mikovitch went across to close the window which had been open all night. He looked out, seeing where his two assailants had gone, the rope snaking down into the alley, ten floors below.

Impossible.

Despite the report which had been filed by the new security guard, no charges were ever laid against Henry S. Mikovitch by the directors of Noraid. They had told the lieutenant from the Boston Police Department that even though their office had been entered illegally by two unknown assailants, nothing had been stolen or interfered with. Yes, they had told the lieutenant, their own organization would tie up any loose ends. No, they had said, we have no wish to file a complaint. Just leave everything to us. They thanked the lieutenant for his trouble.

The young RUC constable was nervous.

Not long out of training, unpolished, he had yet to develop the sense of casual watchfulness so obvious in the other constables and soldiers in the combined patrol. Those who'd got time in, done it all before. Jinking down the street, not even looking as though they were moving fast, certainly not clomping along like him in his squeaky size tens. He supposed it would come to him. Eventually. Once he got used to it.

If ever.

They had put him out on patrol to cut his teeth, to get the feel of it, a bit of experience before he went down to south Armagh, bandit country, where the real action was. He was nervous about going there, too. His father, an RUC sergeant, had told him not to get himself in a tizzy. But the walrus moustache had been moving erratically on his upper lip as he had spoken, a sure sign of the tenseness in him. They'll look after you down there, so don't go worrying yourself. Or your mother. Keep your powder dry, your eyes peeled, and don't shoot till you see the whites of their eyes, his father had joked. It had been small comfort.

He scanned the street, seeing nothing out of the ordinary, people shopping, looking almost normal, going about their business as if nothing were different here than in the rest of the country. Conscious of his raw inexperience, he watched the soldiers as they jigged down the street, the last of the patrol spinning to look behind him as they moved quickly through the crowds. No one spoke to the men in the faded combat suits. The soldiers were ignored, as if they weren't there. They didn't belong.

Alert, he saw a door open in front of him, a good-looking woman step out on to the pavement, head bowed as she pulled the zip across on the big leather handbag she carried over her shoulder. He felt the flush of recognition, his face relaxing, about to smile, speak, to pass the time of day with one of his own. She looked up and saw him, realizing he was going to talk to her.

Her eyes flashed a warning, stopping him, the words catching in his throat, quickly converted into a cough. A tiny shake of her head as she looked past him, down the crowded street, told him to ignore her. He flushed, angry with himself, watching as she turned and walked away, heels clipping on the pavement, the sound dying in the noises of the street.

Resisting the temptation to look over his shoulder, he turned his attention back to the patrol, adjusting the carbine he carried across his chest, making it more comfortable in his hands. He gave up trying to think what the WPC was doing, out of uniform, in this part of Belfast. Instead, he concentrated on scanning the faces hurrying by, focusing his attention, comparing each with the mug-shots already filed in his memory. And the windows. He remembered to look at the windows.

For the moment, he stopped worrying about south Armagh.

About Crossmaglen.

They'll look after you, his father had said.

Jennifer McCauley put the phone down, replacing it in the drawer beside her bed which she then closed. Standing, she rolled her head, easing tired neck muscles, then stretching, letting herself relax. She was tired. It had been a hard day, although her controller had seemed satisfied with her report. Sometimes she wondered if the information she passed on was ever of any use, whether the little pieces of jigsaw puzzle ever fitted when the analysts were compiling the big picture. She had no idea what happened to the information once she had passed it up the chain. One-way traffic, she reflected. No one ever told her if her stuff was useful, if she were earning her pay.

It was lonely, undercover. Her own private war, living on her wits, never sure if there was back-up if she were ever to need it. Alone. No one to rely on.

Only the Walther.

She mixed herself a drink, splashing tonic over Bacardi, then squeezing lemon into it, before kicking off her shoes and curling up in the armchair in the corner of the room. An excerpt on the news reminded her of the incident in the street, when she had unexpectedly bumped into Jamie Rourke as she'd been leaving the newsagents, realizing how close she had come to having her cover blown. Jennifer shuddered. Not long in the force, he still had much to learn. He would not have known she was undercover, only that she was one of his own kind, a friendly face in an indifferent, sometimes hostile crowd.

He was due to move south in a week or two.

She wouldn't be seeing him for a while.

Finishing her drink, she got up, deciding to eat out instead of preparing a meal in the flat. She hated cooking, especially for herself, seldom bothering unless the weather confined her indoors. Her mood suddenly lighter, she showered, dressed, picked up the bag she always carried and walked quickly down the stairs to the door. At the table in the hall, she frowned, puzzled when she noticed her spare key was missing. She tried to remember when she had used it last, but for the moment could not. It was probably in another handbag. Shrugging, she pulled open the door and went out into the night.

She took no notice of the man coming towards her, who turned suddenly and walked quickly across the street.

Green eyes watched her pass, studying her, the roll of her hips under the short, tight skirt.

He had not been expecting her as he had walked up her street, trying to remember if this was the place. There had been much on his mind the last time he had been here, thoughts of what he had done, and what had yet to be done. Memories of her were fresh in his mind, how she had looked bent over the table as he had moved across the room, his jeans tangling around his ankles, impeding him,

It had been good, the warm feel as he had rammed into her, catching her off guard. He'd have given it to her like that if she hadn't yanked at his pubes, digging her nails into his prick like she was trying to choke the life out of it. For him, it had been a poor substitute with the johnny, although she sure as hell seemed to have got her kicks out of it.

He had been debating for weeks whether or not he should try to contact her again. It was a nuisance, her not having a phone, and it had taken time to find her street again, but Donnelly had felt the urge each time thoughts of her had slunk unwelcome into his head. Now, at a loose end, he had decided to chance it.

He watched as she turned out on to the main road, her figure outlined against the fluorescent street-lights, wondering whether or not to follow, perhaps picking up where they had left off. After a few paces, he thought the better of it. There would come a time.

He had to go away for a while. When he got back, he would look her up for sure. He could afford to be patient, to wait until after the job. For a moment he saw the M60 in his mind, gleaming under its coat of oil, the shiny brass cartridge cases, cascading as they tumbled out of the gun, a warm pile forming around his elbows as it burst into life. The sensual lover's kiss against his quivering cheek.

Finger, delicate, caressing the oily surface.

The wetness of her.

Flame, smoke, spurting.

Coming.

Jennifer McCauley.

CHAPTER SEVENTEEN

It was early morning when they left Seattle.

Alex drove south out of the city, on to the Interstate towards Olympia. Neither had slept well on the Boston flight. Richard felt rough, an itchiness in his eyes, perhaps lack of sleep, more likely the Scotch at altitude.

The money in the plastic flight bags had worried him, but with it securely lodged in the hotel safe, he felt less vulnerable. Much of the flight was spent confirming how best to use it.

An easy decision.

The jagged, snow-capped peaks of the Cascades lay to the left, sun glistening on the snow-fields, the sharp crags, teeth biting through icing on a cake. Further south, Mount Rainier alone, thrusting into the sky, majestic, beautiful, sculptured symmetry.

'Some hill.' Richard looked at the mountain. 'I'd like to try it, one day.'

Alex, too, glanced over.

'Jimmy Jamieson, the guy we're meeting. He's been up a couple of times. He said one day he'd take me. Says it's harder that it looks, that, more often than not, everyone visiting Washington has a crack at it, some time or other. It's quite an industry. A team of professional mountaineers, dragging tourists up from Camp Muir.

'Perhaps we ought to think of doing something like that, guiding folk up Ben Nevis, Snowdon, or Scafell when – ' he hesitated, 'when this is over.'

Alex was silent, feeling Richard's doubt, wondering if he might be wavering, uncertain of what he was doing, the enormity of their task at last getting to him. He had known Richard for years, sharing many adventures, wild days as young officers, often in trouble, but always supporting each other. Even after Richard had married Felicity they had remained close, Alex, with his girlfriend, staying over when they'd gone to dinner, too pissed to drive home. The girls would sit after the meal, listening to the two telling war stories.

He would stand by him in this, whatever the personal cost. It had shaken him, learning how close he had been to buying it in the Kaiser-Gebirge, which for him had been a tangle of confused memories. Norris had pulled him off the mountain, got him out of it, never saying a word. No wonder he'd felt so shit scared on the roof. Then, with the guard in the Noraid offices, Norris had arrived, sorting out the mess he'd got into.

Yes. He would see this thing through with him.

'You think Jimmy will help?'

'I don't know for sure. We were good friends at Fort Carson, but this is asking a lot. I've some ideas of my own, things I've been thinking about since the night in Reading. I think I know how we can pull it off, but we need his know-how, a man on the ground, if you get me.'

'I know what you mean.' Richard twisted in his seat, watching Alex as he drove. 'I meant what I said, Alex, back home. I'm going to get him. No way am I going to give up, until it's over. You can bet on it.'

'My life,' said Alex.

They passed the Boeing works, the big wide-bodied jets standing sleekly in the sun outside their hangars. A few days, weeks, if all went well, they would be aboard one on their way home.

They left the Interstate, driving east.

The only traffic seemed headed for the slopes, most cars carrying skis on roof-racks. Richard would have liked to have joined them. But for unfinished business . . .

In Enumclaw they joined Highway 410, turning left, passing the tavern, their rendezvous, a few miles out of the town, set back a little off the road. They were early, but had wanted to be sure of finding the place. Jimmy wouldn't be there yet.

They drove past.

Crystal Mountain Ski Resort was thronging with people. People having fun. They bought coffee and a Danish from the lodge and ate, sitting in the sunshine at a table on the balcony, watching skiers clumping by, lugging skis, standing in line for passes. Chattering, laughing, young kids scampering.

Richard caught his breath. A young man wearing mirror sun-glasses, a wide headband partially concealing straw-coloured hair, laughing, his arm round the shoulders of a pretty girl. Handsome, untidy features, innocent, happy. For an instant, Johnathan. Richard felt a jolt, pain, anguish, the first time he had felt despair since arriving in America.

The young man turned, and walked away.

The moment was gone.

Only the hate remained.

It was warm and pleasant in the sun; neither wanted to leave. Richard scanned the lower slopes, trying to pick out the young man. But he had disappeared, hidden in the crowd.

They drove down, turning right at the bottom of the mountain. On their left, the Chinook Pass road was closed, a barrier thrown across it.

There were a few pick-up trucks and 4-w/d vehicles parked outside the tavern. The King County sheriff's car passed, the deputy talking into his radio, taking no notice of them. It was quiet, except for the sound of the White River cascading over the rocks behind them. Richard followed as Alex pushed open the door and went into the dim interior.

A long bar faced them, a line of men on stools drinking pale-coloured beer, pitchers on the bar. The drinkers were noisy, even at this early hour. The tavern, a warm, friendly place, was decorated with old logging paraphernalia, a pool table in a room to the left. Two bearded men in faded blue dungarees played with casual skill, stopping, leaning on their cues as the two strangers entered. The juke-box was playing a country song which most of the occupants seemed to know, joining noisily in the chorus. Sunlight streamed through the windows casting sharp sunbeams through the dusty air.

Alex immediately picked out the man he was looking for in a booth on the right, a powerful figure, a half-empty beer glass in front of him. His hair was cropped short, in a military style, and he sported a gunfighter moustache, fashionable in the seventies. He hadn't shaved, the stubble thick on his cheeks.

His clothes suited the place, a heavy, check wool shirt, sweat-stained cowboy hat, jeans, an ornate leather belt decorated with inlaid leather thunderbirds, a big embossed buckle which showed the crossed rifles of the US Infantry. The words *Queen of Battle* stood out from the metal. He stood, weight slightly on one foot, pelvis tilted, short. Strong. Someone you would want on your side in a fight.

Alex and the American were firm friends, obvious from the warmth of the handshake. Richard, too, felt the strength of the short-fingered grip.

'Alex, man, you're lookin' good. Filled out some since Fort Carson. And Dick,' Richard winced, 'any friend of this guy is a friend of mine.' Inevitably, Richard felt excluded as the two talked, reminiscing. Jimmy Jamieson sold real estate and was doing well.

'Hey, Dick. You wanna get some more beer? Get a pitcher.'

He poured. They drank, Jimmy taking a long appreciative pull from the thick glass. Then, the inevitable question.

'OK, Alex. Let's have it. In all the time I've known you, you've always gotten straight down to it. No fuckin' around.'

Alex glanced round the bar, seeing they were ignored.

'Jimmy. We want to steal an M60, take it back with us and blow away a bad guy.'

Disbelief, the half-laugh, the beer mug stopping on its way to the American's mouth. Realization.

'Shit. Alex. You crazy Brit. Why?'

Alex turned to Richard.

'Tell him,' he said.

Richard told him, his voice dull, matter of fact. Jimmy Jamieson said nothing, occasionally drinking, or circling with a stubby finger, doodling in a small wet patch on the table. When it was told, he looked from one to the other, shaking his head.

Alex liked this American, had shared a great deal with him. They owed each other nothing. But help would be offered. For friendship. Justice. He hoped.

'Shit,' said Jimmy.

'We need your help,' Alex went on. 'I promise you, no one will get hurt except the target. We'll do all the dirty work. You tell us how, where, when.'

Jamieson paused for a long moment, looking from one to the other, wanting to be sure of what was being asked of him. Alex knew of the doubt, sensed how the American felt, for a moment his own uncertainty nagging. They needed him. Jamieson knew it. He picked up his glass, drained it, wiping his moustache with the back of his hand as he leaned over to look out of the window, first rubbing it clean with his cuff. Quietly he stared out at the sparrows, fluttering noisily as they pecked at the thin layer of crumbs left on the porch for them.

He refilled his glass from the near-empty pitcher.

'What happens to the M60. After?'

Richard told him.

The American nodded, understanding.

'Let me mull it over. Gimme couple days. Meet me here,' he scribbled on a bar slip, 'Thursday. Before six. They serve great clam chowder, and the sunset is out of this world.'

He slid across the booth, stood ready to leave, blocking the sunlight as he was framed in the doorway.

The two watched him.

'What do you think?' Richard was doubtful.

'He'll do it. He's made up his mind. He would have told us otherwise. Jimmy doesn't mess about, keeping people on tenterhooks. I know him too well for that.'

'You're sure?'

'Positive.'

'That's one hell of a load off my mind.' Richard relaxed. A little.

'When did you kick it? The fear?' Alex had been reluctant to ask, but wanted to know. Richard continued to stare ahead, as if he hadn't heard. He answered at last, sucking air over his teeth, shrugging. He chose his words.

'I can't put my finger on the exact moment.' Richard, squinting into the sun, pulled the visor down. 'I watched you abseil from the roof, feeling as though I'd cheated you, forced you to come on some wild-goose chase. I was scared shitless, and I don't mind you knowing. You'd been gone maybe ten minutes, when I started having nightmares about the whole thing. Then I thought about the Provo, Patrick fucking Donnelly, of all the heartache, the despair the bastard has caused, not just to us.' He paused, his mind elsewhere, 'But to all the others. Johnathan wouldn't have been the first.' He glanced at Alex, concentrating on driving, listening carefully.

'Mostly, I remembered Johnathan – he would have been twenty-four next month. The hate in me overcame my fear. I was roping down almost before I knew it, although for a while I froze up there. There was one awful moment when I was balanced on the pipe, getting my balls together ready to step off. A couple of cats got into a fight down below, and a dustbin went with a hell of a clatter.' Alex smiled, remembering. Richard went on. 'It brought me back to reality. I realized then, it was now or never.'

Richard had fallen silent, the memory disturbing. It was a few moments before he could bring himself to speak.

'You'd done all the work, ropes in place, everything. All I had to do was follow you in.' He paused, uncertain, wondering if he had made himself clear, wanting Alex to know how grateful he was.

'Bloody good job you arrived when you did. If he'd got the cuffs on me, I'd have been done for.'

'I was surprised to say the least.' He was chuckling, less tense, glad to be talking this over. 'You were bent over the desk, like he was trying to slip one up you, and I came flying through the window, wondering what the hell was going on. I saw you doing your Schwarzenegger on him. Must have made his eyes water.' This time, both laughed, the tension easing.

'Tell me about Jimmy Jamieson.'

'Not much to tell,' said Alex. 'You know I did a tour in Fort Carson, on an Index P. I loved it, probably why I still talk about it so much. Jimmy was my sponsor, minder if you like. While I was there, he was passed over for promotion. He was really pissed off. They had a system then. Officers had to score virtually maximum marks on their OER – Officers Efficiency Report.' He flicked his eyes up to the mirror, wanting to pass a lumber truck labouring up the hill.

'That year, Jimmy got only 198 out of 200. Shit, that's bloody near perfect.' Alex, seeing the road was clear, pulled out to overtake.

'One morning, I came into work, same as usual, ready to take the piss for them all being in so early, and found Jimmy was an E6 – that's staff sergeant in our Army – when he'd been a captain the day before. The policy was "up or out". Jimmy was allowed to serve out his time as an enlisted man to finish his twenty years for pension. He stuck it for a bit, then told them to piss off. There's no love lost there.' Alex looked pensive. 'Nobody gave a shit about his record in Vietnam, his Silver Star, nothing. I'm pretty sure that's his reason for helping.'

They talked quietly, all the way back to the city. So far, everything had gone their way. Richard knew Noraid would be hurting. A glow of pleasure spread, remembering. And there was enough money left to see the thing through. All of it. He remembered his promise to Nobby Clarke, picturing the grin creasing the mashed features when he heard.

Richard, comfortable, slept on and off, waking each time his head jerked forward as Alex braked. Bad dreams filled his head, short film clips, discarded on the cutting-room floor. As one ended, so another would start, running together into an untidy jumble of nightmares. Each ended on a wet street.

He knew it was Belfast.

They made their way independently to the address Jimmy had given them, a restaurant built on a pier along the wharf. Fishing nets hung from the walls, the bar fashioned from an old whaler. Soft lighting from ships' lanterns gave the place a warm, inviting atmosphere. A baby grand stood in a corner, beside a small intimate dance floor. It was crowded.

Jimmy had already arrived, waving them to join him, a table at the back of the room with a view of the sea.

'Hey, Alex, Dick. How you guys doin'? C'mon, sit down, I got beers comin'.'

It came in ice-cold mugs, and Jimmy waved away the waitress as she made to fill their water glasses, quipping the only time he used water was to clean his teeth. They ordered, letting Jimmy advise, clam chowder, followed by prime ribs, baked potato and salad.

They ate, leaving talk of the M60 until their table had

been cleared. Jimmy told the waitress they were stepping out, that she was to hold their reservation. Out on the pier, they shivered in the unexpected cold. The rain had stopped, a beautiful sunset glowing over the Puget Sound, the Olympia range to the west, a red reflection off the water on to their features. The three of them leaned over the rail. Gulls weaved and dipped into the cold water, their flight controlled, elegant. It was calm, peaceful. Belfast, a lifetime away.

'There's two ways we can get a 60,' Jimmy looked pensive, 'three if you count stealing it straight from the bunker. That ain't easy, impossible, even. You can either take it when there's a unit live-fire exercise, or easier, during PT.' He hesitated, seeing Richard's doubtful look. 'Don't look so surprised. When these guys do PT it's a five-mile run wearing LBE, load bearing equipment, carrying individual weapons. No ammo, though. How much you need?'

'Ten. I only need ten,' Richard said at once.

'Shit, we could probably walk round the ranges and pick up that amount. Else I could buy it. Plenty guys use a 7.62 for hunting. The equivalent sporting shell is the .308 Winchester. Makes a big hole.'

His words had hit Richard brutally. His eyes registered first pain, then hatred. Jimmy Jamieson had never seen its like. Not even in Vietnam.

'Jeez, man. I'm sorry. Fuckin' brain hanging in front of my balls as usual. I didn't mean—'

'Forget it.' Richard was curt. 'Hating keeps me remembering.' He looked out over the water, dyed by the colour of the sinking sun. Red. Like blood. When the heavy bullets drilled into Donnelly.

Jimmy was talking again, pulling a folded map from his pocket.

'The military reservation,' he said by way of explanation. 'You won't be able to get through the front gates without a DECALS, but there's plenty ways in back. Your best bet is here.' He pointed with a dead match. 'You passed it on the way back after meeting me. There's no sentries there. Fridays – tomorrow, is when they'll be doing the next combat run. The next after that is Tuesday. They got a whole brigade out, rehearsing for some visiting NATO brass, wanting to show how fit and combat ready they are.' He looked up. 'You Brits do this crazy running shit?'

Richard thought of the Falklands.

'Sometimes,' he said. 'When it's necessary.'

'They'll be out on the field at 0500, so it'll be dark. Their route skirts the perimeter here.' Again he traced a line with the match. 'So a good place for you to lie up is in this clump of evergreens. You can watch as they go by, work out how best to play it. The formation will be the same Tuesday, so if you find what you're looking for, it'll be there next time round.'

When they returned to the table, the restaurant was even more crowded. They had stayed to watch the sun go down. Talking, they drank more beer, until, at last, Jimmy made to leave. Richard thanked him, awkward in his appreciation. He knew that without the American's help this venture would be much more difficult, impossible even.

Jimmy brushed it aside, saying merely: 'If the 'Cong had taken my boy, I'd be just like you, wantin' to do a Rambo. I love easy, but hate long and hard. I don't owe the Army zip. I got dumped, had to pick myself up and start over. Maybe they'll get their shit together, after this.' He stared hard at Richard. 'Just do what you said with the 60, when it's done. I don't want nothin' on my conscience.'

'You have my word.'

They shook hands and left.

CHAPTER EIGHTEEN

The rain was warm, unusual in January.

From a windless sky, it fell in a vertical sheet, heavy and hard. Immobile, ignoring the water absorbed on their backs and shoulders, two men lay concealed in a clump of evergreens close to the road. Neither wore waterproof clothing, since the sound of rain on such unfamiliar material can be recognized by any careful listener. It was a risk they could not afford to take.

Faintly, over the noise of the rain, something else, distant, unfamiliar. The bigger of the two cocked his head, listening, the sound strange, perhaps an engine shunting, labouring up a steep incline. As the sound drew nearer, both identified it. Men, running. Thousands of them.

It was impressive.

Orderly files of soldiers running in formation, officers in command groups heading the columns. Suddenly, unprompted, a supernumerary chanted a cadence, accompanying the thud of pounding feet, instantly echoed by the men. The two watched the unbroken columns running by, not ten yards from where they lay.

At the back of the formation, after the main body had passed, came the stragglers. It was these they were interested in. Here, they would find what they were looking for.

The sound of the singing was fading. Still the laggers came, walking, some stumbling, weaving as if drunk, or stoned from the weed, even the harder stuff, shot into themselves the night before. These were a far cry from the remainder of the brigade. Formation pennants, flying proud at the front of the column, were missing here. This was the dross, unwanted, ignored by the commanders in front.

Richard and Alex saw him.

He was one of the last, staggering, shuffling, hardly picking his feet up from the road. Occasionally he stopped, hands on thighs, head falling forward, retching, watching the lines of men disappearing, shaking his head, muttering despairingly. Slung across his chest was a weapon. It looked evil, sinister.

An M60 machine-gun.

The man carrying it showed no interest in it at all.

Alex turned to Richard, teeth white in the approaching dawn, grinning.

He pointed.

'That's our man. Tuesday. We take him on Tuesday.'

Richard nodded, sticking up his thumb.

The two men moved backwards through the trees, crawling two hundred yards into the darker shadows, cold now that their watch was over. Richard shivered, the wet shirt clinging to him. Alex offered his hip flask and they sipped in turn, the warmth illusory.

'Let's get out of here. I could use a shower.'

Still shivering, Richard rubbed his arms, trying to warm himself. Looking carefully about, they strode off briskly, weaving through the trees to a track leading to the road, the thicket hiding the car. Richard felt a surge of optimism, almost euphoria, at their recent success. All was going well. Nothing would prevent them. Not now.

They stopped occasionally, getting their bearings, checking landmarks, moving stealthily through broken country, back to the car. At last, its shape loomed out of the semi-light, hidden in a clump of bushes just off the road. Once, they were forced to lie low, a section of soldiers close enough to worry; again, when a deer broke cover, startling them as it cantered out of the trees into the open. Otherwise, no one.

Richard kept watch as Alex gunned the motor, beckoning him on to the road, then slipping into the car while it was still moving. Alex drove towards the main highway, turning left towards Parkway, on to the freeway, back to Seattle.

Richard's hotel room seemed empty and sterile. He had been away the whole weekend. Unlocking the door, awkward because of the bulky parcel he had collected from reception, he entered the room, throwing the package on to the bed. Tearing it open, he examined the contents. There was a brief handwritten note: 'I hope these fit.'

It was signed by Jimmy Jamieson.

He showered, washed without soap, cleaning his teeth without using toothpaste. Nor did he shave, knowing how easily the smell would carry in the clean air of the forest. Dressing quickly in the US Army fatigue uniform, he found the olive-drab T-shirt a touch too small, the trousers loose at the waist. He didn't care. He didn't intend wearing them long.

The car was in the parking lot. As he left the hotel, the headlights came on identifying it. He walked briskly without noticing the cold, feeling better than he had since this venture had started. The difficult part, close now. He briefly nodded to Alex behind the wheel, seeing they were dressed identically.

They drove south, the route familiar.

Parking in a copse about a mile from the original place, they checked, making sure the car was hidden. Satisfied, they crossed the fence into the Fort Lewis military reservation, walking quickly through the darkness towards their earlier hiding place.

It was colder, clouds of condensation forming from their breath as they moved briskly through the pine trees, heading for their hide. Neither spoke, each thinking private thoughts, concentrating on what had to be done. They picked their way, careful as they moved through the trees, feet noiseless on the bed of pine needles. Alex watched Norris in front, following as he floated soundlessly from tree to tree.

Norris stopped suddenly, arm in the air.

Voices.

A group of men talking quietly.

They stopped, breath held, dropping to the ground, listening. Infinitely careful, Alex crawled forward, his shoulder touching. He leaned in close, breath warm in Richard's ear.

'What . . .?'

Norris pointed.

The group, a section of infantry, sat in the clearing where they had hidden yesterday, talking quietly as they ate their C Rations, few sounds other than the scrape of plastic spoons on metal containers, a gurgle as a canteen was raised to drink. Cigarette smoke drifted towards them on the still air. A field exercise, here, in this part of the reservation.

Dammit. Not today.

They lay on the cold pine needles, waiting, not talking, each worrying, trying to control the tension building in him. Norris looked at his watch, then at Alex, the darkness hiding his worry.

The singing started, faint, distant.

Later, the sound of running feet.

Richard sucked in his breath, almost imperceptibly, but knew Alex had sensed it. The head of the column appeared, indistinct, taking shape in the gathering light, gradually materializing from an amorphous, unidentifiable mass into the sharp lines of men in orderly formation. Richard watched them passing, tense, eager, wondering how to get past the section eating a leisurely breakfast just in front of them.

Soon it would be too late, their target gone.

The two looked at one another, trying to decide. Richard gathered himself, made to get to his feet, when, suddenly, the group in the clearing stood, some stamping, crushing the ration tins, others replacing their helmets, hefting weapons, shouldering packs. An order, quietly spoken.

''K. Move out.'

They were gone, a single file, moving tactically, weapons held across their bodies or slung from shoulders, as they vanished into the trees.

Norris was shaking.

Slowly, they got up, crouching behind a pair of wide trees. Units passed, one after another. They waited, shivering, adrenalin flowing.

The lines were thinning. Now, the first of the stragglers, runners, fewer and fewer. They stared, eyes watering. Where was he? Sick? Not running today? Suddenly, they saw him, looking worse than he had done earlier. Without speaking, Richard got to his feet. Alex, a shadow, followed.

Private First Class Damion T. Patterson Jnr was hurting, bad. He was cold, his chest one big pain. Nausea swept through his body. Every hundred yards or so, he stopped, retched, coughing drily as he sought relief from the agony tearing at his chest. His head swam. Hard, focusing, two other stragglers, further ahead in the darkness.

I am dyin', man.

His legs, lead weights, trainers feeling like diver's boots. Muscles aching, head throbbing.

Fuck this shit, man.

He'd felt great last night, injecting into the hardened vein in the sole of his foot, the dreamy ecstasy enveloping him. Morning, waking, summoned to the run.

Now this shit.

The weapon, hanging from his shoulder by its sling, weighed a ton. How many times, since this started, had he thought of dumping it? Leaving it in the trees, coming back for it later?

He sensed two runners come alongside, recognizing authority, trying without success to pull himself together.

The one on his left, a big mean-looking sonofabitch, spoke: 'How we doin', soldier?'

The voice was vaguely familiar, like he'd heard on some black and white rerun.

Gary Cooper?

'Broke dick, sir. I guess I got the flu.' It was gasped painfully, the lie coming easily.

'What's your outfit, son?'

Maybe he ain't so mean after all.

'Second Twenty-Second Infantry, sir.'

'OK. Let me give you a hand with the load. We'll run on in, send out a medic. You look pretty sick, soldier.'

They were walking, the pain easing. Slightly.

Maybe this officer ain't such a shit, like those other mothers in the battalion.

The big guy was holding out his hand for the gun. Patterson hesitated. He wasn't supposed to do this.

But shit, it's heavy, man.

He felt the relief, the weight of the weapon taken from him, the aching in his shoulders easing.

'Rest your ass over there by the trees. We'll get help back out just as soon as we can. Rest easy now.'

Through the pain, Patterson felt a start of alarm as the two officers accelerated away from him. He watched them disappearing into the shadowy half-light. At the side of the road, he sat, knees drawn up to his chin. He hugged them, trying to control his shivering. From his pants' pocket he pulled a misshapen joint, lighting it with a match from a crumpled book, sucking the acrid smoke deep into his lungs.

Man, that is better. Oh shit, that feels better. Maybe the officers were OK after all. Fuck the M60. Who gives a shit, man?

Footsteps in the gravel. He opened his eyes, trying to focus. Two MPs. Staring down at him. Shit. The sweepers. The non-coms who brought the stragglers in. They looked pissed. Where was his weapon? He told them.

'You dumb sonofabitch.'

Then they were running fast, in the direction the two officers had gone with the gun.

I am dead, man. Fuckin' dead.

He let his head fall forward on to his knees.

CHAPTER NINETEEN

It really had been as easy as that.

Richard jogged beside Alex, who was breathing hard, the gun slung across one shoulder. Elated, he couldn't believe it was possible. It had been so simple. He tried to work out where they were, estimating three miles to the car. Now all they had to do was stretch the distance between themselves and the soldier from whom they had stolen the gun, without gaining on the column.

There was a gap in front, to their left, leading to open ground in the direction they wanted. A hundred yards. Their trainers slapped on the gravel road, steady, rhymical.

The gap, fifty yards.

Thirty.

They reached it and turned off, heading for open country, the ground rougher, small stones and patchy scrub making the going more difficult. After perhaps twenty yards they considered slowing their pace, the distance between them and the road increasing with every step. Neither looked back. They were going to make it.

'Hey! You two. Where the fuck you think you're goin'? Get the hell back in formation.'

Richard almost stopped running, nearly losing his stride.

Alex said quickly, 'Don't stop. Whatever you do, don't stop. Keep running.'

Tempted to look over his shoulder, he stared ahead. Who the hell was yelling at them? They ran faster, footsteps loud in the gravel. The shout came again. Unable to resist, Richard glanced over his shoulder. Faintly outlined, two figures standing with hands on hips watching as they disappeared into the darkness. The two who had shouted looked at each other, then together, started in pursuit.

'Alex. They're following. We're going to have to outrun them. How far is the car?'

Alex, breathing heavily, seemed relaxed. But Richard felt the tension in him. Alex was no runner, the strain evident as he forced himself along.

'Two, maybe three miles.' Desperation in Alex's voice. 'Can we push on a bit?'

Richard needed no encouragement. Without being asked, he reached over and took half the weight of the gun, holding the barrel in his left hand to relieve Alex's burden. Together, in step, they pounded along the track, gritting their teeth, wanting but trying not to look back at the pursuing men. Another fifty yards, the temptation was too strong. Norris looked.

'They're gaining! The bastards are gaining on us.'

The angle of the ground steepened. The hill on the way in. They drove themselves hard up the incline. Alex was talking, gasping, the words forced out through lips drawn tight.

'When we get to the top. On the skyline. We'll be silhouetted. Against the sky. When I say. Drop to the ground. Follow me.'

The words came in short bursts as Alex drew air into

his straining lungs. This time Alex looked behind. Their pursuers were about two hundred yards back. One was ten yards in front of the other, gradually outstripping him, his running determined.

The crest of the hill seemed never to get closer. They were both now breathing very hard, and Richard knew that Alex with his greater bulk would be feeling the strain more than he was.

'Almost there. Drop flat. Roll to the right. They'll think we've crossed the summit, on our way down the other side. They may think we're further in front than we are.'

Alex was trying to keep his breathing steady, to breathe every other pace, regulating his air intake, the gun heavy, slowing him. They might have to make a stand. Did the pair chasing them have radios? He hoped not. At the top of the hill, their outline clearly visible, Alex gasped: 'Now!'

Richard let go of the gun as they dropped flat, rolling immediately to the right into low scrub. They lay, panting, listening to the sound of approaching feet, straining to keep the sound of their breathing from carrying, forcing themselves to breathe down into their hands, preventing the tell-tale condensation giving away their hiding place.

The two MPs arrived on the summit, slowing, hesitant, looking about. For the moment they had lost their quarry.

'Hank, you see anything?'

A pause.

'They must have cleared the hill pretty damn quick. C'mon. We're losing 'em.'

Richard, holding his breath, let it squeeze out of his lungs, a silent hiss as the MPs put on a spurt, disappearing from view. They waited, getting their breath back, trying to control their trembling muscles.

At last, Alex whispered, 'I think we may be safe. What do you think? Keep low, off the skyline. Back the way we came. We'll work our way back to the car from the other way. Fucked if I know where we are, for the moment.'

They crawled, low on their bellies, the gun a hindrance, until, below the summit, the darker sky now behind them, making them difficult to see, they got to their feet. They began to breathe easier, although Alex's chest was heaving. They strode off quickly, along a track in the direction of the fence bordering the reservation.

Richard wasn't sure where they were either. Like Alex, he'd lost his bearings during the chase. He looked around him in the gathering light, suddenly picking out the shape of a big evergreen, a landmark he recognized. He was about to point.

'Oh, shit.'

Richard jerked his head to the left.

The two MPs had circled round the hill, coming fast from their left. Had they come the other way, their escape back to the road would have been cut off.

'Damn. The car's another mile, round that bend.'

They started running again, legs heavy, tired, but spurred on by their fear. But the MPs were gaining. If they dropped the gun, they'd have a chance. But neither would ever do that. Not after all they had been through to get it.

Lurching, stumbling, they were ever closer to the road, but its safety was illusory.

Tripping, staggering, still running.

The sound of footfalls, the brush scraping on the legs of their fatigue pants, was nearer. They were going to be caught. Vaguely, headlights on the road running parallel. Maybe the MPs had radios after all and had called up a vehicle to cut them off. It slowed, the dark outline of the driver hunched in the cab clearly visible as he scrutinized them. Suddenly, the vehicle stopped.

Square-shaped. A jeep.

Despairingly they ran, Alex buckling under the weight of the gun.

The jeep slammed to a stop, a screech of metal as the driver strove to jam the gear shift into reverse while it was still moving, ominous in a silence broken only by the sound of their running feet and heavy breathing. The driver found the gear. Tyres spinning on the loose shale, he reversed into a track leading into the trees at right angles to the fence.

The shadows of the running men were picked up in the headlamps. Engine racing, the vehicle drove at the fence, bursting through, dragging posts and wire. It charged forward.

This is it. Nicked. It was all over.

Richard ran on, chest heaving, legs leaden, hauling on the barrel of the gun, trying to force more speed out of Alex.

Suddenly, the jeep changed direction, skidding between them and the two chasing them, crunching to a stop in a cloud of dust. The door was flung open. Richard waited, expecting to see another MP, this time armed. Alex had slowed, looking over his shoulder.

'Alex. For God's sake. We must keep moving. Come on!'

Richard yanked the gun barrel, first one hand, then angrily with two.

'Damn you!'

He tried to tear the gun from Alex's grip, but it was held tight in massive hands. Alex had slowed, almost to a stop. Richard couldn't believe that he would give up, not when there was breath left in his body. This surely couldn't be where it was to end. He wrenched the gun barrel again, desperate, to pull his friend along if need be.

But Alex was unmoving, the beginnings of a smile on his face turning suddenly into a broad grin.

'Well, I'll be . . . Richard. Come on. The jeep. It's Jimmy!'

Richard stared, disbelieving, before he too recognized the American, arriving from nowhere, right when he was needed. Relief.

'Get the fuck in!'

They didn't need telling twice.

Alex threw in the gun, across Richard's lap, then scrambled into the cab, slamming the door as soon as he was aboard. Jamieson was already driving fast towards the road, ignoring the rough ground, humps, ridges, ditches, his jeep bouncing, wheels spinning as it crossed the ditch back on to the black top. Jimmy wrenched the wheel over, accelerating up through the gears.

They were away.

'Where's your car?' he was yelling.

'Up ahead, one, maybe two miles.'

'Jeez. You guys are fuckin' crazy. That's one you owe me, Alex.' He was grinning, his face alight. 'I couldn't sleep. Bin thinkin' about you guys most of the night. Thought I'd better get my ass over here to see if you needed help. Looks like I made the right choice. Those two had you for sure. Alex, you look beat.'

'There. On the right. Just off the road, in the trees.'

Jimmy jammed on the brakes, skidding to a halt, spraying water from a deep puddle beside the car. They leaped out.

'Take the gun. My jeep, it might have been recognized. I'll come pick it up later if need be. We can hide it in my basement until the heat dies down. Call me. You got my work number. Fuckin' crazy.' He was shaking his head in disbelief as he drove off towards the beginnings of the sunrise.

The trunk was already open as Alex lugged out the heavy gun, laying it amongst the tools and spare wheel. Richard slammed it closed. They jumped quickly into the car and with Richard driving sped off in the direction of the main highway, eyes on the mirror for any sign of a vehicle following.

As Richard drove, Alex pulled on blue work overalls. Just before the highway, they stopped, changed places, and Richard did the same, covering the sweat-soaked uniform.

They drove north on the Interstate, merging with the early morning commuter traffic. Gradually their breathing steadied. They relaxed as the miles sped by, stopping for breakfast in a diner north of McChord Air Force Base. Finished, they continued their journey.

They looked normal.

Two men, the early shift at Boeing.

The sky was grey, overcast. The light rain was getting heavier.

Typical Belfast weather.

Although it slashed in heavy drops on to his head and shoulders, the man behind the gun did not let it spoil his concentration. He pulled the butt snugly into his shoulder, nestling it on to its bipod, bedding it in to prevent it wandering when he fired. He waited for the target to appear, pulse steady, his breathing regular, heartbeat a fraction quicker than normal.

This moment, a long time coming. The hatred did not feature in the man's mind. He thought only of the shot he was about to make.

He saw his target appear briefly. It would be there long enough. He did not hurry, his movements lazy, casual, as if he had all the time in the world. Time had been a friend, following in his shadow, letting the target grow ever more casual as the weeks since the killing had passed. It had been forgotten. Except by the man who lay behind the gun, unheeding the rain falling from the sky.

He saw Patrick Donnelly quite clearly. He could not make out the individual features at such long range, but there was no mistaking that it was he.

Richard Norris breathed out, emptying his lungs, then holding steady. He saw the target rise up from the ground, twisting to face him. The left eye closed lightly, not screwed up in a squint, staring unblinkingly through the aperture sight. The eye aligned the aperture with the blade of the foresight, Donnelly's torso a blur behind it. Gently, he squeezed, applying pressure to the trigger. The butt thumped into his shoulder, once, twice in quick succession. He heard the bullets strike.

The target fell.

The radio beside him crackled.

'One hit. High left. I think the second was also high.'

Richard came back to the present, open country deep in the Snoqualmie National Forest, where the loggers had stripped the land of trees.

'Roger.'

Jimmy Jamieson placed the radio down beside him, kneeling close to Richard on the makeshift firing point. He took out a small tool and carefully adjusted the line of the foresight in its groove.

'There. Try that, old buddy,' he said. 'You're high left with one hit. Bring the rear sight down a click.'

Richard did so, pulling the gun back into his shoulder ready for the second of his zeroing bursts.

'Ready? Keep your head down out there. Here we go again.'

Two more shots were fired in quick succession. Two hundred yards away, Alex pulled the target down behind the bank which was shielding him. The radio spoke.

'One hit. Low right.'

Jimmy worked with the tool.

'Keep down. Shots coming.'

Richard fired.

'Two hits. Centre. High and low. You're on Hawkeye.'

'Come in, Mr Marker. I got a cold six pack just waiting to be sampled.' Jimmy Jamieson pushed in the telescopic antenna on the CB radio, waving Alex in. He strode towards them carrying the oblong target fixed to a long pole. They examined the neat holes where the bullets had hit.

'Not bad for an amateur.' The banter was light. 'You sure, Jimmy, that no one will come to investigate gunfire, out here in the middle of nowhere?'

'Alex, this is America. The land God and guns made free. Don't tell me you ain't heard of the second amendment to the good ol' Bill of Rights. *A well-regulated militia being necessary for the freedom of the State, the right of the citizen to keep and bear arms shall not be infringed.* You ask any American to recite the Bill of Rights, an' they'll be able to quote you the second and fifth amendments. Over here, anybody can come out in the woods and blaze away to his heart's content. Nobody, but *nobody*, gives a shit. Except the fuckin' deer in the hunting season. They ain't too happy about all this lead flyin' in their direction, so mostly they piss off back into the high country. They always seem to know when to come back down at season's close.'

He pulled the tab from a can of Oly, handing it to Alex, then did the same for himself and Richard.

'That's the best we can do with the gun. It's going to get knocked around a bit between now and when you need it, but it's designed to have the shit kicked out of it. Just aim for the middle of the body. At two hundred you'll chew him up with a five-rounder.'

Jimmy saw Richard grind his teeth.

Did he have what it would take to see this thing through?

The men sat on the small knoll drinking cold beer in the rain, the machine-gun, for the moment, forgotten. Richard knew it would soon be time to go. For him, a date with destiny. He looked at Alex beside him, drinking from the beer can, ignoring the rain. Jimmy, thumbs hooked into the ornate leather belt, staring into the distance.

The comradeship, tangible.

PART FOUR

CHAPTER TWENTY

Nothing had changed.

The streets wet, the buildings dirty and depressing. Memories. The tension, excitement, a drug, stimulating, keeping him watchful and alert. A time when this street had been littered with the aftermath of the riot. Closing his eyes, he saw exploding petrol bombs, feeling their heat, heard the crack of baton rounds, tasting the acrid stench of the CS gas before the respirator covered his face. Snatch squads charging forward into the crowd, singling out a stone-throwing youth, yanking him by his hair, riot sticks rising, falling.

He had seen it all. Groups of youths, some older men, rounded up and flung one on top of the other into the black Maria until it was full. They had driven off, sirens blaring, returning for another load. The riot, worsening as more suspects were taken away.

A young officer beside him had leapt in a bizarre dance of agony, a petrol bomb exploding at his feet, setting his combat suit alight. The cheers, ugly in their pleasure, as he dashed to smother the flames with his own jacket. The young officer had been whimpering, biting his lips in an attempt to stop the noise. Richard Norris had suffered with him.

The crack of the Armalite rifle changed everything. It had not found a target, but now the radios were alive with voices warning of shots being fired. He had listened to the sound of the heavy rifles being cocked in a dozen pairs of nervous hands, picturing the 7.62-mm bullets feeding from magazine to breech. From that moment there was a palpable electricity, a grimness absorbing the tight knots of uniformed soldiers, the sergeant beside him who had not applied his safety catch.

The whole tone of the riot had changed. The crowd had withdrawn to the perimeter, quieter, more sinister. There was a gunman about. The gloves were off. Come on, you bastard. Show yourself. Just give me a shot at you.

The Armalite fired again, a distinctive sound as the high-velocity bullet cracked overhead.

'Window. First floor. Eleven o'clock. Flash and smoke.' The sergeant. He had his rifle up in the aim, squinting through the SUIT sight. Richard had watched, holding his breath, crouched behind the vehicle, not thinking of drawing his own sidearm, a bloody useless pistol. The sound of the rifle firing beside him slammed into his eardrums, hurting. The sergeant fired three times in quick succession, his rifle angled up towards the window a hundred yards away, the recoil thumping into his shoulder.

The Armalite did not fire again.

The crowd had quietened, beginning to drift aimlessly away. Several youths, those who had not been lifted, jeered and raised their fists before thrusting them into their pockets, swaggering into side-streets and alleyways. Some made their way back to the bars where they had been instructed to assemble before the riot, to boast of their exploits. Did you see the Brit with his bollocks on fire from *my* petrol bomb?

Internment.

The first night.

Richard Norris dragged his thoughts back. The drizzle was cold in his hair and on his face. He had wanted to walk, find this place again and relive the memories. He thought of Patrick Donnelly. What had *he* been doing on that bloody night? In amongst it, probably.

How many times had he pictured the man he had come to kill? Always a body with a head. But the face was blank, a cardboard cut-out at the seaside, the kind people stood behind to have a fun photograph taken, with their face but Batman's body.

The hatred in him was like a slow fuse. The car's engine was still running, and he was grateful for the warmth. Where had Johnathan been when . . .? At the time of his execution, his son's murderer would learn of what he had done. Richard would make sure.

Realizing he was grinding his teeth, his jaws aching, he forced himself to relax, putting the car into gear and pulling slowly away from the kerb. At the intersection with the main road, he waited for a gap in the traffic, then drove off in the direction of West Belfast. The address of a small, private car-hire firm was burned into his brain.

Donnelly's Motors.

Rodney Parade.

It was the sort of night that kept decent men inside. Only those with evil in their hearts were abroad. Rain hammered out of the heavens, cleansing the soul, a wicked earth long past forgiveness. The wind buffeted the rain in all directions, slashing it in irregular patterns on to the car's windscreen. The wipers arced ineffectually back and forth and every few seconds the driver would rub the back of his hand rapidly over the glass to clear it, the demister unable to cope with the combined dampness of the four men in the car.

Two were smoking, thin hand-rolled cigarettes which left shreds of tobacco on their tongues each time they were removed from the mouth, held between fingers and thumb, the tip in close to the palm. Nobody spoke. Inside the car it was quiet, except for the sound of the wipers plunking. Occasionally the silence was broken as one of the smokers coughed. A rear-seat passenger cursed as the man in the front wound down his window to throw away his cigarette butt and spat into the rain.

The city was behind them.

Headlights probing the rainy darkness, the car turned off the main road into a muddy lane leading to a gate and stopped. Each of the men waited for one of the others to get out and open the gate, none wanting to leave the relative comfort of the car. At last, the man in the passenger seat cursed, then yanked his door open, letting in the rain on a gust of wind. Hunched into his jacket, the rain beating down on his bare head, he found the latch and lifted the gate open, cursing when the car drove in, splashing mud on to his trousers. He got back into the car, which bounced down the rutted lane until it reached a rickety barn. It was in darkness, but they knew there was someone inside. The dirty transit van would not have been there otherwise.

The four men left the car, turning their collars up against the weather. They moved forward together, intent only on getting this business finished and returning to the bar.

But this was obligatory. Nobody was permitted to miss this, not when Command had ordered them there. The leading man pulled the door outwards and the four entered the dim interior. Only then was the cover removed from a smoky lamp, revealing a knot of men dressed like themselves, standing over in one corner. In the middle of an area cleared of farm machinery was a solitary chair. A man was sitting on it. His hands were bound. There was a black hood over his head tied at his throat. The material moved, sucked inwards as the man gasped air into his open mouth. All of them smelt the stench. He had opened his bowels.

'You're the last.' One of the group in the corner spoke, his voice flat, impatient. 'Let's get on with it.'

They formed a semi-circle around the chair. The one who had spoken stepped forward and looked down at the man tied there. He had cocked his head to one side, listening. They watched the hood being sucked into the mouth, their eyes hard, unforgiving. They could smell his fear, glad to be standing witnessing rather than sat where he was. The man in the chair twitched at every sound, trying to identify them, knowing one would herald pain.

Or death.

One of the group walked over to the wall. He fiddled there for a few moments, then came back paying out an electric extension cable. He dropped the socket on to the concrete floor in front of the chair, seeing its occupant twitch at the sound. A second of the group bent to a plastic case and took out an electric drill, then, using a chuck, inserted a bit.

It was quiet in the barn. The men shuffled, watching.

The one with the drill held it out towards the youngest of the group. The man in the chair sobbed as the trigger was pressed, the bit spinning, whining loudly, dying into the sound of the rain as the trigger was released. One of the group had stepped forward, hesitant, noticed by the others. He held the drill in both hands. The one who had tested it walked behind the man in the chair and untied the cord holding the hood. He did not remove it. Instead he stood with a handful of the material, then gestured with his head to the man on his right, who lifted the victim's leg, resting it on an empty oil drum. He wrinkled his nose at the stink. He held the leg, preventing it being withdrawn.

The young man with the drill did not want to be in this place, afraid of what was expected of him. He watched in horror as the trouser leg was pulled up. The knee was thin, bony, vulnerable. The man holding the hood beckoned him forward.

He stood looking down, unblinking. Afraid. The drill in his hands shook as he lifted it, holding it a few inches above the patella. The hood was ripped off, the victim yelping as a clump of his hair was torn out with it. He tried to adjust to the dim light, eyes darting in all directions, a terrified animal. The man behind held his head, forcing him to look at the knee. His knee.

'No.' The sob was wretched. They smelt him again as he failed to control his sphincter muscles, a wet stain spreading around his fly.

'Jesus God, no!' He tried to look away, but his head was held in strong, dirty hands. Everyone heard the high-pitched whine of the drill. The man in the chair would be feeling the draught of it

as it revolved an inch above his knee. The leader nodded, once, a sharp dipping of his head. The bit chewed through the flesh, bringing blood then bone as it bored deeper into the kneecap.

The scream tore out of his throat. Still his head was held, restraining, preventing him wrenching his eyes away. His body had strained backward, the spine arched. And still the drill bit spun in his knee. Suddenly, his head fell forward, freed by the hands holding him. The victim had fainted. The driller released the trigger but the drill, embedded, could not be pulled free. He had to restart the drill in order to extract it.

The unconscious man twitched, an animal noise deep in his throat. Then he was still. The bit was removed, thrown clattering into the corner, the drill, wiped clean, put back in its case, the packer coiling the flex tidily, then snapping it shut. At that moment the door slammed against the wall as a particularly strong gust burst against it, startling them.

He came upright in his bed, sweating.

For a few seconds he sat quite still, trying to establish his bearings, listening to the sounds around him. Even after all these years, memories of the kneecapping came back to him. The standard punishment for a host of misdemeanours meted out by Command, the punishment which on that occasion he had been forced to administer. He had not known what the man had done.

Found guilty.

He lifted the sheets and looked at his penis straining out from the curling dark hair on his belly. Without touching himself, he shuddered as the semen jerked out, thick and sticky on to his thighs. For a moment he sat there, savouring the sensation before reaching down to the floor and gathering a pair of discarded underpants. He used them to wipe himself, then tossed them back where he had found them.

Patrick Donnelly rolled over on to his side to see the

alarm clock, its luminous green figures bright in the darkness of the room. Their colour matched the eyes staring unblinkingly at the clock face. Two more hours. Then he was to kill again. He fell asleep without feeling the dampness of the old farmhouse.

CHAPTER TWENTY-ONE

The street looked empty, deserted, different from the last time she had been there. The buildings, artificial, unreal, protected her from the worst of the wind. Nevertheless she shivered, perhaps in anticipation. She was eager, tense, expectant, but could not ignore the wind's icy fingers on her bare thighs, under the short skirt. Without worrying how she looked, she hitched the hem a fraction higher, the move involuntary. Balancing delicately on high heels, she stared down the street, glad she had chosen to wear a leather jacket with a sheepskin collar. Without it, the wind would have cut through the thin jersey material of her dress. A larger than usual handbag hung from her shoulder, her left thumb hooked through the leather loop at the side. The other hand hung loosely, the fingers moving constantly.

She could hear nothing except the roaring in her ears.

They would be appearing soon. Any second.

Despite her anticipation, the first of them took her by surprise, coming fast out of a doorway to her left. She jerked the leather loop hard with her left thumb, ripping open the Velcro. The left side of the bag dropped open revealing a small holstered automatic, the butt angled forward so that she could grasp it with her right hand and draw the gun in one smooth movement – in gunfighter terminology, a cross draw. Two fully loaded clips were held in loops on the stiff leather, but angled backwards allowing them to be withdrawn with the left hand.

Jennifer McCauley brought the Walther PPK/S up into the aim. Dropping into a crouch, she instinctively aligned the rear V of the backsight with the smoked foresight, bringing it sharply into focus. She squeezed off two shots, elated, hearing the 7.65-mm bullets striking home, the empty cases pinging as they ejected on to the road. Jennifer was already sweeping an arc with the automatic, stepping forward, her shoes crunching on the grit, ignoring the target, unmoving after she had fired at it.

Two fired. Five left.

Slowly she moved down the street, arms straight, gun loosely held. Without warning a door to her right banged open, the figure with the Armalite raised in the firing position suddenly visible. She fired three times in rapid succession, the reports of the gun running together. Without bothering to register a hit, she dived to her left, rolling away.

Decision time.

Five fired. Two left.

Change clip? Or wait, see if anyone else is coming at her? Hating the indecision, lying flat behind a lamppost, exposed, she searched the street. Where's the next one coming from? Her breathing was quick, irregular. She strove to control it as she had been taught.

The window behind her slammed upwards. Rolling on to her back, she brought the gun up into the aim, almost firing, until she saw it was a small child, an inquisitive look on its face as it peered from the window. Jennifer rolled quickly on to her knees, changing the clip, all in one smooth action.

Seven available.

Come on, you bastards.

Better. A full clip. She was still dangerous.

Maybe she'd got them all. No, there would be more yet. They came from all directions, forcing her to use all the training techniques she had been taught. She fired from every position, the barrel of the gun hot, susceptible to jamming. Her breathing ragged, she kicked off the high heels, seeing them spin away, not caring where they had gone. Without them she felt the cold street, her stockings a mess, holed at the knees, badly laddered. Now that she had taken the two spare clips, she threw her handbag away, jerking it back-handed from her shoulder.

Another passed in front of her perhaps fifteen yards away, going fast from right to left, towards a group of shoppers. She aimed off half a width and fired three times.

Shit.

The gun was empty.

From the way the slide had not gone forward, she knew it hadn't jammed. She had counted, as she had been taught. A lot of use that was going to do her now. She had been dreading this moment.

Three fired. Bugger all left.

Her arms dropped, still holding the Walther in a two-handed grip, the little finger of the right hand curled round the recess on the magazine. She could feel her heart beating. It was over. Standing at the end of the street, she looked back at the damage she had done. Was it enough? None of them had moved after she had fired. But if there were any more . . .

The loudspeaker crackled as she pulled off the ear protectors and turned back the way she had come.

'Looks like you scored a hundred per cent, Jenny. That's on the electronic scoring. The marker will come out and do a physical so you can see your hits. Nice shooting. Thought you were going to do a Dirty Harry on us for a moment, though.' The amplified chuckle made her smile and, as the echoes of the Range Master's voice died away, Jennifer went round with the marker, counting the neat strikes.

She was satisfied.

The targets on the close-combat range were controlled from a small room overlooking the artificial street. Each was brought into play from a console of switches, according to a pattern set by the man who now stood watching. Jennifer McCauley moved amongst them with a scorer who pointed out the hits, discussing each set of bullet-holes with her.

The Range Master watched her walk away on long legs, his penis iron hard from watching her in action, her skirt damn near round her waist, knickers showing like she didn't give a damn. Jeez, it was enough to give a guy the shakes.

He imagined her knickers coming off as she'd scrabbled to get at targets 3 and 5A. Now, if he'd brought target 7 out then, to come straight up after, she would have had to slide round to her right. That might have done it. He'd seen them, though. Sure as shit.

She could have worn the one-piece coverall, like the other WPCs, but she had argued that if ever she had to shoot in anger, it would be in her work clothes. She wouldn't have time to change into a coverall with some Provo coming at her with an Armalite in his fists. No, she'd do her range qualification in her work clothes. Not that the Range Master minded. He dragged his fingers up his erection, scratching at its tip.

Her handbag was bloody neat. He'd once seen something like it in a spaghetti western, used by some bounty hunter, although he couldn't remember who. He wondered who had made it for her. In all his years as Range Master, he'd never seen a woman shoot as well as she did.

Still day-dreaming, he thought about a target pattern

that might get Jennifer McCauley's knickers off. Now that really would be something.

He thought about it for the rest of the day.

The car cruised slowly forward.

Looking to his right, the driver picked out the building at the far end of the narrow street. Most of the houses looked unoccupied, derelict, a far cry from the smart shops and arcades in the centre of the city. There were a few people, one or two women with supermarket carrier bags stuffed with groceries, the plastic handles of the bags stretched thin, cutting into fingers. A young woman pushed a pram, a big old-fashioned model seldom seen now. He watched through the clear arcs the wipers made on the windscreen as she passed in front of the car, leaning forward on too high heels, head down against the rain. He thought of her going into some bright, warm kitchen, lifting the baby, soft and sweet with sleep, from beneath the big hood of the pram. Would she put him straight into his high chair, as Felicity had always done with Johnathan, while she put the kettle on? Or would she sit with him a while, amusing him with some small toy, resting her cheek against the soft down of his hair?

Richard Norris came out of the dark thoughts flooding his mind. Memories of Johnathan as a baby had brought a momentary happiness, evaporating as he turned his thoughts once more to the reasons for his being here. He did not get out of the car, instead sitting immobile behind the wheel, staring at the building at the end of the street, the wide window, flat, gun-metal, absorbing the light.

Even from his distant position, he could make out the rows of hire cars lined up in the small showroom, the desk, a high-backed chair behind it in the office area to the right. A single light shone, not bright enough to illuminate the whole place. Some form of security light, left on when the premises were empty. There was an air of disuse, as if nobody had worked there for some time.

He slipped into gear, driving till he found a place to park. He locked the car, switched on the anti-theft alarm, then walked back to the road he had just been observing.

He walked directly past the junction, turning his head only briefly to his left, confirming what he had seen there. He registered the name of the street. Rodney Drive. A freshly painted sign, the words standing out clearly, was fixed above the big glass window.

Donnelly's Motors.

There was a telephone number, bright red on a green background, which he memorized, while continuing along St James Crescent, past a house for sale opposite the entrance to Rodney Drive. It was an unimpressive property, unlikely to sell. But it was in the right place. Exactly where he needed it. Norris remembered the estate agent's telephone number, storing it with the other. A short distance further, he turned right then immediately right again, into a narrow lane parallel to St James Crescent. He was now behind the vacant property.

The lane was wide enough for a vehicle, and Richard was able to identify the garage belonging to the house. Backing straight on to a small yard, he guessed there would be a way into it through a door at the back of the garage. He continued, turning right, back on to the main road, glancing up at the bedroom window of the empty house, assessing angles and distances. After a final, casual glance, he went quickly back to the car.

He was getting closer.

Soon, Patrick Donnelly.

Soon.

He was big, an athlete, deep-chested, broad-shouldered, perhaps a javelin thrower in his day. Understandably, he did not look well, the previous four weeks spent in a stormy crossing of the North Atlantic in a fourteen-metre ketch, daunting if, like him, you hadn't sailed before. Still tired, queasy, as yet not fully recovered, he was grateful it was behind him. He parked his car at the rear of the hotel.

There had been a message.

He went straight back to the car.

He called into an estate agent advertising the sale of a house in St James Crescent. From the upstairs front bedroom there was a clear view down Rodney Drive to a garage. He had expressed an interest in buying the property. The estate agent had been both surprised and delighted. Of course he could have the keys to view the house. No, they were more than happy not to send a representative to escort him. Yes, the house was unoccupied. They would check, ensuring the main services were all connected.

He had a duplicate set of keys cut.

He returned the originals.

It wasn't quite what he was looking for.

The woman in the estate agent's offices was disappointed, attracted to him, his soft Irish brogue. She couldn't quite place the accent, the lovely soft burr. It wasn't Belfast, that was for sure.

She wondered where he came from.

Saturday.

Richard walked into the foyer of his hotel, collecting his key from reception. As he crossed the lobby, past the TV lounge towards the stairs leading to his room, he heard a loud burst of applause from a group of men watching the Five Nations Rugby Championship, highlights of the England–Wales game. He watched, standing at the back of the room, nodding when the waitress asked him if he would like a drink. Scotch, he told her.

Red shirts, mingling with the white.

Johnathan.

The roar of the crowd. England had taken a strike against the head in their own twenty-two. They were running out of defence, the Twickenham crowd ecstatic.

In the officers' mess, they talked about the game for a long time after it was over. Bloody wonderful match. The most exciting Army Cup Final for years. Richard had taken the day off. He had sat in the stand and watched his son, proud of him.

Wild cheering. Now.

Johnathan was running.

The white-shirted scrum-half gathered the ball at the back of the scrum. Johnathan's side were eighteen to fifteen up with less than a minute to play. The game was in the bag, unless the opposition scored off this last move. Johnathan broke, almost caught offside. Richard held his breath, Johnathan sprinting across the pitch, angling across the line of players coming fast down the field towards him.

The pass was fumbled, giving Johnathan the yard he needed. The crowd could see the flank forward with the straw-coloured hair was going to clobber the big centre with tree-trunk legs, hard to stop, running with his knees high, straight down the pitch. Richard wondered if Johnathan had noticed that the centre side-stepped off his left foot, that he hadn't come off his right the whole match.

There had been countless discussions between them over the merits of the smother tackle. Johnathan believed in knocking them down hard, intimidating them. The next time they saw you coming at them, they would funk it and blow the pass, had been his argument. Richard had countered, believing the ball to be more important. Take the ball and the man together, Johnathan, he had said. It may not look pretty, hanging off your opposite number, dragged along, but the ball isn't going anywhere. Wait for your forwards to get round and ruck it back. Then counter from this second phase of play.

He wondered what Johnathan would do.

The overlap had been created. If the centre got in his pass . . . He saw his son launch himself at the big centre, who, for the first time in the match, side-stepped off his right foot. Johnathan's hands were high. Well, I'm damned, thought his father, he's going to smother him. He wondered what was going through the boy's mind as he went into the tackle . . .

The crowd cheering brought him out of it.

Belfast.

Johnathan.

They had told him he was dead.

England had scored in the last minute of the game. Just as the opposition had done when Johnathan had been injured in the last tackle of the Army Cup match.

He finished his whisky and took the lift to his room, where he lay on the bed, falling into a restless sleep, dreaming of rugby players without faces and Batman bodies. The telephone ringing woke him.

It was Alex.

CHAPTER TWENTY-TWO

Jennifer paid off the cab and walked the short distance to her flat. The street was empty. No one to see the mess her stockings were in. She had thought about taking them off in the back of the taxi but reckoned the driver, staring into his rear-view mirror, had already had an eyeful when she collapsed into the back seat. Sod him. She had been very satisfied with her performance on the range. But then she practised a lot in front of the full-length mirror in her room, ripping the handbag open, drawing the gun from the spring-clip holster, and dropping into the two-handed stance.

Her father had designed the bag, had it made for her mother, her real mother, before she had left him. She had never adapted to the pressures of being the wife of an RUC man. The late nights, never knowing if he was coming home, listening to the news broadcasts. The constant fear. But she was damned if she was going to carry a gun in her handbag, even if it *was* permitted.

One day, she left.

Jennifer had been twelve.

Once in the privacy of her flat, she undressed, tossing her clothes into the laundry basket. Dressed in a comfortable robe, she took the gun from her handbag and placed it on a newspaper spread on a table against the wall. She sat, staring at the powder burns at the end of the barrel from her practice session on the close-combat range. The inscription *Walther 7.65 mm Indian Arms Corp. Detroit, Mich. USA* stood out clearly.

The gun had been presented to her father when he had been in America. As a young Inspector, he had won a Churchill Scholarship, spending two months with the Chicago Police Department. A blithe Northern Irishman, he had been popular with everyone. They had given him the gun as a keepsake, and to use if he ever got into a jam. It was meant as a joke, but John McCauley had taken them at their word.

Quickly, efficiently, she stripped the weapon and began to clean it, thinking about her father as she worked. Everything she knew about the gun, she had learned from him. PPK stood for *Polizei Pistole Kriminal* he had told her. The weapon favoured by the *Kripo*. It was smaller than the PP, the clip holding seven shots, not eight. He had shown her the little spur on the bottom plate of the magazine which acted as a rest for the little finger of the right hand. He had let her hold it.

He was particularly proud of his unique little gun. This was the PPK/S. The S, he had said rather grandly, meant Special. The 1968 US Gun Control Act required pistols to have a minimum depth of four inches. The PPK was only 3.9 inches, illegal in the USA. But the Walther PPK had proved popular with plain-clothes police, and the company had wanted to take advantage of this lucrative market. As a result, her father had told her, they took the frame of the PP and fitted the slide and barrel of the PPK, giving it a depth of 4.1 inches.

The result, the gun she was now using.

She reassembled it, remembering the sight, the smell, the sheen of gun oil as he had finished cleaning the Walther, slipping it lovingly back into the spring-clip holster. After he had been killed, they had taken her father's gun away. A lot of strings were pulled to get it back. As soon as she'd joined the RUC, there had been no problems with her getting a licence. She held the gun in the flat of her hand, remembering him.

She realized that her father had been dead for almost seven years.

Leaving the gun on the table, she went into the bathroom. Under the shower, warm, relaxed, head tipped back to let the water cascade over her face and body, she heard something. She turned off the shower, head cocked, listening. It came again, ringing, persistent.

Her doorbell.

Puzzled, she shrugged into a robe, tying the belt as she walked downstairs, her hair wet, heavy on her shoulders. Half-way, she heard the sound of a key in the lock.

The door swung inwards, letting in the cold.

*

The spade bit into the brown earth. The man working rested briefly, surveying his handiwork. He had dug a shallow scrape, heaping the soil at one end, then compacted it with the spade. The turf was used to cover the mound, the new earth invisible from the road three hundred yards away. He had chosen well.

The hide, at the leading edge of a small copse, was well hidden, the dark colour of the trees breaking its outline. The sun would rise from behind the copse, low in the sky at this time of year, the sunlight stippling through the trees, camouflaging him. Sunlight, anyway, would blind anyone driving this way along the road this early.

He was satisfied.

Lifting the canvas sheet, he spread it across the shallow trench. Stretched behind the gun, he would be protected from the worst of the dampness. Already water was seeping up through the ground, forming a puddle in which he would otherwise have had to lie.

He picked up the machine-gun, positioning it, projected an inch or so above the low mound in the front of his makeshift fire trench. Looking carefully about him, he stretched out behind it, resting the butt on the ground in front of him, holding it lightly in his hands, almost caressing it. Several times he pulled it up into the aim and peered through the sights. On a fence-post at the side of the road an inverted white polystyrene cup which he had fixed earlier stood out clearly. It was exactly three hundred yards away. He would fire when the target passed this marker.

Gradually it grew lighter. The birds began their dawn chorus, but he did not listen. He lay still. He waited, the pain in the little finger of his left hand the only distraction. After all these years, it still nagged when his hands were cold. He looked down, seeing it sticking up vertically from the butt of the gun, remembering the day it had happened.

The gaffer had taken on a new lad at the site. Donnelly was to break him in, show him the ropes. Big, clumsy, eager to learn, but thick as two short planks. Fuck all between his ears. They were unloading steel girders and Donnelly had been guiding the first into position with a small donkey-winch. Setting the safety lever, he had jumped out of the machine to swing the end of the girder into position because his slow-witted assistant couldn't understand what he was supposed to do.

He was guiding the RSG when the stupid bloody berk had stumbled against the winch, grabbing at the safety lever to steady himself, unlocking it. He wasn't supposed to be anywhere near the winch. The heavy metal had ground down on to Donnelly's finger, trapping it on a pile of bricks. Donnelly had screamed, dropping to his knees, holding his left elbow with his right hand in a futile attempt to stem the agony searing from his hand and up his arm. The lad was looking petrified. Donnelly had yelled, telling him to pull the lever, the one with the yellow knob.

The engine laboured as it took the strain, blue exhaust belching from the pipe. As the girder had begun to lift, Donnelly felt the sweet relief. Before he could slide his finger free, the safety failed. The girder settled back on his finger, crunching, grinding it into the pile. Donnelly had been on his knees sobbing, when at last the new boy had got himself together and run for help.

Command had arranged for him to go over the border to have his hand fixed. They had paid for a private hospital. Donnelly was valuable to them. They had invested in him. But, despite the surgery, the hours of physiotherapy, he was never able to bend the finger again.

He had only just been given the M60. Command was worried he wouldn't be any good.

But he was.

He was their best.

Lighter.

Until now he had not moved. He felt the strain on his bladder and cursed. A basic rule. He should have remembered. Slowly, carefully, he shifted his weight on to his right side so that he could pull open the zip of his fly. Awkward, cramped, he fingered his penis free, urinating quietly, aiming the stream to miss the groundsheet. The steam cloud worried him a bit, but it was unlikely it would be noticed this early.

A car. He couldn't yet see it. Soon it would change down a gear to negotiate the sharp bend before climbing the hill towards him. He tugged at the zipper, readjusting his position behind the gun. A dark-blue Cortina came into view around the bend.

Donnelly breathed out, lips parted, looking through the rear aperture and aligning the foresight. By the time the car reached his marker it would be head on. No need to aim off. Just allow for the angle of the hill.

The sergeant, the Jock, whispering in his ear, as he had lain on the firing point, the whisky sour on his breath, lecturing on the characteristics of NATO ammunition.

'Over three hundred metres a bullet will decelerate from 854 metres per second, to 642. It'll drop a wee 659 mm. With 9.65-gramme, M80 ball ammunition, the streamlined bullet with a lead core will . . .'

Fuck ballistic science.

A burst from this little baby will make any bastard sit up and take notice.

The green eyes blinked twice.

The car drew level with the marker. The dew lay wet on Donnelly's back. He felt the blood forced into his penis.

He blinked again.

John-ny-get-your-gun. John-ny-get-your-gun. John-ny-get-your-gun.

Ejaculating, the windscreen shattering.

Carnage, bullets ripping into the car, chewing into the bodies of the two off-duty RUC policemen, everything spattering everywhere. Fascinated by what he had done, he watched the Cortina mount the bank, flip on to its side, tearing, scraping, sparks from the metal fireworks in the air. The upper front wheel spun uselessly, gravel and mud falling from its treads.

Suddenly, very quiet.

He lay still, uncomfortable on the semen that had pumped out of him, waiting to see if there was any further movement from the car. A light came on in a farmhouse perhaps a mile away, the house still in shadow where the sun had yet to reach. A farm dog barked in the distance.

The wheel stopped spinning.

Satisfied, he gathered in the links of the ammunition belt and stuffed them into his pockets with the shiny brass empty cases scattered on the canvas. Still hot, they burned his fingers. Carefully, he scanned the ground in a one-hundred-and-eighty degree arc in front of him. Seeing nothing, he crawled backwards out of his firing position into the copse, carrying the gun and the spade in both hands, supported by his elbows. He did not stand until well into the trees.

Donnelly strode along a muddy track to a 4-w/d pick-up truck, parked on the edge of a field at the far end of the copse. He did not speak to the driver, instead placing the gun carefully on some sacks under a tarpaulin in the back. He took off the overalls, rubber boots, gloves and balaclava, tossing them in with the gun. Tugging on a pair of old trainers, he slapped the roof of the cab three times, telling the driver it was done, then watched as it sped away down the hill on to the road leaving a pair of muddy tracks behind.

Donnelly turned left, following the tree-line down a re-entrant to a gate which he climbed quickly, glancing along the road in both directions. A small Fiat was parked in a gateway opposite, the driver tetchy, looking up nervously as Donnelly's shadow fell over him.

Donnelly had never seen the teenager before. The engine was running, probably since the gunfire had started. Donnelly was pretty sure that if things hadn't gone well, the Fiat wouldn't have waited. Disgusted, he listened to the tinny sound coming from the Walkman, scowling at the gormless expression as the boy's head rocked backwards and forwards in time to the music, like a chicken pecking in a farmyard.

As soon as Donnelly was in the car, the driver, head bobbing, rammed it into gear and sped off in the direction of Dundalk. They wouldn't use a recognized crossing point. There were plenty of others to choose from.

Crossmaglen was left behind them.

Donnelly let himself relax. He put his hand in his pocket and fingered the brass Yale key warm against his thigh. He dozed in the warmth of the car, thinking of where he would go when the heat of this killing died down.

As he slept, he felt the stirrings of another erection.

Jennifer stopped trying to dry her hair. She was annoyed, unable to think who could be invading her privacy. Nobody ever came here unless invited. She felt anger, was about to yell something rude, when the door swung fully open.

A man stood there, his right hand still holding the key in the lock. He was wearing a suit, light-coloured with padded shoulders. The trousers were creased behind the knees as if he had been sitting a long time. His shoes, though not dirty, needed polish. He looked up, surprised to see her there.

Green marbles stared at her. There was no expression in them. She felt the beginnings of panic, the flush on her face, the coldness in her belly. She remembered in time, forcing a smile on to her lips, trying to spread it to her eyes, showing her pleasure in seeing a lover again.

'Patrick.'

'Jenny.'

He was awkward, ungainly in the doorway. Without being asked, he closed it.

'I was wondering how you'd been keeping, what you'd been doing with yourself. I was at a loose end and felt like coming round to see you. A surprise.' He shrugged, then bent to pick up the evening paper lying on the mat. He held it out to her, like a schoolkid handing over an apple, a gift for teacher. She took it without speaking, letting him stay embarrassed.

'My key. You've got a key to my flat.' She was accusing. He shrugged again, the padded shoulders rolling.

'I picked it up from the table, there,' he nodded with his head, 'when I was here before. On my way out. I probably wasn't thinking. Anyway, my mind was on other things.' The green eyes looked at her.

Jennifer had not seen him so uncertain. This was not the confident whiffler she had picked up in the club and brought home to her flat, who had screwed her without an ounce of passion or tenderness. Despite his discomfort, it didn't look as if he were going to leave. That was for sure.

'You'd best be coming up, then.' She turned and led the way, feeling the marbles on her backside, moving under the thin material of the robe. She opened the door and led the way into her flat.

The gun.

She cursed her forgetfulness.

It was on the table.

It stood out a mile.

A moment of panic. He was behind her. He had put his hand on her buttocks and was trying to push his fingers between her legs. She squirmed away from him, seeing the gun without looking at it. Her mind stampeded.

She walked smoothly across the room, opening the newspaper he had given her, letting it fall, covering the Walther. Temporary relief.

'Drink, Patrick?' she asked over her shoulder.

'Not if it's Bacardi.' He'd remembered.

'I've no mineral water.' Show him she'd remembered too.

There wasn't much to offer. She bent to the cupboard, searching amongst the bottles.

'Whisky, then. Bushmills?'

Without answering, he walked over to the table, stopping to look down at the paper, his glance at first casual. She spoke quickly.

'How about Grouse?'

He wasn't listening.

He was staring at the paper. Perhaps oil stains from the gun had seeped through. Something held his attention. He had put both hands on to the table, leaning forward, taking his weight on them. She poured his drink quickly, letting him hear it splash into the glass.

Turn round, Marbles.

Instead, he picked up the paper, opening it to study something in the middle pages. If the paper folded forward, he'd see the gun. For sure.

Do something. Anything.

'That's not much of a compliment to be paying a girl, looking through the evening paper as if your life depended on it.'

Ignoring her, he continued to read. There was something about him, the way his back had tensed.

'There's an article. Two RUC gunned down in their car outside Crossmaglen. I was interested.'

Jennifer had heard the news, screwing her fists in anger. Another machine-gun attack, quick, efficient, deadly as always. The Provos had a gunner, an unknown, appearing without warning, doing his dirty work, then vanishing back into the shadows, never a clue as to who it might be.

Now, there would be the usual platitudes from the politicians. A bit more high-profile security, then nothing. Until the next time. The endless cycle.

Realizing he was about to close the newspaper, she moved, putting the glass down before crossing the room. In four quick steps she was behind him, wrapping her arms around his waist.

Do something.

She paused momentarily, then slid her hand down to his crotch. Caressing him, she felt his response startling and immediate, a stiffness through the thin suit. Looking around his body, she saw the newspaper fall back covering her gun. He still didn't turn round. Using her left hand, she untied the belt of her robe, shaking her shoulders, letting it fall to the floor. Using both hands to open his fly, she pressed her body into him. He was stiff, warm in her hand. She squeezed gently, then began to rub slowly, teasing him, her fingers lighter now, without pressure.

He still hadn't turned.

She gritted her teeth, then with her hands on his hips, turned him gently to face her. Keeping her hold on him, she pushed down against the force of his penis, holding him between her thighs. She moved gently, feeling the heat.

Green eyes flickered.

He put his hands on her shoulders, pushing her down.

Bastard.

She went with the pressure, down on to her knees. It was huge in front of her. She nuzzled it with her cheek, then ran her tongue along its length. A sharp intake of breath as she reached the tip. She levered him down, holding him with her fingertips, between her lips.

Like playing a clarinet.

Don't come, you bastard.

His hands were resting on the table behind him so close to her gun. It wasn't even loaded. Not like him. She would have laughed . . . Reaching up, she took his hands, placing them on each side of her face. He held her, rough hands, surprisingly gentle.

She undid his belt, letting his trousers drop to his ankles, then slid her hands up the back of his thighs on to the narrow buttocks, encouraging him with the tips of her fingers. He responded as she knew he would. Moving, gently at first, then harder, deeper into her mouth. Hurting her. She gagged. He didn't hear, or if he did, was too far gone to care.

He was nowhere near the gun.

She felt him start to come and jerked her head away, feeling the warmth splash wetly on her neck and shoulders. He was breathing heavily, his chest heaving, still holding her head in his hands.

You bastard.

She stood, leaning against him. The semen would stain his jacket. He didn't notice. She didn't care. Get him to the bed. Away from the gun. She lay down and let him into her. His movements were thrusting, fast, hard.

The Belfast Bonker.

She made the right noises, said the right things, looking at the ceiling, feeling his breath hot on her neck. She could not understand the language he spoke through his teeth, coarse words, tumbling as he drew nearer his time.

'John-ny-get-your-gun.'

Like the time before.

He lay on her for a while until she thought he had fallen asleep. But he was talking into her breast, his voice muffled.

'I've missed you.'

'I've missed you, too.' The half-truth came easily. 'Where have you been?'

'Away on business.'

'What business is that?'

'My business.' He was evasive.

'You've rough hands, Patrick, but soft on a girl's skin.' She held one in her own, lifting it from the bed, running the tips of her fingers across his palm, fingernails lightly scratching the callus. 'As if you did manual work. You told me about your hand, the accident. When was that?'

'I told you. 'Seventy-six. Some thick butcher's boy dropped a bloody girder on me.'

He pulled out of her and rolled on to his back, putting his hands behind his head. He told her then, about the car-hire firm, how a company had sponsored him to get him started, given him a decent living.

He didn't tell her where it was, his precious car-hire firm.

She rolled over on to her side, resting on her elbow, looking at him. His head turned towards her. A stirring in the eyes, not an expression, but a fleeting shadow, a hawk passing in front of the sun.

He rolled on top of her, pushing with his feet, spreading her legs. As he went up into her, she had to bite her lip to stop crying out. He finished, quicker this time, the same thing said at the end. She let his movement stop, then asked him why he said it.

He was up in an instant without warning, pulling out of her, muttering.

She watched him dress. On his way out, he went to the lavatory.

He didn't kiss her.

He didn't look at the newspaper on the table.

After he'd gone, she lay there, her hands screwed into tight fists. Two things worried her.

He still had her key.

She had nearly come.

The bastard had nearly made her come.

CHAPTER TWENTY-THREE

They met in an up-market restaurant in a fashionable part of the city, asking for a booth in the corner where they could see the door. Without paying attention to the menu, they ordered. Alex looked tired. Richard relieved. He had made it home. Not that Belfast could ever be considered that. Richard listened as Alex told him about his North Atlantic crossing in a fourteen-metre, long-keeled, blue-water ketch. It had not been fun. He would not do it again.

'Gales, ice, fog and more bloody fog. Richard, I've never liked the sea much. In a small boat, at this time of year, I hated it.'

Richard was sympathetic.

'How was the skipper?'

'Pissed most of the time. I can't say I blame him. His crew were OK, though. One, a girl, built like a brick shithouse.' He gestured with his hands. 'She certainly knew how to sail, however. Even managed to teach me a bit.' Alex grinned, his face changing, the tiredness gone for the moment. Seeing Richard's look, he went on quickly, 'About sailing, I mean. I picked up quite a lot about Satnav, even understanding a bit about the course.'

The waiter placed avocado vinaigrette on the table.

'We sailed north-east with the Gulf Stream until we

were clear of Newfoundland.' He speared a slice of avocado. 'There's ice there at this time of year, you know. Comes south on the Labrador Current. Once through it, though, it was, to coin a phrase, plain sailing. Just the bloody awful weather.' Alex shivered.

'Any trouble with the cargo?' This had been a constant worry to Richard. He had lost sleep over it. Alex glanced around the room before he answered.

'No. The hire car was where you'd left it. I brought the gun ashore in a sail-bag. There were no customs or checks there. I'll say that about the skipper. He sure as hell knows these waters.'

'He's been around, running dubious cargoes ever since I've known him.' Richard mopped up vinaigrette sauce with a piece of bread. 'How about the road journey down to Belfast?'

'I had to pull the ID card once, when we were on the outskirts of the city. That was a bit hairy. The soldiers were on the ball, but they waved me through the vehicle checkpoint without any questions.'

'And you've left it in the garage. At the house on St James Crescent?'

'Yes. It's stood on its end in a cupboard in the corner, back to the left as you go in. In amongst some old tools and junk. You won't miss it if you know where to look.'

'Alex,' Richard looked at his friend, 'I really appreciate what you've done. At the beginning, well, you weren't too keen yourself to start with.' He paused, searching for the right words. 'I told you it wasn't really your fight, that I had no business asking for your help. I meant that. Anyway, for you it's over. I'll see it finished. Alone.'

Alex put his fork down carefully.

'She was my sister, Richard. Dammit, if it hadn't been for me, you two never would have met. That makes it my fight too. And Johnathan was my nephew. They were my only family.' He looked across the table, jaw jutting, a look on his face Richard had seen often enough before. On mountain routes when neither had been sure of the way, when they'd argued over the route. Alex was about to dig his toes in.

'Alex.' Richard paused, letting the waiter serve the Châteaubriand. 'Up to this point no one has been hurt. No one. But now, I'm about to kill a man. I'm about to commit what is still murder, never mind my reasons or the justness of it. I'll not have you an accessory. That's asking too much.'

'You'll be isolated. No back-up. Nobody to pull you out when the shit is flying around.' Alex was hurt, Richard could see it. But his mind was made up.

'Just make the telephone call. After that, I won't need you, Alex.'

They were silent for a long time, each eating with studied concentration, not wanting to look at the other. Richard knew he had been abrupt, and now he felt the tension between them.

'Come on, Alex. You know I'm right.'

Alex looked unconvinced.

'I tried to do my bit,' he said, 'and perhaps I do feel a bit better about Felicity. Still . . .' He let the sentence trail, sipping his wine.

'What about the offshore accounts?' he asked, suddenly remembering them. 'After we sent old Mikovitch away with a pain where it would hurt. Have you sorted that yet?'

'I sent a fax to the Channel Islands a day or so after I got back from the States.' Richard was glad they were discussing things normally again. The previous tension had eased. 'I had all the information, the spreadsheets from London. It was one hell of a long fax. The recipients should know by now.'

'I'm glad,' said Alex. 'That may help ease away some of

the pain. It can't be traced? And you've kept enough for the finale?'

'With interest. And yes, it's quite untraceable.'

Alex stood, huge in the room. He leaned over the table.

'I'll hang on for a few more days. I'll make your call for eight tomorrow night. You sure that gives you enough time?'

Richard nodded. Alex straightened up, paused, uncertain that this was the end of it for him.

'Go on, you big ugly bastard.'

Richard did not look up to see him leave.

The young RUC man shifted his weight to ease the stiffness in his body. He ached everywhere, his eyes smarting from staring through the powerful wide-angle lenses. The loft of the derelict house where he lay was damp, cold, littered with the mess of the stake-out. His first. He was bored. His partner had the experience, had been on stake-out before. The young constable had a lot to learn.

He took his eyes away from the glasses, trying to focus in the darkness of the roof space. He glanced at his companion, sitting at a small table in the middle of the loft, where there was enough headroom to sit upright. He was wearing headphones. There was an expensive piece of electronic equipment on the table in front of him. It was the untidy apparatus of a phone tap.

It was connected to a number listed as Donnelly's Motors. All calls to and from the number were intercepted and logged. The man at the table read a magazine by the dim light of a tiny lamp. He stopped reading only when he heard the tones in his earphones telling him the extension number to which he was connected was being used. Even then, he would glance up only briefly to ensure that the LED lights were glowing, the needles kicking across the VUs, modulating correctly. Then he would note the tape reading, and record the time and duration of the call. Another recorder was connected to the directional microphone aimed at the front of the showrooms.

Neither man spoke.

One watched.

One listened.

Patrick Donnelly was 'in the frame'.

He couldn't fart without them knowing.

From the bedroom he had an unrestricted view down the length of Rodney Drive to the junction with Rodney Parade. He had pulled the curtains across the window, making a gap of about eighteen inches. On the far side of the room was a table brought up from the kitchen earlier. There was no other furniture in the house. The room was damp, peeling wallpaper exposing patches of plaster, the carpet faded, threadbare, mouse droppings between it and the skirting board. But he was not interested.

His attention was focused on the weapon on the table at the far side of the room. It looked none the worse for its journey across the North Atlantic, gleaming in the thin film of oil protecting it. Richard touched it and shuddered.

He remembered what Jimmy Jamieson had told him about the gun. This was the M60E1, an updated version of the M60 developed in the late 1950s and taken into service in the early sixties as the standard squad machine-gun in the US Army. Jamieson had known his subject. He and Alex had listened intently, drinking cold beer from cans on a rainy day in the beauty of the Snoqualmie National Forest. The American had shown them the workings.

The gun used the feed system of the German MG 42

and the bolt and locking action of the FG 42. A lot of dollars had gone into its development. The early M60 used a barrel with its own gas cylinder and bipod attachment. There was no handle, the crew members using an asbestos glove whenever the barrel needed changing. The M60E1 had overcome these early shortcomings.

It was made by the Inland Manufacturing Division of General Motors, Dayton, Ohio.

It was forty-three and a half inches long.

It weighed twenty-three pounds and three ounces.

It had a 22.04-inch barrel with four grooves in a right-hand twist.

It fired 550 bullets in a minute at a muzzle velocity of 2,805 feet per second.

It was going to spatter Patrick Donnelly all over his office.

They would need a high-pressure hose in there to clean him off the shiny cars laid out in the showroom.

Soon, Donnelly.

Soon.

Unable to concentrate on his work, he stared at the papers spread out in front of him on the desk. At the best of times he hated doing the books, but knew it was necessary to keep his business legitimate. For him to stay clean. Command was not going to see its gunner carted off to court because of a few VAT returns. No record, Patrick, they had told him. So Patrick Donnelly struggled with his books, like countless other small businesses, in order to satisfy HM Customs and Excise.

He was intelligent enough to handle the work, and his education was up to it – the Army had seen to that. Tonight his mind just wasn't on it. The figures in the ledger swam in and out of focus as he tried to keep his mind on his work.

Jennifer McCauley.

Although he hated to admit it, the woman had been on his mind a lot. She had liked what he did to her, he knew that. Writhing about as he pumped in and out of her. Like a fucking wildcat. And, jeez, when she came. Now that was really something. It made him feel good, manly, like he had with Molly all those years ago. No messing with her. Let's get on the couch, Patrick, and fuck our brains out. She wanted no foreplay, she'd said. Just a good hard fuck with that lovely big dick of yours.

Jennifer McCauley was the same.

She loved it too.

He could tell.

She was just another bloody good poke, wasn't she?

So how come I'm still sitting here thinking about her?

The telephone rang.

'Donnelly's Motors. Can I help?'

It was the Irishman from across the border, confirming he would be round to collect the car at eight tonight. Patrick Donnelly made a few notes about the gentleman's requirements, then told him there were no problems with him collecting the car late. No, sir, the flights into Aldergrove were not always convenient. Yes, sir, I'll be here to deal with you myself.

Donnelly had to admit that the car-hire firm was a masterful cover. His instructions were never passed over the telephone. They always came via a customer. The customer was always different. The car always the same. Instructions were left in the glove compartment when it was returned after use.

Got to keep you clean, Patrick.

He looked at his watch. Thirty-five minutes before the car was collected. Would it be the red Cavalier? With a message in the glove compartment when it came back?

The M60.

Jennifer McCauley.

Donnelly felt the heat in his loins.

He switched on another light, forcing his brain to concentrate on the VAT returns. The telephone rang again. He reached for it, only mildly interested.

A voice, unfamiliar.

Alarm, electric, tickled his nerve-endings.

CHAPTER TWENTY-FOUR

The man behind the desk stood out clearly in the brightly lit office. Leaning forward, his head supported by one hand, he worked on some papers, his efforts perfunctory. Occasionally he would stop, throw his pencil on to the desk and put his hands behind his head in an attitude of deliberation, as if his mind were elsewhere. Once, he got up and walked around the showroom, looking everywhere, but seeing nothing. It was obvious his mind was not on his work. The watcher nodded as the man returned to the desk to make another half-hearted attempt at working.

Richard Norris was surprised at the peace he felt now. There had been procrastination, doubt, about this moment of reckoning, from the time he had first embarked on his quest for revenge, his personal nemesis. And Felicity, unable to exist without the person she loved most in the world. He recalled the surge of adrenalin when he had first seen Patrick Donnelly enter the showroom, two hundred yards away, the little finger, stiff, clearly seen through the glasses when he had sat down to work.

St James Crescent, Belfast.

The hatred, the bitterness, driving him half-way round

the world, still spread like poison, strengthening rather than lessening his desire to see this man dead. Strange then he should now wonder about the killing. How it would feel at the instant of firing.

He had killed before.

Aden.

But that had been in the heat of combat, man to man with no time to consider the rights and wrongs. No reason was needed, then. Kill or be killed. Him or you. Or Nobby Clarke. He felt the bayonet in his hand, the shuddering in his arms as the man had gurgled away his life. That had been war. This is peace. For some.

He saw Donnelly look at his watch. Norris did the same.

7.45 p.m.

It was dark except for the showroom window which threw a huge rectangle of light out into the street.

It was time.

A time to kill.

A time to die.

Now, Donnelly. Now.

Norris walked slowly across the room to the table. He stood behind the American M60E1 machine-gun, leaning forward, placing his elbows on the table. His feet formed a triangle with his upper body, a platform. Scrubbing with his feet as if grinding out a cigarette end, he made a firm base to hold him steady when the gun fired. The thin carpet rucked under his feet.

The gun looked ungainly, its sleek ugliness accentuated by the fat silencer. But Norris knew it would do its job. The link belt was already in place, the ammunition glinting dully in the pale light filtering through the thin curtains. He jiggled them, a lover's caress, feeling each bullet with the tips of the fingers of his left hand. Worry beads. As he nuzzled the butt into his cheek, a pulse beat heavily in his temple.

The gun had been cocked.

And locked.

Ready.

The mobile phone lay on the table beside him. Taking his right hand from the gun, he took a deep breath and keyed in the number he had memorized, painted in red letters on a green background. They might have been orange. He couldn't remember. Nor did he care.

Donnelly's Motors.

The ringing tone purr-purred in the small extension speaker and mike he had made in his workshop, a farmhouse outside Cheltenham, so many weeks ago. It was echoed by a faint jingling in the office in the street below. He saw Donnelly glance at the instrument at his elbow, look once more at his watch, then reach out to lift it to his ear.

'Donnelly's Motors,' said a voice.

'He's picking the phone up.'

The young RUC constable on his first stake-out squinted through the powerful field-glasses mounted on a small tripod in front of him. He was stretched out uncomfortably on a door lying across the rafters in the damp loft.

'I hear.'

The Sergeant, experienced, untroubled, glanced briefly at the LED lights on the recording equipment. Satisfied, he adjusted the padded earphones. He leaned forward, holding them tightly against his ears as if he were afraid he might miss something. But the high impedance equipment connected to the phone-tap took only a few milliamperes of current, undetectable by anyone on the line. The recording would be of the highest quality. He would miss nothing.

He noted the counter-number when the tape started to run, his reference when analysing this conversation later. Holding a pencil stub, ready to enter the reading into the log, he suddenly cocked his head, like a blackbird after worms, listening intently. The log was forgotten. Something was up.

'What's he saying?'

'Shut up!' Hissed, a hand held up to command silence.

'What the hell . . .?' He reached out for the telephone at his side, hesitating, his fingers curling lightly over it.

But he did not pick it up.

From his position on the door, the Constable tried to fathom his companion's expression. Satisfaction? Not quite. He shrugged. It wasn't his job to worry about the phone-tap. He was the observer. He'd bloody well get on and observe. He turned his attention back to the field-glasses.

The Sergeant looked at the telephone again.

Listening, he left it untouched.

In his heart he hoped the man who was now talking didn't piss around too long . . .

He'd really be for it if this ever got out. He took a chance. And listened.

'Is that Patrick Donnelly?'

He was tense, alert.

The hair on the nape of his neck moved as if a breeze had blown gently across it. The voice was English, harsh, uncompromising. Donnelly had heard voices like it before, in the Army, when some prissy Brit officer was giving him a bollocking. When he was up on orders in front of the company commander for yet another petty offence. There was authority. And something else. He couldn't place it, but there was definitely something.

'Who is this?'

He kept his own voice hard, unconcerned, indignant at being spoken to like this. But there was fear. The merest hint of it.

'Your executioner.'

'What the fuck you talking about? Just get the—'

'Donnelly, shut up. Your time is short. Don't waste it talking. Just listen.' Donnelly tried to figure, to work out who the caller was. He had no idea.

'November last year. You gunned down a soldier when he was out on the streets doing his job. A young officer. He was twenty-three years old. He loved life. The life you took. You chewed him up with an American M60 machine-gun. You hit him three times, three fucking times, Donnelly.'

What the . . .?

'I don't know what the hell you're talking about.'

'He was my son, you bastard. My son.'

Who . . .?

'Look, mister, I don't know who the hell you are—'

'You're going the same way, Donnelly. With an M60. Except you're going to know. Not like my son. I can see you now, behind your desk, everything. The hair up your nostrils.'

Donnelly looked quickly from left to right, then at the window. Nothing, except the darkness outside.

'Oh, you won't see me, Donnelly, but every move you make, I can see. Pick your nose, scratch your arse, I'll see it.'

Suddenly, Patrick Donnelly knew. Fear crept into his bowels, spreading to his belly. Blood forced into his head, tickling his scalp.

'I've got an M60. You've used one enough. You've no place to hide in there. Drop behind your desk and the gun will chew through it. Try and move and I'll cut you down.'

Donnelly felt panic. His eyes darted around the big room. He was naked. Exposed. Trapped. Wherever he went the gun would get him. He *knew* what it could do.

'This is what it's like, Donnelly. On the receiving end.'

The sound of the plate-glass window shattering

slammed into his eardrums. The double crack passing over his head stunned him. The noise was something he had never heard before. But then, nobody had ever shot at him. Before.

Now he knew terror. He could not believe this was happening. He was Patrick Donnelly. Clean. All these years they'd kept him clean. So how the hell did this Englishman find him?

He remembered the day in November. The day he'd got two of the bastards.

There was a gun in the top left-hand drawer of the desk, a heavy .45-inch US Army-issue Colt. Reaching across, pulling the drawer gently open, he groped for it. It was there, cold, oily. With his index finger touching the cross-hatching on the butt, he inched the gun out. He eased it into his waistband, the movement slow, easy, keeping his upper body still.

A second burst crashed through the window, pock-marking the wall behind him, just above his head. Plaster and dust filled the room, making him cough. Wondering if the shooter had seen him at the drawer, he tensed, realizing he still had the telephone pressed against his ear. The voice, taunting, derisive.

'How do you like it, Patrick Donnelly? Terrorist. Back-shooting murderer. Pissing ourselves, are we?'

Donnelly tried to work out where the shooting was coming from. Probably at the far end of Rodney Drive. He tried to think clearly through the numbing panic.

Think now, Patrick. Think, man.

The post office van.

Due at 7.50. Last collection. The box on the corner of Rodney Parade.

Every evening, without fail.

It was never late.

His watch said 7.49 p.m.

One minute.

Steadier now, he got ready, dreading another burst from the M60.

He hunched over his desk, waiting.

One minute.

It was the longest minute of Patrick Donnelly's life.

'Jesus.'

'What the hell's going on?' The young constable was confused. He had seen the window shatter, heard the stupefying clatter as the bullets passed. It was a sound he'd never heard before. He looked to his Sergeant for direction, guidance.

'Never you mind, son. Just keep looking. And tell me what you see.' Hiding his expression, he half-turned away, looking at the tape.

It was running evenly.

'Jesus,' he said again.

He left the desk, ducking under the rafters, and crawled, wincing as the sharp edges of the timbers bit into his knees. He lowered himself down on to the door, squeezing the other man out. The earphone lead was stretched tight, tugging.

'The glasses,' he said. 'Give.'

Refocusing, he held them to his eyes.

'Well, I'll be . . .' There was a smile at the edge of his mouth.

It didn't reach his eyes.

There were four bullets left in the link belt.

Richard Norris knew exactly how many there were. He had counted. He readjusted his position behind the gun. Cordite, gunsmoke filled the room, stinging his eyes, making him squint to keep his target in focus. Vaguely he heard a vehicle engine, somewhere to his left.

He centered Donnelly's torso on the tip of the foresight.

The time was now.

Johnathan, balanced delicately on a sailboard, muscles hard in his belly as he ran with the wind. Laughter, a young girl watching, waving. The board flipping, the bronzed body, droplets of water cascading as Johnathan surfaced from his ducking.

He moulded his body into the gun.

The sound of the engine was louder in his ears.

Donnelly saw the van appear from the corner of his eye.

Dead on time.

He waited until the moment was exactly right, the moment it would pass in front of his showroom window, shielding him from the man with the gun.

He gripped the telephone tight in his fist.

The Royal Mail van came into his vision.

Now.

Norris saw his victim. Helpless at last before him. He'd waited and worked towards this. His moment of perfect, sweet, cleansing retribution. No judge, no jury is going to save you. Donnelly, in his sights.

Now.

Do it, Norris. Do it.

End this inconsolable sorrow, more than the human spirit can bear. But wasn't the human spirit meant to rise above abomination and anguish? At the moment of unutterable despair, wasn't the supreme admonition human dignity? Wasn't it? If I kill him now, doesn't that make me as vile as he?

Do it . . .

Norris was lowering the gun, his hands relaxing, breath sighing out of him. The voice, flat with the nasal vowels of the Falls.

'I hope the fucker bled real bad.'

He fired.

The last four bullets crackled. The links from the disintegrating belt clattered on to the threadbare carpet at his feet. Donnelly moved, as if in slow motion, diving to his right. Norris thought he saw the body twist as it was hit. He couldn't be sure. A Royal Mail van passed in front of his view almost as he fired. When it was gone, the showroom in front of him was empty.

It was done.

He could not believe anything could hurt so bad.

He lay on the floor. Again, a numbness bringing nausea up into his head, the stunning agony stopping his breathing, bringing sharp tears to his eyes. Agony, preventing rational thought. Nothing could hurt as much as this. Jesus God. My soul to take this agony. He couldn't move, his whole left side paralysed. No feeling at all. Spittle flowed unchecked from his mouth on to the carpet. Dear Jesus, I'm hurting. Stop the hurting. He moaned, his lips close to the carpet. He could smell the dust.

The car.

The Honda Prelude with the automatic gearbox, parked in the yard at the back of the showroom. Got to get to it. Keys in the ignition. Crawl. Keep low so the bastard with the gun can't see you. Shoulder. Can't move my left arm. He looked at the mess. A lump of flesh had been torn out, discarded, flung away. He could see the blood pumping out of him, spreading the pool ever wider. Jesus. Look at the hole in my shoulder.

He moved, whimpering as the pain just forgotten shot through his body. He clamped his teeth together, stifling a moan, shutting out the tears. There had been no more firing since the van had passed. Donnelly crawled, slithering like a serpent, hugging the floor. Moaning, he reached the door that led out of the light. Push? Pull? He wasn't sure, hurting too much to remember. Just get out of the light before he fires again, hurts me some more.

The air was cold on his face.

Sirens, loud in his ears.

Out in the night he got to his feet somehow, favouring his right side. Gathering himself, he lurched towards the car, parked a few yards in front of him, hearing the screech of brakes coming from the front of his showroom. He wrenched open the door of the car. He fell into the driver's seat, pumping blood into the expensive upholstery, not caring, fighting to stay conscious as the shock from his wound set in.

He started the car, then reached across with his sound arm and hauled the automatic into drive. Slamming his foot on to the accelerator, he tore away from this place of his agony.

Somewhere safe to lie up. That's what was needed.

Somewhere safe.

He knew where to go.

CHAPTER TWENTY-FIVE

Richard Norris moved fast.

Time was short, and there were things he yet had to do. He gathered up the empty cases and pieces of link belt and thrust them into a plastic bag. After a quick glance around the room, he hefted the gun into his right hand. He closed the window, and left by the narrow door, down the creaking rickety stairs, out into the small kitchen at the back of the house. It was cold, bare since he had removed the small table and taken it upstairs, a rest for the gun. He thought about replacing it, then dismissed the idea. No time.

Leaving the house, he locked the door behind him, walking quickly across the small yard into the garage which led to the alley. The equipment he needed was in position. The gun was laid on a bench at the back of the room while he pulled on the welder's helmet and visor. The oxy-acetylene torch popped loudly as he lit it. He pulled the dark visor down over his eyes and adjusted the torch so that it burnt with a brilliant blue flame.

He worked fast, aware of the sirens above the noise of the flame, the spitting crackle from the metal as he worked.

He cut the American M60E1 into shapeless chunks.

It would serve no purpose now. Scrap metal.

Collecting the pieces of the gun, he placed them ready to wrap in the sack once they had cooled, to be put in the car and dumped later. As he walked round to open the boot, a small hatch set in the main garage door swung in towards him.

His heart skipped a beat.

The RUC Sergeant passed the field-glasses back to his young companion, who was shuffling about on the door trying to get comfortable.

The Sergeant felt a deep sadness.

So much like his own boy.

Before Crossmaglen.

He had guessed what had happened out on the Rodney Drive. Even if he hadn't heard the telephone conversation, he would have recognized the sound of a burst of machine-gun fire. Although a silencer had been used, the noise of the bullets was easy to identify if the listener knew the signature. The Sergeant knew. He'd heard it before.

He worked his way backwards from the observer's

position, where the tile had been removed from the roof to make the spy-hole.

'Hold the fort. I'll not be long.'

At the recording equipment, he rewound the cassette, stopping it where the telephone had rung in Donnelly's office. His finger poised above the switch. Over his shoulder, he saw the young man's back was to him. He sighed.

He pressed the erase switch.

The tape ran through the cassette until the counter reached the end of the conversation.

He pressed the stop button.

The tape was rewound to its original position.

Reaching round behind the machine he loosened the input jack, preventing any further recording.

When the analysts received the tape, there would be no recorded conversation on Donnelly's extension at 7.45 p.m.

It had never happened. The Sergeant would swear the equipment was faulty. Probably that loose jack plug again.

Climbing stiffly down the stairs from the loft, he told himself for the hundredth time that he was too bloody old for stake-out. The air was cold on his face, invigorating after the stuffiness of the loft, refreshing him as he left the house by the rear door. The dogs started as soon as he was in the alley, the barking half-hearted, as if they recognized a familiar scent. Ignoring them, he went quickly down a path so narrow he could touch both walls.

He moved quickly, looking neither left nor right until he arrived at the intersection with St James Crescent. He knew where to look, where to find the man with the machine-gun. He lifted his jacket, checking his sidearm, then crossed the road in a short dash.

The empty house was in front of him. No lights shone from it. He ducked into the alley behind the house, hearing the approaching sirens, the squealing brakes as the road-blocks were set up, vehicle doors slamming as troops and police dismounted to take up their positions.

The garage was at the rear of the house, an eerie blue light dancing, flashing behind the dirty window. He peered in, but even after rubbing the glass with his hand he was unable to see exactly what was happening on the bench at the back. The figure of a man, partially hidden by a sporty-looking hatchback, was lifting something.

The RUC man crept quietly to the front of the garage. He drew his weapon, and listened at the door. The man had finished working. The purring of the oxy-acetylene torch had stopped. It was quiet. The blue light and cascading sparks no longer showed from beneath the gap in the door.

The Sergeant took a deep breath, then quietly pushed the door open.

Richard Norris took in the squat figure standing in front of him. He had the face of a walrus, normally kindly. His expression now was one of curiosity. Richard was not fooled by the sleepy look in the hooded eyes. Despite the bulk, the man appeared to be light on his feet. He looked as if he had been around. A survivor. There was a small automatic in his right hand, held loosely at his side.

'The machine-gun. Where is it?'

No words wasted with introductions.

Richard was puzzled. Despite the gun in the man's hand, he did not feel threatened. He gestured with his head, and saw the walrus take in the pile of metal pieces on the bench, some still smoking from the heat of the torch.

'Neat,' said the walrus. 'What had you intended doing with it now?'

Richard shrugged.

'Dump it. The river. Who knows. Just get rid of it. Who are you?'

'Never you mind. For the moment thank your lucky stars I'm not a Provee, UFF or the like. Where's the ammo? For the gun?'

'Gone.'

Richard studied the man, beginning to guess who he was. When he spoke again, the walrus moustache, a fat hairy caterpillar, bunched and stretched on the upper lip.

'Donnelly. We had him in the frame. Ever since we got a confirmed ID from the mainland. Every time he shits we know. He can't move without us knowing. But he's clean. The bastard is clean. We have to catch him red-handed, no pun intended, before we can put him away. Then you, Mr smart-arse Englishman, come over to my patch and blow him away. Weeks we've been watching him.'

'He killed my son.' Richard realized now, he was facing the law. For him, it was over. There was no talking his way out of this one. And he hadn't got Alex to help him.

'I heard. So did most of West Belfast by the sound of the sirens.'

Richard nodded.

'And how the hell did you think you were going to get out? The whole area is sewn up tighter than a virgin's hymen. There's no way greased weasel shit could slide out of here.'

'I suppose you're taking me in? I don't care too much. I've done what I came to do.' The walrus didn't answer. Instead he pointed to the car.

'Yours?'

Richard nodded.

'Get in. Drive. I'll tell you where.'

Donnelly drove one-handed, sick with fear and pain. His left arm hung uselessly by his side, the throb in his shoulder unbearable. Blood oozed freely, unchecked, down his arm and into the seat. He sat in a pool of it, soaking through his clothes, clinging to the backs of his legs. The fingers of his left hand were stuck together from it. His vision was blurred, and he had to shake his head every few seconds to prevent himself passing out. His head rolled from side to side as he peered half-blind through the windscreen.

It had started to rain. It was always bloody well raining. He had to let go of the wheel to find the wipers. The car swerved alarmingly, avoiding the oncoming traffic, horns blaring. Steady. Almost there, Patrick.

He had entered the street from the opposite end, at first not recognizing where he was. Confused, his brain refusing to function, he had to study the buildings carefully to find the one he was looking for. Perhaps he had gone wrong, lost his way in the rain in his mad dash for freedom. He'd beaten the road-blocks. But only just.

At last, he found the door and stopped at a place where he could park, bumping over the kerb and hitting a car already in position outside a dingy-looking house. His head fell on to the steering-wheel, the car's horn clamouring into the empty street. Jerking upright, he pulled the car door open, sweating from the effort.

His arm hung limply by his side. He didn't bother to close the door, leaving the rain to blow in on the wind, diluting the blood on the seat. He leaned against the car, letting the rain fall on his bare head. Blood dripped from the end of his fingers and ran in rivulets into the gutter, turning it red.

Who shot me? Think back. How long was it?

He remembered what the voice had said to him. November. Three, maybe four months ago, his brain was too numb to work it out exactly. But he could see it clearly in his mind's eye. The rain slanting down, like now, hearing it on the roof of the van, seeing the door slide upwards as the observer yanked the wires. First the bomb expert, then the stupid sod running to him. Bloody well asked for it. He had thought he had been able to see the bits flying off him as the bullets had hit.

The papers had covered it. Only local papers. What the hell was his name? Horace? Morris?

Norris.

A prissy lieutenant. Did you hurt, like I'm hurting, Mr fucking Lieutenant Norris? Oh God, how I'm hurting. Maybe I'm dying. Is this how it feels to die? So your old man came after me did he, Mr Norris? How the fuck did he find me? I've been clean, all these years I've been clean. And yet, prissy Lieutenant Norris's old man found me.

He walked a few paces, staggered and fell to his knees, the gun in his waistband hurting as it dug into the softness of the lower belly. Tugging it free with his right hand, he used the barrel to push himself up from the wet pavement, not caring about the damage he was doing to the gun. A few more paces, staggering, weaving like a drunk.

At the entrance, he fell against the door. God, let this be the right place. His knees buckled as he slid down, splinters from the rough wood piercing his cheeks, snapping as his body slumped to the ground. He knelt in the rain, shaking his head, whimpering with agony. His body shuddered.

Where the hell is the key?

It was in the left-hand pocket. He couldn't use his left hand to get it, the arm just hung there like meat at the butchers on the corner of Clonard Road, on stainless-steel hooks. Legs of lamb, cold, dead, not bleeding like his arm, warm, living.

With his right hand, he reached across his body, ripping the pocket open, the rain cold on his legs through the tear in his trousers. The key fell to the ground with a musical tinkle, a mischievous chuckle, mocking. I don't believe this shit. Where did it land? Think, Patrick, look for it or you're a goner for sure. There. Glinting in the puddle. Focus on it. Don't blink or you'll lose the thing.

It took all his concentration to bend and pick it up. He almost didn't make it. He lurched to his feet, collapsed against the door, feeling for the lock. Twice, he almost gave up. He would die if he didn't get treatment soon.

He found the lock.

He mated it with the key.

Turn, damn you.

He twisted, falling into the hall as the door swung in on his weight.

Jennifer McCauley, dressed like a tart, stood at the top of the narrow stairs leading down to her hallway. Off duty and going out. Not that she was ever really off duty in her job, but tonight the store manager had asked her for a date. On the spur of the moment she had said yes. He was handsome, like a young Robert Redford or someone, fun to be around. The other girls in the store were envious, but she had ignored the spiteful remarks directed at her.

Sod them.

She had deliberated over taking the handbag, the Walther, deciding in the end she would feel naked without it. She took one last look at herself in the full-length mirror behind her door, pushing a few loose strands of hair back under the combs, picking daintily at the corner of her mouth with a long fingernail, her lipstick not quite as she wanted it. She was ready. Watch it, Mr Supermarket Manager. This could be your lucky night. She pulled open the inner door at the top of the stairs, then turned to close it. Putting on the light, she took a pace forward.

She stopped dead, not believing.

Patrick, never Pat, who had never told her his surname, was collapsed against her front door. He was a mess. His suit was soaked, dirty, and torn on the side where the pocket had once been. The whole of his left side was covered in dark blood, dripping from the end of his fingers on to the hall mat.

There was a heavy automatic in his right hand.

His eyes were closed. Had it not been for the heaving of his chest and the spasms shaking his body, she might have thought him dead, realizing at once that he soon would be if the terrible shoulder wound was not tended. She stared.

'Jenny!' A croak. 'Jesus, I'm in real trouble. I . . . I've been hurt bad. Shot . . . some crazy Brit. I need a place to lie up. A doctor. I . . . I knew you'd help. Thank God I made it here. Will you help me, Jenny? They'll make it worth your while . . . I . . . God. My arm . . .' his voice tailed off.

She controlled her emotions, saying nothing, not trusting herself to speak. Her body trembled.

The sound of Velcro tearing open was loud in the narrow passageway.

Patrick Donnelly heard the slow ripping without recognizing what it was. He looked up at her. He could see her knickers under the short skirt. She knew how she looked to him and spread her legs as far as the skirt would allow, feeling the hem hitch a little higher.

Forget how you look.

The fingers of her right hand were in constant motion.

She reached across her body and drew the Walther PPK/S. The gun that had belonged to her father. Before the IRA took him with a bomb under his car. The only time he hadn't checked. It fitted, snug, part of the living hand. The little finger rested on the spur projecting from the bottom plate of the magazine, as it had when her father had let her hold the gun for the first time. She raised it into the aim, dropping into a half-crouch, holding the gun in a two-handed grip.

The way she'd been taught.

The green eyes that were like glass marbles. For the first time since she had encountered him, she saw expression pass across the shiny glass.

She saw pain.

Realization.

Fear.

He tried to raise the automatic, a ton weight in his hand. It wavered at waist level. It came no higher, until, with a huge effort, he dragged it to shoulder height. He extended his arm. The gun wavered.

Jennifer McCauley fired twice in quick succession. Patrick Donnelly did not move. He did not fall. He stared at the woman who had shot his penis off. The red stain was already spreading across his lower body. He felt the pain then, pain that made his arm unimportant. All his senses focused on where he had been shot. He slumped to the floor, his head thumping against the door. She looked down at him from the top of the stairs. Pathetic. The Provo who had nearly made her come. For an instant she felt where he'd been in her. Then it was gone.

She saw him looking at her as she raised the gun, his head back against the door. She saw the twisted grin, heard his voice, a whisper through his pain.

'Bitch.'

She shot him.

Once.

In the forehead between the shiny glass marbles, turning opaque. She saw the pink splash out on to her wall. Through the gunsmoke she saw the neat entry hole. It looked like a third eye.

There was no expression in it.

No expression at all.

The walrus told him where to drive, how to miss the checkpoints and road-blocks. Apart from these curt directions they had not spoken since entering the car. He was going to make it, helped, now, when he needed it.

He tried not to notice the lights in his mirror. Lights following since he had turned out of St James Crescent, every corner, junction, intersection, once jumping a red to keep close behind. He said nothing to the man beside him.

They had reached the city centre.

The walrus told Richard to drop him at a taxi rank. The car following had stopped fifty yards back in shadow between two lampposts. The walrus got out, then leaned into the car. Richard could smell the damp on him, see the fatigue.

'Go home, Englishman. Don't ever come back to Northern Ireland again. Not ever.'

'I need to know why you helped,' Richard spoke, staring at the car parked behind. The walrus looked at him directly.

'My son. He'd just joined the RUC. They got him with an M60 down in Crossmaglen. Only last week. He was off duty. He never knew what hit him.'

With that he turned and walked quickly away. Richard Norris watched the squat figure as it reached the rank of taxis across the road. He saw him duck to speak to the driver of the cab in the front of the rank. The taxi passed close to where he was stopped. The RUC man was hunched in the back, as if he didn't want to be seen, staring straight ahead. The brake lights flared briefly, reflected off the wet surface of the road as the taxi slowed at the intersection. He raised his hand as if to wave.

But the man wasn't looking.

He looked in the rear-view mirror.

Headlights came on as the car behind cruised alongside. He glanced across as the passenger window of the other car opened.

He opened his own.

'I'll lead, you follow. Don't look so surprised, you silly sod. You didn't think I'd leave you without covering your back?'

'You big ugly bastard.'

They drove off into the rain.

EPILOGUE

The market town looked a little better in the early spring, although a raw wind still blew along its streets, bowling litter before it. Shoppers hurried by, grateful at last to be seeing an end to winter, those long nights, dark mornings, keeping people in the warmth of their bed when they should have been getting up to face the day. But spring was coming. There was a different feel in the air.

The big square van, maroon with gold letters, trundled slowly along the high street, passed a pedestrian crossing, the driver steering to his normal parking place outside the bank. It was collection and delivery day.

The guard jumped down from the passenger side, crossed the pavement and entered the bank, a procedure he knew so well he could do it in his sleep. He made the arrangements for the delivery, then returned to his van. A voice-activated mike attached to his helmet switched on automatically as he spoke. His instructions were acknowledged by someone inside the van.

Waiting on the pavement, the guard was tense, as always at this moment of transfer. He looked to left and right ensuring the street was clear, and was about to speak again when a voice broke into his radio channel, loud in his ears.

'Mr security man.'

He stiffened, his mind on fast rewind.

Christmas.

Panic. Not again. He looked to his right, to the town-hall roof, but saw nothing.

'No. You won't see me up there. But I can see you. Every move you make. You know the procedure, you've been through it before. I give the instructions, you carry them out. Nod to show you understand.'

Jim Dalby, security guard, ex-policeman, nodded, resigned.

'You'll not get away with it a second time.'

'Let me worry about that. How did you twig the town-hall roof? I saw you looking up there.'

'The halyard flapping against the flagpole. I heard it through your radio, the last time. I'm not bloody stupid. Get on with it. Let's get this over with.'

'Clever security man.'

There was grudging respect in the voice.

'Go round to the outside of the van. Stand with your face against it, your back to the road.'

Dalby walked round his van. He looked at the rear door. There was no bomb. Not like before. He tried to think where they might have stuck it this time. Feet braced, he stood as he had been told, trying to guess what might happen next. Everything looked peaceful, normal. Traffic sped by taking no notice of him. He wondered how two robberies would look on his record, whether the company pension would be affected.

He shrugged.

Something hit him hard between the shoulder-blades, winding him, perhaps thrown from a passing car. He looked down at his feet. There were two Securitall bags lying in the road. The serial numbers began with a 4. Not understanding, he stared at them. Dalby bent to pick them up, ignoring the startled, inquisitive voice in his earphones from his partner inside.

He opened the first of the bags, unsure what he might find. Sliding his hand in like at a lucky dip, he pulled out a neat bundle of US dollar bills. Both bags were stuffed full, used, untraceable.

'Well, I'm buggered.'

He sat down on the pavement and started to laugh. He laughed until the tears ran down his cheeks.

Shoppers hurried by wondering what the security guard found so funny.

They couldn't understand it at all.

The envelope was thrust through the letter-box where it landed heavily on the rug just inside the front door. It was not buff-coloured like the others. It was not a bill. The woman walked along the length of the thin carpet in the hallway and stooped to pick up the morning mail. She was not particularly interested in what the envelopes contained. She could see from the logos on the envelopes that most were from the utilities. They would all contain red final demands.

They always did.

And how was she supposed to pay them on the half widow's pension she received from the government since her husband had been killed in Northern Ireland? And her with two kiddies to bring up. She felt the bitterness. The compensation had been paltry, derisory. Almost twelve years he had served. He was coming out. Not going for the full twenty-two. He'd had enough he had said.

She took the bundle of envelopes into the kitchen and threw them on to the table. After seeing the kids off to school, she put the kettle on for another cup of tea, noticing that one of the letters was different, a white envelope with the logo from her bank standing out proudly. It wasn't a statement. Too early in the month.

She tore it open.

Her bank manager, on behalf of the investments advisor, was asking how she would like to invest the large amount of money which had arrived from an offshore account. She looked at the figures, not believing.

She, and others like her who had lost their men in the Province, made enquiries with their banks. They were told that the money had been transferred from a numbered offshore account. The bank thought it most unlikely that they would be able to trace the source. Perhaps a distant relative. It contravened confidentiality to pursue the matter further. The banks were, however, keen to suggest ways of investing the windfall.

The woman looked heavenwards and said a silent prayer, hugging the letter to her breast.

The extension was almost finished. It really had improved the look of the cottage, the natural slate blending with the original stone. Proud of his workmanship, he stood, hands on his hips, contented and at peace. Spring was in the air. There was still snow up on the higher fells, but he had felt the change in these last few days.

His eye caught a slate block slightly out of true. Stepping forward, he tapped it gently with the handle of a club hammer until it was exactly where he wanted it. He sucked on the empty pipe, glancing once more at the sky where the big cotton-wool balls of cloud were galloping, chasing each other.

A woman's voice came from the house, shrill, startling him.

'Nobby! Come quick. The firm. It's on telly. Quick now or you'll miss it.'

Nobby Clarke moved his big body with surprising speed, into the kitchen and through into the living room. He grunted as he hit his head on the low beam at the door. It still caught him whenever he came in too fast or with too much ale in him. The knock always hurt, despite the piece of foam rubber Millie had fixed there.

She was standing in front of the television watching the lunchtime news, short and plump in front of him, drying her hands in her apron. He rested big hands on her shoulders when she leaned back against him.

They listened as the announcer spoke of a robbery in reverse. It had happened down in the West Country, in a small market town.

Nobby remembered the name.

Two bags of US dollars had been tossed at the feet of a security guard as he had been forced to stand facing his van, unable to see where the money had come from. The scene changed from the studio to a small living room where the special reporter on home affairs was interviewing a security guard.

Nobby Clarke recognized the maroon uniform.

'. . . yes, we were robbed just before Christmas by a gang using a hoax bomb, the gang that became known as the Jingle Bell Mob. The money thrown back converts to the exact amount stolen. And the twist is, that interest has been added for the amount of time it was taken . . .'

'What was that you said, Nobby?'

'That calls for a celebration, Milly Clarke. Why not pour yourself a sherry, while I has one of my home brews?' He was grinning all over his face. He went to the cupboard in the pantry where he kept the dark ale he made himself, muttering under his breath. She couldn't be sure, but she thought she heard him call someone a bloody bandit. Yes. He definitely said bloody bandit. He said it twice.

She followed him out to the kitchen carrying her small glass of sherry, warming at the secret smile on her big man's face.

The whisky mellowed him as he sipped from the crystal glass. The sun was dying, leaving a red glow in its wake, silhouettes of distant birds, sharp against it as they sought their resting places for the evening, curling and wheeling. He savoured the moment, the darkening twilight as the sun finally dipped into the shapes of the distant hills. It hung there for one tantalizing moment. Then it was gone. He shivered, then re-entered the old farmhouse through the open French windows.

It was done.

The newscaster had called it another sectarian killing.

The security forces were worried about the appearance of another M60 machine-gun in the Province.

Life, death went on.

Radios came alive in dingy operations rooms. Telephones rang. Patrols left their bases to zigzag along the streets. Groups met in clubs and bars to plot more dastardly acts.

Nothing had really changed.

Except for him.

He was different now.

He looked at the photograph of the officer cadet, one taken at graduation, the boy's mother so proud beside him. He saw the grin creasing the strong, untidy features. In the mirror above, his own face, everything jumbled, the almost blond hair, too long for a business executive.

He saw himself.

The telephone rang.

He thought he would let it ring, then changed his mind.

'Richard Norris.'

He spoke into the mouthpiece.

'If nothing else, Richard, we gave them a run for their money. If ever you need me, you know where I am.'

The line went dead.

Alex Howard.